Praise for
Black Ice

"Linda Hall has another winner. *Black Ice* is loaded with suspense, tension, and best of all, characters that leap out of the pages and into your heart."
—PATRICIA H. RUSHFORD, author of the McAllister Files, the
Angel Delaney Mysteries, and the Jennie McGrady Mysteries

"A body is found. A town is challenged. And Linda Hall has done it again. In *Black Ice*, Hall has given us a story that blends faith with doubt; piety with hypocrisy. And she does it with aplomb. Linda Hall is not only a talented writer and skilled wordsmith, she is a superb storyteller!"
—BRANDT DODSON, author of *Original Sin, Seventy Times Seven,*
and *The Root of All Evil*

"Linda Hall's *Black Ice* should have been titled *A More Tangled Web* as in 'Oh, what a tangled web we weave when we practice to deceive.' With skill and sensitivity, Linda Hall portrays how one lie becomes many and, in the end, can kill."
—LYN COTE, author of The Women of Ivy Manor series

"*Black Ice* is an artfully crafted story with deep, believable characters and a mystery that both entertains and intrigues. I was hooked from the first page to the last. This one is sure not to disappoint. A compelling read!"
—MARLO SCHALESKY, author of *Veil of Fire* and *Beyond the Night*

"*Black Ice* is my cure for the winter blahs! Linda Hall excels at sending her readers down a slippery slope right into the arms of the One who loves us."
—LOIS RICHER, author of *Spring Flowers* and *Summer Love*

BLACK ICE

A NOVEL

BLACK ICE

LINDA HALL

BEST-SELLING AUTHOR

WATERBROOK
PRESS

BLACK ICE
PUBLISHED BY WATERBROOK PRESS
12265 Oracle Boulevard, Suite 200
Colorado Springs, Colorado 80921
A division of Random House Inc.

Scripture quotations and paraphrases are taken from the Holy Bible, New International Version®. NIV®. Copyright © 1973, 1978, 1984 by International Bible Society. Used by permission of Zondervan Publishing House. All rights reserved.

The characters and events in this book are fictional, and any resemblance to actual persons or events is coincidental.

ISBN: 978-1-57856-955-7

Library of Congress Cataloging-in-Publication Data
Hall, Linda, 1950-
    Black ice : a novel / Linda Hall. — 1st ed.
        p. cm.
    ISBN 978-1-57856-955-7
1. Bed and breakfast accommodations—Fiction. 2. Teenage girls—Death—Fiction. I. Title.
    PS3558.A3698B55 2007

                                        2006034361

Printed in the United States of America
2007—First Edition

10 9 8 7 6 5 4 3 2 1

For Kira

ACKNOWLEDGMENTS

A special thank you to my daughter Wendy. I will always remember that morning in Starbucks when we brainstormed this whole idea into existence.

And to my husband, Rik, thank you for being supportive and understanding through all the long days of writing, thank you for always being my brainstormer and first editor.

Thank you Phenny Bryden and Kim Price-Murphy, social workers with the adoption program/Provincial Government of New Brunswick, for answering all my questions and providing much-needed information. Any mistakes in the book are mine.

Thank you as well to Cheryl A. Wilson-Bonner for much help and information on photography.

Thank you, too, to my editors, Traci DePree and Shannon Hill, for getting me to think through everything and turning this into a better manuscript.

Thank you to Danielle, my agent. I truly appreciate all you do.

Two hours after the baby shower began, the baby's mother, anxious to nurse, went to look for her son. Half an hour after that, the police were called.

The day had been unseasonably warm, so the baby was clothed only in a light cotton sleeper. His mother had carefully chosen a blue one with deeper blue designs. Circles. Concentric circles. Circles upon circles. She told all of this to the police when they came and talked with her while she sat in the kitchen of the community hall, a blanket around her. It always reminded her of the circles in the Olympic design, she told them. "That's why I put it on him. He's such a strong bruiser. Big for two months. He's so strong. You should see how he…" Then she put her fingers to her eyes and didn't finish.

The police asked their endless questions, but no one had seen anyone come in, anyone who was not a part of the community baby shower, that is.

There were only two strangers who'd been there, if you could even call them strangers: a niece from out East who was visiting her aunt and a sister of one of the farm wives. There were thirty-seven women at the baby shower, counting the baby's mother, and by the end of it, all thirty-seven would be questioned again and again. But nobody minded. A baby disappearing was everyone's business. Everyone wanted to help. For weeks afterward they brought casseroles to the mother's house and sat with her while she pressed her fists into her eyes. She would never get over this day, she said. Never.

He was a good baby at the baby shower, so content. Everyone commented on his smile. Only two months, and he just grinned and grinned. Such a happy little fellow. Everyone had wanted a chance to hold him, and he was passed from lap to lap while his mother opened the gifts.

"Oh my, aren't you going to be the heartbreaker," one of the older women had said while she held him, his little feet pressed to her stomach and his head on her knees.

"He'll be a good, strong farm hand," the lady next to her agreed.

"Just like his father," another said.

Mothers let their own children hold the baby on their laps if they were gentle—very, very gentle. Pictures were taken, pictures that were later handed over to the police. Someone videotaped the whole thing. That, too, was turned over.

The last thing anyone remembered was the baby falling asleep in his carrier seat. One of the women took the carrier with her into the kitchen and put it on the table while she got the coffee ready. It was too noisy out in the main room, she told them. She didn't want him waking up. But everybody knew the real reason. She just wanted him to be with her for a while. He slept while she got the cream out of the fridge, poured it into four little glass pitchers, got out the sugars, and then took everything out to the main hall. Even though it was warm, she placed his receiving blanket over his chubby legs. Couldn't have him catching a chill, now could we?

No, she couldn't remember how long she'd left him in the kitchen sleeping, she told the police. Maybe ten minutes? Maybe a bit more. She'd put out the coffee and then went to the table where the gifts were laid out. Gorgeous sleepers, cute little shirt-and-pant sets, hand-quilted throws, and handmade sweaters. She'd held each one up and commented. He was one lucky baby. When she went back into the kitchen, he was gone.

But this was no cause for concern. She assumed someone had picked him up, taken him out to the main hall with the others. Maybe his mother decided it was time to feed him. Maybe he needed changing.

In the end, the police determined that someone must have slipped into the kitchen at the precise moment that she had left with the coffee service. Whoever it was probably picked up the carrier and took it out to the main hall and up the stairs and out the back door. *But who could have done this?* they asked each other. They were the only ones there. And just one window in the kitchen, a little square one, high on the wall. The police checked it. It was painted shut and hadn't been opened for years.

The police continued their investigation on the assumption that someone must have seen something. Someone knew something. People in this community looked out for one another. Always had. Farm communities are like that. The community hall, like all of their farm homes, was a bit isolated. The next building was a quarter of a mile away. Still, the police went doggedly from farm to farm. Everyone expressed shock. *Such a shocking thing,* they said to each other over and over. Everyone wanted to help, but no one had seen anything, heard anything.

A blue receiving blanket with baseball players on it was the only thing that remained.

A long time later the official investigation was halted, and it was a long time after that before the baby's mother stopped crying.

1

Another snowstorm was forecast on the day Lenore Featherjohn found the body of the girl out in the back of her B&B. One day later and the girl would have been buried under two feet of snow. Lenore had gone out early to get her groceries, right after the Shop 'n Save opened, so as to miss the full force of the storm, which wasn't expected until midday. But even so, thick flakes accumulated on her windshield as she drove home.

Lenore had two guests at the moment: Mal, a brooding young photographer with two different-colored eyes, and Arnold, a regular who came for two weeks every winter to write science books. This was why she needed to make the trip in the first place. She needed flour, sugar, eggs, bacon, fruit, coffee, cereal—in short, just about everything. Ordinarily she had few B&B guests this time of year, but because of the ice in the harbor, photographers were coming from all over. It was quite a sight to see.

Neither was home when she got there. She parked in the back and called her sons to come help with the bags, but too late she realized they weren't there. Earl and Carl were in the city getting computer doodads. She hated it when they drove in bad weather. But what can you say when your sons are grown men in their thirties?

So that left Lenore to manage the bags herself. Not that she couldn't. She was capable, efficient, organized, and competent. Single-handedly she'd raised three sons, hadn't she? And at sixty-five, her skills at clearing out a leaf-clogged gutter and shoveling snow could rival many a younger person's.

After putting the car in the garage, a flicker of purple by the basement stairs caught her attention. She'd seen this flutter as early as yesterday but hadn't had the chance to investigate. She was particular about her yard. Things had to be neat, even in winter. It would be just like one of her sons to empty his car garbage in the wind and then not retrieve the pieces. Grumbling, she waded through the snow to the basement stairs.

And then she was standing there and looking down, one gloved hand to her throat, unable to move, unable to emit anything but a kind of strangled sound, which was something like, "Ohhh....ughhh....ohhh."

Purple fringed the end of a skinny woolen scarf, which was loosely tied around a dead girl's neck. It astounded Lenore that at a time like this she would notice how the scarf had been tied, with the ends tucked through the doubled-up middle. Last Thursday, at her weekly hair-salon visit, she'd skimmed through an article called "Ten Ways to Tie a Scarf." But this knot was so tight.

She put her hand to her chest and tried to get her breathing back. Then she knelt slowly, stiffly beside the body and stared at the girl's face. Lenore didn't know this girl. She didn't think she'd ever seen her before. The eyes were partially opened, as if she were slowly waking out of a deep sleep. Her lips were white and icy looking. Snowflakes that landed on her cheeks didn't melt.

Lenore hadn't raised daughters. She had grown three sons, so she was a little hazy on the girl's age, but she judged her to be somewhere in her late teens. Maybe seventeen? Possibly a bit older. Was she the same age as the minister's daughter? Lenore leaned forward to brush the hair away from the girl's eyes. Maybe it was the smattering of freckles across her nose that made her appear so young. Or maybe it was the way her pale hair was tied with a matching purple ribbon in a ponytail that fell over one shoulder.

For a long time, Lenore knelt in the snow beside the girl's body in a strange kind of vigil. Later she would tell people it was like being in the presence of an angel, but while she knelt there, her knees becoming wet in the snow and cold, all she felt was fear. "Who are you?" she whispered. "Why are you here?"

She thought about her sons, wondered why the girl was at her sons' door, and was afraid of the answer. So she sat unmoving in that purgatory space of time between the unknowing and the knowing. She kept brushing the flakes away from the girl's cheek, over and over, as fast as they fell. Later the police would want to know why she did this.

"I don't know. I felt sorry for her. It's like she needed someone to sit with her…"

Why had Lenore waited an hour and thirteen minutes before calling the police? Who knew that the time of purchase was printed on grocery receipts?

She would just shake her head at this and say she didn't know why. Shock, maybe? That was part of it, sure. But it was also part of this winter that wouldn't end. And the girl's body brought to her remembrance that other winter.

Three days ago ice had moved into the harbor on the high tide. Large chunks and treacherous slabs heaped against the boardwalk and piled up alongside each other like teepees. The last time this had happened was more than forty-five years ago. Young Fog Point residents who hadn't been here then went giddily down to the boardwalk and took pictures of the ice mountains, while old-timers stayed away and spoke in hushed whispers about "The Last Time This Happened."

Lenore remembered that time.

She had been about the age of this dead girl then. That winter, she was in love with bad boy Harlan Featherjohn, despite her minister father's stern warning. All the girls loved Harlan with his cigarette pack stuck in his rolled up T-shirt sleeve, his leather jacket, and his Roman Red 1960 Chevy Impala.

Funny that she remembered the precise name and color of his car after all these years. He looked like Steve McQueen, with his blue eyes. That's what all the girls said too. She should have stayed away from him.

That winter, she'd gotten pregnant and had to marry Harlan in a hurry. That's how it was done back then. No abortions. No single mothers raising babies. That would have been scandalous. When you "got in trouble," you got married, and that was the end of that.

The wedding was down at the town hall. It snowed like today on her wedding day. The roads were bad, and two people had accidents on the way. One died.

"God's judgment," her father had said.

That winter, old man Browngreen walked out onto the ice floes. His body was never recovered. That winter, Crazy Maizie Nation shot her husband and the family dog out in the chicken shed. She was tired of him stepping out on her, Maizie said, and took matters into her own hand. That winter, a dozen people died of the flu. Lenore had worried about the flu and her unborn baby, and so she stayed in their little apartment.

No one came to photograph the harbor then. People hid in their homes in the winter of 1961.

Now, more than forty-five years later, the ice was back. And Lenore couldn't stop it. She brushed more snow away from the girl's face and began weeping her silent, old-lady tears. Because despite staying inside when she was pregnant and away from all the people who had the flu, despite asking God over and over to forgive her, Lenore's baby, a girl, was born dead.

By the time the police arrived and strung up their yellow tape and tromped their heavy boots through her kitchen and accosted them all with loud voices, Lenore—capable, efficient, and competent Lenore—had carefully worked out a way that her sons would not be blamed for this.

2

The following Sunday, Amy McLaren, the minister's wife, couldn't get warm. The snow, the ice, a chill that wouldn't let go its hold on the land, the senseless death of a girl not much older than her own daughter, all made her feel a cold so deep that she could not be warmed no matter how many blankets she covered herself with or how close she sat to the fire.

She was in her customary place in the church, four rows from the front on the right. Ben, her husband, stood at the front, delivering the sermon. The church was half-empty this morning, which wasn't surprising, what with another blizzard coming in this afternoon. They should have canceled. If Amy had her way, she'd shut this whole place down until spring.

A gust blew snow against the stained-glass window, and it rattled like a coffin full of old bones.

Ben's voice sounded oddly hollow, as if he were speaking from a great distance. He made some comment about the wind, and she wondered how his faith never wavered. No matter what happened, he was a rock.

She drew her wool scarf around her shoulders. As its name suggested, Stone Church was made entirely of stones, one on top of the other, a memorial to some long-ago war. For two weeks a group of congregants had huddled in the basement while cannons fired around them and food for all mysteriously appeared every morning at their doorstep. It was a testament to God, their own manna miracle.

A plaque on the back wall told the story and listed the names of all the people who had been saved within these walls. Some were Fog Point names even now, Nation and Noonan being the most prominent. Not one hair on their heads was singed; that's what the plaque read.

Amy ran her fingers down the edge of the bulletin and wondered if God still listened to parishioners who were just as needy today, just as hungry while cannons of a different sort raged outside their walls.

In the front row on the right, her daughter, Blaine, sat with all the teenagers. Her dark head with its chunky yellow streaks was bent forward, hiding whatever she was doing in her lap. Amy guessed she and her friends were text messaging each other on their cell phones. When Amy was her age, they passed notes, hastily scribbled along the sides of their Sunday school papers. Passing notes in church had become high-tech.

Blaine looked up and sideways at Jana Rikker, who sat beside her. Jana was the daughter of their friend Jake. Jana wore a kind of expectant look, eyebrows raised. The girls had developed an almost morbid interest in the girl whose body had been found, the girl nobody knew. She wondered if that's what they were communicating about.

A year younger than Blaine, Jana seemed so much more innocent than Amy's daughter. She lacked that hard edge that Blaine had already developed and perfected. This worried Amy. It was hard for her to admit that the girl raised in a broken home might have her life more together than the girl raised in the minister's home. Amy looked back down at her bulletin while her husband droned on.

Charlie sat up there, too, in the very first row with a group of young boys. She could see the back of his head, the hair in that spot that refused to lie flat. Just like Ben's.

A blast of freezing rain hit the window beside her. The sound was like a phalanx of mice squealing all over the stained-glass saints, devouring them.

People were already talking about this winter being a judgment from God. These were the same Fog Pointers who believed that people who'd died at sea came to shore from The Shallows on a full-moon, low-low tide, walked along the boardwalk, and went to Noonan's Café and the bowling alley. The day after a full moon, people told each other how they'd seen long-departed family members sitting in the movie theater or drinking lattes at Mags and Herman's Coffee Shop on the boardwalk. Fog Pointers loved their stories. And that's how the rumor got started that this winter was a sign from God. The Tribulation was about to be unleashed. God's judgment was near. The ice was proof of it. The dead girl was the angel in the book of Revelation come to warn the people of Fog Point. Some said she was a ghost, someone's dead relative who'd come in on the ice and couldn't get back.

No one seemed interested in the truth, that she was probably a runaway who came to Fog Point and was murdered here—strangled to death, the news said.

Amy's hands were cold now, and she covered them with her scarf in her lap.

Buzz and Nootie Noonan, owners of Noonan's Café, were in church today too, in the front and to the left. Beside them were a few of the old ladies: Eloise and Pearl and Rose and Enid and that busybody, Lenore Feath-erjohn, the one who'd found the body. Some younger couples along with their children were in church this morning as well, like Colin and Marnie Nation. Their baby daughter, Kayla, sat on Colin's lap, and Colin's parents, Shirley and Gus, sat beside them. But the town boasted so many Nations it was easy to get the branches of that family tree confused.

Amy didn't have to turn around to know that Jana's father, Jake, would be sitting in the back row near the door. Jana was living with him this winter. Amy didn't know how he'd worked out custody with his ex-wife, but Amy was happy for him. Lately, he'd started back at church, carefully, slowly, coming in late and leaving early. He came for Ben's sermons and the reading from Scripture. Not for the social life. Never for the social life. He'd had enough of that to last forever, he'd told them.

The praise team rose and took its place in the front for the final song. Amy stood with the others and sang, and then her husband pronounced the benediction. If someone right then offered her a million dollars, she could not name the song they'd just sung so fervently. She slipped out of her place, took her husband's arm, and the two of them made their way to the back.

As they walked down the aisle, she thought about a Web site she'd found yesterday. It was meant to mimic the tabloids, as if church matters were tabloid worthy. She'd laughed out loud when she read the spoof about a minister's wife who'd hired a clone to take her place on Sunday mornings, leaving her free to stay at home and pursue hobbies she didn't have time for during the week. She suppressed a laugh, and Ben smiled down at her. Maybe the faithful would mistake this sudden ridiculous giggle for joy. So be it.

In a moment she would shake hands with the parishioners. She would hug old ladies and promise to pray for their aches and pains. She would bend down to the children's level and talk to them about every snowflake in God's world being different, and wasn't that simply amazing? (Although, when you thought about it, was this something you could actually prove?)

She'd do other things too. She would continue to teach her ladies' Sunday school class, seeking in her own humorous, unique way to imbue the women with the faithfulness of God. She was a good women's speaker. That's what everyone said. She'd continue to come up with talks and sermons and speak when asked. She and Ben would continue the habit of family devotions, despite Blaine's teenage protests. They would read the Scriptures, and she'd pray at meal times when it was her turn. She would continue to offer her comments on Ben's sermon subjects, suggesting verses and ideas. She'd counsel Blaine to keep herself pure for marriage, which would be to a nice young Christian man, of course. Maybe a minister. Wasn't that the highest calling? To be married to a minister? Wasn't that what her parents wished for her? How lucky Amy was, then.

She would continue to tuck her young son, Charlie, into bed with a bedtime story and a prayer. She'd continue to make brownies for their home-group Bible study. She would smile as she talked about God's goodness and grace that week. She'd even pray when they went around in the circle. She was well practiced at it.

You did all of this when you were a minister's wife. It was expected of you. You submitted, never questioning. You did and you did and you did and you did.

Amy sighed in the deepness of her soul and bent to hug an old lady.

3

J ake worked on his scale model of a Dutch tugboat in the large communal kitchen in the basement of the Purple Church. There wasn't a lot to do during the winter months when you ran a summer business like Adventure Whale Tours and Outfitting, Salvage and Investigations, but little jobs kept him and his partner, May Williams, afloat in bleak midwinter. Last week he'd been called upon to dive under the wharf in the harbor for an outboard motor someone had dropped off the back of a fishing boat.

Jake and Jana had been to Amy and Ben's for Sunday lunch. By midafternoon Jake had come home. But Jana stayed with Blaine. It pleased Jake that Jana was making friends, though it made the kitchen too quiet. Jana had been with him since the summer, after many phone calls to persuade not only his ex-wife, Connie, but Keith, her husband, that he really could take care of a thirteen-year-old daughter and that he really did have her best interests at heart. They relented but not without a lot of caveats. Jana had to go to church and he had to take her; he had to set the example. Plus, any time she said the word, she could, at a moment's notice, go back home to Kentville to live with her mother and Keith and her sister, Alex, and half brother, Mickey. No questions asked.

Jake said he would happily do all that and more.

Keith had said, "Are you *trustworthy*, Jake?"

Jake hated it when the guy used his name. "I'm trustworthy, *Keith*."

"With your history, Jake…"

He let that one go. Then he asked to speak to Connie. After a few "I don't knows" and "How will she get her clothes and things she needs?" it was decided. Jana would stay, and Connie would pack up her winter clothes and ship them. Jana had spent a lot of time on the phone with her mother deciding what to pack and what to leave.

In the six months she'd been with him, he'd gotten used to the sounds of her being there. The stereo, the DVD, the computer, their many conversations, her laughter—things he had missed for so many years.

They lived in the basement of a church that he and May had bought four years ago and from which they ran their business. In the summer, the sanctuary was filled with the things they sold—backpacks, outdoor clothing, kayaks, Sterno stoves, freeze-dried macaroni, sleeping bags, and rain gear. They offered whale-watching trips, kayak rentals and lessons, and tours, where customers paid for the privilege of learning the basics and then went on two- or three-day ocean kayaking trips to islands and back along the coast. To further make ends meet, he and May were also licensed private investigators, and he was a scuba diver, often called upon by the local police to retrieve lost objects from the bay.

They had turned the old Sunday school classrooms in the basement into five apartments. Their summer workers lived there, but now, it was just he and Jana. Early on, he and May had remodeled the kitchen with all new appliances, added a washer and dryer, and turned one of the classrooms that was lucky enough to have a fireplace into a lounge with TV, stereo, and shelves of paperback books. A few years ago, Fog Point encouraged its businesses to add colorful murals along the outsides of their buildings, so Jake and May had hired a local firm to cover their church in bright purple, and then they'd hired an artist to paint a large mural of a whale along one side. It was known to all in Fog Point as "the Purple Church" ever since.

The business was still technically open in January, but you could count on one hand the number of people who actually bought something. After Christmas, many Fog Point businesses just shut down and went on vacation for two months. Florida was clearly the destination of choice. But for Jake this morning, Florida was a distant dream as snow blew sideways at the basement windows and rattled the boards.

And while the wind blew, Jake sat in the kitchen and listened to a blues radio station while he painted little figures for his tugboat. He heard the sound of feet upstairs. Then it was quiet. Was Jana back from the McLarens' already? But she usually charged down the stairs full of words and exclamations. He put down the sailor, wiped his hands on a cloth, and went up the stairs that led to the sanctuary and to his and May's office, which in its former life was a sacristy.

May was sitting at the computer, clacking furiously on the keyboard. Her cane leaned against the wooden table, the front of which was inscribed with *In Remembrance of Me.*

"My laptop's in the shop in Ridley," she said without looking up. "Stupid thing needs a new motherboard. Had to come here." She wore the ball cap she always had on with the word *Squirrels* imprinted across the front.

"You came out in this?" He pulled up a chair, sat beside her, and strained to see the computer screen.

"Had to. I told you."

In the years they'd owned Adventure Whale Tours and Outfitting, Salvage and Investigations, May had become like an older sister to him, a best friend and a trusted business partner.

"*Purple Whale* work?" Jake asked her. He leaned closer, adjusted his glasses.

She shook her head. "No. It's about that girl."

"Ah."

The police discovered that the girl, who'd been dubbed "the Frozen Girl" by the media, had been staying at the Dew Drop Inn out on the highway, two miles from town, and had registered as Irene Johnson from 209 Sea View Drive, Maplewood, New Brunswick, Canada. Police checked it out, of course. There was no such person as Irene Johnson and no such place as Maplewood, New Brunswick.

The only identification found on the girl was a slip of paper with May's name and number. This had been buried deep within a zipper pocket in her jacket. It was the only identifying mark she wore. Even the tags of her clothing had been torn out. They were clever, whoever they were. The police were at a loss.

The police had questioned May incessantly. Did May know the girl? No, she didn't. Why would May's name and number be on a slip of paper in her inside zipper pocket? May had no idea. Jake suggested that perhaps she'd come to Fog Point about a summer job. That seemed to satisfy the police.

"I still go with the summer job thing," Jake said, sitting down beside her.

"I don't think so. I just don't think so." She kept her fingers on the keyboard. "Since when do summer students come traipsing out here in the middle of winter without telling us they're coming? Has this ever happened before?"

"Always a first," Jake said.

May snorted and turned back to the computer. "I think it was something else. I think there's another explanation."

But Jake knew what she was doing on this cold and wintry Sunday afternoon. May was looking for a connection between this girl and her husband's death. Six years ago, May's police-chief husband was killed by a sniper's bullet while he was filling their truck at a road stop in Pennsylvania. The bullet had killed him and left May disabled. The police never found the Allentown Gas Station Sniper, but May never stopped looking for him.

4

E ven though she had grown up with it, Amy hadn't gotten into the habit of the institution known as The Sunday Afternoon Nap. When her parents and everyone else in her childhood home went to bed from three o'clock until five, she would sit on her bed and cut out paper dolls.

She had a collection of them, and when the dolls didn't come with the right clothes, she made her own, scissoring them from white paper—always remembering to add the little tabs that folded over and kept them on—and coloring them in with her box of Crayolas. The two hours went by quickly and left her with many dolls with lots of multicolored clothes.

These days she didn't make paper dolls, but on Sunday afternoons while Ben slept, she would make herself a full pot of herbal tea and read novels. After the Sunday dinner guests left—and there were always guests for dinner; that was part of her job description—she and Ben cleaned up the kitchen. Then he headed off to his nap, and she went to the window seat in the living room. Her time.

Jake and Jana had been there for lunch. This was an easy lunch because they were friends. No sense of having to try to entertain them or engage them in pointless conversation. Witnessing Ben's yawns, Jake had left a little while ago, but Jana had stayed; now Jana and Blaine were down in Blaine's room. Seven-year-old Charlie, who was fighting a bit of a bug, had crawled into bed with Ben.

Amy, her feet tucked up underneath her and covered in her grand-mother's afghan, was reading a novel. Or she wasn't reading it. Mostly she sat in the window, listening to the storm as snow blew against the pane. If this kept up, school tomorrow would be canceled. The more snow days they had, the more they would have to make up in the summer. Amy taught fifth grade at Fog Point Elementary School. She hated making up those snow days.

Something made her suddenly draw back, close the curtain, and wrap the blanket more securely around herself. It was as though a shadow had fallen across the land. She thought about the dead girl again and about her own daughter. Was there a mother out there somewhere who sat at a window and wondered where her daughter was? Why couldn't they find her?

A little while later, Amy went into the kitchen, closed both doors, put on a Bonnie Raitt CD, and began making brownies for their home Bible study, which was supposed to meet here tonight, if it didn't get canceled again. Which it probably would. Still, it might be nice to have brownies if the four of them were snowed in tomorrow. Or maybe Blaine and Jana would like them when they came upstairs from watching videos. She could hear them talking loudly about something.

The phone rang, and she raced to answer it, but Ben beat her to it. A few minutes later he came into the kitchen in gray sweats, bed-headed and yawning.

She didn't look up when she asked, "How long've you been awake?"

"Twenty minutes. Working on tonight's Bible study a bit more. I wanted to give the whole first chapter of Ephesians another look."

"And you're thinking we should still have it? Are you aware of the weather, Ben?"

Ben didn't say anything as he opened the refrigerator door.

Amy stirred in more cocoa and asked, "So, who was on the phone?"

"Rube. From the board." He took out the mustard and the ketchup and the mayonnaise and an almost empty container of orange juice and plunked them down on the counter.

"What did he want?"

"Don't know." He bent down, pulled more items out of the fridge. "He wanted to come over now and talk with me about something."

"Today? He wanted to come today? In the snow?"

He straightened to full height and regarded her. "Yes, Amy. Today."

"It must be important if he wants to come over and talk to you on a day like this. So is he coming?"

"I told him not to. In light of the weather. And yes, Amy, I am aware of the weather."

"Don't call me *Amy* like that, and what are you doing with all that stuff out?"

He turned away from her. "I'm trying to find the coffee. And why shouldn't I call you Amy? It's your name."

"But not the way you're saying it."

"How am I saying it? Never mind. Just never mind." He found the coffee can and pried off the lid. "I don't want to get into anything now."

"Neither do I, *Ben.* So you don't know what he wanted."

"I already said that." He spooned coffee into the coffee maker.

Amy went back to her brownies and wondered. Last week she had seen Rube in deep, frowning conversation with Lenore Featherjohn. Lenore repeatedly came to Stone Church and then got her feelings hurt and left for a while and then came back again. Most people just winked and nudged and said, "That's Lenore for you." If there was a gossip in church, it was Lenore. A close second was Enid, her neighbor.

"We need to keep a firmer hand on Blaine," Ben said thoughtfully while the coffee filtered through. "I saw her down in the front pew text messaging or whatever on her cell phone during the sermon. That isn't acceptable behavior in church."

"Did you ever think, Ben, that maybe it's your firm hand that's causing some of her problems?"

"Amy, that's unfair."

She shook her head. "I grew up in a minister's home. You didn't. I know what it's like to be a minister's daughter. It's hard. There's a lot to live up to. Let her find her own way, Ben."

Deep lines creased Ben's forehead. He opened his mouth to say something but must have thought better of it, because he closed it again.

Amy poured brownie batter into a pan and didn't look at him. No one was perfect, yet Ben demanded perfection. Everything had to be perfect, even food items in the refrigerator had to be arranged just so. Thing was, up until now, he *did* have the perfect family.

She said, "I'm making brownies. I'm going out to the living room to finish my novel."

"I'll bring you some coffee."

She left without saying anything. Amy was all out of things to say to him.

5

L ater, after Bible study was canceled and Jana went home, Blaine appeared in the kitchen and poured herself an oversized mug of coffee. This was new with her, this coffee drinking. She eyed her mother, but Amy wasn't going to say anything. She was choosing her battles. Coffee drinking by a fourteen-year-old just didn't make it to the top of the list.

Blaine lingered in the kitchen while Amy cut the brownies and placed the squares on a plate and pretended not to notice. That's what Amy did when Blaine was around. Too effusive and Blaine would be back down in her room with the door closed for a week. Even a smile dispensed at the wrong time had her glaring and saying, "What're *you* looking at?"

So Amy took the cautious route. She arranged the brownies artfully on the plate and said with a sigh, "Boy, would you look at that snow."

"Mom?"

Amy turned.

"Can I talk to you for a minute?"

"Why certainly, sweetie." What parent refused that offer?

"It's about Jana and me…"

Amy looked at this tall, thin daughter of theirs. Already she was taller than Amy and almost as tall as Ben. Amy looked at the way her knit pants rode low on her hips. And the small top she wore revealed her bare midriff and the belly-button ring even in this weather. But the thing that troubled Amy was the way Blaine looked so much older than her fourteen years.

Blaine shifted from foot to foot and said, "You know that girl? The one who froze to death? In the snowbank?"

"Yes?"

"Do you think she's an angel?"

"Why do you ask?"

"People are saying she's an angel."

"I know what people are saying, but people around here say a lot of strange things. That doesn't mean it's true."

"Jana thinks she's an angel."

"Jana does? That surprises me." Amy shook the crumbs from the pan into the sink.

Blaine stirred three tablespoons of sugar into her coffee and rolled her eyes. "Jana has a lot of weird ideas."

"She's not an angel," Amy said. "She's just a poor runaway girl who got lost and ended up here. Soon the police will find out who she is, and her parents will come."

"No, they won't." Blaine took a long drink of her coffee. "Ew, who made this?"

"Your dad did."

"Well, that figures. He always makes it too strong."

"He likes it strong."

"Well, he could think of someone else for a change."

"Blaine. Don't."

"Don't what?"

But Amy merely shook her head and placed the brownie pan in the sink, squirting some dish soap into it. "Have a brownie if you'd like."

"Can't, Mom. I'm a vegan. You know that."

"Blaine, they're brownies, not steak burgers."

"Do they or do they not have eggs in them?"

Amy didn't feel like arguing. She could say all sorts of things. She could say how concerned she was for Blaine's health. Fourteen-year-old girls needed milk and meat and lots of good protein. It wouldn't do any good; one never won an argument with Blaine.

Hearing Ben in the living room, Blaine automatically pulled down her shirt. Ben had hit the roof when Blaine showed up with a belly piercing. But he passed the kitchen and walked down the hall to the bathroom.

Blaine ran a hand through her chunky hair. Her nails were navy blue. "What a dork!" she said.

"Blaine! Don't talk about your father like that."

"I'm not talking about him, Mom. I'm talking about Jana."

Amy sighed. "Blaine, she's your friend. Please be nice to her."

"She's not a school friend, Mom. She's a church friend. That's all. And she's so *young*. You have to admit that."

"She's exactly one year younger than you are."

"I know, but…" She examined her fingernails. "She has all these weird ideas."

"About angels, you mean?"

"About *everything*. And then today I made this mistake. I'm text messaging her about something, and now she's all, 'Oh, we have to go to the police! We have to go to the police!' "

Amy looked at her. "What are you talking about?"

"I'm talking about the girl who died, the so-called angel. She's not an angel. I know because I talked to her. And so I text messaged this to Jana to get her off this stupid angel thing, and now she's saying I need to go to the police. Or tell her dad or something. Like I'm going to go over there and talk to Jana's dad."

"You *talked* to that girl? When *was* this?"

"It's not like I'm the only person she talked to when she was here, Mom. And besides it was nothing. And I only told Jana because she's all into this angel thing, and…now she's even thinking that *my* dad should have a funeral for her at the church."

Amy put her hand up. "Back up, Blaine. When did you talk to this girl?"

"Oh, I don't know. Like maybe a week ago. I can't remember exactly."

"You *spoke* with her?"

"Yes, Mom, weren't you listening? I spoke with her."

"Where?"

"She was all by herself on the boardwalk. And she sees me and we start talking."

"Blaine! They're saying that anyone who has any knowledge of her needs to come forward. That's been all over the news."

"Like I watch the news."

Ben stood in the kitchen now and stared at the two of them. "Blaine, you talked to her?" His hands around his coffee cup trembled, and the crease between his brows deepened.

6

When Lenore heard the doorbell, she wiped her hands on the sides of her apron and made her way down the hall. She'd been doing up a batch of cinnamon swirls and watching a cooking show on the little television in her kitchen. Was this the police again? She had talked to them so many times over the past week she'd memorized what they took in their tea. Bill, the one who seemed to be in charge, liked his black. But he always left half a mug. Lenore guessed he didn't like tea to begin with and was only being polite. The woman officer, Angela something-or-other, liked milk and sugar in hers. She always drank hers down. Lenore could imagine her heading home to her one-room apartment and her cat and making tea after work. The other young officer liked three spoons of sugar. He never finished his either. Maybe he thought lots of sugar would make it palatable.

Lenore's story never wavered. She'd found the body like that, hands together in prayer. Just like an angel. She was so stunned by the sight she didn't immediately know what to do, so she sat there in the snow for a while next to her.

She didn't tell them she was crying. She didn't tell them the whole thing reminded her of her baby who had also died. No one needed to know that she sat in the snow weeping until her knees were so cricked she couldn't get up without groaning. No one, not even the police, needed to know that bit of foolishness about her life.

"I'm coming. I'm coming," she said when the bell rang again. "Hold your horses."

If it wasn't the police, maybe it was someone to see one of her boys. But you'd think their friends would go to the boys' entrance rather than her front door.

But it wasn't the police. It wasn't some girlfriend of Carl's. Standing there was the mother-and-daughter duo of Rose Nation and Pearl Sweet. They were bundled in coats and rubber boots and scarves, and Pearl held an umbrella. Pearl was stomping her feet while she waited.

"Oh my," Lenore said. "I didn't get the walkway swept yet. And here you are on my front porch. Come in. Get yourselves in out of the cold. I'll make some tea. Come in, come in. My boys haven't got the driveway shoveled yet. But do come in for tea."

She led them in and took their coats and hung them on the brass hooks in the foyer. What did they want? Was this about the church? She knew Rose and Pearl were regulars at Stone. Was there some trouble there that they needed her opinion on? She had lots of opinions and wasn't stingy in giving them out. Especially if it concerned Stone Church. She'd already given Rube a piece of her mind about that minister and the way things had gotten over there lately.

"Thanks, Lenore," Pearl said, leading her mother by the arm. "We won't stay long."

They followed her into the kitchen, which was warm from the oven. Lenore knew Rose a bit. Way back in the dark ages they went to school together. Pearl, her only child, had never married. A long time ago now, Pearl got pregnant and the child was put up for adoption. When Rose's second husband died of heart failure, Pearl moved in with her mother.

"We wouldn't normally bother you," Pearl said. "But Mother's arthritis has been acting up something fierce. That's why we came."

Lenore raised her eyebrows at that one. What in the world did they think? That Lenore could do something about arthritis? "Tea might be nice, then…"

"Tea would be nice. Mother would like tea."

Lenore filled the kettle and set it on the stove. The two women sat close together at the kitchen table. While the kettle boiled, they looked at each other, then out the window to the backyard, and then back again at Lenore. They weren't saying anything. The whole thing was rather disturbing and confusing, and Lenore kept flitting from her tea to the cinnamon swirls and back again to the tea.

As Lenore pulled a tray of cinnamon swirls from the oven, she kept saying, "Well, well," to the women, and then, "You're in luck. A fresh batch!"

Finally Rose said, "Tell her, Pearl. We need to tell her why we're here."

Pearl looked at her mother, took a deep breath, and said, "Okay, we want to see the snowbank where the angel was. We think it might help Mother's arthritis. Look at her hands. Show her your hands, Mother."

Rose held out her hands. They were knobby and swollen and red, and Lenore flinched at the sight of them.

"We came here because it's Mother's last resort. I want to take her out back and have her touch the snowbank."

Lenore was still confused. "You want to what?"

"Touch the snowbank. The one where the angel was."

Lenore made a sound in the back of her throat. A half grunt. A swallow. She blinked her eyes rapidly several times.

"We think her presence might still be there. Like an imprint," Pearl said.

"An imprint of the angel," Rose said.

Baffled, Lenore kept making little noises in the back of her throat.

"It's our last hope," Pearl said again. "The doctors can't do anything else for her."

Lenore still hadn't said anything.

"Can you show us exactly where she was?" Rose asked.

Lenore took a deep breath. "The snowbank's all covered up with new snow. The police have been digging around like it was buried treasure. Nothing's like it was."

"But she was praying? Right?"

Lenore nodded. "That's what I said." She was careful not to look straight at their eyes when she told them.

"Could we go out there?" Pearl leaned forward, her eyes wide. Her curly gray hair was still wet in ringlets from the snow.

"Let's have tea first," Lenore said. "Let's just drink our tea." She poured the hot water into the floral china teapot that had been her mother's. She said nothing while the two women talked about how everyone was saying this was God's judgment—this weather, along with the ice. And now this angel had come to offer them all a chance for redemption. They were actually sitting in her kitchen and saying this. That this was a chance for hope. A tiny angel child who was praying for the whole town of Fog Point. Lenore kept silent.

Later, after they'd finished their tea and cinnamon swirls, Lenore got their coats and boots for them and put on her own, and they traipsed out the back door to the snowbank.

"There," she said pointing. "That's where she was. Where I saw her that morning. Just like she was praying. Like an angel." Lenore stood back and watched as Pearl held her mother's arm. The two of them stood and stared into the snowbank. They stood for a long time while snow rained down on them.

And then Rose did a strange thing. With a strangled cry she collapsed to her knees. She began to cry. Loud sobs. After rocking like that for a moment, Rose leaned forward and fell into the snow.

"Rose!" Lenore shouted.

"It's okay," Pearl said to Lenore. "Let her be. It's okay. She's worshiping." Then Pearl knelt next to her mother, who was moving her arms in the snow. Lenore thought of the snow angels that she and her friends used to make back when they were girls, but they bore little resemblance to this wrinkled woman with the gnarled fingers making a horrible parody of a snow angel.

Lenore watched, her feet becoming colder and colder in her boots as she shifted from foot to foot. Wouldn't it be funny, she thought, if Rose's arthritis actually did go away?

7

Bible study group was canceled, Ben had told Jake on the phone. "Don't bother coming out on a night like this," he'd added. "It's only going to get worse."

Jake didn't tell him he hadn't planned on going anyway. They always asked. He never showed up. Even though, aside from May, Ben was probably his closest friend. On mornings when the roads were plowed, the two of them ran the length of the boardwalk. When they felt really inspired, they ambled up the cliff path to the gazebo and back again. It was a good work-out. Jake liked these early morning runs, which usually turned into early morning talks where they solved all the problems in the universe, or at least talked about them. They also had a standing lunch date on Mondays. But going to a Bible study with a group of people from church, well, that was another matter entirely.

Wasn't it enough that Jake had started back at church, something he said he would never do?

He'd grown up in church, even went to Bible school for a year. Met his wife there. Got married. Toyed with the idea of being a missionary. Had all the pamphlets and had gone as far as working through the application form. Then Connie got pregnant. Which was okay, too. So he went to the police academy. Law enforcement had always been his real dream, anyway.

They had two beautiful daughters, a wonderful life. Then, six years ago,

Connie ran off with the head of the church board. They were married now and had a kid of their own. They all still went to church there. No doubt Keith was back to being the head of the board. That's how things worked in that world. Which was why Jake left it.

Jake was painting struts on the side of his model tugboat, which was laid out on the Ping-Pong-table-sized kitchen table. A few doors down, in the lounge, the television was on. Jana was watching a video. They didn't have television reception here. He seldom watched it and so hadn't bothered to hook up the cable. When Jana would ask, "But, Dad, can't you get cable?" he'd answer, "Why?" They owned enough videos to open up a rental store. He had an extensive collection, and the summer students and boaters who stopped in to use the laundry and showers traded videos and books, and they always ending up leaving more than they took.

When it was determined that Jana would live with him this year, he'd come downstairs and weeded through the videos and turfed the R-rated ones. Sometimes the cruising boaters who came through weren't very discriminating. He didn't need Connie and Keith getting wind of this. That would be all they would need, that he was contributing to the moral demise of a minor, they being such examples of high moral ground themselves.

With thick white cotton thread, Jake attempted to tie a miniature Turk's-head knot for the front of his tugboat. He examined his work. It did sort of look like a Turk's-head, if he did say so himself. He had just taken up this model-building hobby. Pop Maynard, who ran the only marina in town, had a lot of scraps lying around that he'd said Jake could have for the taking, tiny pieces of teak, perfect for his tugboat. Plus Carrie, Pop's daughter and Jake's on-again, off-again girlfriend, had given him a book on model ships for Christmas.

This was his first attempt at building one.

"Hey, Dad?" Jana stood in the doorway.

Jake looked up at his very beautiful thirteen-year-old.

"I was thinking." She shuffled. She paused. "You want some popcorn?"

"Love some."

She got out a bag from their stash of microwave popcorn, which seemed to be a staple in their kitchen. They had all kinds, from the low-fat, low-salt, low-taste to extra butter and sweet. While it popped, she sat down across from him.

"You're good at that." She tucked a hank of brown hair behind one ear.

"It's kind of fun. What're you watching in there?" he asked.

She shrugged. "An old movie." She looked away from him. "*Fifty First Dates*. It's kind of cheesy but cute. I'm not really watching. I'm mostly doing homework." The microwave dinged. She got up and took the bag out of the microwave. It never failed to amaze him how much Jana looked like her mother. She was shrugging and pouting and not looking at him.

"Is everything all right?" He picked up his paintbrush again.

She shrugged. It was that expression, that slight pout, the little pixie look, the expelling of air through the lower lip that was so like Connie. "Sort of."

She poured a bit of the popcorn into a bowl for herself, left the rest for him, and headed for the door.

"Jana?"

She turned.

"What's on your mind?" he asked.

"Why do you think something's on my mind?"

"Because you get a certain look in your eye when something's on your mind. Your bottom lip comes out." *Just like your mother,* he wanted to add but didn't.

She brought her popcorn bowl back into the kitchen. "Can I ask you something, Dad?"

"Shoot."

She sat down across from him, fiddled with a few unpopped kernels. Something was wrong. It worried him. Was living here not what she expected? Did she want to go back to Kentville and her mother already? "Jana?"

She moved her chair closer to the table, leaned across it as if she were afraid someone else would hear. But they were the only two in the whole building. "Blaine told me a secret about a dead person. I told her she needs to talk to the police. But she doesn't want to. She says it was a secret."

He blinked at her. "What's this about, Jana?"

"It's about Blaine."

"Yes."

"And the girl that died."

"Okay."

"Blaine told me in church that they were friends. That they knew each other. And that the girl came 'specially to Fog Point to see Blaine. Like she knew her. From the Internet."

Jake stared at her, a handful of popcorn in midair. "Blaine told you this?"

Jana nodded. "She's going to be so bummed when she finds out I told you. But I kept telling her how important this is…"

"It is important, Jana. It's very important. The police will want to know this. We're going to have to tell them."

8

My breath fogs around me like ghosts on this cold morning. I'm sitting at the dilapidated table in the unheated barn, and my palms are down flat on top of it. I should have remembered to wear gloves. I look at my hands. They are the withered and deeply veined hands of an old, old man.

It's early, much earlier than I ever get up anymore. But I'm worried, and when I worry, I don't sleep much. Last night it was the sounds of the house contracting in the cold that kept me awake.

Back when the farm belonged to Glad and me, not to my sons, I got up early all the time. Four o'clock and I'd be out doing the milking. I leave that to Tim and Ashe now. Tim and Ashe are my sons. I have five children. There's Tim and Ashe and Roger. Those three live out here and run the farm now, with their wives Bobbie, Suze, and Meredith. I'm surprising myself that I can remember all their names. Maybe the cold is good for this old noggin of mine.

Then there's Pam, my only daughter. She's married to a hog farmer, and they live down the road twenty minutes or so.

The only one missing from this great family conclave is Philip, my second youngest, who went off to university and now lives in the middle of the city a thousand miles away, where he works in computers. He's already on his second wife, who's painfully allergic to farms, she says. "Anything green? Forget it!" she always says. They seldom visit.

I have lots of grandchildren and even one great-grandchild, a boy who lives here at the house. His mother, Gabrielle, is my eldest granddaughter. She had him when she was still in school. His name sometimes goes out of my head, but I think it's Jonah. My granddaughter lives here too. It's a big farm house.

Ashe works here in the dairy operation and lives with Suze and their kids in the old hired-man's house that they redid a few years ago. Roger and Meredith built themselves a house on the property, about a ten-minute walk away, down by the water. They have a few kids too. There are always kids around. Too many of them, I think sometimes.

I'm still in the main house. They haven't kicked me out of here. Not yet anyway. Tim and Bobbie sleep in the master bedroom that Glad and I conceived all of them in. My room now, the old-man's room, is a small one off the family room that gives out onto the kitchen. The room I'm in isn't meant to have a bed. It's supposed to be an office. It'd started off being an office and will probably revert back to being an office after I'm gone.

I know their thinking. A room on the main floor doesn't require the use of so many stairs, and one has to think about such things when dealing with an elderly parent in the first stages of Alzheimer's. I can manage the stairs very well, thank you very much. But I comply. That's what you do when you're old. You comply.

Plus, Glad's not around anymore to fight all the battles. Glad was always the strong one, the opinionated one. She was the one—I credit her for that—who took us from being poor dirt farmers to the huge, modern dairy operation we run today. And now that people are drinking milk again and shunning the transfats or whatever they are and eating real butter instead of that margarine slop, profits have never been better.

It's quiet in this old shed-barn. The only sound is my cold breath. I'm sitting at the table that Glad and me used to have in the kitchen. I like the quiet. The house with all its different people and their friends is never quiet. Even when I close my door, I hear everything. Tim and Bobbie arguing the way they do. The little tyke of a great-grandson going on about something. My granddaughter fighting with her mom and slamming the doors. The video games and the television and the computer. My son Ashe may look like Glad, but Tim is most like her. Always arguing. Always having to be so right about everything.

It's funny. You want your sons to grow up and take over the family business, but then when that happens, there's a part of you that wishes it hadn't.

"What're you doing out here, Dad?" I am roused from my musings by my eldest son, who stands haloed in the light from the door, rubber boots, a black wool cap pulled down over his ears. His milking costume.

"You're letting all the cold air in," I tell him.

"Which is kind of funny when you think about it," Tim says, coming inside and closing the door. "Since it's the same temperature in as out."

"But not as windy," I answer. "You're letting the wind in."

"Are you okay, Dad?"

"Fine, son."

"Coffee's ready."

"I'll be in in a minute."

"You need to come in, Dad. It's too cold to be out here."

"In a minute, son."

I watch my eldest son, the one who is so like Glad, blow out a breath and close the door behind him. I've come out here because this is the one place I can think. All my life this has been the place I come to when I'm worried. Even when it was me and Glad raising four sons and one daughter, and I worried about the farm, about money, I would come out here and think and pray. This building was a proper barn then, too, and not this shed, which is the catchall for everyone's junk. It's become the place they keep disused tractor parts, former bicycles and skates and tables and chests of drawers and sleds and wagons, and this old antique wooden table and chair, where I sit now. Tim keeps threatening to pull down this old barn, but I won't hear of it. When I'm gone, I'll bet it'll be torn down, the stuff all sold at some big auction.

It still has the same barn smell, though—the hay, the wood. It's a smell you can almost feel on your skin. A smell that has a color, even. A kind of brown with gray and shot through with something bright. Like yellow. Or pink even. Or maybe a certain shade of blue.

The cold seeps through my pants and boots and long johns that I wear all the time now. I should go in. Before they all start worrying. Before they all come out. Or call the doctor.

A long time ago, long before The Terrible Thing happened, it would be Glad who'd be in the kitchen, whipping up big batches of pancakes and fried eggs for me and the hired men. I can still picture her in her skirt and stained kitchen apron, flipping pancakes and eggs for them all. Between giving orders, whistling. And then telling me and the hired men what to do. Where to farm that day. As if we didn't know. I'd wink at the men, like I always did.

Thing is, I hadn't minded her orders when we first got married. I thought she was competent and capable. Hadn't she been the one who'd orchestrated the purchase of the adjacent farm for far less than market value? Everyone in the whole family had her to thank for that.

She always whistled. Women don't often whistle. Women usually hum. She's long dead now. Yet, sometimes if I listen carefully, I can still hear her whistling.

I sit at the table and stomp my cold boots on the wooden floor. We have newer barns now; sleek, modern things with proper ventilation and lighting and heating in the winter and air conditioning in the summer, all run by computers even. A place where the cows line up factory-like and surrender their milk.

But the place is unchanged from this past summer when I came in to find the girl camping out and using this as her table, her backpack and things piled neatly in the corner.

I always thought it was strange that out of all the sheds she could have chosen to set up her squatter's existence, she chose mine.

9

D id you hear? Rose Nation's arthritis got cured."

The Fog Point Garden and Flower Club met for lunch the second Monday of every month. They had just listened to a visiting horticulturist talk about rootings and cuttings and were now finishing up their lunch.

Lenore choked on a mouthful of coffee and managed, just barely, to keep that mouthful firmly in her mouth instead of spurting it all over her slice of Nootie's blueberry pie. And then, when she did manage to swallow, she coughed and placed her hand to her chest. Because of her distress, everyone's attention focused on her, and she apologized to the ladies and gentlemen of the Fog Point Garden and Flower Club. She was fine. Really, she was. Just a bit of coffee down the wrong way. It happens. I'm fine.

After that was settled, after Lenore patted her chest and steadied her hands, the conversation, of course, went back to Rose's arthritis. At the end of the table, farthest away from Lenore, Beth leaned forward and said, "What do you mean? Her arthritis got cured?" Beth suffered with something called gout.

"She called me this morning," Beryl said. "She woke, she said, without pain for the first time in many years."

"How did it happen?" asked another. "Was it the bracelet?"

"My sister, you all know Millie Whaley?" said another. "She got one of those bracelets off the Internet. Said it didn't work. Said it wasn't worth the price she paid for it."

A dozen members of the club were sitting around the table in Noonan's back room, the room reserved for groups and meetings. AA met here twice a week, as well as the Garden and Flower Club, the Ministerial Association, the Fog Point Tourist Association, Weight Watchers, and the chamber of commerce. The oblong room's walls were decorated with not very good paintings of lighthouses. It was the closest thing Fog Point had to a convention center. Conventioneers could stay at Lenore's B&B and then come over here and have their meeting in the back room at Noonan's Café.

"No, it wasn't anything like that." Beryl looked toward Lenore. "It was the angel. Tell her, Lenore."

Lenore blinked her eyes. Felt hot. Felt her face redden. Swallowed. It had been years since she had suffered from hot flashes, but she suddenly wished she hadn't worn her heavy cardigan. Enid, beside her, helped her take it off her shoulders, get it on the back of her chair. "Warm," was all she said. Enid nodded. Enid lived across the street from Lenore. They'd known each other since they were girls.

"The angel chose to manifest itself to Lenore," someone else was saying, and everyone continued to look at her.

"I think we are truly blessed," another said.

"Oh my. Oh my, oh my, oh my," Lenore finally managed to get out.

"The story," Beryl said, "if Lenore is too modest to say, was that Rose and her daughter went yesterday to Lenore's snowbank. To hear Rose tell it, she could actually feel the angel's wings. She felt them fluttering by her face."

It was the snow, Lenore wanted to say. *The snow fluttering by her face. That's all it was.*

"She said the pain didn't immediately go away. Like, not right at the snowbank. But this morning when she woke up, she didn't feel a shred of pain. She called me right away."

Nootie came in with a tray of pie slices on plates.

"Nootie, what do you think about the angel?" Enid asked.

"Did anyone think it was merely the cold that did it?" Nootie said. "Caused the pain to end?"

"Cold doesn't cause arthritis to end, it only intensifies it," someone said.

Lenore looked down at her blueberry pie. Normally, she had to restrain herself from eating two pieces. But now, this pie held no appeal. She wondered how it could be that she was cold and hot at the same time. She struggled into her sweater again. She should go. She should never have come out on a day like this in the first place. So cold. Coldest February on record. A good half dozen of their members weren't even here. Her hands felt so cold. She put them in her lap, clutched them together. Maybe she was coming down with something. So many people were sick. It was the ice.

But Beryl kept talking. "Rose says God has worked a miracle upon us. A miracle upon us."

"Well, that would be a good thing," said Brill, one of only three men in the garden club. "You get people going to church, that's never a bad thing. Look how many people started back to church after 9/11."

Lenore took another sip of coffee. This sip managed to descend the proper way. Unfortunate though, because as soon as it hit her stomach, she thought she was going to be sick right there, upchucking her coffee and blueberry pie all over the table. Oh, the embarrassment of that! *But it would serve me right,* she thought. *For what I did. Strike me dead. Strike me dead right here.*

"Are you okay, dear?" Enid patted her shoulder.

"I'm fine. Thank you, dear. Yes. I just think I may be coming down with something."

"So many are sick this time of year, and, Lenore, you just go. You go home and get some rest."

Lenore shook her head. "No time for me to rest. I've got guests at the B&B."

"This time of year?"

"Come to see the ice, I suppose," Lenore said.

"Oh, my dear, you are working yourself to the bone," Enid said.

Across the table someone was saying. "God is visiting his wrath upon us, and one little angel comes to pray for us."

"I think we should be grateful," someone else said.

"His wrath?" another asked.

"For sure, his wrath. Look at all the things that could have happened. Without the angel, oh my, the ice could've covered us like that tsunami. Fog Point could've been completely covered in ice."

"Bert said more came in yesterday," Brill said.

One of the other men, a skinny man named Ty, who was a retired fisherman, leaned his elbows on the table and looked at them. "I don't believe all of this. You people, she's just a girl. A girl who came out here, for whatever reason, and found herself lost and somehow got in with the wrong people and got herself killed. Strangled, they say. At somewhere other than Lenore's backyard."

Lenore patted her stomach, seeking to quell its stirrings. She looked at Ty. They all did.

He opened his palms. "It was on the news this morning. Something about the position of the body. They could tell it'd been moved or something."

Lenore gasped but tried to hide it behind her hand. "I have to leave, have to go…" She got up, grabbed her purse, and fled from the room.

10

Blizzard watchers crowded Mags and Herman's Coffee Shop, one of a few businesses that stayed open during the winter, when Ben and Jake stopped in for lunch on Tuesday. Almost all the tables were full, and the place was noisy; the windows steamy from conversation and homemade soup made it impossible to see the bay. Jake didn't know a number of the faces, strangers with cameras on their tables. He guessed some of them might be newspeople.

Mags and Herman's was a place where you could get sprout sandwiches on something called Ezekiel bread and organic tea and fair-trade coffee. Not that Jake was into whole foods. Ben had ordered a ham and cheese on homemade rye, and Jake was chomping his way through a corned beef and sauerkraut.

But Jake and Ben were not talking about the ice or the newspeople. They talked instead about Ben's meeting the previous evening with his daughter and Amy and Bill, Jake's friend on the police force.

Jake picked up his sandwich and asked, "How did it go?"

Ben's eyes darted around the room, finally settling on Jake. He picked up his coffee and took a long drink. He mumbled something, and Jake had to lean forward to hear.

"They came over—Bill and another officer."

"Bill's a good man. He'd be gentle with Blaine."

"He was," Ben said and then went on with his story. It had been after ten when Bill knocked on their door. He'd driven through the blizzard in the police 4 x 4 to get there. He arrived when the storm hit its highest. Amy made a pot of decaf and set out a plate of brownies.

"We had no idea," Ben said to Bill, "that our daughter had spoken to her. If we'd known, we would have come forward sooner."

"It's probably nothing," Amy said, fluttering her hands as she set out napkins. "Blaine only talked to her that once. Bumped into her actually. Down at the boardwalk."

Blaine, in her pajamas, covered with a throw, sat huddled in an easy chair.

"That's not what I understand," Ben said. "I understand that our daughter had a relationship with this girl, a friendship they struck up on the Internet."

"That's not true!" Blaine said. "I don't even know her name! I don't even know who she is."

Amy shot him a look. But what was he to do? Blaine had text messaged Jana that she'd had a long e-mail friendship with the dead girl and IM'd regularly.

Bill put his glasses up on his forehead, as though he had a second pair of eyes up there, and opened up a notebook and took out a pen, all very methodical movements. He seemed to be in no hurry despite the lateness of the hour. "We're still trying to figure out who she is," he said. "And any conversation anyone had with her, however brief, might be of value in locating her family. So, Blaine…" He leaned forward, smiled, his hands on his knees, and faced her. "Can you start at the beginning? Tell me about talking with this girl."

His gentle manner seemed to have the right effect on Blaine because she said, "Okay, it was a couple of weeks ago. I was taking a walk down by the boardwalk and looking at the ice, and up walks this girl. She asks me where to find Featherjohn's B&B, so I tell her."

"And that was all? She just wanted to know where the bed-and-breakfast was?"

Blaine nodded.

Bill raised his eyebrows and wrote in his notebook.

Ben didn't believe a word of what Blaine said. He couldn't remember the last time Blaine actually went for a walk. He knew she was lying but didn't know why, and that worried him.

"I was given to understand you had a long friendship with her...don't lie," Ben began, but Bill put up his hand, then turned toward Blaine.

"When was this?" Bill put his pen down and took a drink of coffee.

Blaine shrugged. "I don't know. Couple weeks ago, maybe."

He reached into his pocket and produced a little calendar, which he handed her. "Would it help you to look at the dates?"

"It might." She took the calendar, studied it a minute, and then said, "Last Tuesday. The Tuesday before this past Tuesday. After school." She handed the calendar back to him.

He asked, "Had you had any contact prior to that meeting?"

She shook her head and said, "I just made that up about the Internet to get Jana off my case about the stupid angel. I made the whole thing up. And then she's all weird, thinking it's all true. Stupid..." Blaine muttered into the blanket she had now drawn up to her neck.

"Can we perhaps see your computer?" Bill asked. "That would help."

"I need it for school. Can I go now?"

Ben said, "If the police need your computer for an investigation, Blaine, you're going to have to give it to them. You don't have a choice in this."

"I can't, Dad. I need it for school. And I told you. I had to make up this big story to get Jana off my case. We never IM'd. I don't even know her name."

Bill smiled, rose. "It'll be all right," he said to Ben. "We'll let you know if we need to see her computer. Right now, we're just trying to identify her."

Bill had left then, and Amy had taken the plate of uneaten brownies into the kitchen.

The noise level in Mags and Herman's had risen as even more people piled in to get coffee and look at the ice, but Jake was looking intently at his friend. There was something wrong here, something Jake couldn't figure out. Ben had hardly eaten a bite of his sandwich. And he kept looking around the room and raking his hand through his hair. Something was troubling him.

"Ben, what is it?" Jake asked.

"What if…," he paused. "What if we're all in danger?"

"How could we all be in danger?"

"But what if we are?"

Norah Waterman, who ran the Inner Healing Shop two doors down on the boardwalk, came over, carrying a cup of coffee and wearing a winter coat that looked as if it used to be a blanket. She sat down across from Jake and Ben, disrupting their man-to-man. "Do you mind if I sit with you gentlemen? Look at this place, every table full. Everybody's come to see the ice. The world is in a mess, and the ice is the proof of it. It's like we're living in a Stephen King novel. Do you know that in other parts of the world"—she put down a steaming cappuccino at their table and shrugged out of her coat, underneath which she wore a sweater that obviously hadn't been too long off the back of a sheep—"the West in particular, they are getting *no* snow this season? And these are places that need snow because of skiing. They're crying for snow out there!"

Jake said, "We could ship some to them."

"Don't laugh," she said. "It may come to that. I heard Brill from the chamber actually talk about that very thing like it was feasible."

"They've got snowmakers out there for their ski hills," Jake said.

"Yeah, but, you guys…" She put her hands flat on the table. "Think of all the publicity for this little town. 'Ladies and gentlemen, the snow you are about to ski on came directly from Fog Point, home of the ice and the angel.'

Because now we have the whole angel thing working for us. I say we use it. I'm getting a bunch more angel pins into the store." She leaned back. "And now that we've actually had a 'healing'"—Norah made fake quotes in the air—"the world will be beating a path to our door. We'll be as famous as Lourdes…did I mention I'm getting more angel pins?"

Ben and Jake looked at her, mouths agape.

"Oh, you guys didn't hear? Apparently some lady went to Featherjohn's, touched the place in the snow where the girl's imprint was, and was instantly cured from arthritis. Now people are lining up behind Lenore's B&B for their healing touch."

Jake couldn't respond, but the feeling that something was wrong wouldn't leave him. What if, as Ben suggested, they were in danger?

11

B en was quiet. He'd been quiet and strange since their meeting with the police. Amy was clearing the supper table, and Charlie was helping her and telling her how he and his friend were inventing a video game. Amy tried to pay attention to her son, but she kept thinking about the meeting with the police. Ben didn't believe Blaine. He'd made that clear. At the meeting with the police he'd practically accused her of lying. Blaine had her challenges, but to accuse her, embarrass her the way he did. There was no excuse for that. After Bill had gone, Ben had turned to Blaine. "It's one thing to lie to your parents; it's another to lie to the police."

Amy's mouth had dropped open. "Ben?"

He shook his head. "You need to be truthful about talking to this girl. Nothing is served by withholding information." Ben twirled a pen in his hands, running it in and out through his fingers. Amy had found the gesture distracting and wished he would stop. "Nothing is gained by lying. Nothing at all."

Blaine had merely shrugged, gotten up, the throw still draped around her shoulders, and headed downstairs to her room.

Amy had said to Ben, "Why are you saying this? Why are you accusing Blaine of this?"

"I know our daughter," he'd said. "I know when she's lying and when she's telling the truth."

"...and then we have these red guns that shoot sideways," Charlie said, "When you have these special bullets, and the way you get these bullets is you sneak behind enemy lines. But you have to get in and not let anyone see you. It's really hard..."

Amy filled the saucepan with water and placed it in the sink to soak. "Bullets?"

Charlie grinned and his eyes sparkled. She could see the smattering of freckles on his nose. All those freckles always made her feel soft and warm, like a mother should feel. Chatterbox Charlie, his grandmother called him. Charlie, their miracle child. That's what she called him, never to his face, and never even to Ben, but to herself, that's what she called him.

Amy could hear the television in the living room, even though the volume was low. Ben was catching up on the evening news. From the kitchen she could see him on the edge of the couch, hands on his knees, gazing intently at the screen. What was it with him lately? He usually wasn't that interested in the news.

Blaine was already in her bedroom with the door closed. Father and daughter hadn't spoken since last night's visit with the police. It was silent downstairs, and Amy guessed Blaine was in there, her headphones plugged into her iPod. Why should she come up and join the family? She had her music, her own TV, and now her own cell phone. Another sore spot between her and Ben. Ben said she had to earn a cell phone by good behavior, and Amy said a cell phone in today's world was a must. "We need to keep track of her, Ben."

In the end, Ben had relented.

"...So, Mom, do you want to see a prototype?" Charlie was looking up expectantly. "It's just pictures we drew. But I could show them to you."

Prototype? Was this normal language for a seven-year-old?

"I'd love to, Charlie."

So that's what they did after they finished clearing the dishes. She went up to his room and looked through the drawings he and his friend had come up with. Intricate drawings punctuated by a lot of POWs and ARGHHs!

She tousled all that cowlicked hair of his and said, "Don't you think your game could be a little less violent?"

"But all the good games are like this, Mom." He looked up and grinned. "You want to see how it works?"

"How about homework, Charliekins?"

"All done, Mom."

"All of it?"

Again he grinned up at her. "All except for one problem."

"Let's have a look at it then. Your old mother isn't a teacher for nothing, you know."

He opened his book, and five minutes later he'd figured out long division with two numbers.

With a prayer and a kiss, she tucked him in. *Bless this house. Bless this child. Bless both my children. Bless this family.*

Next, she went down to Blaine's room and found her daughter sprawled on her bed and pushing buttons on her cell phone. "Blaine?"

"Mom, I'm busy. Just a minute."

Amy sat on a chair in the corner and watched her. Blaine glared at her. "Mom? I'm on the phone."

"Your homework?"

"I did it in school. Mom, I gotta go…"

And the look her daughter gave her made her feel small and tired and sad. Amy was tired of fighting, tired of feeling this way. She closed Blaine's door behind her and went back upstairs.

The news was off. Ben was in the kitchen. The kettle was on.

"I need to talk to you, Amy."

She sat down at the kitchen table. She'd wait, without talking, until Ben decided to tell her whatever it was he wanted to tell her. He folded his hands on the table. He looked so like a minister with his long lean body, his narrow glasses; plus he favored dark turtlenecks, which always made him look like he was wearing a clerical collar even when he wasn't.

"I think," he said to her, "I think, Amy, that you should tell me what's wrong. I know something is. I think you should tell me."

She stared at him, mouth open. "You're asking what's wrong with *me*?"

He cleared his throat. "You seem so...how shall I put it? Unhappy."

She stared at him. "What's wrong with *me*? You accuse Blaine of lying, and you ask what's wrong with *me*? When I try to stick up for her—"

"Can we not make it about Blaine for once? Why does it always have to be about the children?"

"For the simple reason that it *is* always about the children, Ben."

"I don't think it has to be."

He reached across the table, took her hand. She fought the urge to pull it away. "You just seem so distant lately. Like you're not here."

"I still can't believe you think there's something wrong with me. You're not speaking to your daughter, and you're asking what's wrong with *me*? Doesn't that seem a little weird to you, Ben?"

"No, Amy, this started way before the incident with Blaine. And we've always stood together as far as the children were concerned. But this is from before that."

There *was* something wrong, something she'd never shared with him and something she never would. If she could admit it to herself, this whole thing with Blaine had given her a convenient excuse. She hated that he was figuring that out.

"Life gets crazy," he said to her. "Maybe what we need," he said playing with her fingers, "maybe we need a date night. You and me. Dinner in Ridley? Maybe take in a play at the theater there?"

She smiled, just a little. Would it be wrong if she went and pretended to be happy?

"I love you, Amy. No matter what happens, I love you."

His searching gaze finally found her, and she felt herself weaken. How was it that Ben's love for her had never faltered? Through almost twenty-five years of marriage, his love for her was like his love for God. Steadfast, pure, unchanging. Solid. She wondered how he did it. He never faltered, while she faltered all over the place. She grabbed a wad of Kleenex from the box on the table and dabbed at her eyes, then stopped. *No matter what happens?* She put the Kleenex down and looked at him. *What was going to happen? What did he mean by that? It has to have something to do with Blaine and the girl and the police.*

"What do you mean, 'whatever happens,' Ben? What?"

"It hardly bears repeating."

"So repeat it anyway."

"It was just rumors."

What was he talking about?

"Okay." He spread his hands wide. "You were asking about Rube, right? And the rumor?"

Her eyes went wide. What rumor?

"You want to know why he called, right? And what's been on my mind, right? Well, turns out he heard a rumor I was resigning, moving to a pastorate out west."

"What!"

"That's what I said. Sometimes I don't know how these things get started. I told him it was totally false."

Amy stared at him, her mouth open.

"Probably someone heard something, got their facts wrong, and then went running to Rube."

"Really?" On top of Blaine and the police and the dead girl, there were rumors like this? "Who went running to Rube? What are you talking about, Ben?"

"Apparently Lenore Featherjohn heard it somewhere and asked him whether it was true or not," Ben said.

"Ah." Lenore Featherjohn. That explained it.

"Why the 'ah'?" he asked.

"That woman has not liked us from day one."

"She's lonely, old, and afraid, Amy."

"Afraid of what?" Amy said, getting up. "She's got the whole town at her beck and call, and now she's spreading rumors?"

"She doesn't mean half of what she says. She just says things off the top of her head."

"Okay, Ben, this is it. This is exactly what I'm talking about. You are giving Lenore Featherjohn, a busybody, the benefit of the doubt, but not your own daughter."

He was quiet for a while; maybe her words were sinking in. But then he said, "Do you know she has a son in the ministry?"

"Of course I know that. Everybody within earshot of Lenore at any given time or place knows that. Everybody also knows that the famous son of hers was a candidate for Stone, but then the church in its wisdom wanted you. Yes, Ben, I know that. I also know she was so miffed, she quit Stone after that for a while. What are you getting at?"

"I'm just saying that rumors have surfaced but that the board is dealing with them. Just in case you hear anything. It will all die down soon. I'm confident of that."

But Amy knew in her soul that this was only the beginning.

12

S o here's what we know so far," May told Jake. "A girl no one can identify is found in Lenore Featherjohn's backyard. She has no ID. Police check the room she's staying in and find no ID, nothing. She comes here and sees Blaine McLaren and asks where Featherjohn's B&B is. But…" May thrust her Magic Marker at the air. "But we know she wasn't going there for a room, because she was already checked in at the Dew Drop Inn. So what was her business at Lenore's? And so she goes there. And dies. Plus, the only thing she has on her is a slip of paper with my name and number."

With each point she made, May stabbed her black marker on the opened-up brown paper grocery bag where she'd drawn circles and arrows and radiating lines and more diagrams, all in various colors. She always worked this way, and Jake found it fascinating. He mostly sorted everything through in his head.

It was Wednesday evening, and Jake and Jana, along with Carrie, had just enjoyed a huge pot of May's late husband's famous chili at her little cottage down in The Shallows.

Jake hadn't known Carrie would be here, but May was sure her two best friends—Carrie and Jake—belonged together. It wasn't Jake who disagreed with that.

"Hey, Jake," Carrie said when she saw him. That was Carrie, bright and cheerful but always skirting the point. He would have preferred that she look slyly away or ignore him or look nervous and uncomfortable around him. *That* he could deal with.

At Christmas he'd asked her to marry him. He had a ring and everything. Her response: "I can't, Jake. I love you. You are my dearest friend. But I can't."

My dearest friend. Not good enough. Tonight at supper, she'd gone on and on in her cheery way about the weather and the ice and the boats her dad was taking care of. And Jake realized this was her way of dealing with things—put on a cheerful face.

He knew she had disappointments in her life. She'd had to leave a high-profile news job in Detroit to come back home to manage her father's business after her mother died. She had a schizophrenic brother who was a constant concern. If this is what she had to do, then let her be.

And this was what May had told him after dinner as his gaze followed Carrie and Jana walking on the ice and laughing.

"She'll come around," May said.

"I'm sorry, May." He looked back to her. "You wanted to talk?" Even though May was his closest friend, he didn't feel like talking about Carrie. There wasn't anything else to say.

He watched Carrie and Jana in comfortable conversation out on the shore. The tide was coming in, sweeping over the ice statues in the bay.

May was one of those people who didn't mind shoptalk, and after the meal was over, she had said, "Okay, Carrie, you and Jana go out for a walk. Jake and I have work to get at." The wind was blowing snow along the marsh plains. Everything was white. Jake saw Carrie raise her eyebrows and smile at Jana. They grabbed their coats, mitts, scarves, and hats from a wooden coat-tree beside the door, pulled on their boots, and left. The ground was lumpy and frozen and wild, and Jake watched the two of them through May's window, his daughter and his girlfriend. No, not really his girlfriend—his friend.

One last look at Carrie and Jana, and he had turned his attention back to

May. He was sure May wanted to discuss ways their business could make money over the winter, such as selling and renting cross-country skis or snowshoes. Instead, she'd opened up this paper bag to show him all her work.

"I was doing some research today," she said, "on the Allentown Gas Station Sniper. I'm not ruling that out of this equation. I know what you're thinking, Jake, that this is a long shot. But she had my name. She was looking for me."

"She was also looking for Featherjohn's B&B."

"I'm having the handwriting analyzed. See if it matches anyone that had anything to do with the sniper."

His attention drifted again to Carrie. He watched her in her big red coat, her hands in her pockets, and the matching red earmuffs she wore. Most of the time, Carrie seemed to favor clothes from places like L.L.Bean, but she also bought clothes regularly on eBay, old things. And sometimes she showed up in vintage jackets, scarves, and boots she'd gotten deals on.

"…assuming we take the case. Pro bono, if you will," May was saying. "I need to know what you think of that."

Jake looked at her. He needed to pay better attention. "Pro bono," he said.

"Yes, Jake, pro bono. The police, well, she's just one of many cases, and her parents aren't coming forward. Why not? Wouldn't you move heaven and earth if Jana or Alex were missing?"

"I think this is a pretty high priority with the police now, May."

"Right now it's a priority," she said aiming a purple Magic Marker at him. "But it won't be for long. Before long, they'll be moving on to something else, and she'll just end up in a Jane Doe box marked Unsolved."

"It's only been a week, May."

"That's a long time for a person to be missing, especially a teenage girl. If the police don't find out who she is, I propose we offer to help out. I know Bill and his crew would be happy for an extra couple pair of hands. He's already mentioned as much to me."

"Free doesn't pay the bills."

She looked around her. "Neither does sitting around on our duffs building model tugboats. What else are we doing this time of year, Jake? I'm willing to do this. Because," she looked down at the sheet of paper, "who else does she have?" She paused a moment and then straightened. "Okay, I'm going to see if we can get a complete copy of the autopsy report when it's ready. Bill's already told us lots, but I'd like to read it for myself."

Jake nodded. He had to admit, the case intrigued him. And it just might be what he needed to get his mind off Carrie and her inability to commit, and Ben and his problems.

13

I t was hard to find a time when both her sons were gone from their apart-ment, but on Thursday morning, after her B&B guests were fed, Lenore made her way down to the basement. Earl was on his way to Ridley Harbor doing who knew what. Probably he'd come home with some sort of new computer gizmo. How he could afford it all, she didn't know. Well, that was his business, wasn't it?

Carl was off doing some community service, court ordered, stemming from an illegal sale of a firearm last summer. But since his quick thinking resulted in the saving of at least three lives, the judge had been lenient, and Carl got off with community service. So, on Monday, Wednesday, and Thurs-day afternoons, Carl was down at the Boys and Girls Club in Ridley Harbor.

Ten minutes after Earl left, Lenore made her way down the kitchen stairs to where her sons lived. They called it an apartment when they referred to it, and that's how Lenore talked of it too, "My sons live in the apartment in my lower level." In fact, it wasn't an apartment but the entire level underneath her rather large Victorian bed-and-breakfast. It was a cellar, really, with no inner walls, whose rooms were defined only by the placement of furniture.

They didn't pay rent. If they wanted a proper apartment, a proper room—and she had plenty of those—they'd have to *pay* her. As long as her grown sons, both of them in their thirties now, stayed in her cellar, they could live there for free.

When she'd first initiated this rule, she thought it would be a good way to get them to pay her something for living in the good rooms upstairs. Instead, they took her up on it and decided to move downstairs. What could she do?

Plus, they seemed to like it here. At least they never complained. Earl moved all his computer equipment down here, along with their huge flat-screen TV. But, of course, this was only temporary for Carl. Just as soon as his house down on the water was finished, he'd be moving in there.

But Carl had stayed. They'd both been living here for almost a decade, which was how long the foundation of Carl's house on the water had been dug. People were beginning to complain. She knew that. It was an eyesore, some said, that unfinished place, all the boards lying around. A hazard, too. Lenore would be inclined to agree if the talk weren't about one of her sons.

"Carl's just had a few setbacks," she'd tell people. "When he gets on his feet, that place will be up and it will be beautiful. You just wait."

The cellar floor underneath her feet was uneven concrete topped with an old carpet, which was damp and mildewed in places. You could smell it down here. The only room with a real set of walls was the bathroom, and it smelled the worst. Every time she cleaned it, it reverted back to its basement-bathroom smell within a day.

The plumbers she hired to get the smell out told her the smell was in the pipes themselves. Because it was in the basement, which was really a converted root cellar, water in the toilet and sink had to be pumped up and out of the house via a sump pump. And therein lay the problem. If the pump wasn't working one hundred percent, water from the sink and shower and toilet stayed in the pipes. She'd had a new sump pump installed, but it hadn't solved the problem. "A toilet down here," one plumber told her, "isn't meant to be used on a daily basis."

Alongside the toilet was a little tin shower stall that always smelled of stale water and rusted pipes. There was no tub, and Lenore wondered how they could stand that. She grew up in a time when people bathed. They didn't shower. She enjoyed her baths in her old claw-foot tub, complete with bubbles of varying scents.

To the left of her against the far wall were their single beds, on opposite sides of the room and separated by a wall of dressers. Beds unmade, of course. On Mondays, when she came down here to collect their laundry, she made their beds with clean sheets. Those boys of hers, if left to their own devices, would probably never change their sheets! Once a week she gave the place a good once-over, scrubbing down their cubicle of a bathroom and vacuuming every inch of the carpet. Her fingers itched to make their beds now, just toss up the covers. But she didn't dare. Not today. Today she was down here for a different purpose.

On Earl's side of the room, a huge American flag covered the cement block wall. Carl's tastes ran to movie posters, and pictures of female singing stars graced his side of the room. He did so like his music. She still had the piano upstairs, where all three of her sons had taken lessons. Of all her sons, Carl had shown the most musical promise. Not even Norman showed the talent Carl did. MarieAnn, Norman's wife, played the piano, so that was good. It's nice, she thought, when a minister's wife can complement her husband's ministry that way.

She stood in the cellar of her house and sighed. She reached up and wiped the sides of her eyes with the edge of her sleeve. She tried and she tried, but sometimes it wasn't good enough. Sometimes nothing she did was good enough. Like now, like sneaking down here to see if she could find any connection between the dead girl and her sons. Why couldn't these two be like Norman?

Ahead of her was what Earl called his office. It was little more than a large table that came from the church basement. *Stone Church* was stamped into the side. Well, that was fine. In a roundabout way the church belonged to her anyway. And her sons.

The church property from which Jake Rikker and May Williams ran their business originally belonged to the congregation, of which her grandfather had been their fire-and-brimstone preacher for forty-five years. When he died, his widow was given the church building, since the small congregation had merged with the congregation at Stone Church and moved into that structure. Lenore's father was the next preacher at Stone Church, and he had been there fifty-five years.

Lenore was an only child, so there were no sons to carry on the ministry tradition. Lenore was supposed to marry a minister, had been engaged to one actually, a short, bespectacled seminary student she didn't love. Instead, she married Harlan.

It was only right that items like this long fold-up table, covered now with computers, cables, and odd pieces of equipment, be in her possession.

She hardly ever wandered over here. She usually didn't even vacuum here, afraid she would scoop up pieces of computer cord.

What mother doesn't try to save her own sons?

A week ago she had found the body of a girl crumpled against the doorway that led to the basement entrance to this room. Sitting with the girl, holding her hand, and running her fingers through the dead girl's hair, one fact became clear to Lenore. The girl had been trying to reach one of her sons. What would it mean for the future of her sons if this fact were known? They would surely be implicated in her death…

Using all her strength, she had grabbed the girl by the shoulders of her jacket and pulled her toward the back of the yard, away from her sons' door, away from any inkling that it was her sons the girl was trying to reach. It was snowing heavily by the time she placed the girl in the snowbank in her garden.

The heavy snow had completely obliterated her tracks by the time the police arrived. The girl looked so like an angel with those freckles that Lenore laid her on her side and placed her hands together in prayer.

Her sons knew something about this girl. Something neither one of them had shared with the police. And the police had been here many times since it happened. Her boys said they had no idea who she was. But they were lying. A mother always knows when her sons are lying. She wondered if the police could tell that or not.

Through the years, both Earl and Carl had been arrested on various charges. Usually small things. Once Carl had been found with one marijuana cigarette in his glove compartment. Well, anyone could have put that there; why blame Carl?

She always paid their bail. What else could she do? She was their mother, after all. What mother didn't pay her sons' bail? Because when you got right down to it, none of this was their fault. If their father hadn't been the town drunk, if their father had been a better father, none of this would've happened. None of this would be happening now.

And now the phone calls were starting. By the time Lenore got home from the Garden and Flower Club, a half dozen Fog Pointers were in her backyard, kneeling in the snow. She'd made tea for them all and given them cinnamon swirls.

Now she stood in front of Earl's computers. She didn't know what she was looking for. There was a low hum, and a screen saver on one of the monitors flashed multicolored fireworks. The other two computer screens were black. Stacks of paper and business cards covered the folding table—she leafed through these. All people she didn't know, with names and addresses all over the country.

An old chest of drawers leaned into the folding table. She pulled the top drawer open. Paper clips, thumbtacks, pens, pencils, odd bits of paper, more business cards from strangers. Nails. Some old passports from people. A whole lot of old passports. Why did Earl have these? Well, he did passport photos. Maybe when you did that, you got to keep people's old passports.

She closed that drawer and pulled out the next, which was filled with white photocopy paper. Several more drawers yielded nothing.

Underneath some invoices at the bottom of the next drawer, she found a couple of plain manila envelopes. She pulled out the contents of one. And found herself looking into the face of the dead girl. Lenore's fingers trembled as she picked up the photo. She'd been expecting this, hadn't she? Some connection to her sons? She saw again the freckled face, the grin, the long blond hair draped over one shoulder. The girl was very much alive in the photo. She was a cute girl. You couldn't call her pretty, but cute, certainly. Spunky, maybe.

Paper-clipped to it was another photo. This one was a baby, chubby cheeks, the mouth in a bit of a crooked smile. She thought of her own sons and felt sad. She turned both pictures over. Nothing was written on the back of the baby picture, but on the back of the picture of the girl was a name— Tolita Shenk—and a telephone number. The name meant nothing to her, and Lenore was good at remembering the names of guests. She grabbed a piece of scrap paper from Earl's garbage and wrote down the information. And then, after several false starts, she figured out how to get Earl's photocopier to make copies of the pictures. She paper-clipped the originals back together again and put them where she'd found them.

Hands trembling, she closed the drawer.

She looked through a few more drawers and the bedroom dresser and found nothing. She went over to their sleeping area and fingered carefully through their clothes, the things on their nightstands, underneath their beds. She looked inside the small bar fridge they kept, found nothing. Then to the other far wall, where a sloppy couch faced the huge flat-screen TV hooked up to satellite. She went through their box of DVDs. Nothing.

Lenore went upstairs and put the photocopied pictures in an envelope and put the whole works under her breadbox and made some tea.

Two more people were on their knees in the snow outside her kitchen window. And later, of course, she invited them in. She put the kettle on and got out some cinnamon swirls, all the while listening to the chatter about the amazing miracle of Rose's healing. Every so often she glanced in the direction of the breadbox. As her tea guests talked, Lenore worked out scenarios in her mind.

The girl had been a girlfriend of either Earl or Carl. Carl, most likely. He seemed to attract the ladies more than Earl did. She'd had her baby and come back here for child support. Or maybe she had resorted to blackmail. The latter was the more probable. The one flaw was, where was the baby? *Her* grandchild? That thought made her gasp suddenly, and Gert, who'd just been telling Lenore about how the angel had healed her bunions, no doubt thought it was because of that.

"Yes!" Gert said. "My bunions. All gone. You want to see?"

"No, thank you," said Lenore, but even the hot tea she was drinking could not keep the cold out. But that was it; surely, the girl with the odd name had had a baby and that baby was Carl's.

She needed to call that number, find out where the baby was. Her grandchild!

14

J ake was concerned about ice on *Constant*, his sailboat. No matter how many tarps he strapped around her, the next time he went to the boatyard, the wind had blown them askew. He also worried about ice inside his boat. Prior to the winter he'd forced antifreeze through the engine and pumped potable antifreeze into the holding tank and sinks. Still, he fretted when it was this horrendously cold and every bit of liquid everywhere froze. Including his blood.

May was back at the office of the Purple Church, continuing her Internet research, and Jake was down at the boatyard looking at *Constant* with Pop Maynard, Carrie's father. Jake had two boats, his sailboat *Constant*, plus *The Purple Whale*, which he co-owned with May. The latter was a refurbished lobstering boat they used to take tourists out to see the whales. *Constant* was outside in the boatyard, while *The Purple Whale* was inside Pop's huge heated boathouse. Pop was the best marine mechanic for miles around and had the reputation of being able to fix anything. "If man made it, man can fix it" was his motto. It was something he said so often that Carrie once told Jake she thought she would do it up in a cross-stitch and give it to him for Christmas.

"She'll be all right," Pop said to Jake. "That antifreeze is good for sixty below. It's not sixty below, only feels like it."

"So much for global warming," Jake said, looking out at the ice coming in on the tide.

Jake had brought rope, and they talked while they wrapped lengths around *Constant*'s hull, tying the tarps in tightly. Jake's fingers were cold through his gloves. To his right, grotesque gargoyle ice was still heaped up in the harbor, and the cold showed no signs of going back to where it came from. Already fishermen had missed a week of fishing, and none of them were too happy about it. They hung around Noonan's and the bar and complained. Boats that hadn't gotten iced in completely were motored out past Thunder Island and taken the thirty miles down the coast to Ridley Harbor, which was bigger and had a more open harbor than Fog Point, and were fishing from there. Thunder Island provided a natural windbreak here in Fog Point, and when ice came in, it stayed.

Jake felt a fresh burst of wind on his face. In his four years of living here, the wind blew, the temperature dropped, the freshwater puddles and ponds froze, but the salt water stayed clear, and fishing was carried on all year long. But this year, mini-icebergs floated through the harbor, making it dangerous for fishing boats. On the boardwalk, people with cameras and tripods had gathered. Jake stopped to watch them for a minute. No doubt these pictures would end up on many of next year's calendars.

"Look at them," Jake said. "Still out there taking pictures."

"They're crazier than us," Pop said.

Way out past the ice, a few boats were moored. One was completely iced up and listed dangerously in the frigid water. He knew most of the local boats, but through the blowing snow and snow fog he couldn't make out which boat this was.

The sky was a steel gray and odd looking, like before a tornado. It was as if the entire town of Fog Point had been transported to some alternate reality. Norah Waterman was right. They were living in a Stephen King novel.

"Looks like we're in for another storm," Pop said.

School would probably be canceled again tomorrow, Jake thought. That would be twice in one week. He didn't mind that so much. Yesterday Jana had helped him work on the tugboat. She'd sat beside him at the table, offering suggestions of paint colors for this and that, while they drank mugs of hot chocolate and ate microwave popcorn.

Connie would have a fit if she knew Jana was subsisting on mostly frozen microwavable dinners, popcorn, and hot chocolate. But they did have fruit. Lots of fruit. Oranges and apples and anything they could get this time of year. Jake insisted on that one thing. They might eat microwaved chicken dinners, but they always had a salad and apples for dessert.

He liked having Jana around. He had missed about three years of his daughters' lives. And winning them back had become his goal. With Jana it was fairly easy, but he was having a harder time with Alex. When he would call, she wouldn't be there, and he wondered if that was always the truth. His e-mails to her went largely unanswered.

"You guys need a hand?" Colin Nation tromped through the snowdrifts toward them.

"Yeah," Pop said. "Grab this line, will ya?"

He did so and tied it into a neat clove hitch against the boat's cradle.

"I thought you'd be out fishing," Jake said to him.

"Soon," Colin said, grinning. "I got me a little job sweeping snow off some of the summer people's boats. In a bit, as soon as I'm finished here," Colin continued, "tide'll be in, and I'm taking my boat down to Ridley."

"De-ice it first. Be careful," Jake offered.

"Always am."

You couldn't live in a fishing community without knowing the statistics—more people died in fishing accidents than in any other kind of occupation. It was an occupation fraught with danger in the summer and even more so in the winter. Icing was a dangerous and potentially fatal problem. The careful fisher took the time to completely scrape off the ice before venturing out.

"Just thinking about that girl that was murdered," Colin said. "Some sad, eh? Really makes you stop and think. Gets me thinking about Kayla. Like what would I do if she was missing? If something happened to her?" He shook his head. Jake thought about Colin's baby daughter and knew he was asking the question everyone in Fog Point was asking. Why was it taking so long for her parents to come forward?

After the boat was satisfactorily secured, Jake climbed into it and checked the batteries.

An hour later, when Jake got back to the Purple Church, Lenore Featherjohn was sitting on a folding chair in their office, drumming her fingers on her lap. Across from her, May was writing in a notebook.

"Hey, Jake," May said, indicating with her pen. "Pull up a chair."

Lenore's ringed fingers kept fluttering from her lap to her throat and through her bright red hair. She said, "Jake doesn't need to know about this. I didn't want this to be Grand Central Station, May. This was just between me and you. You doing a little job for an old friend. I'd do it myself, but the number's disconnected..."

May said, "Lenore has a phone number and a name she wants to attach an address to."

"Should be easy enough," Jake said.

"That's why I didn't want to involve a lot of people," Lenore protested. "It's such a small thing now, really."

"If it's a phone number you're looking for, why don't you ask Earl?" Jake said. "I'm sure one of your sons would have the resources."

"I can't!" Lenore protested. "This concerns him—him and Carl!"

She lowered her eyes to her hands in her lap and muttered something he couldn't hear.

"Tell him, Lenore," May said.

"I...uh." Lenore cleared her throat. "I have reason to suspect someone might be blackmailing one of my sons, or maybe both. Probably both."

His eyebrows shot up.

Lenore's voice was weak, breaking. "It's to do with a baby." When she didn't say anything, May continued for her.

"Lenore says either Earl or Carl fathered a child, and now the mother has come demanding child support."

Jake scratched his nose. So Earl or Carl was in trouble, and now Lenore had come to bail them out. No surprise there.

Lenore shifted in her chair and fingered the strand of red costume pearls she wore around her neck. In her earlobes she wore matching red globes. "I need to find out about the girl's family. They may be behind this whole thing. You understand, I need to be careful of my money. There are unscrupulous people out there who'd love to get their hands on my money. This is not the first time people have come sniffing around my sons for my money." Lenore was rubbing a fingernail on her left hand with her right thumb. "And then there's the baby. I need to find out about this baby, my, uh, grandchild."

"This is the baby in question." May pointed to a photocopied snapshot of a baby.

Lenore went on, "I was collecting my son's laundry and found this picture. So I copied it on his machine. There was also a name and a phone number written on the back of it, so I wrote them on another piece of paper. Neither of them has been himself lately, and Earl recently asked me for a large sum of money." Lenore sniffed and blinked rapidly and looked away. "So I thought I would see what I could find out about this baby's mother. Her family."

Jake picked up the photocopy. A smooth, round cherubic face with a tuft of pale hair and a large, crooked smile looked out at him. "Okay, so what you're saying is that this Tolita Shenk"—he read the name on the piece of paper—"had a baby by either Carl or Earl and now she's blackmailing him? That's her name, Tolita Shenk?"

"I know," Lenore said. "It's an odd name, but yes, that's exactly what I'm saying."

"And you have proof of that? E-mails, perhaps? Threatening letters? Bank statements? What do you have?"

"Just this picture and this name and this phone number."

"If what you say is true, why aren't your sons here instead of you?" Jake asked.

"Because they wouldn't, would they? I mean, boys like that…" She let her voice trail off. Then just as quickly she rallied. "Well, I can't very well ask them, can I? They'd suspect something. You see. I have to do this. If anyone got wind of this, well, it could affect my business. I've built up a name. I don't need it besmirched by some little"—she motioned with her highly ringed fingers—"whippersnapper just wanting his money. My money."

"Why not call the police?" Jake asked.

"Oh, I could never do that. I've my business to think about. Something of this nature, this scandal." She shook her head. "I just couldn't do it."

Jake squinted down at the ten-digit phone number. He didn't recognize the area code. The whole thing seemed rather odd. Lenore Featherjohn, the biggest busybody of the Fog Point busybodies, was hiring them to track a phone number. The woman must be desperate.

"What happens when you phone this number?" he asked.

She made a noise between a huff and grunt. "Well, I get a message that it's been disconnected, don't I? I mean, if someone answered at the other end, well, I wouldn't need to be here, would I?"

"And you don't have a picture of the mother?" May asked. "Just her baby? You're saying you don't know her, have never met her?"

"No. I don't. I don't have a picture of her. No picture of her." Lenore grabbed a handkerchief from her handbag and dabbed at her cheek. Jake couldn't figure out whether these were tears or if she was just suddenly too warm.

"No pictures of her and Carl together?" Jake added.

"I already told you, no. My son wouldn't have known her for very long."

"Long enough, by the looks of it," May said. "You know you really haven't given us very much to go on."

"What about the original photo?" Jake asked, picking up the flimsy photocopy again.

"I can't very well bring you the original, now can I? Earl and Carl would know something was up."

Jake looked down at the picture again and knitted his eyebrows together. It seemed somehow familiar, the set of the smile, perhaps. Or maybe it was something about the eyes. It was a face he'd seen recently. Somewhere. Where? He shook his head, tried to jog whatever it was to the surface, but whatever it was, it was gone. He squinted down at the chubby-cheeked face, the lopsided smile, and it looked like every other baby he had ever seen.

15

I have forgotten how to do my e-mail. And I know by this time there should be plenty of messages waiting for me. When Tim and Ashe are out in the barns and Bobbie's gone to her job in town at Fabricland and Suze's gone to the day care where she works, I try to remember how to do it. I can't. I know there must be e-mails waiting. She promised she would send me e-mails.

My great-grandson would know. Jonah. I remember his name now. That little tyke is on the computer all the time. Maybe someday I'll ask him to help me.

It was late in June when Tully came into my life. I'd gone out to my shed, just to be alone for a while, and there in the corner was a heap of cloth. Had the grandkids come in here playing? I walked over and saw Oreo cookies, a bag of jellybeans, a sleeping bag, a couple bottles of water, and a thick Harry Potter book. I lifted up the sleeping bag.

It's not uncommon for vagrants to take refuge in barns and sheds. Happens all the time. The Blexfords had had a homeless man sleeping in their grain bin for three months before anyone found him. When the police look for runaways or criminals, they scour the local barns and sheds first.

Leaning up against the wall was a pale pink backpack, dirty but still functional. I opened it up and felt through it. Socks and T-shirts. At the bottom was one of those cell phones and next to it what felt like a wallet. It was red and plastic.

What local farm kid had decided this would be a good place to camp out? I opened it up. And then I stared down at the driver's license. And kept staring. And kept staring. When I saw who it was issued to, I dropped it like it had burned me. Was this a joke? Was the Almighty playing some sort of cruel prank?

Despite the June warmth, I felt cold to my toes. I stood there for a long, long time. I could not stop the trembling.

That's why I didn't go right to Tim or Bobbie with what I found. Because it was Tully. I was still standing there when I heard footsteps. Her? Tully? I found myself backing against the wall like a skittish calf.

"What's going on?" It was Tim who'd stood in the doorway that day last summer. Tim would know nothing about The Terrible Thing. Or did he? Did they all?

"What? What do you mean?" I stammered at him.

"What are you doing back here?"

I moved out from the shadows, back to the light.

"Just checking on things," I said. "Just checking on things. Just…"

"You okay, Dad?"

"Fine. I'm just fine."

Tim had shrugged, like they all do with me. I'm losing my mind, after all.

"I came to get you for your doctor's appointment," Tim said. "Everybody's looking for you."

"Doctor's appointment," I said. I walked out of the barn then. Tim hadn't seen the sleeping bag, the backpack. And that was good. That was very good. That was the way it would stay.

Later, when I sat in the waiting room of the doctor's office, I stared at a painting of a tree on the opposite wall and thought about Tully. Nothing wrong with my memory as far as that is concerned. I can remember the day that baby disappeared, that awful day. And the part I played in it. And now Tully had come to my shed. My shed!

"You seem anxious, Mr. Black. Are you okay?" the doctor asked me. She looked as young as my granddaughter. Her hands were gentle on my shoulders. I'm an old man, and people are gentle around me. I wonder if they would be so gentle if they knew everything about me.

"Fine, fine, fine," I told her. "Fine," I added once more for emphasis.

Did Tully know? Is that why she'd come here? Did she somehow know?

"Something wrong, Dad?" Tim had asked on the way home.

"I'm fine." I kept saying it. Maybe if I said it enough times, it would turn out to be true.

As soon as I got home, I went back to the shed. The backpack was gone. The sleeping bag was gone. So were the water bottles, cookies, and jellybeans.

It was true then. My dementia was getting worse. Demented. I'd imagined the whole thing.

And now my fingers tremble on the computer keyboard. I no longer remember how to turn it on.

I have imagined the whole thing. All of it is part of my shadowed thinking, but what if even part of it is true?

16

"Are you and Carrie ever going to get married, Dad?"

Jake and Jana were out walking. May was back at the Purple Church seeing what she could dig up on Tolita Shenk—which at the moment wasn't much. Jana had come home talking about the fresh batch of ice that had come into the harbor. They had talked about it at school, and she wanted to walk down to see it. When Jake suggested he come along and maybe the two of them could end up at Mags and Herman's for hot chocolate, a smile lit up his daughter's face. But his plan was double-sided. It was dangerous on the boardwalk now, people were saying. Parts of it had been closed off two weeks before, and now town councilors were calling for a complete shutdown of the boardwalk. But businesses like Mags and Herman's and Norah Waterman's shop, plus the bookstore and a few other places, only had access from the boardwalk.

So far nothing had been done. No one had been hurt yet, but a town that depended on tourists for its bread and butter could not afford even one mishap. He grabbed his wool coat, pulled his wool cap down over his ears, and away they went exploring.

"This is so cool!" Jana exclaimed as they tromped through crusty snow toward the boardwalk. Ahead of them lumps of ice wafted in lazily with the tide. "Look at them!" she said. "They look like potatoes."

"Potatoes?"

"Like potatoes in lobster stew, like what May makes."

Jake cocked his head and looked at the bay with new eyes. Yes, perhaps the entire bay looked like a great cauldron of lobster chowder.

On the boardwalk, their booted feet chunked along the cold wood. She continued, "Back with Mom and Keith, cool things like this never happen."

Back with Mom and Keith. That's what she said today, not *back home.* He smiled inside. This was good, being with his daughter, having her talk to him like this. Maybe there was forgiveness in the universe, after all.

Her voice called him back. "So? You didn't answer me. Are you guys going to get married?"

"I don't know, Jana. Would you like that? Me marrying Carrie?"

"She's really nice."

"I think so too."

"And you should be happy."

"I am happy. I'm happy you're here."

"No, I mean *really* happy. Like if you were married. You know what I think would be neat? If you and Carrie got married and had a baby."

Jake almost choked.

They had come down to the far end of the boardwalk, where ice had left a gaping hole in this section of the walk and shattered pieces of wood and ice stuck up like knife blades. To the right of them was an empty building that used to be a jewelry studio. Until the jeweler, whom Jake thought he was falling in love with, turned out to be someone else. A For Rent sign hung crookedly in the window.

He didn't have great luck with women. He didn't have great luck with a lot of things.

He looked away from the boarded-up building and back to his daughter, who looked small and lovely in the new ski jacket he'd bought for her in Ridley. Her hands were in her pockets, and eagerness shone from her eyes as she gazed out toward Thunder Island. He stood close beside her and thought about all the bad decisions he'd made, all the wrong choices, all the stupid mistakes, the bad father he'd been to both his girls, the way he'd run away when Connie had left him, not realizing that running away from her meant running away from his daughters. He was very definitely the black sheep in the family. The only divorced son in a whole family of Christian Rikkers, some on the mission field, most in the pastorate.

But having his daughter back with him on this cold day in February was worth the effort it was taking. Maybe second chances were not only possible but probable in this strange world where bad things happened to good people, where good people died and bad people prospered. And that somewhere in this strange and crazy world there was room for a father and his long-estranged daughter to find peace.

Jana leaned out over the railing.

"Be careful there," Jake said. "I wouldn't count on that thing holding you up."

"I think you should pray to her."

Her statement startled him. "What?"

"Maybe if you prayed to the angel, Carrie would say yes."

"Jana, you know you can't pray to an angel."

"Lots of people have, Dad, and lots of people are getting cured. It's on the news. And maybe you and Carrie could have a baby."

"Jana, I don't think that's going to happen."

"I could baby-sit."

"I know." He narrowed his eyes as he gazed out over the harbor with its ice chunks and seaweed. He saw in his mind the baby picture Lenore had given them. Who was that child and why was he suddenly thinking of him again?

A little while later Jana asked, "What will happen to her, Dad?"

"What will happen to who? Carrie?"

"No, the girl, the one who died in the snow. Like, will there be a funeral for her?"

He looked down at his daughter. It had started snowing, and lazy flakes had settled on her shoulders, her hat, her eyelashes. He said, "When her parents find her, I'm sure they'll have a service for her."

"But what happens if they don't? If no one comes?"

Jake shrugged. He didn't want to tell her that the girl's body would be kept on ice until such time that the police determined the case was not a high priority. Eventually, if no family was found, she'd be buried in some grave marked only by a number, courtesy of the state.

"I think she should have a funeral," Jana said. "I think Blaine's father should do the service, so I'm trying to get her to talk to him about that. And she's trying to persuade me to get *my* dad—you—to do something for her."

He looked down at her. "Your friend Blaine wants me to do something for *her?*"

"She wants you to find her mother for her. That's the only reason she's hanging around me lately."

Jake felt momentarily confused. "Where is Amy? Not at school?"

"No. Her real mother, Dad. I'm talking about her birth mother."

Jake said nothing. Just looked at his daughter.

"Dad?"

He didn't say anything for a while.

"Dad, you didn't know Blaine was adopted?"

Yes, he did know that. A long time ago Ben had told him they'd adopted Blaine after many years of trying to conceive.

"So Blaine wants to find her biological mother?" Jake asked.

Jana nodded. "That's all she talks about."

Out ahead of them on the sea, Colin Nation's fishing boat, *Colin's Dream,* wended its way through the mini-icebergs toward Ridley Harbor, the diesel engine thunderous in the cold calm. The tide was coming in; already it had moved forward several inches during the time they had stood there. "Are you cold, Jana? Maybe we should head to Mags and Herman's and get a hot chocolate."

"Okay."

They walked away from the end of the wrecked dock and the ice thorns toward the warm coffeehouse.

"So, Dad, will you help her?"

Jake shrugged, thrust his hands into his pockets. "Why does she want to do this?"

"Well, because she feels like Amy doesn't understand her. She's always felt *different* in that house. I mean, just look at her. She's already as tall as her dad. She thinks her real father's a pro-basketball player who was already married, and her mother was a native Indian who had an affair with him. She deeply loved him, and he loved her but couldn't do anything about it. Couldn't leave his wife for her. So she had to give the baby up."

"A native Indian?" Jake looked at her questioningly.

"She thinks that's why she has black hair and is so tall. Don't you think she looks like a native warrior?"

"You've concocted quite a story."

"It could be true. She thinks it's true."

"Does Blaine's mother know about this?"

"Amy? No, she doesn't. So will you help her?"

"No, I will not help her. What I think Blaine needs to do is to make peace with the mother who raised her and loves her before she goes looking for the mother who gave her up."

"Dad. It probably wasn't like that. Probably it wasn't. Her biological mother maybe had to give her up because she was too young to take care of her."

"Maybe."

"So you're not going to do it?" Jana asked as they entered Mags and Herman's. "You're not going to help her."

"No, honey, I'm not."

"But lots of people look for their biological mothers."

"A lot of people who are older and not teenagers who are having problems with their real parents."

Jake ordered a coffee for himself and a hot chocolate for Jana along with one of Mags's gigantic cookies.

"You know what I like about being here?" Jana said as they sat at the round table near the window. "We get to eat stuff like this all the time."

"Just don't tell your mother."

He was glad their conversation had veered into safer territory. He listened half-smiling while Jana related other things she liked about being here, but one thought kept intruding through her happy chatter.

He took a long sip of his coffee and wondered again why the face of an unknown baby was haunting his waking dreams.

17

Freak! Freak! Look at us, freak! Look at us lookatus lookatus.

At night when the girls were all in bed and asleep and it was late and the house was creaking with the cold, the voices of the children sometimes came to him on the wind. *Look at us look at us look at us.* And he would be back to that time with them all circled 'round him, their voices in his ear so loud that he couldn't think, and so he would look at them. And they would run away screaming, *Freak! Freak! Say something! Say something! Fa-fa-fa-freak!*

Mother told him to stand his ground, don't let them walk all over you, you stand up and fight back, she said. But he couldn't. She didn't know what it was like to be him, to not be able to think of the things to say when it was time to say them. To fumble over words, to start to say something and then not have it come out right.

Mother told him all that name-calling would build character in him, and he would be the stronger for it in the end. Maybe Mother was right, because now look at all the responsibility he had! Mother had given him the task of taking care of all the girls. This was the first time she'd trusted him so. He even lived in the same house with the girls. It was a room off the kitchen that she said used to be the maid's quarters back when this house was brand new. But he was no maid! No, he was the security guard, and their complete and total safety was in his hands.

Freak! Freak! Look at us, freak! Look at us, look at us, look at us.

He turned up the volume with his television remote. If he kept it loud enough, he could drown out the voices. He was watching *Lost,* and he tried to concentrate. Sometimes if he concentrated really hard on things, the voices went away. And besides, he had work to do soon. At the end of the show, even when the credits were running—he never stayed to watch scenes from next week's episode—he'd be up and checking their rooms, the locks on the doors, all of the windows too. It surprised him how many of the girls tried to escape through the windows. Afterward, he would go outside and "secure the perimeter," he called it, which was something he picked up from television. It actually meant walking around the house twice to make sure no one was spying or trying to get in or out. Every night he walked it once in a clockwise direction and then the second time counter-clockwise, checking, checking, checking.

That Mother would trust him with the girls made him want to scream at his childhood tormentors, *See? See? You thought I would be nothing, and I'm something! I'm something!*

He had to make sure all of the girls were accounted for and safe and that they stayed healthy. Healthy, that was the main thing Mother stressed. Even so, every so often he'd have to march downtown where he'd find a girl in a bar or some other unsafe place. And he would take her wrist and pull her home, all the while screaming at her, "What are you doing? D-d-don't you know drinking is b-b-bad for you? It's bad for you! You need to be in bed. It's for your own good!" Sometimes when the anger came, he forgot how to speak.

And they'd argue and hit at him and hiss at him and call him names—he knew what they called him. But he was their guardian. It was an awesome responsibility and one that Mother didn't take lightly.

Sometimes sitting in his room late at night, the girls safely inside and the doors and windows double locked and checked twice and the perimeter secured, he pretended he was King Solomon and they were his harem. When this happened, when these good thoughts came, he could almost forget the childhood taunts, the voices that stayed in his head no matter what he did, the voices that made him lash out and kill things. And then Mother would scold him and put him in the cellar for three days.

But all that was a long time ago. At the last place. At this place of girls he was going to do better. Mother was trusting him more, sending him out on errands. Stealing things from doctor's offices, for example, files he had to carefully look at and photograph with the camera Mother gave him. Sometimes she asked him to put things through the shredder. Sometimes it was drugs Mother needed. And all of these errands, no matter what the task, he took most seriously and did them meticulously, down to the minutest detail.

And in this new place of girls, he would finally, finally prove himself to Mother. He would never be locked in the cellar again. He would make her proud of him here.

18

In the beginning they took me to the doctors because I forgot things. I sometimes forgot where I was or got mixed up with names. They also said I made things up, delusional, they called it. I wasn't. That wasn't it at all. But they wouldn't listen to that part. It was just sometimes I forgot things, recent things, like I got the names of my grandsons mixed up. But who wouldn't with all the *J* names they insisted on naming those kids. All boys they had, too. I might forget recent things, but I remember the important things. Those are the things I remember. I remember The Terrible Tragedy like it was yesterday.

That first night after I went back and Tully's sleeping bag was gone, I tried something. I took a leftover roll from the kitchen and a bit of real butter, because you can't have a roll without real butter. I also spooned a little of the evening's stew into a bowl, cut a piece of the peach pie and put it on another plate, poured a glass of milk, and then put everything on a tray and put a cloth over the whole works and carried it outside. And as I did so, I remembered all the times that Glad did this very thing for me. Out in the field, me working alongside my sons and the hired men, and out would come Glad, driving the old truck across the ruts with plates of hot food covered with tea towels.

I left the tray on the wooden table. Then I went back to the house, to my room, and watched television. I have my own television in there, a Christmas present from them all last year. I know the real reason they got it for me—they don't want me sitting out in the family room with them.

The next morning when Tim left for the barn and Bobbie went to Fabricland, I headed out to the shed. The food had been eaten. The bowl was neatly stacked on the plate, the utensils inside of it, the cloth folded in squares next to it.

For five nights I put food out, and five nights it was eaten. I had to do this stealthily, so Bobbie wouldn't suspect. The third night I had a close call. Bobbie caught me carrying in an empty plate. I thought she'd gone to work. She hadn't. She looked at me curiously and then at the plate with the scraps of last night's supper on it.

"I wanted to eat out in the shed last night," I told her. It was the first thing I could think of to say.

"But you had a full dinner with us, Dad."

"Yeah, well, I get hungry, you know."

She shook her head and frowned. I'm sure she thought I was really losing it then. She took the plate from my hand, rather roughly, I thought, and placed it in the dishwasher alongside the breakfast dishes.

I would have to be more careful.

The sixth day was Sunday. The rest of them went to church, but I didn't go. I told them my knee was bothering me and I was having trouble swallowing. I didn't know what it was, it just came on. I like doing this, making things up: an inability to swallow, a pain behind my left ear like a hot, poking needle, the little finger on my right hand going completely numb, a shadowy film over half of my left eye. Today it was an inability to swallow and a sore knee. I knew, though, that they were just as happy to leave me home on a Sunday. Didn't want the old coot embarrassing them in church—snoring or burping or farting or anything.

So I do them all a favor and make up symptoms most every Sunday morning so I don't have to go. As soon as they left that day, I arranged a tray with coffee, fried eggs, two pieces of Bobbie's homemade bread with butter and jam, and cut-up fresh tomatoes; they were just beginning to come in. I took the works out to the barn.

She was standing at the back of the shed, leaning over her backpack when I came in.

"Hey." I surprised myself at the gentleness in my voice.

"I…oh…," she stammered, straightened, looked at me, looked eagerly at the tray of food then back at me. "I…I didn't mean…"

"I brought you some breakfast," I said. "Figured you'd be hungry."

"Thank you. Thank you for bringing me food."

"It's okay. There's plenty of food in the house. No one's missing any."

"I thought you would be in church."

"Nope. Not me. You're the Shenk girl, aren't you?"

She nodded.

"Anyone ever tell you you're the spittin' image of Coralee?"

She shook her head. Then nodded. She looked like some wild thing, her hair in two hayseed plaits down her back. There were smudges on her face, and her eyes shone like she was really afraid. I wanted to assure her that there was nothing to be afraid of. She swallowed several times, looked at the tray of food I still held. I put it on the table, and she walked toward it, her eyes on me.

"Go ahead. Eat. You must be hungry."

She nodded. "I am hungry. I'm only getting this one meal a day."

"Well, good thing I brought this. Don't know what you take in your coffee, though. Here's fresh cream."

She shook her head. "I don't drink coffee."

"Do you mind if I have it then?"

She handed it to me, and I seated myself on a wooden box and watched her. "So, you running away from home, I take it?"

She shook her head. "I would be running away from home if I had a home to run away from."

I nodded. "How long you planning on staying here?"

She talked between bites. "As soon as I figure out what to do. I got to get a job. I might move to the city. Maybe Vancouver. I know someone out there."

"Home life not suiting you?" But I already knew the answer to that. Coralee was a mess. Alcoholic by all accounts. And her husband, Tully's father, was dead. A whole lot of water had passed under the bridge since The Tragedy. At the thought of that, my hand shook a bit, and I choked on a mouthful of coffee and lowered the mug to a wooden box beside me. I really *was* having trouble swallowing, prophecy coming true. I closed my eyes briefly. Loss of memory would be a blessing if you could forget certain things.

It was quiet in the barn then, just the outside sounds of birds, the sound of a dog barking in some far-off field. A little bit of breeze, you could hear the trees rustling. It was summer outside and warm in the barn, but I felt cold. So cold.

When her plate was cleared, Tully turned to me. "Nobody's in the house?"

I shook my head. "Everyone's in church."

"Do you think…do you think I could go and maybe, uh, have a shower?"

A little waif, she looked like. "Sure. Why not?"

She piled the plates on top of each other the way she did, small plates on top of larger and the coffee cup on the top, and carried the tray inside the house. I led her to the family bathroom on the second floor. There was shampoo up there, nice soap, dusting powder, things a girl might want. My own bathroom, the little one off my room, only had one kind of soap. I wash with Dove soap only, use it on my head, everywhere.

It was while she was in the shower that I began to realize why she'd come, why she'd been handed to me like this. It was a sign, an omen, that she'd come to *me*! Maybe her coming would give me some sort of a second chance. Maybe I could take everything that Glad did wrong and make it right again.

19

Two in the afternoon and Amy was home from school. They'd closed the schools early today because a storm was coming. Blizzard number about two dozen, but who was counting? It had started at nine, picked up by ten, and by eleven they were in whiteout conditions with blowing snow and drifts. Five years ago a school bus had skidded off the road, and two children had been injured. No one died, thank God. But ever since that near miss, the school board couldn't risk hurting children. The kids loved the time off until it came to the end of the year and they had to make up the days. At this rate they'd still be in school in July!

Blaine was still in school. There was no high school in Fog Point, so Fog Point kids were bused forty-five minutes each way to the regional high school in Ridley Harbor. It wasn't closing early, probably much to Blaine's unhappiness. And Ben was still at church, so it was Amy and Charlie here at home.

Maybe she'd make a nice meal for the four of them tonight. Something special. There was a recipe for seafood lasagna in yesterday's paper, or was it two days ago? She rooted through the recycle box until she found the paper. Now, to make sure she had the ingredients. She had a bit of lobster, frozen pieces of it waiting for just this sort of recipe. She also had scallops in the freezer, given to them by Jake, who got them off the ocean floor while diving. In the freezer she found a package of some sort of whitefish. Kind of freezer burned, but it would be fine for a lasagna. And she had cheese. She always had copious amounts of cheese in her fridge, which probably accounted for the extra few pounds she was never quite able to lose.

Still, this might be nice. The four of them. At home on a snowy evening with a comfort dish like lasagna. She needed to get them together, eating lasagna.

Ben kept after her, "Talk to me, Amy. Talk to me, please. Let's try to work out whatever it is."

It was Blaine, she kept saying. The whole thing was Blaine. But it wasn't, not totally; some of it was, of course, but it was a whole lot more. Plus Ben had to shoulder some of the blame. He was doing his share of being secretive, too. The first night had been right after the girl's body had been found. He'd been out presumably at the church until almost eleven. She'd put Charlie to bed by herself that night.

"Where's Dad?" he had asked.

"Oh, you know Dad. A meeting."

He'd nodded. Charlie understood about meetings. That was what ninety-nine percent of being a minister was, going to meetings and not being there for your children.

There was also something wrong with Blaine. A year ago Blaine had been helpful, obedient, and cheerful. She'd taken a major role in helping with the church's vacation Bible school program and also helped the third-grade Sunday school teacher. But since the fall, she'd gotten a tattoo and her belly button pierced.

Amy blamed the influence of the high school, with its drugs and peer pressure. Amy also blamed the long bus ride. "I'm too tired," Blaine would say when she got home. Too tired to help in Sunday school or go to youth group. All the girl did was lie on her bed and text message her Ridley Harbor friends. Amy felt powerless to do anything about it.

The only bright spot, the only positive influence, was Blaine's friendship with Jana. But, as Blaine was quick to point out, the two of them were church friends only. Fog Point friends only. Jana was still in middle school, and there was a world of difference between the last year of middle school in Fog Point and the first year of high school in Ridley Harbor.

And then there was Charlie—dear, sweet Charlie, the apple of Ben's eye, the one he doted on. When she told Ben that she thought the games Charlie was writing might be a tad too violent, he'd just said, "Oh, let the boy grow up. We all played cowboys and Indians when we were little. He'll grow out of it." Which, according to Amy, was part of Ben's double standard. Charlie, his perfect little son, would be allowed to grow out of problems, but Blaine was not. Ben just couldn't see it, no matter how Amy tried to tell him.

Amy set the water on to boil for the lasagna noodles and got a can of tomatoes from her cupboard. The recipe didn't look too hard. She turned on the radio and became engrossed in a political discussion on NPR. Something about war. *There. Think about something else for a while, something calm and pleasant to take your mind off the real problem.*

"Mom?" Charlie stood in the doorway, papers in his hand, feet astride. He looked so like Ben with his wide forehead and little chin dimple.

"Hey, Charlie, how's it going?"

"Mom? I wrote a story."

"Hey, great!"

"You want to read it?"

"Well, sure, Charlie." She wiped her hands on the sides of her jeans. When had women eliminated the very good idea of aprons? "Let me finish up here. I'm almost done. Then I'll have a look at it. I'd love to read it."

"Okay." He placed the papers on the table and sat on the stool, dangling his legs and watching her.

"You getting your homework done, kiddo?" she asked.

"I did it at school." His legs swung back and forth.

"You can help," Amy said. "Can you grab the milk from the fridge for me?"

He walked over, opened the door. "Which one?"

Which one indeed? They had three varieties of milk in there. Skim for herself. Two percent for Ben, and whole milk for Charlie. Vegan Blaine had sworn off milk, much to Amy's consternation. She wouldn't let herself think that Blaine would also veto the lasagna.

"The skim."

"Skim, yuck." But he complied.

"You won't even taste it."

"If you won't even taste it, then why put it in?"

She assembled the lasagna, put a layer of foil on it, tucked it in around the sides, and then wiped her hands on a dishtowel and said, "Okay, Charlie, let's have a look at that story of yours."

"It's the people in the video game I'm writing about."

"I bet it's really good, then."

She sat down, picked up the three sheets of paper, looked at them, and dropped them onto her lap as if she'd been burned.

"What's this, Charlie? What *is* this?"

"It's my story, Mom."

"No. No, what *is* this?"

On the paper, centered in all capitals, was:

FINDING MY REAL MOTHER

1. Internet, all the places from before.
2. Talk to that lady again. (Make an appointment.)
3. Get Jana's dad to help. (That means being nice to Jana. Yuck!)

She put the paper down carefully on the table.

"Mom, not that! Turn it over!"

She did. There was his story, neatly printed. But all Amy could say was, "Charlie, where'd you get this paper?"

"Mom," the impatience was evident in his voice. "It was in Blaine's garbage. I needed paper. You need to read my *story*."

"This was in Blaine's garbage?"

"Mom?"

A shiver began somewhere in Amy's feet and made its way through her knees. What had her daughter gotten herself into? And why suddenly did Amy feel such fear, such dread?

20

L enore shoved her hands into the sudsy sink to warm them as much as to wash her pots. Everything about her felt so cold. First, there was the snow and the girl. And now this rumor.

Rube had called this morning. He and another church-board member wanted to come by and see her, he said. At first he didn't say about what, but when she pressed him, he finally told her. It was about that stupid rumor. Where had she heard it? She wouldn't mention names. She wasn't a gossip, and she wasn't about to pass on names. Truth was, she couldn't remember, couldn't remember if it was something she'd actually heard. Or maybe it was something she dreamed. Had Enid told her this? Maybe not. In any case it wasn't something she was going to tell Rube. She pushed back her hair with a sudsy, rubber-gloved hand and realized too late that she'd just gone and wrecked her hairdo. Outside, in her backyard, people had lined themselves up again for a chance to kneel in the wet snow where the girl's body had been.

And what could she do about it except invite them all in afterward for tea and cinnamon swirls?

So she baked more, made more tea, and kept her smile on. She scrubbed a stubborn stain on a baking sheet. With all that had gone on, she'd burned a batch of cinnamon swirls. She had three guests staying with her right now. Arnold was still there, as was a young woman with a cane, and someone from a science magazine. The quiet young photographer with the two different-colored eyes had checked out. She couldn't remember his name. And she needed to make another batch of cinnamon swirls as well as muffins. Maybe pies. Guests who came to this little town and this place expected homemade pies. The third thing that was getting away from her was the police. They kept coming, always with more questions. They acted as if they didn't believe her. Didn't they know who she was?

Her father's name meant something at one time. Time was when she knew all the police in her town. *Her town.* Funny she still called it that. She'd grown up here, and yet other people were coming in from the outside and taking it over, pretending it all belonged to them.

Outside, a young woman knelt in the snow while two little girls in matching red snowsuits stood beside her. One turned to look in the kitchen window, and Lenore saw a snippet of upturned nose, a grin. And this made Lenore think of her own granddaughter, Norman's daughter. How she missed her grandchildren. She sighed so loudly that one of the guests at the dining-room table who was reading a book, the girl with the cane, looked over at her. Lenore managed to stifle the sigh into a cough and get back to her dishwashing.

This little girl in the snowsuit was so like Alyssa—her grandchildren were parts of the pieces that she couldn't gather into her and put together.

By rights, Norman should be the minister at Stone by now. Wasn't it time for Norman to come back here? Hadn't enough time passed?

She pulled the plug in the sink and wiped the counter with a rag and heard voices in the hall, loud voices. "Helloooo. Anybody here?" Then a quieter voice said, "I don't know, Teddy, there might not be anyone here. They should have one of those little bells you can ring. You'd think an establishment like this would have one of those little bells."

Lenore hastily wiped her eyes on a dishcloth and made her way to the front hall. "Coming," she called.

Two people stood there, a woman with coifed blond hair and an expensive fur coat and a man with a gray beard and a jacket with lots of pockets.

"Can I help you?" Lenore said. She hoped her eyes didn't look teary or red.

"We'd like two rooms if you're not booked up," said the woman, pulling her gloves off one finger at a time.

"I've got a few rooms available right now," Lenore said. "You'd like two?"

"Yes." The woman smiled again. "I'm Jeanine Bowman from FN News, and this is Ted Sorensen, my cameraman."

Ted stood slightly behind her.

"It's nice to meet you." FN News! Imagine! "You must be here to take pictures of the ice, right? For the TV, right?"

"And the angel. Isn't there something about an angel?" the woman asked.

Lenore put her hand to her throat. "I guess. And, well, yes, you've come to the right place. Well, uh…come, ah, into the office here, and I'll get your sign-in information."

They followed her into the alcove office off the foyer where she kept her guest registration.

"How long will you be staying?" she asked.

"One night," Jeanine said. "One night should be all we'll need."

When the woman leaned over the counter and flashed a white-toothed smile, Lenore could see she was much older than she appeared at first. Lenore thought she could see the faint tracings of face-lift scars along her jaw line. Her teeth were exceptionally white and large. In fact, everything about the woman was large and loud.

"Well, let's sign you in, and then we can go upstairs. I'll show you the rooms I have available, and you can take your pick," Lenore said.

Jeanine filled out the card and guest book and threw a Visa card on the table. Lenore ran it through the machine and handed them their receipt, then said, "Follow me," as she walked toward the stairs.

"What about our bags?" Jeanine asked.

"Well, you can bring them with you, of course."

"No, I mean, don't you have someone here who will manage them?"

"Oh, ah…" Lenore looked at them, confused. Then Ted winked at her and said, "My esteemed colleague is not used to carrying her own luggage."

"Oh, well, I'm sorry. Here let me help you." Lenore lugged two of her bags while Ted managed another plus all the camera equipment.

"Ted!" she said harshly. "I've another in the car. Get that, too, for me."

Ted left the suitcase and camera equipment he was carrying in the foyer and went out to the car.

"And no elevator?" Jeanine asked.

"No, sorry," Lenore said.

"What kind of a place is this?" The woman looked around her.

Jeanine and Ted ended up choosing rooms next to each other on the second floor. Jeanine said she didn't want to carry her luggage up any more flights of stairs than she had to, thank you very much, when it was Lenore and Ted who'd carried them.

The rooms they chose were two of Lenore's best, big with king-sized beds, desks, private baths, and views of the water. Jeanine chose the bigger, the one with three windows, and Ted's next to it had one window. She took off her coat, carefully folded it, and laid it on the bed. Underneath she wore a crisp beige suit. Lenore kept looking at her and then said, "I watch FNN all the time. Would I have seen you?"

"Maybe. Maybe not." The woman folded her scarf. "We're with one of the affiliates."

"An affiliate. Oh, my." Lenore had no idea what an affiliate was. "Well, then, I'll leave you two. When you're finished unpacking, come downstairs, and I'll show you the rest of the place."

Lenore had time to get the tea and some cinnamon swirls set out on one of her prettiest patterns, one that belonged to her grandmother, before the two came down. "Breakfast is between seven and nine," Lenore told them, "and I also do lunches and suppers, but I need prior notification for that. Plus that's a bit extra on your bill. There's always tea and coffee any time of the day, and sometimes I have special treats. I try to make my guests as comfortable as possible."

"Coffee would be good," Jeanine said. "Wouldn't it, Ted?" He nodded.

Lenore showed them through the various guest lounges, one with books and one with satellite television, although their rooms, she hastened to add, had their own televisions.

"They're in the armoires against the far walls. You also have wireless Internet," she added.

"Well, that's good," Jeanine said.

"My sons set that all up. Both of them are very handy with technical things."

They were in the dining room now, and Lenore served them tea. The cups tinkled slightly as she carried them to the table.

"We'd like to meet them, if it's not too much trouble," Ted added. He'd taken off his vest with the pockets of film, revealing an open-necked, short-sleeve shirt. A camera was slung around his neck, making him look like a tourist.

Lenore looked at him. "You what?"

"I'd like to meet your sons. I'm interested in technology myself."

"No, Ted, you don't need to do that," Jeanine said. "I think we'll be kept busy enough around here without that."

Lenore looked at them both, secretly glad that they wouldn't be talking to her sons. She didn't need newspeople fiddling around in her family's life.

21

The police were at the door when Amy answered it after supper. There were two of them, someone she knew as Bill, a friend of Jake's, and a tall curly haired woman who introduced herself as Angela.

Ben was suddenly behind her, although when he had come up from his study, Amy didn't know.

"We need to talk with you, Ben," Bill said.

"I know." Ben opened the door without a word to Amy, who stood to the side, and let them in.

"Ben?" she finally managed, but the three of them were already down the stairs and in Ben's office with the door shut before she could register what happened. So she sat by herself in her window seat and looked out at the snow. Later she graded papers and got Charlie to bed and prayed with him and said goodnight to Blaine and then went to bed. All before Ben came back upstairs.

When he did, his feet heavy on the stairs, his face was white. He sat on the side of the bed and took off his socks. Amy didn't watch him do this. She'd been married to him long enough to know he always did this first. He didn't say anything. Amy got up and came around to face where he sat. She leaned against the wall and looked at him.

"What were the police here for?" she asked.

"It was a police matter, Amy."

"Well, obviously, it was a police matter. I didn't think it was a plumbing matter or a snowplowing matter. They're here about Blaine, right?"

"Why do you ask that?" He pulled off his turtleneck, folded it carefully, and placed it in his bottom drawer, straightening the sweater beside another dark turtleneck. His movements, his fastidiousness infuriated her tonight. She wished he would throw something, anything, instead of being so restrained.

"Because you think Blaine's lying to the police. Did you tell them that? Is that why they came back—and why aren't I a part of the discussion? I'm her mother, after all."

"They just needed my help with something."

"Why did they stay so long, then?"

"They weren't here all that long. Maybe half an hour. They left through the basement door." He placed his socks in the clothes hamper.

Amy walked out, went to the bathroom, and took a long, hot shower.

Later, when they were lying side by side in bed, each on a far edge, the middle of the bed an invisible barrier, Amy said, "Blaine is looking for her real mother. And I don't believe in God anymore."

Ben didn't answer her. He was either asleep or hadn't heard. Or maybe she hadn't really said it out loud at all. Maybe she'd only thought it.

The following day at school, Amy retrieved her plastic container of yogurt and sandwich from the staff refrigerator. It was what she ate every day.

"They're calling this the great mystery town." The fourth-grade teacher placed a boxed lunch in the microwave.

Amy poured coffee into the mug she always used.

"Who's calling it the mystery town?" someone else asked.

"The newspeople, CNN, they're all here now, getting pictures of people praying to the angel. FNN, too, I think."

"Whatever works," someone else said. "That's what most people are thinking. If nothing else works, why not give this a shot?"

"Well, what if this isn't a bad thing?" The fourth-grade teacher removed her microwave lunch and put it on the table. The place smelled of cooked chicken with sauce. "I mean, I do believe that God is all around us," she said. "Who's to say he or she didn't manifest himself or herself through an angel? Why don't we think of this as a gift?"

Cue Amy. At this point the director's hand would certainly be pointing at her. This was where Amy, the minister's wife, should have been saying something profound and biblical. She should have given some word of testimony. Instead, she spooned powdered cream into her coffee and stirred it in. A long time ago, Amy would've said something. A long time ago, Amy was sure of her faith, confident that the God of her fathers and mothers, the biblical God, was enough and that everyone else was wrong. She ripped opened a packet of Splenda and dumped it into her mug.

Amy "grew up in a Christian home," as the phrase went. Her father was a pastor. She went to a Christian elementary school, then a Christian high school, and then on to Christian Bible school, where she met Ben, who became her Christian husband. They got married in a Christian church. He went to a Christian seminary after that, and since she wasn't getting pregnant, despite their best efforts, she went on and finished her teaching degree at a Christian liberal arts college.

She took a sip of her coffee while Randy, another teacher, wildly guffawed. "It's a dead girl! And as soon as CNN gets her face on the news, her mother and father will come running to this little outpost to claim her. She was a runaway, probably a hooker. And since we're speaking about God and worshiping snowbanks, where was God when this girl was out there dying in the snow?"

Amy took a sip of her coffee. Amy took a bite of her sandwich. Amy ate a spoonful of yogurt. Amy finished her coffee. Amy didn't say anything, because Amy had completely forgotten her lines.

22

"At least we've got the area code," May said to him. "That's a plus." Jake and May were on their way into Ridley Harbor in May's SUV. Jake was in the passenger seat, listening to ice crystals feather against the windshield. It wasn't snowing, not exactly, and Jake wondered if this misty ice was some sort of new precipitation only available in Fog Point. It wasn't a dull day, though. The sun was haloed with mist but still shone down in the stillness. May maneuvered her SUV through plowed highway, snowbanks high on each side. Ahead of them, a snowplow cleared the way like Moses leading them through a Red Sea of snow.

They were in Ridley Harbor because Jake needed boat parts and May wanted to check on some cross-country skis that were on sale. An outdoor-recreation shop was going out of business, and all of their winter skis and equipment were selling for at least half off. May said, "If you can't beat 'em, join 'em. We may as well make the most of the snow to generate some business." But they were also going to the mall phone store to see if anyone could help them with the number. It couldn't hurt, Jake thought, but May was certain that all the information they needed was on the Internet, if only she could find it. Already she had found out the obvious, that the area code was for the northern half of the Canadian province of Alberta. May looked up the Shenks in Alberta, but there were hundreds of them; she'd call them all if she had to, she said, but it would be nice to narrow it down a bit.

"You know," May said, gripping the wheel and expertly guiding it past the snowplow, "I could always ask Sol."

"He's too expensive, May."

"Still, he'd find that number in about five minutes compared to some phone store geek who's not going to know his foot from a hole in the ground."

"Humor me, May. Let's see what the phone company says."

Sol was May's Internet contact whose specialty was finding people who didn't want to be found. Jake always thought of him as a shadowy presence who lived inside the Internet. But he was also handy to know when they needed quick information on someone. It had been six years since May's husband had been the victim of a sniper's bullet. The police were no closer to finding the killer. Books had been written about the sniper. He'd been the speculation of many a news article and mystery novel. Even *Law & Order* had done an episode that bore a striking resemblance to the incident. Police figured he had died or been killed in an unrelated incident, and that was what Jake felt. After her husband died, May sought refuge on the Internet, making connections, getting to know the sniper's victims online, setting up several Web sites for victims of the Allentown Gas Station Sniper. They shared information, always searching for that one clue, that one missing piece of evidence overlooked by the police and everyone else. Sol's brother had been killed by this madman, so he was as interested in finding him and bringing him to justice as May was. Only Sol was not above using illegal means to sniff out whatever information he needed. The sad irony was that Sol could find out just about anything about anybody, except the Allentown Gas Station Sniper.

"Okay," May said. "You win. We'll go to a phone store first, but if they're not able to deliver, I'll e-mail Sol tonight."

At a phone store in the Ridley Mall a high-heeled, dark-eyed woman told them with a flourish of her ringed forefinger that one of her associates, a guy named Ryerson, might be able to help them. He was a computer student at Ridley Tech and knew everything there was to know about phone technology. If they wanted to wait, have a look around, the store had a whole batch of wonderful new phones on special this month only.

She left them alone with the cell phones tethered to the walls like lights on a Christmas tree. One wall featured custom covers. There were sky blue phones, red phones, phones the color of mustard, phones speckled like robin eggs, and ones with lightning zigzags of gold.

Jake picked a camera phone from a large wall display and began pressing buttons on the keypad and suddenly "Dixie" blared through the empty store.

"Just what we need, Jake," May said.

"But this is cool," Jake said. "This is a camera. We should get a couple of these. All the good PIs have camera phones. We're operating in the Dark Ages. Plus, this one can do e-mail."

"Just what we need, camera phones that play the Confederate anthem. Won't we be popular."

"You've got to admit, May, it might be a good idea to get some new phones."

"There's a simple reason we don't have them, Jake. We can't afford it."

He put it down. "Such a spoilsport, ruin all my fun. It would be nice, though, to have a snazzier phone than my own daughter's. Jana has this phone that rings differently for each of her friends."

"Just what we need," May said.

Jake looked at the phone again, and May said, "Let's wait until next summer. See what kind of a season it is. Then we'll invest in some new business phones."

They both looked up when a jock of a guy with a shaved head emerged through the back door. When they told him what they wanted, he grinned and said, "No problem." He clicked through a series of commands on his computer and said, "Ta-da!"

"Ta-da what? Just like that you found the person at the other end of this number?" May asked.

"This number," he said waving the piece of paper at them, "is for the province of Alberta. That's in Canada!"

May took off her Squirrels cap and rubbed her eyes. She stared at him for a few seconds and then at Jake and rolled her eyes. Then she looked back at him and said, "Your mother name you Sunny?"

He looked at her for just a moment before saying, "You want me to see if I can find out who this number belongs to?"

"That's the idea," May said. "You figure it belongs to a cell phone or what?"

"Let me work on this, and I'll get back to you."

"If it belongs to a cell phone," Jake said, "is there a directory anywhere? How can we find that out? Would the person be in Alberta, then?"

"Maybe, maybe not. You can get portability with numbers now. Someone wants a cell phone for business, then moves and doesn't want to change the number. He can do that now. This number could be from anywhere. People pick up a cell phone in the mall, use it for a while, then move, then either cancel it or stop using it, or use it and pay the roaming charges. If you're willing to pay the roaming charges, you can move all over the planet. Who's going to stop you?"

"Why would someone be willing to pay the roaming charges?" May asked. Jake knew she liked to account for every penny in their business.

The guy grunted. "A whole lot of reasons. This could even be a terrorist phone."

"A *what* phone?" Jake asked.

"Totally untraceable. The police call them throwaways or disposables. You walk into Wal-Mart; you buy a phone with minutes on it; you don't even need a resident address or land line. And if you pay cash, they can't even trace you by your credit card."

Jake hadn't thought of this possibility. He knew how difficult it was to trace these types of phones. When he'd left the police force just before 9/11, this technology was just in the baby stages.

"Let me see what I can figure out for you guys," Ryerson said. "I love a challenge. This some person you know?"

"Something like that," May said.

Jake gave him their business card and said, "Can you show us those camera phones over there?"

"Hey, we got a special on them, guys. First three months, text messaging is free."

"Great. Just what we need, text messaging," May said.

An hour later, Jake and May walked out with two brand-new camera phones. They got the business plan, which Ryerson explained was an even better deal than the home plan, with free calls between them.

"Jana's going to flip when she sees this." Jake played with it all the way to the outdoor-recreation shop.

They drove home to Fog Point with the two new cell phones and two dozen pairs of cross-country skis, poles, and boots in various sizes, which all fit snugly in May's SUV.

"You know anything about cross-country skiing, May?" Jake said on the way home, still pressing buttons on his new phone.

"Jake, I know looking at me, it doesn't seem possible, but a long time ago I was an athlete. A long time ago, I did more than cross-country ski; we called it back-country skiing then. We strapped on long wood skis and tie-up boots and put on our wooly pants to the knee and away we went. Today they call it extreme skiing. We just called it skiing." She added, "But that was before my husband was murdered and my knee got buggered up beyond repair."

Jake didn't say anything as May went on about the joys and agonies of skiing. Instead, he was looking down at his new phone, wondering how easy it would be for someone to disappear.

23

Someone needs to tell Tully about The Tragedy. I need to. I need to before I lose my mind completely to the Alzheimer's. Already it's getting bad, already I'm forgetting simple things, like where my room is. I walk through the front door, easy as you please, and then up the stairs to the master bedroom, like I've done a hundred times in my life, a thousand. But then I stand there, in the doorway, wondering why everything looks different and wondering what Glad has done to it. That isn't her housecoat hanging on the back of the door. Or did she get a new one? Where are my slippers? Not where I left them on my side of the bed. Who put that blue spread on the bed? And the curtains are different. When had all this happened? And I stand there yelling, "Glad! Glad! Glad!"

Then a woman takes my arm and leads me down the stairs, through the kitchen, into the family room to the little pigeonhole of a room, sits me down in a chair, and turns the television on.

Then I remember.

This is my room now, and the woman is my daughter-in-law. Her name is Bobbie. Bobbie and Tim sleep in the master bedroom now. And Glad is dead.

Sometimes I sit here in my chair and wonder if the whole Terrible Tragedy was something my failing noggin made up. But then Tully came. I didn't make that up. Seeing her made me remember it all again.

Glad was a coward for not doing anything. So was I. When you got right down to it, my actions were the most cowardly. I was the man of the house, after all. In this one important thing, I'd failed.

She'd provided shelter for her niece then; that poor, sad, crazy girl who wasn't right in the head. Not since the rape. Not since her own baby died. Her own mother putting her out like that. Glad and I had to take her in, didn't we? It was the Christian thing to do, wasn't it? What else was the poor thing going to do? Go out and sleep in the grain bin? Glad'd felt sorry for her. At least that was what I thought then. But as the years passed, I got to wondering if Glad had done what she did, not out of sympathy for the niece, but to save her own good name in the community. How would it look, after all? That was Glad's main concern. Always had been. How things would look.

Sometimes I think about God's judgment. I sit in this chair, with the television on, and wonder about the cancer that came for Glad. The awful pain she endured in the end, the endless vomiting, her bitterness through it all. All a part of God's judgment.

Now the Alzheimer's is coming for me, as slowly and as surely as the sun rises each morning and sets each night. And day follows night, which follows day, and each day it gets just a little bit worse. All a part of the judgment of God for the part we played in the destruction of the Shenk family.

24

A day seldom went by when there wasn't someone kneeling in Lenore's snowbank now. The fact that every night the wind whipped the snowbank into new shapes, like wind on sand, only intensified visitors' interest. The people kept seeing new shapes: an angel, a cross, the star of David, the Madonna, even the yin-and-yang symbol.

And more people were staying at her bed-and-breakfast, almost more than she could handle. Along with the FNN people who decided "to stay a few extra nights, and we hope that's okay," the young woman with the cane, whose name was Violet, was still there, along with Arnold and two photographers who chased all over the country after strange weather phenomena for their weather calendar, they told her.

The FNN people, now, they were a strange pair. Lenore knew very well there was something going on between them. They had two different last names, so they weren't married. Ted's bed hadn't been slept in, and his towels had migrated over to Jeanine's room. Well, that was their business. If they wanted to pay for two rooms and use one, well, who was she to complain about that?

So it was busy. In the summer, she always hired students to help her. But now, with her two summer workers away in college, Lenore had to do it all herself. This morning, for example, she'd been up since five, making muffins with blueberries she'd frozen last summer. With all of her guests around the table, the muffins disappeared quickly, along with another jar of her home-made apricot jam.

Then in the middle of her breakfast fixings, May had called about the photo. Could Lenore spare a moment or two?

Lenore dumped the used coffee filter into the garbage and readied another pot of coffee. If these people were anything, they were coffee guzzlers. One of the photographers had asked her if there was a Starbucks in town, and when she shook her head, he asked her if she had an espresso machine. No, she did not. Well, what she *did* have was one of those little espresso double-decker pots that you put on the stove. She never used it, didn't know how. Didn't even know where she'd gotten it. She climbed up and got it down from a back cupboard, and the photographer patiently showed her how to make espresso that way. It was slow going, but with the addition of a handheld milk frother, she ended up making a passable cappuccino that pleased her more urbane guests.

If there was one good thing about the angel and the ice, it was that all the businesses were doing well. Rose Nation said this *proved* she was an angel.

"The angel was praying for us, and it's working. All the motels are full. Photographers are here. And, of course, I'm the first one to tell them about my arthritis. Did you see me on television?"

"It's still cured?" Lenore had asked.

"What do you mean, is it still cured? Of course it is! Once you're cured, you can't get uncured from something."

"Well, that's good, then, isn't it?"

And now May was banging on Lenore's kitchen door with her cane. Her first words were, "I'm going to need the original of that photograph," in a voice loud enough to wake the dead.

Lenore ushered May through the kitchen and into her own room and shut the door. Her private quarters were a combination bedroom and sitting room. It was the place Lenore retired to each evening after her work was done. She had her own television here, her phone, a computer, and of course her wall full of pictures of her grandchildren.

Lenore said, "What's this about needing a photo?"

"We need the original. The original would tell us a lot."

Lenore looked at her, a feeling like ice in her knees. "I don't know if I can get it. It's in Earl's desk, and I don't want him knowing I'm doing this."

May said, "There seems to be a date alongside the photo that we can't make out. The original might even lead us to where it was developed. It would only be for a day or two."

"I just don't know. May, if I can be frank, it's the child I'm interested in. Not the mother. I want to know about that child." Already Lenore was wondering if she'd made a supreme mistake in getting May involved. May was smart, and so was Jake. He used to be a police officer, after all. It wasn't going to take them too long to put two and two together. Plus, she knew May. That woman had this uncanny ability to tell when people were lying. So Lenore kept her hands in her lap and her eyes down.

"You're wondering whether the child is your grandchild," May said.

Lenore nodded, still not looking up. Maybe May would just think she was distraught. Well, she was. She wasn't lying there. May didn't say anything for a while.

"There are a dozen people lined up in your backyard, Lenore. Do you know that?"

Lenore followed May's gaze out of her window where a few more cars had pulled in.

"It's the angel. They just keep coming," Lenore said quietly.

May pulled off her Squirrels baseball cap and ran her fingers through her gray hair. "They'll get tired of it soon. When the magic wears off."

"Did you notice the fog this morning? They think the fog has something to do with things now. That's why it won't stop snowing. Enid told me that."

"Crazy people."

"You get anything on that phone number?"

"We've localized the area code, but it might be a cell phone. We have someone looking into it. The area code is for the Canadian province of Alberta. That may or may not mean anything."

"Alberta? Oh, my." Lenore put her hand to her chest. "That would be as far away as Nebraska?"

May raised her eyebrows.

"Norman lives in Nebraska."

May took a drink of coffee. "I know where Norman lives."

"You know that Norman's a minister in a megachurch, now? Have I told you that, May? His church has more people going to it than the whole population of Fog Point and then some. They have twenty ministers—"

May rose. "Just get that photo for us—"

"The head minister there, well, I'm sure you've heard of him. He's quite famous. He's written books. I have two of them. Norman sends them. His wife—MarieAnn—she works in the Christian bookstore that's attached to the church..." Lenore was aware she was blathering on, but she couldn't stop. When it came to Norman, when it came to her grandchildren, she couldn't stop.

May took off her glasses and rubbed her eyes. "Yeah, well, as soon as we get this photo—"

"He relies on Norman quite a bit, the head minister does. Norman is quite successful."

But May was up and adjusting her Squirrels baseball cap and shrugging into her heavy canvas coat. "Lenore, you know my opinion of Norman, now, don't you?"

After May left, Lenore frowned and opened the door to the basement and made her way downstairs, terrified of what May might find when she gave her the picture.

25

The word on the street is that we're officially in *The Twilight Zone*." May hummed the theme song from the TV program as she came into the warm office at the Purple Church and shook off the cold. Their new skis were leaning against the far wall of the office.

Jake was at the table, going through possible ad ideas for promoting their new ski-rental business.

"Crazy," she ran her fingers through her hair and put her baseball cap back on. "I am totally convinced that everyone in this town is certifiable."

He didn't quite know whether she was talking to him or her dead husband, so he said nothing. May often did that, talked out loud to Paul. She was one of those people who mumbled constantly, and usually these mumbles were prefaced with "Paul." So far, Paul'd never answered back. At least not to Jake's knowledge.

"Did you hear me?" May said.

"You're talking to me, are you, May?"

"Of course I'm talking to you, Jake. Who else would I be talking to?"

On a row of hooks next to the door, she hung up the heavy canvas coat she always wore. She'd never told Jake, but he was certain it had belonged to her late husband.

She took off her glasses, breathed on them, and cleaned them on the edge of her sweatshirt before sitting down in front of the computer. The office computer belonged to both of them, of course, but he seldom used it. From day one, it was May's territory. Jake had his own laptop he kept downstairs and used for e-mails when May was working on the office one. And of course, May had her own laptop she kept at her cottage.

She was still mumbling. "We've got an idiotic gaggle of newspeople setting up cameras down at Lenore's as we speak. Plus, she's acting weirder than I've ever seen her. Citizenry are lined up from here to Ridley, and she's going on and on about Norman."

Jake adjusted his glasses. "Who's Norman?"

"Her bum of a son."

"I thought he was the minister, the only nonbum of the group."

"If you ask me, he's the worst bum. He's the one that takes after his father the most. Even looks like him, if you saw him. Plus, what's with the snow fog? Everybody's going on like this is something important and eerie. Like we're in some alternate reality or something."

"Maybe we are."

She hummed a few more bars of the *Twilight Zone* theme while her fingers flew on the keyboard. "Let's see, any messages, any messages…and people praying, actually *praying* to a snowbank. Now tell me, have you ever in your entire life heard of anything more ridiculous? Like Tom Hanks worshiping his volleyball in that movie."

"He didn't really worship the thing, May."

She shrugged and said, "You ever see *The Crawling Eye*?"

Jake flipped through the notes he'd taken earlier. "Another movie?"

She turned to him, her hands still flying on the keyboard. "Probably before your time. An old black-and-white jobby about a radioactive cloud that engulfs a mountain."

"Sounds interesting."

"It's a cheesy movie. But around here people are beginning to talk like that, like this is some strange phenomenon." She waved her hands in front of her and hummed again for a few moments. "I'm expecting any day now for the scientist with the white coat and the shirt pocket full of pens to come along and analyze the situation, and for the pretty maiden to need saving, and the townspeople to all rally in the street, and the handsome guy to come in and save the town, ending up in bed with the pretty maiden. If we're in the middle of a B-grade movie, we may as well do it up right." She adjusted her baseball cap. "Plus, what's with your friend Ben these days?"

He looked up. "What about Ben?"

"I saw him today, almost bumped into him. He barely acknowledged me."

"I think he and Amy are having a few challenges with Blaine. There could also be church things. I don't know what all."

"*Church things.* One good reason to stay away. Two, if you count people worshiping volleyballs."

"Nobody worships volleyballs at Ben's church."

"No, but they do worship snowbanks. People from the church you've lately been attending are lining up in Lenore's backyard, and don't tell me they're not. I was there. I saw them."

She had him on that one. "Paul was a Christian, May. You've told me that."

"Yeah, and look where it got him. By the way, I saw Carrie too."

He put down the papers he was perusing. "Carrie was there?"

"No, not at Lenore's. Give her some credit. I was in Noonan's, grabbing a paper, and there she was. I said, 'Carrie, why, why, *why* don't you bring a bit of sense to this town? You're a journalist! Get that defunct *Fog Point Lighthouse* newspaper going again.' She could do that, Jake, you know she could. So I said to her, 'Write an editorial that brings some sense to these crazy people!' And well, she screwed up her face and backed away from me like I had just told her to run screaming naked through the streets. It's possible that the cloud of fog has affected her brain as well."

"Carrie's kind of sensitive when it comes to her newspaper writing, May. You know that."

She shrugged. "I know. I *know.*" She put her hands in the air. "She had to leave that great job at the *Detroit News* to come out here to this backwater and manage the boatyard, and she misses it. She's told me she misses it. But if she misses it so much, well, I say do something about it. Start up a paper here."

"You about finished?"

"Yep."

"Ryerson called. He's located where the cell phone might be from."

"Why didn't you tell me this sooner?"

"Couldn't get a word in."

"Okay, what've you got?"

"It's in the central part of the province of Alberta. Near Edmonton. A place called Barrhead."

"Okay."

"Ryerson's going to try to get us a list of recent phone activity. Plus, I took the liberty of looking at an online directory while you were gone," Jake said. "And there are a whole bunch of Shenks living in Barrhead. But way less than the entire province, which is what we were dealing with before we contacted Ryerson."

"Great work, Jake. You're a good detective."

"Thank you, madam. I told you it wasn't a stupid idea going to Ryerson."

"You call any of them yet?"

"I left that for you, May. I know how you love that sort of thing."

26

Any mother would do this, Lenore told herself as she stepped into her sons' lair for the second time in as many days. She stood at the bottom of the stairs, and the smell of the place assaulted her nostrils. What she needed to do was bleach that bathroom of theirs again.

She breathed through her mouth and made her way quickly to the desk drawer and opened it. It was still all there, in the bottom drawer—the pictures of Tolita Shenk and her baby, with the name and phone number on the back of Tolita's. From the looks of things, Earl hadn't even opened this drawer since she had taken the pictures out and photocopied them. Well, good then. They might not be missed.

She glanced down at the baby. Such a cute little boy with his crooked, gummy, old-man's smile. There was something about it that so reminded her of Carl. Could this be Carl's baby?

When her boys were small, she dressed the three of them in sailor suits and lined them up on the piano bench to take their picture. She still had that photograph. It was framed on her wall right next to the pictures of her grandchildren. She ran her finger across the face of this baby, wondered where he was. Nothing told her this was a boy, but she'd raised three boys. She knew boys. She thought of her other grandchildren, Alyssa and Jonathan and Bradley, and a choke rose in her throat. How had her life come down to this?

She looked down the side of the photo where May said the date was. Yes, there was a date, or what used to be a date. It was a blur now.

Next she looked at the picture of the girl. *What did you want when you came here? And where is your baby?*

Sometimes it worried her that she was keeping all this from the police. But, really, how would the knowledge that Earl had this girl's photo in his drawer really help their investigation anyway? And so *what* if she moved the body? The girl was already dead, wasn't she? Strangled? That's what Enid had told her. Enid watched FNN all day long. The thought that the poor girl was strangled stopped her, and she put a hand to her throat.

She put the girl's photo back and put the original baby picture in the pocket of her sweater. Carefully, she closed the bottom drawer, but the jarring of it brought the computer above to life. She glanced up at the screen and *Freesia,* her boys' whale-watching sailboat, came to life. Another business venture of theirs that had failed. Lenore had had her doubts about that, even when she'd fronted the money for it.

They had taken a few people out, but as for seeing whales, they saw nary a one. Carl blamed it on the boat. It was just too slow to get to the whale grounds. They might see a whale blowing in the distance, but by the time they got there, the whale was long gone. Halfway through the summer, they dropped the words *Whale Watching* from their signage and offered just schooner cruises. But the people who had signed up on the Web site expected to see whales. And then when their boat sank at the wharf one night... Well, that was another story.

Jake and May did very well, however, with their boat. Well, of course they would; it was a faster boat. Maybe all her boys needed was a faster boat. Maybe she'd suggest that to them.

Before she went upstairs, she made a quick tour of the rest of the basement. And in the smelly bathroom she found a container of unfamiliar pills in the medicine cabinet behind a can of shaving cream. How had she missed this before? It was a plain, brown, plastic bottle like the kind dispensed in pharmacies for prescriptions, yet there was no label on this one. It frightened her. Had the girl been drugged before she was strangled? She searched her mind to remember what the news had said. Maybe she should ask Enid about that. Enid knew everything in town, even more than Lenore did. And even if the news didn't say she'd been drugged, she knew that sometimes the police withheld crucial facts in their public statements, things that would help them later. Maybe this was one of those facts. And it wouldn't be long before the police got a search warrant—frankly she wondered why they hadn't already—and would come down here and find these pills and the picture of the girl and arrest her sons. She dumped the entire vial of pills down the toilet and put the plastic container in her pocket next to the picture.

Upstairs, Lenore opened the door to the kitchen and entered quietly. She heard voices. Those two from FNN were making their way downstairs for midmorning coffee.

"It was your bright idea," she heard the woman, Jeanine, say, "to come here in the first place. What were you thinking? Fog Point of all places?"

"Damage control," Ted said. "You said it yourself."

"Damage control, damage control—if the lug had listened to me carefully in the first place, we wouldn't be in this pickle."

"But looking for it will be like looking for a needle in a haystack."

"I know that, but we have to try."

And then they saw Lenore and immediately stopped talking.

"Hello, hello," Lenore said. "I imagine you'd like some tea? Or coffee? I've a fresh pot of coffee, and tea is just a boiled kettle away."

"Coffee," the woman said. A red scarf was tied around her neck, and Lenore couldn't look at it for long. It reminded her of the way the girl, Tolita, had tied her scarf.

"Cappuccino," Ted said.

"You should really invest in a proper cappuccino machine," Jeanine said.

"I can't imagine running an establishment without one in this day and age." They entered the guest dining room and pulled out a *New York Times*.

"I would like the front section, Ted," she said.

Obediently, he gave it to her, and the two began quietly reading.

Two elderly women from Ridley, whom Lenore didn't know, were already at the table, drinking tea that Lenore had earlier prepared. They had been kneeling in the snowbank, and one of them still shivered and kept blinking. Lenore had to wonder how good it was for sick people to sit in snow for extended periods. *Next thing you know, I'll be sued for this.* Violet, the girl with the cane, sat drinking coffee and staring out at the snowbank where worshippers still congregated.

At that moment, Earl came through the back door, bringing the cold with him. Every time Lenore looked at him, she swore he was bigger than the time before, if it were possible for him to get bigger. He couldn't fasten the buttons on his coat, so it was opened, revealing a huge stomach in a blue tent-sized T-shirt. He carried with him a family-size bag of Doritos.

Could he be the father of that baby? It had to be Carl. Carl was charming with the ladies, just like his father before him. Yet, the pictures were in Earl's desk. Maybe Carl had gone to Earl, saying, "Fix this." And Earl had. How had he done it? Had he put those pills in her drink and then strangled her? She didn't know if she could imagine him putting those big chubby baby hands around her neck and squeezing.

And then she had a thought—how soon before the screen on his computer went back to screen-saver mode? Five minutes? Fifteen? She didn't know, so the only way to keep him upstairs was to offer him food.

"Have some coffee, Earl," she said. "I put on a new pot not more than half an hour ago. And cinnamon swirls. I just made a fresh batch."

He grunted, put down his bag of Doritos, and eyed the sheet of swirls.

"Help yourself," Lenore said. In different respects, both Earl and Carl were like her husband. Carl possessed Harlan's charm and raw appeal, while

Earl had his addictions. Harlan died early of liver disease while waiting for a transplant. Because of the way he drank, he wasn't high on anybody's organ-donor list. He'd likely have drunk his way through a second liver if he'd been lucky enough to get one. Which he wasn't. And Earl would surely eat himself to death one day when his heart decided it couldn't support the body that surrounded it.

Earl grabbed two cinnamon swirls, took them into the guest dining room, and sat down at the table.

"Earl, I don't know if you've met our guests, Jeanine and Ted from FNN," she said proudly, "and Violet. And," she indicated the two women, "I don't remember your names; I'm sorry."

"Wilma and Katherine," said the nonblinking woman. The blinking woman kept blinking and looking at her cup of tea. It looked to Lenore as if she hadn't drunk any of it.

"Hey," Ted said, rising and extending his hand. "You're the Web wizard, I hear."

"Yep. Web wizard." He burped loudly and Lenore scolded, "Earl!"

Ted merely smiled. "I'd like to see your work someday. We're in the market for a Web site."

"FNN wants to get Earl to do their Web site. Wow!" Lenore announced to the room at large.

"We're with an affiliate," Jeanine corrected and went back to her paper. "And we've already talked about this, Ted," she said quietly.

"I'd be happy to oblige," Earl said. "I'll bring my laptop up later this evening, and you and I can look over the sort of stuff I've done. Is this evening okay?"

"That would be fine."

Violet, at the window, sighed.

"Are you okay, dear?" Lenore asked.

"Fine," she said quietly. She looked at the two shivering women and said,

"I was hoping that coming here would make a difference. I thought…I even went out to pray. Yesterday…" Her voice trailed off.

"Did you know that girl?" Jeanine asked, looking at her suddenly.

Lenore gasped and hoped it wasn't audible. She put hand to her chest. It fluttered there for a while. "I never saw her before. Until that day, I mean."

"I was asking Earl," Jeanine said. Her lips looked as though she had just devoured a juicy steak, and Lenore thought of all the vampire books she had ever read.

"That girl?" He shook his head. "Don't know her from Adam. Or should I say Eve. Never met her in my life."

Lenore studied his face when he said this. He looked Jeanine in the eyes and shrugged as if he truly had never met the girl. Maybe she had misjudged him. Maybe it was all a big coincidence. Yet, she was quick to remind herself, the dead girl's picture was in his desk drawer. There was no coincidence about that.

Earl added, "So, you finding lots of newsworthy news up here in this godforsaken part of the planet?"

"Plenty," Ted said with a laugh. "Just plenty."

"The parade of idiots," Earl said. "The news at six. Look at all the idiots out there." He yelled through the closed window. "Hey, you! You in the green ski jacket. Your village called! Their idiot is missing!"

"Earl," Lenore said sharply. "Be respectful."

He grunted and ate a cinnamon swirl in two bites.

The others around the table—Violet, Wilma, and Katherine—barely looked at Earl when he said this.

A few moments later, Lenore thought of something. "You know, if you're ever doing a story on churches, you should visit my son Norman's church. It's a magnificent building."

"Is it around here?" Jeanine asked.

"No. It's in Nebraska. They have eight thousand people who come to their church every Sunday. I could give you the Web site. If you ever do a story on megachurches, I could give you Norman's name and number."

"Give it a rest, Mother, will ya?" Earl said.

"Oh, you be respectful of your brother. You're just peeved because they didn't hire you to do the church Web site. That's what your little protest is all about."

"Megachurch, huh?" Jeanine seemed to be mulling it over. "And an angel comes to *his* mother's backyard…"

"Guy's a scag," Earl said. "That would be your real story."

"It would be a good story; I know it would." Lenore's hands shook. She turned and faced her son. "He's a good man. You'd do well to follow your brother's example."

27

The wind, and the banging noise it made on the side of the house, kept Amy awake at night. She was used to the sounds of this old house. The settling of wood and timbers in the cold, the cracking like old joints. Usually she slept through it, the noise providing a kind of backdrop to her dreams. But not lately. Lately she was finding it more and more difficult to sleep. Every little thing kept her awake. She kept seeing things, shadows. She thought of Blaine and Blaine's biological mother. Her daughter wouldn't find her mother. It was illegal. Adoption records couldn't be opened to anyone under nineteen. She'd checked that out today on the Internet. But still it worried her. A lot of things worried her these days. Blaine. Ben. Her family. Was there any chance for her and Ben?

Beside her, Ben slept soundly. After what he had told her after supper, she wondered how he could do this. But he did. He always did. He'd knelt by the bed and prayed and gave everything to God and then climbed under the covers and went to sleep. She marveled at that.

She glanced at the bedside clock. Two-thirty in the morning was too late to take a Tylenol PM. Not unless she wanted to sleep until ten. And by ten, she'd be deep within a math lesson with her class.

Two people in her household had met and spoken with the dead girl. It astonished her that in both cases she didn't hear about it until way after the fact. First there was Blaine. And now Ben.

Amy rose quietly from the bed, shrugged into a robe that hung on the side of the door, and realized it was Ben's and not hers. She put it on anyway and smelled the smell of him, a smell she knew like her own skin.

She walked past Charlie's darkened room, went downstairs, sat in the shadows, and looked out onto the woods across the street. It was a clear night, windy, and the moon was full. The misty snow fog of the day had lifted. Maybe this would be the end of it.

Across the street, a deer nosed its way through the drifts. He seemed to sense her, and although that could not be possible, he looked up and faced the picture window and stared at her, his snout covered in snow. She hugged Ben's robe closer to her and thought of that biblical psalm about the deer panting for the water. *There is no water to be found in this land*, she wanted to tell it. *All of it is frozen. All of it has turned to stone.*

Her husband truly believed that God would never leave them, that anything bad, whatever tribulation befell them, God would rapture them out of it just in time. But something deep and dark inside of her told her that wasn't going to happen this time.

Ben didn't know what she knew, that God didn't always answer prayers. It wasn't that he didn't answer prayers the way they wanted; it was that he didn't answer prayers at all. If there was a God.

If there even was a God.

She stared out at the deer across the street and watched him paw his way down to find grass under the high banks of snow and then move away from her view.

Right after supper, Ben had taken Amy's hand and said they were going for a ride in the car. And they left, to the surprise of Charlie and Blaine. They took off and drove to the library parking lot and sat in the car, the engine running.

"I need to tell you two things," Ben had said.

"Okay."

"I shouldn't keep things from you."

"No, you shouldn't."

"There are two things you need to know. First, the police. The girl that died came to me. She came into the church."

Amy stared at him.

"She wanted directions. That's what I kept trying to tell the police. She wanted to know where Featherjohn's Bed-and-Breakfast was. I thought she wanted to stay there. That was all."

"She came in wanting directions? She asked Blaine the same thing, didn't she? Why did she want directions?"

"I don't know, Amy. I'm just telling you what I told the police."

"So why didn't you tell me this sooner, like last night? Like right after the police came?"

"I'm trying to protect my family—"

"From what, Ben?"

He'd merely shrugged.

"You said there was a second thing?"

"About the rumor that we were moving. This one's nothing. I just wanted you to know that. Rube took care of it. He talked to the people in question."

"You mean the person in question."

"Person, then."

There was a sound now, like walking, coming from the room below. Blaine's room. Up and about at two-thirty? She went quietly down the stairs and stood outside her daughter's door. A knife blade of light shone under the door.

She stood there and tried to listen. She heard the quiet clatter of fingers on a computer keyboard. Then silence. Then more typing. Then nothing. Homework? Or something else? Messaging with friends? But who would be up at this time? She knew Blaine had some sort of boyfriend at school, a junior who was too old for Blaine. Yet what could she do? Especially when Blaine looked so much older than fourteen.

A few weeks ago, Blaine had said, "I have a boyfriend, but don't tell Dad. He'll freak."

Amy kept her secret. One more in a growing garbage pile of secrets between husband and wife. And while she had chided him for keeping secrets from her, her secrets from him were different. She needed to maintain her relationship with Blaine, and she agreed with Blaine: Ben would freak.

She pressed her ear closer to the door. Another mother would knock and ask gently, *Everything all right?* Another daughter would smile and answer, *Yes, just up for a minute.* Another mother and daughter would share a moment or two of quiet heartfelt chat, just the two of them sitting together on the edge of the bed in the middle of the night. Another mother and daughter would take each other's hands and pray.

But Amy wasn't another mother. Amy was a mother who didn't know how to be a mother to a fourteen-year-old daughter who didn't want to be her daughter anymore and who was looking for her real mother. Her *real* mother. Amy wasn't real. She was a vapor, a piece of gossamer, a snowflake. A ghost. A piece of snow fog.

She held her hand against the door for a moment, a sign not of blessing but of yearning to be a different mother, the real mother. She left the door and crept back upstairs.

28

I found something," May said to Jake in the morning. "It's not a lot, but it's something. At least I feel like I'm on the right track."

There were deep bags under May's eyes this morning and a slump to her shoulders. "Tell me, May," he said, sitting down. "Tell me you got some sleep last night. That you didn't go home and spend the entire night on your laptop."

She shrugged. "You know me, Jake."

That was the trouble. He did.

As it was, the two of them had worked together until close to midnight, making a list of Shenks in Alberta and looking up names and businesses. They decided not to call any until they'd compiled a full list and checked them out on the Internet. Also, they could find no one named Tolita among any of the Shenks.

"I tried to get to sleep, but I kept thinking of things. I thought with an unusual name like Tolita she'd be fairly easy to find something on…"

"Tell me you didn't…"

She looked at him, wide-eyed. "Didn't what?"

"Hire Sol."

May grinned. "I didn't. Thought about it, though."

"Okay, tell me what you have."

"I found a Tolita Shenk." Theatrically, she laid the printout in front of Jake. "Ta-da," she said.

It was a short newspaper article, not more than an inch in length and dated almost a year ago from the *Barrhead Leader*, Barrhead, Alberta: "Police are still looking for Tolita Shenk, who disappeared from her foster home in early May."

"Where'd you find this?" he asked.

"The online archives. I had to pay, but it was worth it."

"Any more references to her?"

May shook her head and looked at her watch. "And as soon as it's not the middle of the night out there, I'll start calling all those Shenks. If she's a foster kid, she'll be in the system somewhere. Maybe we can find out something."

"Social Services isn't going to tell you anything, May. You can't get anything out of them without a dozen warrants in triplicate. Even the police can't."

"I'll do it. Trust me, Jake. I'll call the paper. I'll call the mayor. Somebody knows where this kid is. And her baby. And then, as soon as we know, we'll bundle up the information and give it to Lenore so she can go out and get her grandson and bring him home. That's what she really wants, after all."

Jake raised his eyebrows.

May said, "I've known Lenore a long time. She dotes on her grand-children. If there's any question of a grandson, she'll be right there. So with that done, I'm back researching the dead girl. I got curious about this whole angel business. I wanted to see if there was historical precedent for this thing." She showed him a printout. "Look what I found: here's the imprint of Jesus on the side of a Tim Hortons restaurant in Nova Scotia, and here're people finding Jesus and angels in everything from grilled-cheese sandwiches to what all. This one sold on eBay for twenty-eight hundred dollars. It had a bite out of it, so that probably lowered its value, but you can clearly see the imprint of

Mary. A guy bought it for his casino and keeps it under glass, so people can have good luck. You'd think the casino owner wouldn't want it there. I mean, how many casino owners actually want their patrons to have good luck? Peo ple have seen Noah's Ark in their tortillas. It's true," she said between yawns. "We are all this close to bowing down before our own volleyballs."

"Go have a nap, May. Downstairs. Take your pick of the summer students' rooms. The beds are all made up."

"Oh, I just might." She got up, groaned with her hands on her knees, and grabbed her wooden walking stick. She didn't like to call it a cane. On her desk was a bulging file folder. Jake knew this was only a fraction of what she'd collected through the years on the Allentown Gas Station Sniper. At the top was the list of all the victims. And he knew why May had been up all night—trying to find a link between the girl who died and the Allentown Gas Station Sniper. He wondered if she would ever stop looking.

An hour later and still no sounds from the basement. He hoped May was getting some sleep. Jake would wait until she woke up to call Alberta. She'd probably never forgive him if he made the calls himself.

Just a couple more things to clear up on this case. Jake mentally checked them off. (1) Call out west to get an address for this Tolita Shenk. (2) Get the original photo from Lenore, look at it, and find the baby.

He tapped his finger on the photocopy of the baby and looked at it again. There was a line from the center of the top to the center of the right. It looked like a bar of some sort. He squinted at it. Probably part of a crib or something, or maybe a defect in the paper itself.

He picked it up and peered at it. There it was again, that feeling that he knew this picture and this baby. And somehow he kept thinking of Jana in connection with this. Or was it that this baby picture reminded him of Jana when she was a baby? What was it? He shook his head and went back to the computer where his e-mail icon was jumping up and down.

This one was from his other daughter, Alex.

Hi Dad, How are you doing? We don't have any snow here.
I hear you have lots. It's even on the news. I made the
basketball team. Here are some pictures.

His other daughter. The daughter he felt most estranged from. One shouldn't have favorites among one's own children. Yet, this other daughter, the younger one, eleven-year-old Alex, was, when he got right down to it, more like him than his favored child, Jana. Alex even looked like him—tall, athletic, with straight, fine hair—while Jana looked so like Connie with brown, wavy hair. Yet it was Jana who sought him out, who wanted to live here, who forgave him his years of neglect. *How can you not have favorites when one daughter begs to live with you and the other begs to stay away?*

He looked at the two digital pictures she'd sent. One was a posed shot of her basketball team in blue and gold uniforms, she in the back, of course. She always stood taller than most of her peers.

How had all this happened? He never expected to raise his kids in a broken home.

He answered Alex's e-mail and uploaded a couple of photos of the bay for her and one of Jana.

Here are some pictures I took. Look at the water. You're not
going to recognize it!

While he was writing, the e-mail icon flashed again. After he hit Send for Alex's, he opened it. A couple from out west was coming here for their honeymoon. They'd seen Fog Point on the news recently, and it looked so nice and remote. They wanted a good recommendation for a place to stay, and they would like to sign up for a day's kayak adventure. He'd pass this on to May. She was the one who took care of the bookings.

A loud knock on the office door got him away from the computer, and he opened the door to a very irate Lenore Featherjohn.

"How come your office is locked? Here I am in the cold, knocking and knocking out there." She huffed her way into the office. She wore a fur coat, and the collar was dusted with snow.

"Sorry, Lenore, the door's usually unlocked. I didn't know it was snowing again."

"It's not snowing, just blowing, blowing a gale out there. Snow is all over the road, and nothing's plowed. I pay good taxes, and you'd think that would cover decent snowplowing. I barely made it here in one piece."

She handed him her coat, and he hung it up on a hook by the door, right next to May's canvas one. "Is May here?" she asked.

"She's resting. She worked late into the night."

Lenore sat down and pulled off her hat, a fur thing that tied under her chin. She laid it on her knees, where it looked like a quiet lap dog. She reached into the purse beside her and handed him an envelope. "I brought the photo for May, the original. You can give it to her."

He took it, and pulled out the snapshot. It was smudged and soft and creased down the middle as though it had been folded forward and then back on itself. But the photo itself wasn't remarkable. Jake guessed it to be about three-by-five inches, and to his inexpert eyes it looked as though it had been taken with an ordinary thirty-five millimeter camera. He ran his hand over the edge. What had looked like a date in the photocopy looked merely like a smudge in this original. He looked down into the face of the baby again, try-ing to evoke the feeling he first had when he looked into this baby's face, but whatever it had brought to his thinking when he first had seen it was gone. "It's bigger than this in the photocopy," he said.

Lenore shrugged, stroked her hat. "I don't know anything about that. I just put it in Earl's photocopier and pressed buttons."

"He must have had it set on enlarge." He turned it over. Nothing written there. Then he remembered something. "There's nothing on the back," he said.

"Why would there be?"

"You said that Tolita Shenk's name and phone number were written on the back of the picture."

"I did?" She twisted a ring on her right hand. "Well, I certainly didn't mean it, did I? When I came in to see May, I was so distraught I might not have remembered everything correctly." She kept twisting that ring. "What I meant to say is that I found Tolita's name and phone number on a slip of paper that was paper-clipped to the picture."

Lenore's eyes kept darting. She never looked at him square on. He'd been a police officer once. He knew what darting eyes meant. She grabbed her coat from the hook, threw it on, and huffed out into the snow, a whirlwind of fur and mutterings. He watched her strut her way down the roadway to her car, get in, and drive away. He knew she was hiding something bigger than a lost grandson. He wondered what it was.

29

How *dare* he!" Lenore muttered to herself as she drove home on the newly plowed streets. At one point, she was stuck behind the plow. She cursed as the convoy of cars made its way up Main Street. *How* dare *he!* she thought. *Accusing me of lying, of hiding something. May wouldn't treat me like that. Giving me that look of his. Who does Jake think he is, anyway? I know a little something about that Jake. And it isn't pretty. What if I were to blab that all over the universe?*

At one nasty intersection, she swerved dangerously on black ice, but then managed to right herself. She said a word then, a word that would surely have her sainted mother rolling in her grave clothes. Her mother would have no idea that sweet Lenore even knew such words.

"And there are more words where that came from," Lenore said out loud as she gripped the steering wheel and righted the car. "I learned them from Harlan. He's the one should be blamed for all of this!"

But the real truth was, she was mad at herself. Obviously, this whole bogus plan of hers was just plain stupid. May and Jake were good investigators. Look what they'd discovered in just a few days. It wouldn't take them too long to figure out just what it was she was hiding. And then what? More police. More questions. And she would be in trouble, of that she had no doubt. Because what if, with all of this trying to help her family, it all came out wrong anyway? That's all she wanted to do in the end, wasn't it? Help her family?

She tried pulling her car around the plow but faced oncoming traffic, so she pulled back into her lane and cursed again, a ribald word, one that Harlan, and now Carl, used with regularity.

She was finally able to turn right, and the snowplow went straight, but when she got to her house, the plow had been by and she was met by a three-foot bank of snow at the end of her driveway. More words.

Even in her present anger she would never be able to forge her way over the bank with her car. Those no-good sons of hers. Where were they? They were supposed to keep the driveway snow-blowed at all times. She parked her Town Car in front of Enid's house across the street and then set off on foot, climbing over the snow wall. Thigh high. Another not-too-nice word when her left boot came off and stayed in the snow pile and, sock-footed, she stepped in the snow. She looked up. Enid wasn't standing at the window. She was sure Enid would have something to say about her language—if not to her, then to everyone else at church.

She wrested her boot from the snow, wiped off her foot, and put the boot back on.

"*Earl!*" she screamed as loud as she could. "*Earl, get your fat butt out here and snow-blow the driveway!*"

"Yoo-hoo! Hello. Yoo-hoo!" Enid had just stepped out of her house with a broom to sweep off her stoop.

Lenore turned, smiled sweetly. "Enid, hello dear, how are you?"

"Lumbago's acting up again."

"My dear, you need to try fish oil." Lenore brushed off her fur coat. "I'll bring you a bottle next time I come over."

"That would be sweet of you, dear."

Lenore made her way across the street toward her friend. "Enid? I wonder if you've heard something…"

"About what?"

"I was just wondering…uh," Lenore climbed Enid's steps. "You, um, I know you watch a lot of news…" Which was a nice way to say that the television was never off at Enid's. Even now, through the lace-curtained window, she could see the flickering square blue of the set.

Lenore continued, "Have you heard anything about drugs being a part of that…that poor girl's death?"

"Drugs?" Wide-eyed, Enid looked at her.

"Like have you heard she was poisoned? Have the police said that? Do you know? Has that been on any of the reports?"

Enid shook her head. "It was just on. A program about angels helping people and various places where this has happened. But I haven't heard anything about poison. Or drugs. No, can't say that I have, dear."

"Thank you. And next time I'm by, I'll bring you some fish oil. I'm sure you'll find it some help," she said as she waved and then walked back across the street.

She climbed over the snowbank and walked down the driveway. She expected to see a line in her backyard, but the only ones there were a young mother and her small daughter. Lenore knew this pair. The woman's name was Sharla, and her military husband had died in Iraq just before Christmas. Their only daughter, Amber, suffered from a kind of asthma so severe it defied all known medications. Lenore had heard about the many midnight runs to the hospital and the once-a-month trips to Children's Hospital.

"We're sorry," Sharla said as Lenore approached. "This must get tiresome, everybody invading your backyard."

Lenore looked down at the little girl, all in pink, the big eyes, the way she held on to her mother's hand and looked up at Lenore. Lenore looked away. What had she *done*? It was Lenore who had moved the body. It was Lenore who had placed the hands together in prayer like that! Lenore seemed incapable of movement. Her wet foot was numb with the cold.

"I'm sorry," Lenore said through chattering teeth. "I don't see how this will help. This snowbank. It's just *snow.*"

Someone had placed a wooden cross in the snow, and flowers, as though it were a grave. The sight of it depressed her.

"We know that," the woman said. "But it represents hope. And we've just about run out of hope. We're not worshiping the snow, you know. We're worshiping God. This just represents something. Hope and God. It did something for Rose Nation. And I'm hoping this will work for us. And it's not so odd. God can work in all sorts of ways. Look at Lourdes, the Pool of Siloam. There is a long history of God working miracles in this way. How can we limit God when he chooses to act like this, when he chooses to heal through something as ridiculous as a snowbank?"

"But you don't understand. This is—"

"God chose you, Lenore. How important and fortunate you are! God *chose* you for this!"

Lenore coughed into her scarf and backed away. She would surely be punished by God for this. What would that do to her reputation? To Norman's reputation? She had done one little lie—moving the body—and now had to lie and lie and lie. She could not keep up with the lies. "I have to go in. I got my foot wet. I have to find my son. Get the driveway snow-blowed out. Or you'll never get out of here."

"It's okay, Lenore. It's hard to be a single mom, I know that. And you raised two fine children. I only have one."

"I have three," Lenore said, suddenly stopping and turning. She needed to correct people on this. "*Three* children, three sons. My oldest, Norman, is a successful minister. He doesn't live here. He's a minister."

"Oh, I'm sorry. I didn't know there was another Featherjohn son."

"There is. My eldest, Norman, is a minister in a megachurch."

"That's nice." Sharla laughed a little. "If I even know what a megachurch is."

"A megachurch is called that because so many people attend. More people attend my son Norman's church than live in the entire town of Fog Point."

"Oh my goodness, he must be *really* busy."

"In that church," Lenore pointed out, "they have around twenty ministers. That's more than Stone will ever have."

"You must be very proud of him."

"Oh, I am. I am." She looked down at the little girl in front of her and thought of her own little Alyssa. "I have a granddaughter your age," she said bending down. "When you're finished here, why don't you come in? I'll make some tea. Maybe some milk and cookies. You'll have to wait anyway, until I can get Earl or Carl to snow-blow the end of the driveway."

Amber said, "I'm not 'lowed to have milk."

"Allergies," Sharla explained. "She's allergic to a lot of things. But we'd love to come in. I have cookies for Amber in the car. And rice milk. I'll get them. I always carry food she can eat with me."

Lenore said again, "When you're finished, come in."

Inside, Lenore put the kettle on. Then she opened up the basement door to get Earl. That kid needed a torch underneath him to get him to actually do anything around here, anything except for his computer work. She usually ended up weeding the entire garden herself, mowing all the lawns, and at sixty-five, she wasn't getting any younger. She could even operate the snow-blower when it came right down to it.

The light glowed in Earl's office, so she went quietly down the steps.

But it wasn't Earl who sat at the desk, staring into the monitor, a hand on the mouse. It wasn't Earl who moved back and went through the drawers, flitting through them like she had.

It was Jeanine from FNN.

Lenore watched her, her long neck leaning in toward the computer for several seconds, before she went back up the stairs to the kitchen to make tea.

As she filled the kettle, she berated herself for not marching right down there and confronting her. Why didn't she? Even now, there was time. She didn't know. It was one of those decisions in a long line of decisions Lenore couldn't explain.

30

What I should've done right away was call the police. The first time I saw Tully there in my barn, I should've called the police, no questions.

"She was a runaway. Why didn't you call someone? Didn't you think anyone would be looking for her?" I imagined the police asking me.

But I didn't. Well, I have a good excuse. I'm in the early stages of being demented. So, what can they do? Send me to prison? They don't send people to prison when they do stupid things because they have Alzheimer's. I've never heard of that in my life.

Every morning after Tim went down to the cows and Bobbie went to Fabricland, I went out to the barn to fetch Tully and bring her inside. Together we would whip up eggs or pancakes or french toast. And milk. Always lots of milk in this house.

"Girl your age needs milk," I said to her. "Milk builds bones."

We would eat our breakfast around the table, and then she would take a shower in the upstairs bathroom and check her e-mail. She always spent a lot of time on her e-mail.

"You have a lot of friends," I told her once.

She pulled away from her chair, scraping it across the wooden floor. "I don't have any friends," she corrected me. "Not here anyway. Everyone here hates me. Why do you think I'm running away? Because it's such a wonderful paradise here? No, these are friends I've met online."

"Isn't that dangerous?"

"I'm really, really careful and I'm really, really smart. I've been on my own practically since the day I was born."

I nodded. I knew that to be true. Everyone around here knew that to be true.

"Do you know my mother?" she'd asked me once. "You said I look like her."

Dangerous ground, but I responded anyway. "She's a nice lady."

"Nice, my foot!" Tully stomped around the small room. "She's the reason I'm leaving." She stopped, looked at me. "She's the total reason I'm leaving. I barely live with her as it is."

"Your mother had a lot of heartache in her life."

"Tell me about it! And I was the biggest heartache, the fact that I wasn't a boy! I've been told that all my life, that I was supposed to be a boy!"

"It was your father dying, too." I didn't know this for sure. But it was a good guess.

"People die. And it's been how many years? He died when I was two. That's sixteen years ago! And it was a stupid accident, a stupid farm accident anyway. And I want to scream at her, 'Get over it!' But no, she lies in bed all day, and then periodically she signs herself into the psych ward. I think she likes the food. Or the attention she gets there."

While she went on, I sat very still on the couch and looked at her and thought about the past. I knew her father, too, and about the terrible accident that had taken his life out in the wheat field. I was about to tell her the truth about that, trying to formulate the words in my mind, when she said brightly, "You should get e-mail! Here, come here and I'll set you up with e-mail."

"What would I ever need e-mail for?" I said.

"You can e-mail your grandchildren."

"But they're all right here."

"Oh, come on. It's just fun to have. Maybe you can meet people. Not hang around here all by yourself. Plus, we could e-mail when I go."

"Where are you going?"

"I told you, Vancouver."

Today, with Tully gone, I wonder if I can remember how to get my e-mail. So far I've not been able to. She wrote down the instructions somewhere. I don't know where I put them. And I need to find her. I know she's in danger. I place my fingers on the keyboard, but it feels so strange. Lately I'm having more and more trouble remembering how to do these little things. I'm forgetting lots of things, many more things than before. Simple things, like how to open the fridge and how to get ice from the freezer. They have a nurse coming in three mornings a week for me.

Can I remember this? This e-mail thing? I need to find her. I don't know how I know, but I know she's in danger.

31

A couple of hours later and May was still downstairs sleeping. The snowplow had just gone by, so Jake decided not to put off the inevitable any longer. He pulled on his boots and jacket and got out the snow blower from the shed beside the Purple Church.

Through the tree skeletons, Jake could see the ice sculptures in the bay, like huddled people going nowhere. Past the ice, fishing boats glinted in the sunlight. A path wound its way down from the side of the Purple Church to the boardwalk, which in the summer was lined with greenery and flowers. May demanded that for her customers. And she demanded that the path be kept clean, mowed in the summer and plowed in the winter. When he finished the end of the driveway, he'd get to the path. In a couple of days, if all went well, they'd start renting cross-country ski packages, so the place had to be shipshape.

He fired up the snow blower and wondered about Lenore. Jake was always surprised at the number of people who hired him and May and then lied to them. *If you spend good money to hire a PI,* he thought, *why lie?* Yet people did it time and time again.

And why did that child look so familiar to him? When May woke up, he'd get her thoughts on it. Maybe tomorrow he'd head into the photo studio in Ridley Harbor with the picture. He was sure someone there could shed some light on this photo for him. He wondered if it was possible to find out where it had been taken and when.

A few minutes later, still mulling over these ideas, he looked up and saw in the distance a tiny figure trudging down the road toward him, her backpack low on her back, her jacket open, her feet dragging in the slightly pigeon-toed way she had of walking. Jana. He glanced at his watch. She didn't usually come home this time of the day. He was surprised to see her and stood watching and waiting with the snow blower off. She waved and so did he.

"Hey, it's nice to see you. How come you're home?" he said when she was closer.

"It's just for lunch. I didn't have anyone to sit with, so I came home."

"Well, I can leave this end of the driveway till later. Let's go inside and see what we can rustle up."

"Rustle up?" She giggled. "My weird dad. I already have my food. In my backpack."

He grinned at her, but suddenly her expression changed.

"Something the matter, Jana?"

She shrugged. "I don't know. Nothing, I guess."

"You want to talk about it?"

"I don't know."

"Come on." He put his hand on her shoulder. "Let's go on inside. Let's get that lunch."

Jake didn't say anything until he had dumped a can of chicken noodle soup into a pot on the stove. "Now, tell your old dad what's wrong."

"I don't know," she said.

"You can tell me, Jana."

"I said, I don't *know*."

"Okay, then."

She sighed, put her chin in her hands. "I have no friends here, Dad."

"Of course you do. What about Blaine?"

"But she's not at my school, Dad. And she's not my friend anymore. Not since you won't help her find her real mother."

"But you two were fast friends last summer." Why was he trying to convince her? He clamped his mouth shut. *Just listen to her,* he admonished himself. *Good fathers just listen.*

"Last summer was last summer. This is now, and she's different now. It's like, one minute we're friends if she wants me to do something for her, and the next minute she decides not to like me. I have to go along with whatever she says. It's like everything's all her."

Jake nodded and stirred the soup while Jana unwrapped her sandwich. "I've had friends like that," he said.

"Now she says she doesn't need me or you, because she's found these *new* people who are going to help her find her real mother."

"So she found a new friend."

"Not a new friend, Dad, I told you. She said she found someone who's going to help her find her real mother. That's why she doesn't want to be my friend anymore. Because she doesn't need *you* anymore."

"Where'd she find this person?" Jake buttered the toast, got out some sandwich meat.

"I don't know. She didn't tell me. I think the Internet."

"You know what I think?" he said, sitting down. "I think she's just bluffing, just to get your goat."

"Get my *goat,* Dad?"

He grinned, ruffed his hand through her hair.

Jana chuckled and said, "You're going to rustle up some lunch so I can get my goat?"

He took a spoonful of soup. "Eat up," he said.

"Dad?" Her hands were folded on the table in front of her.

Midslurp he looked up at her. "Yeah?"

"What about grace, Dad?"

"Grace? Grace who?"

"No, I mean grace before meals."

"Forgot. Sorry." He took her hand, they bowed their heads, and he said a quick prayer, thanking God for the food and their time together. Jake always added that.

Jake grew up with grace at every meal, plus the institution of family devotions. Every evening, no matter how busy their schedules, his father read a passage from Scripture and they'd pray. His father expected all of them to pray out loud.

Married to Connie, they prayed at every meal but sometimes skipped family devotions. They kept trying. He kept trying, but they could never get into the habit and make it stick. They'd go for a week or two, and then life and activities would get in the way, and they'd quit. But they always said grace.

"So," Jake said when they'd finished their prayer. "It's nice to have you home for lunch."

"Dad? I sort of miss my friends from Kentville. And Mickey and Alex too."

Jake put his spoon down. Here it comes, the speech where she would ask to go home. He waited, then took a deep breath. "Jana? Do you want to go back to Kentville? You know you can. I can take you back this weekend if you want."

"You could?"

He nodded, swallowed, found it hard to look at her. So he didn't.

"Dad?"

"Jana? If this is something you want—"

But she pushed her chair back quickly and, without looking at him, fled down the hall to her room. He didn't move for a while. What was he supposed to do now? What would the childrearing manuals say? He didn't know, so he got up and knocked on her door.

She lay on her bed, face in her hands, sobbing. He sat down on a chair across from her. He said, "Jana, I want you to be happy, and I want what's best for you. I don't want you to stay here if you don't want to. I won't feel bad. I really won't. Don't worry about me."

She looked at him now, through bleary eyes. "Are you trying to get rid of me? Are you saying you don't want me anymore?"

"Jana. Of course not!" He moved to sit on the bed with her. "That's not what I'm saying. I don't want you to go, not for one minute. I just want... You said you missed your friends, so I just thought..."

"Dad." She came into his arms. "I don't *want* to go back to Kentville. I really like it here. Don't think I want to leave, just because Blaine is mad at me and nobody at school likes me. It doesn't mean I want to go back to Kentville. I love it here, Dad. This church is a totally cool place to live. My friends in Kentville are so jealous when I send them pictures. And I like May. It's just..." She held on to him tighter.

In his arms she felt so small and tiny and birdlike. He let her continue to cry into his shirt, his protecting arms wanting to shield her from all the world's hurts. He vowed once again, as he did so often when he was with her, to be a better father.

32

L enore was entitled, wasn't she? After all, the woman had done it to her son, hadn't she? Snooped in his desk? Jiggled the mouse on his computer? Therefore, on this day when Lenore took clean sheets and towels around to all the rooms, what would it matter if she looked a little through Jeanine's things? It would be so easy. Jeanine and Ted were gone this morning. Earlier she'd seen the two of them take off in their van with all of Ted's camera equipment in the back. More ice had come in. That's what the photographer had told everyone at breakfast. That's probably where they were headed.

What was that blasted woman looking for in her son's room anyway? And that wasn't all. This morning, early, when Lenore had risen to get a head start on her cinnamon swirls, that Jeanine woman had been kneeling in the snow. At first Lenore thought she was praying, and the sight unnerved her slightly. But when Lenore had peered more closely, it looked like the woman was sifting through the snow as if looking for something. She kept this up the whole time Lenore had kneaded her dough and added her special blend of cinnamon and real maple syrup.

What was that woman doing? Perhaps she was working on one of those exposé news stories. Lenore didn't think there was any way for Jeanine to figure out that Lenore had moved the body. She could have found the picture of Tolita Shenk, though. She wondered if Jeanine had discovered some connection between Tolita and Earl or Carl. *Oh please,* Lenore half thought, half prayed, *let me please see my grandchildren just once more before they cart me off to prison.*

Lenore's hands trembled as she unlocked Jeanine's door. She entered, sat on the bed—the towels and clean sheets in her lap—and looked around her. Jeanine had arrived with two fairly large suitcases, a computer case, and a handbag. The computer case and handbag weren't in the room. The larger of the two suitcases was open on a luggage stand. It contained folded clothes and underwear. A peach scarf lay across the top as if thrown there. The other suitcase was closed, on its side in the closet.

Lenore sighed and took the towels into the bathroom and exchanged the dirty ones for clean ones. She once-overed the tub and sink and toilet with her cleaning rag. On the edge of the tub and the vanity were full-sized bottles of salon shampoo and conditioner. Bottles of expensive makeup lined the vanity. Lenore provided her guests with little shampoos and lotions and soaps she got in bulk from a hotel supplier, yet from Lenore's years in the business, she knew that many people preferred their own. She picked up the bottle of shampoo and looked at it curiously. The labeling was in both English and French. This particular brand was manufactured in Montreal. Canadian labeling was in both English and French, yet the address Jeanine had given upon registering was FNN in the U.S. Did that mean anything? Had she gone to Canada to buy these products? Had she been there recently?

She wiped down the mirror and went back to the bedroom. Once again she sat on the bed. Another glance out the window assured her their van had still not returned. Of course, yesterday their van was gone and there was Jeanine, easy as you please, down in Earl's office. Lenore closed the door and locked it. Then she walked over to the opened suitcase and fingered through it gently, aware even as she did so, that she was violating everything she ever held as important as a B&B hostess. She was aware, too, that if she ever caught one of her summer workers pawing through a guest's lingerie, she would fire them on the spot. No questions. No second chances. But Lenore kept looking. After feeling under every bit of lingerie and going through all the zipper compartments, she found nothing of interest.

Lenore then went through the bureau drawers and other folded sweaters and slacks. Again, nothing. She eyed the other suitcase, the one that was zippered up and on its side. She really had to do this, she told herself. She really had to.

Hardly breathing, she shoved a chair up against the locked bedroom door, the way she had seen on TV. If Jeanine did return, the sound of the key in the lock would alert Lenore, but Jeanine wouldn't be able to get into her room unless Lenore moved the chair, at which point she would declare that she was giving the room a good sweeping. But the whole thing would buy her time to pack up the suitcase and put it back the way she found it.

She lay the suitcase on the bed and unzipped it all around. Empty. Wait a minute. There were zipper compartments all over it. The side zippers yielded nothing, but from a zipper compartment in the lid, she pulled out a large manila envelope. Carefully, so carefully, she dumped the contents on the bed. Baby pictures. Lots of baby pictures. Small wallet photos. Larger five-by-sevens. Portraits that looked professionally done. Snapshots taken by home cameras. White babies, black babies, Hispanic babies, Asian babies. Lenore went through the pictures one by one. But the one that made her stop, that made her sit there very still and put her hand to her forehead and utter a small, "oh," was the picture on her lap right now. Tolita's baby stared up at her. The same picture she'd found in Earl's desk, the same picture she'd photocopied and given to May.

What did all this mean? Who were all these children, and did they have anything to do with Tolita Shenk? This had to be the story Jeanine was working on for FNN.

Tucked in the middle of the pictures was a pink and blue threefold brochure. On the front, a teddy bear capered and children's blocks spelled out the words, Tender Moments Adoption Agency.

She opened it up and read:

We are in the business of bringing together children with prospective parents who want them. If you have been look-ing and praying for a baby, God may have you in his view. Many babies need you just as much as you need them.

One of the folds was labeled Prospective Parents, and the next column read Pregnancy and Maternity Services. Under Prospective Parents, she read:

Are you desperate for a child? Contact Tender Moments. We have many babies and children who are looking for parents just like you!

In the Pregnancy and Maternity Services part of the brochure she read:

Are you facing an unplanned pregnancy? Choosing adop-tion is never easy. That's why in all of our homes we provide counseling and the best of medical care. All at no charge to you. Contact us. We can help you in the most important decision you will ever make.

Was Tolita Shenk putting her baby up for adoption? Was that what this was all about? Her *grandson*? She shoved all the pictures and papers back into the envelope. Her fingers trembled so much she almost missed the small Post-it note that had somehow adhered itself to the inside of the envelope. She pulled it out and read: *I did what you said, Mal Barcklay.* Something about that name was familiar, the combination of the *c* and *k* and *l*. Then she remembered.

Quickly she placed everything back in the manila envelope, zipped that in the suitcase, and placed the suitcase back in the closet the way she had found it. Then she pulled the chair from the door, changed the sheets, and vacuumed, all the while her mind raced.

As soon as she finished cleaning the other guest rooms, she went to her cubbyhole office off the foyer and went through her guest book. Yes, Mal Barcklay was the young man who'd been here when the girl had died, when Tolita had died, the man with the stutter and two different-colored eyes, the one who never looked you straight on. He'd paid by cash and given no address. She was one of the very few hotels in all of Fog Point that didn't require a charge card imprint when guests arrived. Carl was always getting after her for that. Yet, if people paid in cash, what more did she need? She had given him an address card, but he'd never filled it out. It was for advertising purposes more than anything else. She trusted people. Was it a crime to trust people?

She looked at Jeanine and Ted's Visa payment. The payment, in Jeanine's name, had come through, no problem. Lenore double-checked.

Unlike Mal Barcklay, Jeanine had left an address in New York. Lenore shoved the receipt and registration card into her sweater pocket.

She didn't know why, but she suddenly felt very afraid.

33

May agreed with Jake. Obviously, this photo wasn't a new one. But how old was this child? Jake decided to take it into Blake Filmore's photo studio in Ridley Harbor. Blake had taken all the pictures for their Purple Church Web site and felt he was in Jake's debt after they took Blake's family out on *The Purple Whale* for a complementary whale tour. Blake's four children were ecstatic when they saw three minkes. Now Blake couldn't, it seemed, do enough for Jake. Perhaps it was payback time. Maybe Blake could get a firm date on this photo for them.

May wasn't going with him, she said. Instead, she'd stay and make more calls to the Shenk families in Alberta. She planned to call the first on the list of Shenks and keep going down until she found, and spoke to, Tolita Shenk. "Plus," she said. "I misplaced my case notebook. I can't find it here."

As he was getting ready to leave, he asked May what she was working on so intently. She had a small magnifying glass and was looking at something on the table.

"Handwriting analysis," was her reply.

"I didn't know you knew anything about handwriting analysis."

"I don't. I got a book," she said. "From the PI Mall Web site."

He walked closer, peered over her shoulder.

"The note," she said. "The one that was in the dead girl's pocket. Bill was nice enough to make a copy for me. I've already put out a message to Sol."

"So you're going to Sol after all."

"If it has to do with the sniper, he works for free."

"And you think this has something to do with the sniper."

"I do." She bent her head over the note.

"May, if I don't get home before Jana does, can you poke your head downstairs every once in a while?"

"No problem. I'll get her to come up and help me. Hey, watch for black ice on the road," May said. "That's what they're saying on the radio."

He put the photo with the envelope in an inside pocket of his parka and then had an idea. He called Carrie.

"Hey," she said.

He could never figure out the signals in Carrie's voice. Was that a friendly "hey"? He decided to barrel on ahead. "I'm heading into Ridley on business. You want to come along? Grab a coffee?"

"Ridley?" He could hear the hesitation in her voice. He could read that at least.

"Come on. What else are you doing?"

"Going through my father's shoe box of receipts, trying to get stuff ready for the tax gods."

"Then a break would be a good thing."

"Maybe you're right. I'd love to be dropped at the mall for a bit while you take care of your business, if it wouldn't be too much of an inconvenience for you."

"It's never an inconvenience to have you along, Carrie."

This would be good, he thought. Just the two of us. Maybe we'll have time to have a good talk on the way in.

On the way out to his truck, Colin Nation yelled over, "Hey, May says you might be going to Ridley today. Can I get a lift? My boat's there. Had to take it over there, on account of the ice here."

"Well, sure then."

Twenty minutes later, the three of them were in Jake's truck heading into the city. Jake felt very much like a chauffeur. *Just put me in a black suit and hat,* he thought. So much for long, private talks with the woman he loved. Carrie wore her red coat and a hat made of some kind of fur and shaped like a beret. With her funky brown glasses, she looked like some artist who lived in a loft and painted brooding self-portraits. She was pretty, amazingly pretty today. He wanted to tell her so. He wanted to talk about a lot of things with her. He wanted to ask her why she was so afraid of commitment.

Instead, the three of them ended up talking about the ice and the murder and the angel and everything else Fog Point had been experiencing of late.

Colin said, "You know that lady from FNN?"

Carrie turned to Colin in the backseat, "You mean the one with all the hair?"

"You've met her?"

Carrie shook her head. "Only seen her from a distance. But you can't miss the hair."

"That would be the one. Well, she's creeping Marnie out."

Jake looked at Colin through the rearview mirror. "What do you mean?"

"She's called like three times asking questions. I've never been there when she's called, or I would tell that lady to bug off. Marnie's given her my cell number, but she never calls me on that."

"Maybe she's doing a story about fishing," Carrie suggested. "I know how these newspeople work—sometimes they can get a bit in your face."

"But that's not it," he said. "She's not asking questions about fishing. She's asking all these personal questions, like have I ever talked to that girl who was murdered behind Featherjohn's? Like, did I know her? Did I ever talk to her? Had she ever contacted me? And it's totally freaking Marnie out."

"Really odd," Carrie said. "Why would she think you would know this girl?"

He shook his head. "I have no idea."

"It could be," Carrie said, "she's asking these questions of everyone in town for her story."

Colin asked, "You think that's all this is?"

"Could be."

But as Jake drove down the highway, listening to Colin, he wasn't so sure.

34

Amy didn't go straight home after work. She needed to think. She needed time alone. Charlie had indoor soccer after school, and it would be hours before Ben or Blaine got home. Plenty of time for Amy to grab a quiet cappuccino at Mags and Herman's. She felt guilty about doing this, of course. A good mother would go straight home and prepare dinner for her family and get caught up on laundry.

Amy read a book once about a mother out on a beach picnic who just got up and walked away from her family. And kept walking. Sometimes Amy thought about that—getting in her car one morning but instead of driving the too-familiar path to the school, she would keep on going, out onto the highway toward Ridley. Then past Ridley. She would keep on driving until her car ran out of gas. Then what? She never had an answer to that, so she drove, as always, to school and then home again.

"A cappuccino," Amy said to Mags at the counter. "Nonfat," she added. "In a mug."

While she waited, she grabbed the newspaper from the rack and found a window seat. There were others in the coffee shop, a few tables of people Amy didn't know. Tourists, she supposed, people come to see the ice and pray to the angel. She was still on the first page of the paper when Mags brought over her cappuccino.

"Just bad news, all of it," Mags said with a chuckle and walked back behind the counter. Amy watched the friendly banter between Mags and her husband, Herman. Mags was a big woman who wore loose cotton dresses and kept her long gray-brown hair in a braid down her back. Herman with his brown ponytail was as thin as Mags was big. Amy looked at the way they teased each other, the way she patted his arm, their smiles. Here was an unchurched couple who had more going for them than she and Ben.

Yesterday Blaine had come to her and asked how long she had to keep going to church.

"Blaine, this is not negotiable. You go to church with the family."

"I just want to know if there's an age. Is it sixteen? Can I quit when I'm sixteen?" The dangly pair of dream-catcher earrings, which Amy had never seen before, hit her cheeks when she shook her head.

"There's no *age*, Blaine. This family goes to church."

It was so unfair, Blaine said, stomping away. So unfair. And so *typical*, she added.

What Amy didn't say, what Amy would have said if she were being totally honest was, "I'm with you, Blaine. I want to quit church, too. But if I have to go, you have to go."

In her twenty-four-year history of being a minister's wife, Amy had met only one wife who didn't go to church with her minister husband.

Amy thought this was remarkable and strange. She met her once when Amy and Ben attended a banquet and found themselves at the same table as this couple. Eve was cordial, nice, and it was plain to see they loved each other—the way he held her hand, the way she looked at him. When she got up, Amy excused herself too and followed her into the ladies' room.

The woman exuded something exotic and foreign in her bearing. Maybe it was the sweep of her hair, the blond streaks at a time when ministers' wives didn't do such things to their hair. Amy had suddenly felt doltish and fat, cowlike and simple next to this woman in her sleek black business suit and heels.

"I hear," Amy said falteringly. "That you don't go to church. I was just wondering—"

"How a minister of the gospel can possibly live with me?" Eve smiled broadly, showing a lot of white teeth. "My husband and I have an arrangement. I don't go to church, which is his job. And he doesn't come to the insurance office where I work, which is my job."

Out the café window, a man set up a camera and tripod on the wharf. Amy watched the man methodically prepare the shot, shadowing the top of his camera with a piece of cardboard. She wondered about his life, whether he had children who were happy to see him, whether a wife waited for him. Did his wife keep secrets from him? Amy looked at him for a long time, her hands around her mug of coffee, and wondered if she would ever find the words to tell Ben her secret. Oh, she had whispered it once in the darkness of their bedroom, but he had never responded, so she was sure she had whispered it to unhearing ears. *Will I ever have the courage to say it to him out loud? I no longer believe in God.* That was her secret. She was married to a minister, and she no longer believed in God.

She was so intently staring at the photographer that at first she didn't see them, but when she did, her hands became like cement around her coffee. It was Blaine, Blaine who should be in school now, and there she was at the far end of the boardwalk, talking to a woman that Amy recognized as someone from one of the news stations. Amy watched the way the woman bobbed her blond head forward and made gestures with her hands. And Blaine standing there, nodding and nodding. The woman reached forward and gave Blaine a little hug, and Amy gasped at the implied intimacy. Why was this woman touching her? Blaine stiffened and backed away. Amy knew the gesture well. Lately, when Amy had tried to reach out to her daughter, Blaine shrank from her, almost recoiling at her touch. So Amy stayed where she was, her hands around her coffee mug, watching instead of running out to rescue her daughter.

35

Blaine knew a lot of things. And all of this knowing was giving her a stomachache. At first she thought it was cramps—she sure had her share of those—but they kept on and on. She'd sort of felt this way ever since Tully had been killed two weeks ago, sick to her stomach, like she could throw up any minute.

Blaine knew why Tully had been murdered. She didn't know the whole thing—she didn't know who'd done it, just why.

Tully had come to Fog Point on a mission, and somebody didn't want her here, so they killed her. Tully was smart, she could figure things out, and because Tully was her friend, Blaine could figure things out too. But Tully was dead, and Blaine couldn't tell anybody what she knew, because, as Tully had said, anyone who knew Tully's secrets could die too.

Blaine and Tully had been e-mailing since the summer when Blaine visited that adoption Web site chat room and found someone asking questions about Fog Point. Blaine couldn't imagine anyone wanting to come here on purpose, so she e-mailed her. The girl wanted to send Blaine a picture of the person she was looking for and had tried scanning it into the computer she was using, but she couldn't get it to work. It wasn't her computer, she explained. It belonged to the people in the farmhouse where she was staying for the summer. She couldn't get their scanner to work. The old man who lived there with her didn't know how to work the computer stuff.

Only a couple of people knew why Tully came here. The first was Jana. Jana didn't know her name was Tully, though. Blaine had never mentioned the name Tolita Shenk to Jana because Tully had asked her not to. Actually, Tully had said not to tell anyone *anything*, so Blaine had already violated that little request.

When Blaine told her, Jana promised not to tell "on pain of death," she said. That statement had new and frightening meaning when Tully actually died. After that, Blaine decided she couldn't be friends with Jana anymore. Jana already knew too much. And Jana's dad used to be a cop and had all these cop friends. Jana and her dad were probably already on the hit list. Blaine was afraid if she hung around her too long, she'd end up telling Jana everything just to have someone to talk to, and she couldn't risk that.

"But my dad could help," Jana had said right after Tully died.

"No!" Blaine had screamed at her. "The only thing your dad would be good for is to find my real mother!" She hadn't meant it, of course. It just slipped out, to put Jana on a new course.

The other person who knew Tully's secrets was that newslady. A madman was on the loose, that's what the newslady had told her, and Blaine would be wise to keep her mouth shut about the things she knew.

Part of what was making her so sick was that she had told a lot of this secret stuff to the newslady. That lady had come to her so sweetly with her big smile, and Blaine had ended up trusting her. The lady said she was doing a story on adoption and knew all about Tully, she said. All Blaine had to do was fill in the missing pieces. The fact that the newslady knew Tully's name surprised her and made Blaine trust her.

But then the newslady started showing up in the weirdest places, like she was stalking Blaine. It freaked her out. If the woman knew Blaine's bus stop, what else did she know about her? Maybe too much. Maybe she'd known too much about Tully too. Blaine started staying away from school so she wouldn't run into her while she waited for the bus. She had skipped school a lot lately. Sometimes she would leave for the bus stop and then not show up there. She'd walk around the boardwalk for a while until she was sure that the house was empty, then she'd go home and stay in her bedroom for the day. No one ever went to her room anymore, so she was safe there.

Blaine had this wish that her mother would come down to her room in the middle of the night when things were really scary and sit with her and hug her, like she had when Blaine was little and got nightmares. Her mother would come down and pray with her then. Then her mother would hug her until she felt better. Her mother never did that anymore. And, of course, she could never ask her mother for a hug. She'd rather die. So she just hid in her room and pretended she didn't care.

The whole idea that got it started in the first place had been so stupid. She and Jana were watching an *Oprah* show about adoption when Jana suddenly asked, "Do you ever wonder who your real mother is?"

It surprised her a little that Jana remembered this. She had told her a long time ago, when they first met, as a way of impressing the younger girl. She pondered the question. Sometimes she wondered about her real mother. But not a lot. If she thought about her at all, they were hazy thoughts, like dreams. And usually, in her mind, the mother who had given her up was just not there. It wasn't like she was dead, but more like she never had been.

They wrote down some of the Web sites from the show and went on them just for fun. On the Web sites you were supposed to be over eighteen, so Blaine faked it, said she was. But Jana pointed out that that was stupid, because how would her real mother know it was her if she was really fourteen?

But the truth was that Blaine didn't really want to find her mother. She wouldn't admit it to Jana, but the whole idea frightened her. What if her mother didn't want to be found? Maybe her mother would tell her she was glad she'd given her daughter away, like she was throwing out the garbage. Or worse, what if she was a really nice lady who would have been a better mother than the one she ended up with? It was all too complicated to imagine. Yet something pulled her to search anyway.

It was on the Victims of Adoption Fraud Web site that Blaine met Tully for the first time, Tully who'd been strangled in the backyard of Featherjohn's B&B. Strangled. It was unbelievable that one of Blaine's friends had been murdered. And who had done it? It could be someone Blaine saw every day, someone she trusted, someone she *knew.*

She pulled the covers over her head and lay in her bed in a ball. She didn't like being afraid, but she was afraid all the time now. Afraid for herself and for Jana. Afraid for her mom and dad.

She wished she could get her stomach to stop hurting.

36

After dropping Carrie at the mall and Colin at the wharf, Jake high-tailed it over to Blake Filmore's photo studio on Water Street. Jake was the only customer on this chilly morning, and Blake beamed when he saw him.

"Hey, Jake, how you doing? What can I do you for on this blustery day?" He'd been arranging cameras in a glass display, which he now closed and locked.

"I have something I'd like your opinion on."

"Anything. Just name it. My boys still talk about the whales they saw that day."

"It's a photograph, but I'm hoping you can tell me when it might have been taken, or even where. Anything about it."

Jake followed Blake to the counter, past walls arranged with wedding photos, grad photos, and photographs of lighthouses and boats. He pulled the photo out of the envelope and laid it on the counter.

Blake took a pair of skinny glasses from a case in his pocket and perched them on the end of his nose. He picked it up and examined it. "It's got a bit of a reddish tinge, do you see that?"

"I noticed that too."

"That happens with age sometimes."

"Age?"

"Or environment." He turned it over. "Where did you get this?"

"It's part of an investigation."

"Oh, in that case, I should really direct you to the best. There's a guy I use sometimes. He's a collector of photo memorabilia and knows just about everything there is about dates and cameras. I know he could give you a definite date. Can I have him take a look at it?"

Jake left the photo with him.

Half an hour later he was drinking coffee with Carrie at Starbucks in the Ridley Mall. The place was crowded; university students along the wall hunkered down over textbooks and binders, while at tables, groups talked seriously as they sipped their Frappuccinos. On couches, mothers jabbered to one another and nursed their babies discreetly under blankets while older children with crayons worked their way through coloring books on the coffee table in front of them. Those with laptops checked their e-mail or downloaded music. Starbucks—the communal living room of the twenty-first century.

Jake and Carrie were lucky to find a recently vacated table in the corner by the fireplace. They sat across from each other with their coffees, a slice of cheesecake, and two forks.

"This is nice," she said. "The fire is nice." She pulled off her hat and fluffed out her hair and pushed it behind her ears. There were a few gray strands. He looked at her, at the freshness of her, and he remembered Christmas Eve, when he'd been ready to get down on one knee, if that was what it took. She had said no. He was quite certain she had no idea that in his pocket had been a diamond engagement ring.

Today they talked about the weather and the angel and Jana. He told her he was worried about his daughter. Early in the year she seemed to be making friends, he told her. He shook his head. "I don't know. Her friend Blaine's going through some stuff, and I think it's affecting Jana. Jana takes things so personally."

At the table beside them, a couple of young teens were playing a game of checkers and arguing with great animation.

"She's a very sensitive girl," Carrie said.

"I feel fortunate to have her this year." He tried his coffee. Still too hot. He put it down. The "No no no, you can't do that," from the next table overpowered their own attempts at conversation. So much for a good heartfelt at Starbucks. "She likes you, Carrie. She thinks you're cool," he told her.

"Oh, I am *so* cool," she said putting down her coffee. "This coffee is hot. Good, but hot."

"You ordered extra hot, didn't you?"

"So I shouldn't complain, right? You mostly get what you order in life." She looked down at her coffee. "Sometimes it cools down too fast…"

Jake looked at her fingers playing with the handle of the coffee mug. A lot of things cooled too fast. He resisted the urge to reach out and touch them. She looked up then, and for a moment their eyes locked. Then she laughed, a nice lilting sound, picked up her coffee, and continued. "When I was working up in Detroit, sometimes I would go into Starbucks and get a coffee. And usually it ended up getting cool before I was finished. So I got in the habit of ordering extra hot. So"—she put down her coffee and took a forkful of cheesecake—"how'd your business go here?"

"Fine. I'm trying to date a photograph."

She grinned. "Wouldn't it be nicer to date a real person?"

"Yeah, but when the person I want to date won't go out with me, well, I have to resort to photographs…" He looked at her.

"Jake," she began, and then from the other table came, "Excuse me! Hey, *excuse* me!" It was the checkers players again. The bushy-haired young man leaned back in his chair. "You guys know anything about checkers?"

Carrie said, "I'm an old checkers player from way back."

"When a person gets kinged, you can move backward and forward, right?"

"Oh yes," Carrie said, "that's one of the main rules."

He turned back to his partner, a skinny blond with long hair in a ponytail. "See, I *told* you."

Later, on their way home, Carrie said, "I'm wondering about that FNN person."

"What are you wondering about her?"

"Jake, I was in the news business for a long time and, I don't know, something about her just doesn't seem right."

"But you say you haven't met her."

"No, but something about what Colin said strikes me as odd, asking personal questions like that. If she's doing a story about the angel or the ice, that's one thing. I'm going to make some phone calls."

37

S he was such a little bit of a thing, that Tully. But such spunk. She
favored her mother in that regard, although a lot of the spunk went out
of Coralee a long time ago. Some days Tully looked like an angel, I thought,
with her yellow hair, the edges of it wisping out around her face like a halo,
like those pictures you see on Christmas cards of the Madonna with the halo.
That's what she looked like sometimes in the mornings when I would come
out with her coffee and eggs.

Now, on these cold, cold mornings when my bones feel old and weary
like I've already lived too many years on this earth, I think about summer
mornings and Tully.

I don't know where she is now. She wanted to go to Vancouver. But I
know she ended up going in the opposite direction. And sometimes I can't
remember her name. When I remember it, I say it over and over again so I
won't forget. *Tully, Tully, Tully.* But then the next time I try to remember, I've
already forgotten.

Two nights ago I asked the little tyke in the family room, the one with the
J name, if he could help me. "I have messages from a girl," I told him. "I don't
know where she is! You need to help me! I need to get on the e-mail." The little
boy looked at me oddly and then ran to the woman in the kitchen. Then the
woman put down her pots and came and lifted me by the arms and walked me
to my room and sat me down on the chair and turned on the television.

As I sit in my chair this morning, I can remember plain as day about the girl and last summer.

Tully and I ate in the kitchen on summer mornings, and she would ask questions, which I would answer as best I could. I still hadn't brought myself to tell her about The Terrible Tragedy and my part in it. And Glad's. I needed to tell her. I owed her that much. I knew it, yet somehow, when I got to that part in the narrative, I would stop and take a veer, never quite hitting it on the nose. Not a solid blow.

After breakfast, Tully would wash the dishes, all of them by hand—I told her it was necessary to do that; the extra dishes in the dishwasher would certainly be questioned—she volunteered to be the one to do it. And while she washed, she would ask more questions.

"Tell me about my father," she asked me one day. "Did you know him?"

"He was a fine farmer," I said. "A handsome young man and a hard-working son. He was one of Gabe Shenk's sons. Middle one, I think."

"I know who my uncles are, but I never see them. It's a weird family. Nobody talks."

I nodded. People, family members especially, like to distance themselves from a tragedy. It would do no good to tell Tully about the Shenk brothers and the way they pounced on Henry and Coralee's land after Henry died. How would that help her now, to know these things?

"You should know the truth of it," I found myself saying one day, "the truth about his death. People shouldn't keep things from you. You should know what really happened."

She put down the plate she was drying and looked at me. For a while I didn't say anything. I can remember that day as clear as the sky. The story was that he was out in his field. Something wasn't running right, so he got off, and while he was working on it, a blade tore off his arm and he bled to death.

The truth was much simpler. He'd merely taken a gun with him out into the field, got down from his combine, sat down in front of it, and shot his brains out all over the field of winter wheat. He left a young widow with a two-year-old child, a child who would not remember her father. When townspeople talked about Henry and Coralee, they spoke in hushed tones about The Terrible Thing. Coralee had that awful spell after Tully was born. It happens sometimes with mothers. Poor Henry, he just couldn't cope with her any longer. Plus there was the blame he felt. They always look to the father when something like that happens.

Two weeks after the funeral, a neighbor found Tully in a two-day old diaper in her crib, whimpering and hungry while her mother sat, stone-faced, on a chair staring at the wall. Social Services placed Tully into foster care immediately and the mother in the psychiatric ward.

No family members stepped in to help. In a community where people usually helped, no one did. Tragedy heaps on tragedy sometimes, and there comes a point when people become afraid to help, afraid the tragedy will define their lives as well.

Tully had grown up with strangers. And now she's gone. And I can't get on the e-mail and find her.

"I need to get on the e-mail," I keep muttering, and finally the woman comes into my room and brings me coffee. "I need to get on the e-mail," I tell her, but she just pats my shoulder. The little tyke has gone back to his television game. I can hear the pows and screams and beeps of it.

All the Shenk brothers, and not one of them stepping in to help, not one of them missing her. Them with their wealthy, big computerized farms and that big shot Shenk now the mayor and all.

A new woman is standing in the doorway now and smiling at me.

"How're we doing today, Mr. Black?" she asks. Her voice is loud and officious. She's the nurse-housekeeper they have coming in. Maybe she'll help me. I rise, move slowly into the family room. "I need to get on the e-mail, but I don't remember how to anymore." I sit down at the computer.

"As far as I know," she says, wiping her hands on a cloth, "you've got a system that's connected all the time. Did you want to surf the Web or something?"

One thing nice about this woman is that she never just bundles me away in my room. No, she's all for getting me to remember things, and going on the Internet would be right up her alley. She writes things down in big letters. And she's always going through pictures with me. *This is Bobbie. This is Tim. And you know Jonah? And Gabrielle?*

"You just hold on a minute, Mr. Black. I'll get this kitchen cleaned up, and I'll be right there."

She always speaks slowly and loudly to me in simple words as if I'm some little child newly on the planet instead of on my way out.

She comes and sits down next to me.

"Let's see, did Bobbie or Tim write down your password anywhere?" She's sitting so close to me, yet she's practically shouting in my ear.

"No!" I shout right back at her.

"Now, Mr. Black, there's no call for that tone. How about we move over to the couch and read a book?"

"No," I say it more quietly and feel tears of frustration well at the corner of my eyes. "I need to find my e-mail. I need to find the girl."

"Okay, okay. Now let's see what we have here."

She gets a number of Web sites, pictures of animals for me to look at. She's found some place on the Internet that has zoo animals, thinking this is what I want. Zoo animals!

I look at the screen and begin to cry.

38

When Jake got back to the office, May had emptied all the desk drawers onto the floor. Stacks of paper littered the tables, and Jana was in the process of going through the contents of their recycling box.

"I've lost my notes," May said.

"Hi, Dad," Jana said, putting down a heap of recycled newspapers.

"Hey, kid."

"My notebook," May said. "All of my written stuff." May kept meticulous shorthand notes of all phone conversations and research in small spiral books, a separate one for each case. She carried them with her everywhere. "Do you have it, Jake? Do you think you might've put it in your backpack by mistake?"

"I'm certain I don't, but I'll check." He dumped the contents of his backpack, found his own notebook, but not May's.

"What's that on the table?" he asked.

"That's a new one. I've had to start a new one." He opened it up to the first page. There were notes from a telephone conversation there.

"So, you called Barrhead?"

"Yeah. I've lost all my notes, every one."

"What about your computer notes?" Jake asked.

"You know me, Jake. I save e-mails, sure, but I always write everything else down."

"It's got to be around. When's the last time you had it?" he asked.

"I can't remember *not* having it. It goes with me everywhere when I'm on a case." She sat down and squared the edges of a stack of paper in her lap. "I searched my entire house. All night. It's not at my house. Anywhere. So, I thought I must've left it here. I'm always so careful, Jake."

Jake opened the cupboard that contained their paper, ink cartridges, and office supplies.

"Don't bother looking in there. I've been through it a hundred times."

"Is it in your SUV?"

"Checked. Looked under the seats. No. It's not there."

"Is this it?" Jana said, holding up a duotang folder from the recycle bin.

"Afraid not," May said. "What I had was a spiral notebook."

"Oh." Jana put it back.

"So tell me," Jake said. "What did you find out about the Shenks?"

May sat. "Okay, maybe I need a break from all this looking. Yeah, sit down and I'll fill you in. I got a hold of the managing editor of the *Barrhead Leader,* someone named"—she reached for her new notebook—"Tom Grasion."

"And?"

"And he knows the Shenk family. Big family, he told me. Lots of Shenks all over the place. I already knew that and told him so. It seems everyone in the whole town has a Shenk in their family tree. The mayor of the town is even a Shenk."

"Did you find Tolita Shenk? Talk to her?"

"The editor at the paper didn't know her. Knew of her, but not her. So I consulted a Web site for the town. Sure enough, there is a Shenk who's a real estate broker. Bob Shenk Realty. So I called him. He's one of those garrulous salesmen. I finally was able to ask if he knew who Tolita was." May consulted her new notebook. "And then he's real quiet. So I repeat my question, 'Do you know Tolita Shenk?' He calls her Tully and then proceeds to tell me that she's a runaway kid in and out of foster homes, with a father who died when she was a baby and a mother who's been in and out of mental institutions. I got the impression that our Tolita, or Tully as they call her out there, was born into the wrong wing of the Shenk family. So now I know that this girl, the one blackmailing Lenore, is not from what you'd call on the right side of the tracks. That's what I'm figuring out."

"Police record?"

"None I could find."

"You ask about her baby?"

She nodded. "Well, this Bob Shenk, he laughed and said this certainly wouldn't surprise him. No siree, not one bit. Not knowing those Shenks."

"His name is Shenk and he said 'those Shenks'?"

May nodded. "Like I said, weird Shenks. So I asked who reported her missing to the police, because somebody did or it wouldn't have been in the paper, and he said he didn't have a clue. Oh, and you know what else?" She stabbed her new case notebook with her pen. "I called the police. Yes, she's a missing person. And no, it doesn't seem to be high priority with them either."

"And no one knows where she is?"

"I'd love to talk with her foster parents. That's next on my list. After I find my notebook, I'll find out who they are and talk with them. Meanwhile, Tolita Shenk seems to be missing."

That niggling feeling scratched at the back of his neck again, so much so that he actually put a hand to his collar. "May," he said then. "Do you see a similarity or am I the only one? This wild-goose chase that Lenore has sent us on—perhaps it's to divert us from what's really going on. That the girl we're supposed to find, this Tolita Shenk, is the same girl who died in her backyard."

May sighed loudly, pulled off her cap for a moment, looked at it. "I've had that feeling all along. I think we'd better call the police."

Jana sat very still, a stack of recycled papers on her lap. "She was looking for her brother," she said simply.

Jake and May looked at her.

"I wasn't supposed to know this. I promised not to tell. But Blaine told me. The girl who died was looking for her brother."

39

Y*ou make one mistake,* Lenore thought, *one foolish choice, and you end up having to live with it for the rest of your life. There's no changing it, no going back.* Lenore had made a lot of foolish choices in her life, marrying Harlan being the grandest, letting her sons sell the old church to Jake and May another, and most recently, dragging the body of that poor girl away from the entrance to her sons' apartment steps and into the snowbank.

She vacuumed around the grandfather clock in the dining room and thought about all that had been taken from her. The dreams of her youth, a family that loved her and appreciated her for all she had to offer, instead of these ungrateful sons she'd been stuck with. She lifted her head to gaze at the majestic clock her mother had left her. It was a good thing she'd held on to this piece of furniture, that she hadn't let Earl or Carl get their paws on this one. It had to be worth quite a lot. They didn't value anything from the past, it seemed. It was all new with them. Some new piece of computer equipment and they were happy. Some new big-screen TV with a remote that kept them from ever leaving their chairs and they were in their glory. Lenore sighed. Vacuuming done, she lugged the old upright to the corner and then squirted a bit of wood oil on a white cloth and got to work on the clock, fingering the cloth into the crevices and creases.

Everything in this house belonged to her predecessors, she thought. Even the house itself. All her life she had struggled to be a good Christian woman and try to hold all the important things to her—her religion, her family, the status of her name, her furniture, the church furniture, the collection of Hummels that she dusted on the shelves of the glass-fronted cupboard. But none of this stuff was hers, not really. She sniffed at the oily smell of the furniture polish and sneezed twice.

Wasn't she the most hospitable person in all of Fog Point? Her name was even once in the Grape Vine column in the Ridley paper as Fog Point's most hospitable hostess when they did that big article about her B&B. She never neglected her religion. Every morning without fail, she read *Our Daily Bread* along with her Bible. A wave of fatigue so debilitating that her knees weakened forced her to sit down.

Pearl from church had called earlier. Her mother's arthritis was back and worse than ever. The doctor was furious that Rose had been neglecting her meds while she went on about how Lenore's snowbank had healed her.

Lenore had tried to placate the woman, but she was livid. Was Lenore to blame for that, too? Did she force people to kneel in her snowbank? She wondered if she could be sued. Stupider lawsuits had happened in this crazy world. She'd read about them in the *Reader's Digest.*

She heard a knock on the door and saw through the window that it was the police again. She sighed and opened the door and invited them in. "I'll put on tea," she said.

It was that detective Angela, along with Bill. Big Bill, was how she'd begun thinking of him. He towered over her. Bill said they hadn't come for tea.

"Well, I know that, don't I? You've come to ask more questions about the girl who died in my backyard, and I've told you everything I can possibly remember and then some."

They sat down at her kitchen table without being invited to, which in a way galled Lenore. But they'd been here so often they even took the same seats they always did. Angela sat across from Bill, who ran his hand over his face and said, "It's the *and then some* that we're here about."

"If you would just tell me what you want." She wiped her oily hands on a dishtowel. "I'm rather busy dusting. I've a business to run."

Bill said, "Maybe it's time you told us the whole story, Mrs. Featherjohn. Everything. Right from the beginning."

Lenore plugged in the kettle. "Well, even if you're not going to have some tea, I feel like some."

"Mrs. Featherjohn," Angela began.

Lenore spun. "I have told you everything I can. What more is there?"

"The truth," Bill said.

"What truth?"

"The name of the girl who died in your backyard is Tolita Shenk, the one you've been sending Jake and May on a wild goose-chase to find. And don't deny it. Her picture has been sent out to Alberta, and it's the same girl. I just want to know how you knew and where you got that name and number, and who is the baby in the photo?"

Lenore opened her eyes wide. "Really? I had no knowledge of that. You mean to tell me that the girl who was found and Tolita Shenk are one and the same? Yes, well, that's what you just told me, isn't it? Well, how about that! I happened upon that name and thought maybe she worked here during the summer. I wanted to contact her. It was a simple custody matter. I was thinking of the baby, you see. I had no idea she was the same, oh my. If the child is a relative of mine, I wanted to do the Christian thing and support him. You know, financially. And in other ways, too. I merely asked my good friend May to look into this matter for me."

Angela raised her eyebrows, and Bill said, "Your good friend May tells a different story."

"My, my. Well, okay. Yes, I imagine she would. I merely thought Tolita's baby might be my grandchild." She opened her arms wide. "That's all! I just wanted to do my duty to the child. A case of mistaken identity. I thought the child belonged to Tolita. I didn't come to you, well, because this is a sensitive matter to me. My family is…"

"You knew the name of the girl who was found dead, and you never contacted the police," Bill said. "That is a serious matter."

"Well, of course I didn't know they were one and the same!" Lenore fairly screamed this. "Weren't you listening to me? You telling me now, well, this is the first I've heard. I just want to do right by Tolita's baby."

"Tolita has no baby," Angela said. "She's never been pregnant."

"What?"

"Tell us about the baby, Lenore." Bill said. "Who is the baby?"

"I have no idea. I assumed it was Tolita's. And now you're telling me that Tolita was the girl I found? This is a lot of information to assimilate in one day. Oh my. Oh my, indeed."

They asked about the picture and the telephone number, and she told much the same story she had told Jake and May, except she made sure she told them that the name and number had been on a separate piece of paper rather than on the back of the photograph. They wanted to see the piece of paper, and she told them she had given it to Jake and May. If push came to shove and the police asked Jake and May for it, it would buy her time to write something out herself. All the while she talked, she kept eying the breadbox, under which was the real picture of Tolita Shenk.

The kettle boiled, and she made a pot of tea in her grandmother's teapot and set it out on the table. "Sometimes, well, I'm a stupid old woman sometimes. Obviously, I put two and two together and got sixteen hundred. Obviously, there was no blackmail scheme. Can I ask you one thing, officers? That you not tell too many people about this. I'm so embarrassed for thinking this."

Lenore had to think fast, and she hoped she wasn't painting herself into too many blind corners. Already, she worried that she'd contradicted herself.

Lenore had a theory that if she kept talking, they would soon tire of her or be so confused that they would call her a crazy old woman and leave. Which actually almost worked. Except when they demanded to talk to her sons.

"Well, Carl's not home," she said. "I'm sure he's not home. As I've said, he's a charmer with the ladies. He has a new girlfriend." She grinned. "And well, Earl's probably asleep. You really shouldn't wake him. He needs his sleep. He works so hard, that boy does."

But Bill opened the door to the basement and called down that they were on their way. Lenore heard Earl grumble, "Yeah? What?"

They tromped down the stairs, and she followed, wringing her hands. Earl was not in bed but was sitting at his computer in huge gray track pants and an undershirt.

"Tell us what you know about Tolita Shenk, Mr. Featherjohn," Bill demanded.

Earl ran his hand over his greasy face. "Who?"

"Tolita Shenk is the young woman who was killed in your backyard. Do you know anything about her?"

"No, I've already told you that."

Bill pulled out the picture of the baby. "What about the baby in this picture?"

Earl squinted at it. "I've never seen that before."

"Do I need to come back here with a search warrant?" Bill asked.

"You can, but you won't find anything here. Nothing," he said opening his hands palms up. "I'm a businessman trying to make an honest living, and I'm hassled left, right, and center. I've got nothing to hide. Here." He faced his computer, opened up to his e-mail program. "Here, take a look." He wheeled himself away from his screen. "I've got nothing to hide. No hidden drug deals, no kiddie porn here. I'm not even after an online love affair. But," he wheeled himself back, "if you want to take this computer with you now, you're going to need a search warrant. I need it for my work."

Bill and Angela left then, but on his way out, Bill looked at Lenore for a long time. "We're going to get to the bottom of this, Mrs. Featherjohn. With or without your cooperation."

"Well, I certainly hope you do, officers. This has gone on long enough, in my opinion."

After she shut the door, she sat trembling at the table. She wasn't the only Featherjohn who was lying. She knew Earl was lying about Tolita and the picture of the baby. She had proof of that. But he was hiding something else, hiding something very big.

40

They were ten minutes late for church, which caused his daughter extreme consternation.

"What if there's no place for me to sit? What if there's no room in the row? And what about Blaine? She's already mad at me as it is. I have to talk to her. Explain…"

"Honey," Jake tried to reason. "Blaine was keeping information from the police. You just don't do that in a murder investigation."

"I know, but, Dad…oh, I hate this. I hate walking in late, and she's going to know it was me who told—"

"I'm sure it will be fine, Jana. You did the right thing."

They were in Jake's truck, and the closer they got to the church, the more agitated his daughter became.

Two things brought on today's tardiness. Number one was the fact that all of them, including Jana, were up late the night before. Their first call had been to Bill on the police force, who was very interested in what they had to say.

For his part, Jake was happy to turn the entire thing over to the police, including the fact that the original baby picture was being examined by a photo expert. He gave Bill the contact information for Blake Filmore.

The second thing that brought on today's tardiness was a flood in the women's bathroom at the Purple Church, which had been caused by a rusted piece of galvanized pipe that hadn't been replaced by copper when everything else in the old basement was redone and refitted and refurbished.

He hadn't noticed the water because, while Jana was getting ready, he was up in the office, still trying to locate May's lost notebook. May was worried she'd left it at Noonan's or Mags and Herman's. "If that fell into the wrong hands, Jake…," she'd said. "Even by accident. Especially now…especially with all we suspect about the girl."

"But can they read your writing? Don't you use some kind of shorthand?"

She'd shrugged. But Jake knew, from past experience, that she was the only one who could read her scrawl.

"It'll turn up," he'd said. But he'd looked in all the places they'd already looked and still didn't find it. And so when he'd come back downstairs, there was Jana wearing her pj pants and a T-shirt trying as best she could to mop up the floor with towels. It looked as though every towel they owned was on the floor.

"Dad, where *were* you? I was calling and calling." She was whimpering, shaking from the cold as much as from anything else.

"Upstairs, honey. Looking for May's book again."

"I don't know what happened. I turned on the shower, and all this water came from everywhere. I didn't do it, Dad. I didn't do anything. The water just came. And I've got to get to church today. Blaine's not answering her text messages."

He turned off the mains and surveyed the damage in the women's bathroom. "It's okay, Jana. It's okay, sweetheart. It's not your fault. It's just this old building has a mind of its own sometimes."

They managed to get the place mopped up sufficiently, and Jana was able to shower happily in the men's shower room since there were no summer workers in the apartments.

When they finally got into the sanctuary, Blaine wasn't even there, and Jana ended up sitting with Jake in the back.

From his perch in the back pew he could see the entire congregation. Lenore Featherjohn was sitting five rows in front of him on the left, with a group of older ladies, none of whom he knew. Her red hair frizzed out from a center part. She looked frazzled and unhappy.

When Ben moved to the pulpit to read from the Scriptures, he began to cough. Someone brought him a glass of water, which he quietly drank. There was an awkwardness in this moment. Jake couldn't figure it out. He would have expected Ben to make some sort of joke about this, to say something, but he didn't. His friend quietly put the glass down and resumed reading the passage. It was a flat recitation, without inflection, without emotion. His whole sermon after that was the same way, as if he were preaching by rote or reading it.

Later, on the way out, Jake shook his hand. "Hey, buddy," he said.

"Jake," Ben said.

Jake made to move on, and then Ben grabbed hold of his arm. "Jake, wait," Ben said. "Can we get together? Can we talk?"

"Yeah sure, anytime. Tomorrow? Today?"

It had been weeks since Jake and Ben had met for a Monday lunch or a morning run.

Ben nodded. "It's important." Then he whispered, "The police came again last night."

"How'd it go?"

"I don't know. That's why I need to talk."

"You want to come over this afternoon?"

Ben stood for a moment, considering, then said, "I'd better not. I'd better stick around home today."

"Tomorrow? Breakfast? Noonan's?"

"I'd rather it be somewhere else, somewhere not so close to Fog Point. The Dew Drop Inn? They have a coffee, a coffee shop."

Jake looked at Ben's fluttering lips. "What is it, Ben?"

"Tomorrow, Jake, tomorrow."

41

Thick clouds gathered around Lenore this Sunday morning like snow haze, like ice. She sat in her customary pew but couldn't concentrate and wondered why she'd bothered to come this morning in the first place. Well, she had to, didn't she? How would that look if the night after she'd been questioned by the police she stayed away from church?

She hadn't slept well at all. She kept thinking about Earl. And Carl. And the baby who wasn't Tolita's baby, but a picture that Earl had nonetheless, which was the same picture Jeanine had. She sat back and listened to Ben fumble up there, and that made her think of Norman. She was quite confident this sort of thing wouldn't be tolerated in Norman's church. And that got her thinking about something else. If Norman were the minister here, things would be different. She looked at the drums up there on the platform and wondered how long they'd been there. There was also some sort of red shiny guitar on a stand. Time was those instruments were reserved for the dance hall. Lenore twisted her fingers together in her lap.

If Norman were here, he would know what to do about people bowing to the angel. She could tell him what she couldn't confess to the police. She wouldn't have to worry about Tolita Shenk and angels and babies and sons. She clenched her fists together. *Focus on something else. This isn't the time to be thinking about all that.* She focused her eyes on Ben up front. But even there she found distress.

The pulpit itself, a wooden structure her grandfather had donated and which bore her family's inscription in a bronze plaque on the front, was gone. Instead, Ben stood behind a small lectern that ushers moved to the side when the singers and musicians went back up on stage. Since Christmas, since coming back here, she tried to ask a few people about it, and all she got were shrugs. It was as if they didn't even want to answer her or acknowledge her. It was a long time ago, sure, but when people donate some exquisite piece of furniture, it shouldn't be locked away in a basement, gathering dust. That pulpit was part of this church's history. It was meant to be up there. If Norman were here, the church wouldn't be in the state it was, with her family's carved wooden pulpit in the basement under a thick layer of dust.

But even more than protecting the history of Stone Church, if Norman were here, he would make sure his brothers were on the right track, and Lenore wouldn't have to lie to protect them all the time. This incident with Tolita could take its proper place. That's what older brothers were for.

One of the Browngreen girls, Kimberly, if memory served, was up at the front of the church, singing along with a tape-recorded background and not doing a very good job of it. Already she'd had to have the guy in the back begin the music again so she could start over. Lenore was fairly certain that sort of thing wouldn't be tolerated in Norman's church. When Kimberly finally did get going, she was singing too loudly and too much like they did on *American Idol*, without Simon Cowell to tell her to sit down and put everyone out of their misery.

"Used to be," Lenore whispered to Eloise beside her, "soloists in church had to be professional musicians. And you sang with a real organ, not with all these tapes. You had to be trained."

The whole thing was upsetting to her, the unprofessionalism of it all.

Lenore looked up to where Amy was sitting, leaning into the pew, probably embarrassed for her husband, who was up there coughing and coughing.

What was the matter with him, anyway? He was someone on the way out—that was evident to anyone with half a brain.

And Ben's sermon, she couldn't make hide nor hair out of what he was saying. People would be so much happier if Norman were here. Nine years was a long time, wasn't it? Nine years was long enough for any minister to stay in one place.

She'd call Norman today. If Norman were here, she would be having none of these problems with Earl and Carl. This time it might work. Surely, Norman was ready for a change. He could come here and be the head pastor and not one minister among many. Surely that would appeal to him.

Plus, it would be nice to have her grandchildren closer, have them over for milk and cinnamon swirls in the afternoon. She'd have to learn what their favorite snacks were. She didn't even know. Yes, they'd be a distance from MarieAnn's parents, their *other* grandparents, but wasn't it her turn now? The thought of her grandchildren reminded her of the other child, but she couldn't bear that. Why had all this tragedy knocked on her door?

The congregation was singing, something fast and unfamiliar, the words of which were projected on a big screen at the front. When did it happen that the hymnbooks her family had donated had quit being used? She looked down at her hands folded on her lap like thick and gnarled pieces of wood.

Next to her, Eloise was singing. How was it that Eloise knew this song? The lady was Lenore's age! They'd gone to school together, right here in Fog Point. Lenore took a deep breath, looked at the screen, but her eyes filmed over. She'd call Norman today. How she missed them! Sometimes it was such an ache that she thought she would not survive it. And whenever she thought about this—the ache in her soul—her thoughts traveled to the envelope in the back of her dresser and the plain white legal-sized envelope she'd kept there all these years.

Eloise put her hand on Lenore's arm. Lenore shrugged it off. She didn't need comfort.

And then Lenore thought about what Sharla had said, about her being chosen for the miracle of the angel. Chosen. No. She bowed her head. They were praying now, and she folded her hands so that her grandmother's rings showed. She was sniffling, ever so quietly.

Eloise again put her hand on Lenore's. This time Lenore didn't shrug her away. "Allergies," Lenore whispered.

Eloise smiled. Lenore saw it from the corner of her eye.

"Something about this old building," Lenore whispered. "Every time I come here, my eyes water. That's why I quit coming."

Ahead of her, Amy was sitting in the place where MarieAnn should be. She tried to imagine MarieAnn there, and the three children sitting in that exact pew, and Lenore would be sitting on the other side of her. Of course she would, and she'd bring crayons and coloring books for the youngest one. Church can be long for children. Yes! As soon as she got home, she would call Norman!

If they needed a place to live, well that would be no problem, would it? She had all these upstairs rooms. She would gladly give up her entire B&B business to have her whole family together. Norman and MarieAnn in her deluxe suite upstairs, the one the FNN lady had now, and then she'd let the children choose which rooms they wanted. She'd get them repapered. Or painted. They could choose the color. And she would remain in her downstairs apartment to give them some privacy. And her other sons in the basement. They'd get together for meals. That would be nice. She'd cook for all of them. Give MarieAnn a chance to do church work. And if MarieAnn wanted to work at a Christian bookstore, well, there was one in Ridley Harbor. Surely they would hire her.

A tear dropped onto her bunched and veiny fists. Wasn't it time for her now?

42

I t's a different sort of day today, and the differentness confuses me. I want to ask the woman about it, but I can't remember her name. I've been trying to think of it all morning, ever since I got up. All of them are sitting around the kitchen table when I walk out, still in my pajamas. And where's that woman who comes in every morning now to fix my coffee with fresh milk and to clean the kitchen?

"Where is she?" I ask.

"Where's who, Dad?"

"The woman who comes."

"You mean Betty? It's Sunday, Dad," Tim says. Tim. I remember his name now. "She doesn't come on Sundays."

"Church," I say. That's why today feels different.

"Yes, Dad, church. Which means you'd better get ready if you're coming with us."

"I'd like to go to church."

"Good." Tim gets up from the table, puts a hand on my arm, and leads me back to the little room off the family room and helps me change out of my pajamas. "I need a tie," I say.

He finds a tie in my closet, but I tell him I want the blue one. "And a white shirt. I have to have a white shirt. Did Glad iron any?"

"You have a closet full of white shirts, Dad. And they're all ironed."

"The girl," I say. "Has anything happened to the girl? Has anyone found her?"

"Dad, we've been through this before. There *is* no girl. Here, let me help you get that shirt buttoned up."

"When did they do this?" I look around my room.

"Do what?" Tim asks, tying my tie. I'm glad he found the blue one. Against a white shirt it looks nice. A man's not dressed for church unless he's in a white shirt and tie and wearing a proper suit.

"When did they put up the wallpaper in here? I don't remember it."

"Dad, that wallpaper's been there for years. If I recall, Mom put it up."

He's lying, of course. Glad would never do such a thing. Not this paper, the vines with the eyes that keep looking at me. Then Tim takes my arm and leads me back into the kitchen.

"Here's your breakfast, Dad," says the woman who is Tim's wife.

"We have to call the police," I tell her. "About the girl."

"Come on now, Dad. Let's have some scrambled eggs." She takes my arm, helps me to sit. "We all have to get on to church soon."

But I am insistent. I have to be. I stand and pace to the other side of the room. "She was here last summer. She lived in the barn. All summer. She was here. She's in danger. We all are. You, too. And me. She found it on the computer. It's all on the computer. But I don't know how to find it." The woman, the one Tim married, grabs at my arm and walks me around to the kitchen table again where eggs are laid out on a plate.

"I have to get her food now. I can't sit down. It's time for me to get her food."

But the woman says, "Come on, Dad, let's settle down and have some breakfast. We have to leave soon. Jonah, up you get. Go brush your teeth." The little tyke gets up. I sit down and put fork to mouth, fork to mouth.

"He gets so agitated," I hear the woman say quietly to Tim. "I don't know what we're going to do."

"Keep him as comfortable as we can."

"He's keeps on about that girl. Do you have any idea what he's talking about?"

"He's confused," Tim says.

"I changed my mind." I push the rest of my breakfast away. "I have to find her. I can't go to church today."

"Dad!" The woman's voice is harsh, sharp. She doesn't often speak like this. "Come. Sit down. I'll get you some coffee."

"I always gave the girl lots of milk. I took it out to the barn."

"Dad! There *is* no girl! There never was a girl. Tim, what're we going to do?"

And she has my arms and leads me back to my little room, and I feel this awful dread. Something terrible has happened to her. Again, I am too late for the Shenk family. Again, it has happened. I sit down. There's something wrong with this room. Maybe it isn't the wallpaper. Maybe it's something else. A feeling when I enter it. Like someone has lived here before and then died here. And then I remember Glad and The Terrible Tragedy. "It's on the computer. I have to get onto the Internet."

"Dad, you don't even know how to use the Internet."

I am crying now because I can't remember her name, and it is so vitally important that I remember her name. Maybe if I sit really quietly the name will come to me.

"God is punishing me," I tell her. "For what I did. For what Glad did. And Reeny…"

I surprise myself by saying that name, a name I have not said in many, many years, a name I never expected to say again. Now Tim is in the doorway. "What made you say that name, Dad?"

"Betty's been going over the albums with him," the woman says to the man. "That's probably where all this is coming from."

I reach for the photo album. The woman who is here during the week leaves it right on my nightstand. I am looking through the pictures. I am looking for Reeny.

The woman puts a blanket on my knees over my good suit and sits beside me. "Tim, I'll stay with him. I don't think there'll be any church for him today. I don't mind staying."

And when the others leave, we look through pictures. "Here, Dad, look at the pictures. Here's Tim, and Roger. And look here. Here's Pam when she was little." And she points to each picture in turn. The ends of her fingers are red. I wonder why. I want to ask her if she's hurt herself somehow. "Look, Dad, here's you and Mom. And here are your sons. You have four sons, Tim and Ashe and Roger and Philip, and one daughter, Pam."

"Philip," I say.

"Philip lives in Toronto."

"Where's Pam?"

"Here's Pam. She lives down the road. She comes to see you."

"Reeny."

The woman leafs through the photo album. Reeny's picture is near the beginning. "Here's Reeny, Dad. But Reeny died a long time ago."

"Her baby died. She killed her baby…" I know I am agitated, but I can't help it. There's so much that people need to know, so much that has been covered up all these years. And now the girl is in danger because she knows it all, has it all figured out. I shouldn't have done it, told her all those things. I should've kept the book in my closet and not brought it down. I can't look at the picture of Reeny. I want to close the album. I never want to look at it again. I grab the edges. I need to fling it from me. I grab hold of the edge and wrest it out of her hands and fling it from me, but before I do, I catch a glimpse of her surprised face, and I begin to shake and tremble.

"She killed her baby. She killed her baby." And my face is in my hands, and I am shaking, and my words are coming out wrong. I know they are, but I can't help it.

"Reeny's dead, Dad. She died a long time ago." The woman gets up and gets the photo album from the floor, straightens it out, closes it, and puts it on the table beside my bed. "She died a long time ago. There's nothing to be afraid of."

I need to be Samson, I think. One more burst of strength before this house comes tumbling down. I need to remember. I need to tell them. *Help me, God, to tell them.*

43

B en was coughing and couldn't seem to stop. Amy wondered what was wrong with him. Someone brought him water. She looked over to where the young people sat. Blaine wasn't in church this morning, and it had been with great reluctance that Amy had allowed her to stay home alone. The police had come late last night and asked about Tolita's brother. Did Blaine know anything about that?

She'd nodded. "Yes, she told me she was looking for her brother when we spoke on the boardwalk. I just forgot to tell you."

"You forgot," Bill stated.

She shrugged. "Yeah."

"Blaine!" Amy said.

"What*ever*," she said.

Last night was the beginning of Amy's feeling afraid, really afraid. Some-one had killed this Tolita. Tolita had spoken to Blaine. Could that same person be a threat to Blaine? And now Blaine was home alone.

This morning it had been hard rousing Blaine out of bed. "Church in one hour," Amy had said.

Blaine groaned, turned her head away, and said something indecipherable.

Fifteen minutes later she'd gone back in. "Church in forty-five minutes. No more arguing. Get up." It usually took Blaine at least half an hour to get ready. But lately it was taking much less. Lately, it seemed, she'd get up, pull on a pair of what looked like pajama pants, and go to church, her hair in disarray.

"I don't want to have to come back in here," Amy said. "Up in five."

"I'm sick," Blaine muttered.

"I want you up in five."

"I said I'm sick."

"You will come, Blaine. This is not up for negotiation. Sometimes we have to do things we don't want to do."

Blaine muttered something and pulled the covers over her head, and Amy wondered when Blaine had started using black nail polish. A big chunk of white hair stuck up out of her blanket.

"I'm sick. I have cramps."

Amy wanted to reach forward and touch that streak of white-blond hair, wanted to suddenly take this half-grown young woman in her arms, tell her it was going to be okay. She was the daughter they had waited so long for. "Are you really sick? You're not lying?"

"Why does everyone around here *assume* I'm lying?"

"All your father and I have to go by is past experience, Blaine."

"I'm not lying. And he's not my father and you're not my mother."

It was a jolt. "*What* did you say?"

"I said you're not my mother." She put her hands to her stomach, curled up on the bed and faced away from her.

They had never hidden the fact from Blaine that she was adopted. They had chosen her, they often said. Chosen, like God chooses us. We're not God's children by blood, but by his choice. That's what they were fond of saying. Today she wanted to scream all of this at her daughter. She wanted to take this girl that they had loved beyond all loving by the shoulders and tell her she was their daughter—no matter what, she was their daughter. But she couldn't. She stared at Blaine, and for one horrible instant, the girl was a stranger to her. Amy said nothing, turned away.

Blaine said, "I can't go to church. I'm sick. I'm really sick."

"Okay. I believe you. You're sick."

"I have cramps."

"Fine. Stay in bed then."

Amy stood there for a while, staring at this daughter under the covers. And then she saw it on her nightstand. A pink-and-blue brochure about an adoption agency. Scrawled across the front were a name and phone number. What was this? Blaine had done this, found this, without telling Amy. That was the part that hurt the most, that Blaine could choose to include her in this search for a birth mother, but didn't. They had always been honest with her about this. Why this secrecy on Blaine's part now?

Perhaps she had put it there so her mother would see it. And be shocked. And be reminded that she was not Amy's "real" mother.

"What's this?" Amy asked her.

"What's what?"

"This name. This number. This *agency*? Who is Jeanine?"

For someone who was sick with debilitating cramps, Blaine tore out of bed and grabbed the brochure from her mother's hands awfully fast. "That's mine! That's my business! That's the trouble with you, you're always in my business."

"Who is this, Blaine? Who is Jeanine? Is she the woman you were talking to?"

Blaine glared at her. "How do you know about that?"

"I saw you, Blaine. Who is she?"

"She's just someone who wants to help me, something you have no concept of." Then she muttered something under her breath that sounded like a curse.

"*What* did you say?"

"Nothing."

"It wasn't nothing, young lady. I know what I heard."

"Whatever." She got up, and this tall beauty of a daughter made her way through the doorway. Then she groaned suddenly, clutched her stomach, and fell forward toward the wall.

"Blaine!" Amy rushed toward her daughter, and for a moment, only an moment, Blaine seemed to melt into her arms, but then just as quickly she flinched away from Amy and said, "I told you I'm sick, and you didn't believe it. Now you know. You always think I'm lying. I'm sorry I didn't remember what that girl told me. I'm not perfect. I'm sorry I'm not good like Charlie. Like your *real* son."

Amy looked down at her daughter leaning against the wall and felt a jolt so fresh as to immobilize her. Maybe all this was her own fault. Maybe Amy hadn't loved her enough, done enough for her, been a good enough mother. Ben was firm with her; Ben took no nonsense from her. That may work with Charlie, but it wasn't working for this girl. Maybe through the years she hadn't been there enough to soften Ben's firm hand. Maybe she had failed.

These thoughts raced through Amy's mind while she listened to the girl who was singing up front. Kimberly was Blaine's age, used to be Blaine's friend. But while Blaine wanted to know when she could quit church, this young woman was one of the leading teenagers. She helped with the Sunday school and even sang in the choir. Even if she wasn't one of the most remarkable singers on the planet, and she did seem extraordinarily nervous this morning, but at least she was trying. Maybe it was good Blaine wasn't here today. Amy was sure they'd hear about Kimberly's lame attempts at singing all the way home.

She and Ben had wanted lots of children. Ben was an only child, and Amy had only one sister. So they determined their own family would be filled with laughter and children. Lots of them. It didn't happen. And after more than ten years of trying and many, many trips to fertility clinics and doctors, they'd decided to adopt. Blaine came to them the day she was born, and there weren't two happier parents. It was an entirely closed adoption, at a time when adoptions were increasingly open. They knew only one thing: the mother wanted her baby placed in a Christian home.

And now Blaine had grown into this tall, hard-edged fourteen-year-old who looked eighteen.

Sometimes Amy wondered whether some other family would have done a better job of raising Blaine. You don't wonder about that when it's your biological child. Why should you? They're part of you, but when you adopt, you wonder if the next couple on the list, the next in line, would have done a better job.

When Blaine was seven, Amy found herself inexplicably pregnant. Charlie was easy and healthy, and Amy breastfed him for eleven months, something she hadn't been able to do with Blaine.

Amy tried to pay attention as Ben spoke, but her thoughts kept flitting to the brochure and the name *Jeanine*. Was this the woman she'd seen talking to Blaine on the boardwalk that day? Wasn't she that TV person? What was her business with Blaine? There should be some law against newspeople harassing teenagers.

As she sat there in her pew, suddenly she knew. The random bits of information fell together, and she intuitively fit together the interlocking pieces. She *knew!*

44

The first time Lenore punched in Norman's number, it was way too early and she got the answering machine. Well, of course, silly me, she thought, looking at the clock. Given the time difference, they would still be in church, he being the minister. Knowing Norman, they were probably the last out of the building. She didn't leave a message. Three o'clock, she told herself, I'll wait until three.

She kept glancing at the clock while she cleaned out the coffeepot to make more. It was all she could do to keep up with the coffee drinking of her guests. *These newspeople!* she thought. Carl sat at the kitchen table, reading through the *Ridley Harbor Sunday Times* and grunting every so often. She wished he wouldn't make that sound.

Lenore decided to ask the question. "How would you feel," she asked, "about your brother being here?"

Carl grunted. "Earl? Now getting him upstairs to eat gentlemanly-like at the table—that'll be a feat."

"No, I meant Norman."

"Norman! What happened—his church kick him out for being the jerk that he is?"

"Be quiet about your brother! He's serving God! He's not on probation like some people I know!"

"And speaking of being on the wrong side of the law, Mother, why're the police so interested in you?"

"None of that is my fault."

Carl grunted and took a long drink of his coffee.

"You'd do well to follow your brother's example and go to church every once in a while."

"Spoken like a true soldier of the cross, someone who quits church every other month." Carl put his coffee down and shifted in his seat.

"Don't speak to me like that. I always have good reasons for what I do."

"You never answered my question—Norman's church finally kick him out?"

"No, his church did not kick him out. Of course they would not kick him *out*. He is indispensable there." She poured fresh water into the top of the coffee maker. She was pouring so fast that some of the water spilled onto the counter. But she couldn't help it. Carl was making her so angry, and she needed time to think. She had to practice in her mind what she was going to say to Norman.

Norman, I know you weren't very interested in Stone Church back nine years ago, but if the pulpit were to suddenly be vacant, would you consider coming out?

The coffee ready to go, Lenore went into her room. She'd try phoning again. Maybe get them when they were just walking in the door. Would that be a good time? Maybe not. Norman might be angry that she phoned then. She'd force herself to wait. While she did so, she got down the photo album of Norman and MarieAnn's wedding. It had been a lovely ceremony, out in Nebraska where she lived. Lenore had taken months to find the perfect dress, the one that would best complement her coloring. It'd been such a beautiful day. And Norman looked so strong, so sure of himself, and MarieAnn so beautiful. Everyone said they would make a fine couple, and they were.

She had three photo albums, one for each of her grandchildren. She started with Alyssa's and went through the pictures from the day Alyssa was born until just yesterday, when MarieAnn had sent some more by e-mail. Here was a new one, Alyssa in a lavender snowsuit and standing beside a sled. Lenore tried to calculate. Would Alyssa be five now? Time flies. That little girl had such a pretty smile. There. This was a much better thing to do, she thought, than thinking about the police and Tolita Shenk and worrying about what the FNN people were up to.

She got down Jonathan's album. *Oh, my goodness, he must be ten by now, standing there in his boots and winter jacket in front of their big house in Nebraska.* No hat, she noticed. She hoped MarieAnn didn't let him play outside that way. Maybe this was just for the picture. Maybe he was allowed to take his hat off just for the picture.

The third album was little Bradley's, the seven-year-old. What a rascal he was. All boy, that one. His picture was taken inside, where he was holding up the truck Lenore had sent for Christmas.

Sometimes the pictures overlapped, and she didn't know quite which album to put them into. Holiday pictures were an example of that. She looked down at their most recent Christmas pictures.

Their family always went to MarieAnn's parents' place for Christmas. There they were, all sitting around the Christmas table, smiles everywhere, the Christmas dishes spread on a festive tablecloth. There was one of the Christmas tree. What a big tree that was! MarieAnn's family always went all out. You could tell by the size of tree they always had.

Lenore closed the book, got up, and went to her dresser. *Don't do it, Lenore,* she told herself. Don't get out that envelope. Just leave it. Or throw it out. You should finally, finally throw the thing away. But she couldn't. She just couldn't. She opened the top dresser drawer. This wasn't the regular bureau where she kept her everyday clothes. This one held special things, mementos and things she wanted to keep safe: her grandmother's jewelry, a few old photos, the one of Harlan and her on their wedding day, Harlan looking so handsome. From underneath her grandmother's creased and ironed handkerchiefs, she pulled out the envelope.

It was an old envelope, soft, the way paper gets after many foldings. She opened it up and pulled out the plane ticket and looked at it, although she had every word of it memorized, even the fine print. It was dated for six years ago.

At one time, Lenore saw Norman and MarieAnn every year. Once a year Lenore would purchase a plane ticket, fly to Omaha, and then take a taxi to their home.

Six years ago she was set to go, had her plane ticket purchased and her suitcase packed when Norman called. It wasn't convenient to come just then, he said. They were in the middle of a missionary conference. Bradley was a rambunctious one-year-old, and Jonathan was in preschool church day camp. It was an incredibly busy time. And wouldn't you know it, it was the week of the annual Blow Out Sale at the church bookstore and MarieAnn couldn't get off. Rotten timing, but there it was.

"I could help out," Lenore had said. "While you're busy, I could be with the children. I could baby-sit little Bradley. And of course, I could cook your meals. That might take the pressure off. I love to cook. You know, I've won ribbons for my cooking..."

"It's just not going to work. We're going in ten different directions."

"But I already have my ticket."

"I'm sorry, Mother. We've got a lot of things happening here. It's just a madhouse. You wouldn't enjoy yourself. Maybe you could cash in the ticket and come another time."

Lenore never tried to get any kind of reimbursement for her plane ticket. She put it in the top drawer in her dresser and unpacked her bags, unpacked the toys and clothes she'd bought for the boys. She'd rewrapped them all in Christmas paper and mailed them a few months later for Christmas. She never asked to come again, and they never invited her.

She sat on the edge of her bed and waited for three o'clock.

45

Amy barely stayed focused and civil to all the people who wanted to hug her and shake her hand on the way out the door. She stood at the door with Ben but put a hand to her head. This whole charade was too much. She couldn't do it anymore. Her family was falling apart; God was not a part of her family anymore. And she needed to be home to see about Blaine. Especially since she knew who that woman from the news was and why she was really here. It made perfect sense to her. That person from the news had been here for many days. How long did newspeople stay in one location? Maybe one day? Not as many days as this woman had been here.

It was a mercy that today they had no guests for dinner. She'd grab something from the freezer for the family, and that's what they'd have for lunch. She wasn't even hungry. She doubted whether Blaine would eat anything. Plus, she had to do something this afternoon, something she couldn't tell Ben—or Blaine—about.

When she got back from her errand this afternoon, she'd make peanut butter brownies. Blaine's favorite, especially now that Amy had learned how to make this particular recipe without eggs.

She hoped Blaine was feeling better. She had such an awful time with cramps, and so far nothing the doctor prescribed seemed to work. Maybe it was time to head back to the doctor's. That's all the outburst was about this morning. It was the cramps talking. And maybe she *had* forgotten what the dead girl had told her about looking for her brother. They'd arrive home and there she'd be, wrapped in a fleece blanket in front of the television. Everything would be okay.

But when they got home, the family room was empty and the television was off. The house was quiet. Too quiet. Maybe she was really sick and was downstairs asleep in her room.

"Blaine?" Amy stood outside her daughter's closed door and knocked lightly. No answer. She opened the door a crack. "Blaine? You okay?" Amy opened the door wide, looked around. Empty.

She was not in the bathroom or any of the rooms in the basement.

Amy raced back upstairs. "Blaine? Blaine!" She checked in all of the rooms, the attic, the garage. She opened the front closet, rifled through the coats, and gasped. Blaine's coat was gone. And the thing was, she didn't want to tell Ben. She *couldn't* tell Ben that Blaine was missing. He would go overboard like he always did with her. Still, how was she to hide the fact that Blaine wasn't here?

Amy ran downstairs and into Blaine's room again. The brochure on her dresser was gone. Amy stood for a minute, put a hand to her throat, quelling a rising nausea. Jeanine. She needed to take care of that errand now.

"I need to go." She brushed past Ben at the bottom of the stairs. "I'll be back. I have to go and get something."

"Where are you going?" Ben asked.

"I'll explain it all later." She had to get out. She had to grab the keys and push past her husband and get out the front door and into the car and drive away before he could stop her.

She motioned with a hand. "Get the tacos going. There's hamburger in the freezer. Put it in the microwave. The taco shells are in the upstairs freezer."

"Amy! What are you *doing*? Where's Blaine? Down in her room?"

She had never done anything this remotely defiant before, leaving Ben like this. But as soon as she brought Blaine back and explained about Jeanine, he would understand. Thing was, she couldn't tell him. Mothers do what mothers have to do, she thought as she drove away.

A mound of snow a foot high edged the end of the driveway to Lenore's B&B, but Amy drove right over it and parked next to a large, dark blue van. She chirped the lock with the remote and moved quickly toward the back door. A line of people was kneeling in the snowbank. Amy leaned on the doorbell. A man was taking pictures. Carl answered her knock.

Amy kept her voice even. "I'd like to talk to the woman from FNN."

"Haven't seen her today at all, darlin'. Why don't you come in out of the cold? My mother might know where she is."

Amy entered. The kitchen was warm and smelled of coffee. He offered her some. She refused and stayed standing with her coat on. A few guests were drinking coffee and talking. Amy stood in the center of the room and tried to calm her thoughts. What was she doing here in the kitchen of a woman who disliked her so intensely?

"My mother's in her apartment," Carl said. "She's working herself up to calling my deadbeat brother. And any conversation with my deadbeat brother is sacrosanct. I'll go and check her room if you want to wait here."

He disappeared around the corner.

Amy swallowed and went into the dining room.

"Did you happen to see a girl here?" Amy asked a man who was sitting with a newspaper in hand. "Maybe earlier? This morning? My daughter is tall, has dark hair with blond chunky highlights in the front. She may have come here."

He looked over his half glasses at her. "I don't think I've seen her. Not in here anyway."

"Do you know the FNN people who are here?"

"Seen them," he said.

"I'm looking for the woman, Jeanine. I don't know her last name."

"Haven't seen them today," said another.

"I think they left," said someone else.

She paused and looked out the window at the line of people. "Are all those people for the angel?"

"Yes," said a young woman beside the bay window. "Some of them are getting healed."

"*Some* of them?" Amy asked.

The girl turned to her with wide eyes. "Those with enough faith are. It all depends on your faith. If you have enough faith, God heals you. If you don't have enough faith, then he doesn't."

"What kind of a God is that?" said Amy "Who makes it all depend on *you?*"

"But that's how God is!" the girl protested. "You need faith! It says so in the Bible."

Amy shook her head at this. She needed to get away.

Carl returned and said his mother "couldn't be disturbed." He'd also knocked on Jeanine's door, but there was no answer. Did she want to leave a note?

Amy shook her head but then changed her mind. "Sure, give me a piece of paper."

On it she wrote, "Please call me at your earliest convenience," and she left her name and number.

She would talk with this Jeanine. She'd have it out with her. It was unfair that Jeanine should come for Blaine now, after all these years. The adoption had been closed, making Jeanine's actions illegal and morally wrong, and Amy intended to tell her so. Jeanine was Blaine's biological mother, and Amy intended to let her know that her secret was out.

46

W hen they got home from church, it wasn't immediately apparent to Jake that Blaine was in his daughter's room. He'd been mulling over the strange church service and Ben's odd behavior, so when he heard voices from Jana's room, he thought she was on her phone.

He busied himself cleaning up the floor from the earlier mishap. He was mopping near her room when he heard, "I'm really sorry! It just popped out! But I don't know what difference it makes, Blaine. So what if she was looking for her brother? I don't get what the big *deal* is."

"The big deal is we could both end up dead. *That's* the big deal, Jana."

On that note, Jake knocked on Jana's door and entered. Jana was sprawled on her bed, and Blaine was lying along the back of the couch, her long body curled around it. "End up dead? What's that about, Blaine?"

She stretched her tall body catlike. "Nothing," she said.

"Blaine, it's something. What do you know about the girl?"

"Nothing. I already told everybody everything I know."

Jake shook his head and frowned at her. He and May had already talked through various scenarios around Tolita's brother. Perhaps Tolita was looking for a younger brother, thus explaining the photo of the baby. The police squashed this one, however, when they reported that Tolita was an only child.

May had suggested that sometimes a good friend is considered a brother. "Maybe that's who she was looking for, someone who was *like* a brother to her."

So far they, along with the police, were stymied. As for the baby picture, Bill had told him they were not putting too much credence in Lenore's testimony about it.

Jake said, "Blaine, I didn't see you come in."

"I snuck in during church."

He raised his eyebrows. "Your parents know you're here?"

"I'll get home before they do. My dad's always the last one out anyway."

Jake handed her his cell phone. "Call your parents and tell them you're here. We'll drive you home."

Jake grabbed his keys and heard Blaine's words again. *End up dead.* Was Blaine being overly dramatic, or was she speaking the truth?

47

Precisely at three o'clock, Lenore punched Norman's number into her cordless phone. It was answered on the second ring by a tiny voice. Little Alyssa? Lenore looked down at her picture in the album and tried to imagine her on the other end of the phone. "Is this Alyssa, dear?"

"Yes."

"Well hello, Alyssa. This is your grandma calling."

"My grandma?"

"Yes, dearie, this is your grandma. How are you?"

"You don't sound like Mamam."

"This is Grandma Featherjohn, dear."

"Mommy!"

Lenore heard the phone being handed to MarieAnn, who explained that Alyssa had strict instructions to hand over the phone if she didn't recognize the voice. She laughed and said she hadn't meant that to include Lenore, of course.

"Well, that's wise," Lenore said. "You never know in today's society. How are you, dear?"

"Oh, I'm fine, just fine. We're just sitting down to lunch."

"Well, I won't keep you then. Is Norman there?"

A few seconds later she heard a scuffle, some arguing in the background, and then the voice of her son.

"Hey, Mother, how's it going?"

"Fine, Norman, just fine. Well, busy as all get out." She told him about the newspeople and the Frozen Girl and how silly some people were. Didn't he agree?

"Yeah, hey, yeah. I gotta run here. We're just about to sit down to lunch."

"Norman." She stopped. "Norman, there was another reason I called."

He was immediately concerned. "Is everything all right, Mother? Are you all right? You're not sick, are you?"

"Yes, I'm all right. You know me, healthy as a horse. I was just wondering... Well, I had some people staying here with me in the B&B..."

"Yeah, and...?" He sounded impatient.

"They were from FNN. I told them about your church, your megachurch. And I sort of convinced them they should call you. They might be doing a story on megachurches and they may phone you."

"I wish you hadn't done that, Mother. You know how those people twist things."

"But this is FNN, Norman."

"I don't care if it's the queen of England."

"Norman!"

"I'm sorry, Mother. You did what you thought was right. Your intentions were good and that's what matters."

She softened a bit. "I...I had another reason for calling. It's about Stone Church. You know Stone Church."

"Of course I know Stone Church."

"It looks like Ben McLaren might be leaving."

"Really! That surprises me. He's a good man. Where's he going, do you know?"

"I called because—"

"You want to know if I know any good men. Who's the chairman of the board there? I'll give him a call."

"No, um…I was thinking of you. I know you weren't interested nine years ago, but what about now? Can I mention your name to the search committee? You could live here with me. I've plenty of room. Well, you know this house, Norman. You know the potential for Bible studies and small groups and dinners…" She ran her fingers down the edge of a snapshot of Alyssa.

He laughed then, and his laughter suddenly reminded her of Harlan. Her husband had always laughed like that. "Oh, Mother, you get such *ideas*! The kids, the family, we're pretty settled here. And MarieAnn, well, she couldn't bear to be that far from her mother."

No, of course not. Lenore sighed, closed the photo album. "I was wondering…then, when will you be coming to visit?" She sounded whiny. She knew it and tried to stop herself.

"We really have to plan for that. Maybe this summer. Let me look at the family calendar and get back to you."

That was what he always said. They said good-bye, and she put the photo albums away.

48

"If I know something," Ben asked Jake, "am I obligated to go to the police with it?"

"If you know something about what?" Jake asked.

It was Monday morning early, and they were eating the Dew Drop Inn's breakfast special: two eggs any style, two pieces of toast, bacon or sausage, hash browns, and as much coffee as they could manage. Even though they were the only ones there, they had chosen a booth in the back to ensure privacy. Ben had wanted that.

"If I know something, say a secret, about someone who is dead, am I legally obligated to go to the police?"

Jake leaned across the table. "Ben, you're beginning to sound like your daughter—all these secrets. If you know something about what?"

"About anything. Hypothetically speaking."

Jake had never seen his friend quite like this—jittery, eyes darting, breathless, coughing, nervous. "Hypothetical is a language I have trouble understanding, Ben."

Ben nodded, brought his mug of coffee to his mouth, but then put it back down on the table. "Not thirsty," he said. "Stuff gets to my stomach these days."

Jake waited.

"Okay," Ben said, drumming his fingers on the wooden table. It was a hollow sound in the empty restaurant. "I know the rules. They just seem to come into conflict in this case. Do you know what the seal of the confessional is?"

Jake took off his glasses, folded them, and placed them on the table. "Sure. It means a priest can't violate what he's heard in confession. But you're not Catholic, Ben."

"Right. For priests, the confessional is sacred and cannot be violated for any reason, even death. For ministers—and lawyers, I think—confidentiality may be breached, even should be breached, if someone's life is in danger."

Ben looked out the window, where ice crystals were misting the air. "But, what if this…this minister's family was in danger? What if the danger comes, not from withholding the truth as in confession, but from revealing it to the authorities? Let's say the person who confessed is now dead, murdered, and this person said that if the minister went to the police, his family could be in danger. The same danger, I might add, that got her murdered in the first place."

Jake looked at him. Blaine had talked about people being in danger yesterday.

Ben rubbed his hand where his wedding ring was, and the skin there looked red and raw, as if he had been rubbing it for a long time. He opened his mouth to say something, but then closed it when the door opened and a couple of journalists made their way past the two of them. Ben waited until they sat down at a far table. Then he said, "Jake, I don't know what to do."

"I understand, buddy."

"I don't know if I can share this with you. With anyone."

Jake put his glasses back on and leaned forward. "Ben, you are my friend. You can tell me whatever it is you need to tell me. You've done the same for me so many times. When I came here, my life was a mess. I'd basically run away from life for three years. I was sleeping around with anyone who wanted to share my bed. I had no relationship with my daughters and hated their mother's new husband. But I now have my own business. I'm not sleeping around, and I think I'm in love with a nice girl, although whether she loves me is another matter. And I have a fairly good relationship with one of my daughters at least. Plus, even though I don't ever want to be best buddies with Keith, at least I don't feel like murdering him anymore, and I've even started to go to church on Sundays, which is something I said I would never do again.

"And it's because of you." He looked Ben in the eyes when he said, "You never gave up on me, no matter how wretched and awful I was. You accepted me as your friend and even trusted me with your sermons.

"Now you're in trouble," he continued. "I don't know what it is. I've heard things too. I know about Blaine. I know you're having trouble right now with her…"

When Jake said the name *Blaine,* a groan escaped Ben's lips.

Jake continued, "I can be here personally as a friend, Ben, and just sit and listen. And I can be here professionally as a PI. There, friend, speech finished."

Ben looked at him for a long while before he said, "When the police came at first, I told them nothing. I told them she merely came into the church to get directions. But that's not the truth."

Jake put his cup down. "Tell me."

Ben had been alone in the church one evening when there was a knock on the door. It was night, and the knock jarred him. He'd been alone, praying for his family. Especially for Amy. He didn't know what was the matter with her, but something was. And with Blaine. He was so worried about Blaine. She'd changed recently, and he didn't know why. She'd become sullen, and he seemed to be getting lost in the jumble of emotions coming from the two females at odds in his home.

When he heard the knock on that snowy night, for half a second he thought it was the hand of God. The stories of Samuel, of Paul, who were visited by God, came to his thinking. Ben made his way from his office, turning on lights in the sanctuary as he walked to the front of the church. A girl with blond hair, a purple scarf, and a faded pink backpack stood there, a dusting of snow on her shoulders.

"I need to see you," she said simply. "It's about Blaine."

He opened the door, and she came inside. She was shivering and wet and looked tired. She told Ben she was staying at the Dew Drop Inn, and Ben got the idea she'd walked from there.

"What about Blaine?" he asked.

She stood there awhile, looking at him as if she didn't know how to start. He invited her to his office, and she followed him and sat in the chair he indicated. She kept her coat on and shivered. He turned up the thermostat.

By this time he began to believe this was one of Blaine's friends sent to play some sort of practical joke, but the nature of the joke eluded him. He'd wait. He sat behind his desk and made a tent of his hands and watched her. "Are you one of her friends?" he finally asked.

She blew air out of her lips and said, "You might say that."

"What do you want?"

"I need to warn you about Blaine."

What was Blaine into now? he wondered.

"Okay." The girl slid the backpack off and placed it on the floor beside her. "She's getting herself involved with the wrong people. I thought you should know."

Tell me something I don't already know, he thought.

"I came all the way out here. It took me a whole long time and a long, long bus ride, and the closer I got, the more I realized that neither Blaine or I should have gotten involved with these people. They're more dangerous than I thought."

"What people?" But Ben was still thinking this was some sort of joke, his daughter sending a friend to mess with his head. Well, it wouldn't take much.

He took off his glasses. "I don't know which friend of Blaine's you are, but I want to know why you're here." And then another thought occurred to him. Here he was, a minister alone in an office with a young woman. What was he thinking? He got up. "I'll walk you out," he said. "Do you have a place to go?"

"Please!" Her eyes got wide. "I'm trying to tell you! And don't go to the police. That's the surest way to get her killed. And if I were you, I wouldn't take that chance. They steal babies!"

"Who steals babies? What are you talking about?"

"I have proof! I have lots of proof!"

Ben began to wonder if the girl was mentally ill. He asked her name, but she wouldn't tell him. At the door, she turned to him for one last entreaty. She only said that she would be back tomorrow and would convince him of everything. She had a book, she said, and pictures. Just before he ushered her out—and she wouldn't accept a ride anywhere—she asked for the name of a good private investigator. And she would prefer a woman. Ben had written May's name on a piece of paper and handed it to her.

"Ah," Jake said, taking a forkful of eggs.

"She left, and in the next two days I forgot all about this drama-queen friend of Blaine's who came to me for whatever reason. She never came back with her information. And then two days later, she shows up dead. Murdered."

Jake said, "And you've told no one else this story? Not the police? Not Amy?"

He shook his head.

"And you knew all along who the murdered girl was."

"Well, not her name."

"Ben, this isn't good."

"I know."

"You should have gone to the police."

"I know. But I just couldn't take the chance of something happening to Blaine. I'd give my life for that girl."

"I know that, buddy. I know that." Jake shook his head.

But he couldn't get over what Ben told him—who would be stealing babies? And why would they want to kill Blaine?

49

It ends up being Jonah who helps me get my e-mail. The little tyke shows remarkable patience with this old man. Bobbie isn't there to whisk me away to my room with the chair and television before I show any signs of demented strangeness. She is outside shoveling off the front porch, and I'm on the couch with the photo album and looking out onto the fields, which are dusted in snow. She's a strong woman, that Bobbie is, and I can hear her shovel hitting the wooden porch slats. She and Tim had had one of their arguments about whose responsibility the front deck was. Tim said he had enough to do with the barn and the driveway, and Bobbie said how could she do it all with her work at Fabricland and still take care of his dad. I hear all of this, of course. But they do this a lot, talk about me like I'm not there. They don't think I can understand them.

"He's *your* father, and I've got all his care!"

"You don't have *all* his care, as you say. Who dresses him? Who makes sure he takes a bath? And you know you can call Pam any time to come and help."

"I don't want that woman in my house, Tim."

"She's my sister and he's her father!"

"I still won't have her in my house!"

"Well, fine. Don't complain then that you've got all his care!"

Then my granddaughter Gabrielle comes in and there's more yelling, and I'm surprising myself that I can remember their names. I remember their names today. I remember everything.

I hear the shovel hitting hard on the deck and hear Bobbie stomping her boots. Jonah sits on the floor in front of the television, his hands around a contraption that he presses with great speed and force. On the screen, army men shoot one another with guns.

The little tyke seems to ignore the words between his grandparents. He's grown up with it. Well, so had his grandfather, Tim, with the fights Glad and me used to have all the time.

When I woke up this morning, I remembered. I got up and looked over to my left, and there on my nightstand, underneath the clock, right where Tully had left them, were the instructions she had so patiently written out for me. I picked up the paper and unfolded it.

"Here, Mr. Black," she said last summer. "I'll write it all down for you, how to get your e-mail. So when I'm on my trip to find out where Seth is, I'll e-mail you and you can e-mail me back. We can even IM. And I'll tell you the progress I'm making."

I have the piece of paper in my hand. I've had it with me all morning.

"Can you help me with this?" I finally break into the little tyke's game.

"Help you with what?" He doesn't look up from the beeps and squawks of his game.

"My e-mail. I probably have a lot of messages waiting for me."

I show him the slip of paper Tully had written out for me. "Can you figure out these instructions for me?"

Jonah scans the note. "Sure. This is cinchy, Grandpapa." He puts down the contraption with the buttons and climbs into the chair behind the computer, does some fast typing. "Is this you, Grandpapa? RoryB22?"

"That's me." I say it proudly. "My name's Rory, and my last name's Black, and I was born in 1922."

"Wow!"

I don't know whether the wow is because I'm so old or that an old codger like me actually has e-mail. Jonah's fingers are lightning fast. "Hey! You've even got messages, Grandpapa," he points to the screen. "Who's this," Jonah scrolls down. "NancyDrew2?"

"Can you print them off for me, Jonah?"

"There's *tons* here!"

"Can you print them all off? In big letters so I can read them with these old eyes of mine?"

There are about two dozen messages, and the most recent was sent a month ago. Nothing since then? That worries me, and I run my hand over my stubbly chin.

"Thanks, little tyke," I tell him when the printing is complete. I call the guy *little tyke*. I used to call all my boys *little tyke*.

I sit down with the printed sheets on the couch. When Bobbie comes in, I hear Jonah say to her, "I helped Grandpapa with his e-mail. He got tons from Nancy Drew!"

I gather up my papers and take them into my room. But my mind is misting over. I cannot stop it. I cannot remember.

50

Lenore was still upset about Norman on Monday morning when she went down to collect Earl's and Carl's dirty laundry. It was all that MarieAnn, that's who it was. If it were up to Norman, he would move back here. Having to be out there near her family. Well, wasn't it Lenore's turn by now? And Norman didn't grow up that way. Norman grew up in Fog Point, where family counts for something, where family *means* something. And then he goes away to Bible school and meets that MarieAnn. She was the one putting all these ideas in his head.

She tore the sheets from the beds rather gruffly, ignoring Earl, who was sitting at his computer. "How can you stand the smell down here?" she muttered to her fat son whose backside hung over the sides of his chair.

"Ya get used to it," he mumbled without looking up.

She stuffed the sheets and her sons' dirty laundry, which she had to collect from all over the floor, into her basket. What did he do all day down here, besides eat? There were several empty chip bags around him. Lenore picked up these as well and stuffed them into the black garbage bag she carried.

"I was getting to those," Earl said. Just like when he was a boy. *"I was getting to those."* And as she picked up a bag of Fritos and an empty McDonald's burger container that lay beside him on the floor, she looked up at the computer where Earl was clicking away. She stopped, held herself, put her hand to her chest. The same pink and blue logo she had seen on the folder in Jeanine's suitcase was on the computer screen.

"Oh my! Oh dear! Oh, Earl!" She couldn't keep herself from saying it out loud.

Earl turned toward her. "What?"

"It's just. You…uh…you have so many chip containers on the floor. You should eat more healthy…ah…um…"

"Why should I?" he said.

But she could not move her eyes from the computer screen. It was a giant collage of baby pictures, the ones she'd seen in Jeanine's room. She also saw that—and needed to catch her breath—the picture of Tolita's baby was there. So far Earl hadn't seemed to have missed the original, but what would happen when he realized it wasn't there? She wondered how long Jake and May needed it.

She needed to ask Earl what all this was. Who that baby was. She needed to ask him about this Web site, but she just couldn't formulate the words. Couldn't get them out. "What are you…?"

"Mother? Something the matter?"

She fled upstairs with the laundry basket and garbage bag. Two police officers were knocking on her kitchen door. She gasped, cried out, put her basket and bag down, and put a hand to her heart to stop its rapid beating. Were they here to arrest Earl? Had they come with that search warrant now? She didn't know how Earl was going to get out of this one.

Lenore calmed down enough to answer the door. "Come in, come in," she said opening the door. "Will you have tea and cinnamon swirls?"

"Mrs. Featherjohn," the one named Bill said. "We need to speak with you."

Not again! What did they want this time? "I already told you everything…"

"We're not here to question you this time. This is Guy LaPointe. He's a sketch artist who's come up from Boston."

"A sketch artist…oh my." Lenore put her hand to her chest. She thought of the artists who came in the summer and set up their easels at the gazebo. She looked at him and said, "That's very nice then. An artist." She motioned for them to have a seat.

"We're very interested in a young man who stayed here at your bed-and-breakfast during the time the girl was found outside your house."

She got out her basket of herbal tea bags.

"His name is Mal Barcklay," Bill said.

Lenore remembered the name. Jeanine had written it on that adoption brochure. He was the one with the two different-colored eyes. "Why are you so interested in him?" she asked, arranging cinnamon swirls on one of her grandmother's plates.

"Well," Bill folded his big hands and placed them on the table. "For starters, there is no such person in any of our databases."

"Oh." Early on, she'd given the police a list of all the people who'd stayed with her since Christmas. All the hotels in Fog Point had had to do that. Lenore put the plate on the table. "I don't have his address either. He paid with cash."

Bill spread his hands wide. "Now, do you remember what this guy looked like?"

"He was big with little ears and little eyes. Very strange. I remember thinking his head was too big for all his features. Very odd man. Quiet. And when he did talk, it was with a kind of stutter. I got the idea he was quite shy. Didn't mingle with the other guests. Well, I only had one other guest at the time—Arnold, who comes every year and who is a bit of an oddball himself. So I had the two of them in there not talking. There was something weird about Mr. Barcklay too. Wouldn't look you in the eye. On the last day, I noticed he had two different-colored eyes. It was funny, I didn't notice that until the last day."

Bill leaned forward, studied her when she said that.

"We want to find this guy. We don't know who he is, and that's where we need your help. Guy is going to draw the man's face; we just need your help to fill in the details."

"Oh, my. I've never done this before."

"No problem," said Guy. "We'll talk you through it."

Guy opened up a laptop computer and brought up a rather plain head shape.

"I thought you were an artist," Lenore said.

"I am, but this is mostly done by computers now," he said.

So for the next half hour they tried on various eye shapes, ear shapes, noses, and hair until they ended up with a pretty good facsimile of Mal Barcklay. For her part, Lenore was so happy the focus was off her and onto this new person that she happily complied.

But as they were finishing up the drawing, a new thought began niggling at her. What if they caught the guy and he admitted to killing Tolita, only to tell them he never moved the body to the snowbank? Maybe she shouldn't have been so accurate in her description. She might be implicated in this. She might even go to jail!

51

*I*t's funny how you can fake some things when you know all the right words, the correct language, how to say things. Amy had been born into this life with a language she'd known since childhood. How easily the right language slid off her tongue as she stood in front of a group of women at the Ladies Missionary Circle meeting. The passage for tonight was Matthew 11:28, "Come to me, all you who are weary and burdened, and I will give you rest." Amy stood at the front of the room and spoke. She could do this. She was a teacher after all.

On command she could make herself teach even when all was turmoil at home and in her life. She had learned how to turn all that off and stand up there and go through a math or a spelling lesson. This was no different.

"When we're physically tired, the only thing that will revive us is a good night's sleep," she began. "But what do we do when we're spiritually weary? If you're like me, we just keep on, don't we?" She smiled for effect. "We're mothers, we're wives, we have full-time jobs, *and* we have to come home and make supper. We don't have time to get away on some spiritual retreat, do we?" That got more smiles and nods, a few laughs. "We don't have time to be with Jesus."

Oh, she knew the language all right—that and some help from the Internet late last night and she had the lesson down pat.

"I teach in the public-school system," she said. "And if there's anything that's exhausting, it's that. Oh, those children! They can really tire a person out. Even though I love them to death, my fifth graders…"

She stopped, had to consult her note cards. What had she meant to say here? "…I love them to death and…," and she went on with her prepared speech. In front of her, twenty-five women sat in rapt attention, smiling, their Bibles opened on their laps. Eloise was there, and next to her, Lenore. Amy's eye began to twitch. She touched her eyebrow. Rose Nation was there along with her daughter Pearl, and sitting next to her was Kate Nation, who taught in Amy's school with her. "I was called by God to be a missionary in the public-school system." Those were words that usually shut people up when they asked why she wasn't teaching at a Christian school. "I feel God has called me to make a difference." And as she spoke, she interwove personal anecdotes with humorous stories about weariness. And the women in front of her smiled and nodded and laughed at all the right points.

The truth was, she had entered the school system many years ago with the idea of making a difference, but did she still believe that? She didn't know. It was a job to her now, a job she was good at, but still a job. She'd always been able to make people laugh with her stories. She'd always been happy and jolly, the class clown. Listeners said she could make any Bible passage "come alive." So it wasn't difficult to stand up here and tell them all about a wonderful God who sustained believers during the tough times, who touched the weary and lifted them up.

"When I first chose this path, some well-meaning Christians tried to warn me away from the public-school system, but I always responded with, 'If my faith is that fragile, if my faith cannot withstand the slings and arrows of the world and its beliefs, then it's not a faith worth having.'"

That got a bit of applause from the ladies. Too bad Amy didn't believe it. All along she felt her faith a fragile thing. Even at the Christian college she had attended, she had more questions than answers. But if she married a Christian, especially a minister, certainly that would protect it. Maybe she'd be safe then. And it worked for a while. But now Blaine was a teenager and challenging everything in Amy: her faith, her marriage, and even her own self. Amy didn't know who she was anymore. She didn't know what she believed, what she wanted out of life, even if she'd made the right choice when she'd married Ben.

But when she got right down to it, in her twelve years of teaching in the public-school system, had she made a difference, as she liked to say? Had she led anyone to the Lord? No. Had anyone come to know Christ as a result of her wonderful testimony? No. Had her faith withstood the so-called slings and arrows of modern science and contemporary culture? Not really.

What had she actually learned? The first thing she learned was that Christ doesn't make a difference in marriage. She had always been told that a marriage without the foundation of God was sure to fail. Well, that wasn't exactly true, now, was it? Because a whole lot of Christian marriages supposedly based on the "sure foundation" failed miserably, and many others not based on Christian principles somehow found a way to make it work. The divorce rate among Christians was about the same as the divorce rate among nonchurchgoers. Look at Jake and his ex-wife. They met in Bible school, just like she and Ben had. And then look at Mags and Herman. She had never seen a couple more devoted to each other. She wondered if she and Ben would get along as well as Mags and Herman if they worked side by side, making soup and baking bread, day after day like that. Yet they, by their own admission, felt that all faiths were worthy. Mags once asked her, "These many different belief systems and denominations, couldn't they all be right? Isn't God big enough for that?"

Ben had been with her when Mags asked that, and of course he immediately began to witness about Christ. But Amy had backed away, not saying anything, because a part of her was asking the same question.

The truth was that there were good people throughout the entire world who believed in various religions with just as much reverence as she did. Or used to. And now Blaine was looking into native spirituality, convinced she was part native Indian. Yesterday she had come home, her hair completely dyed black, the blond chunks in the front gone, dream-catcher earrings, and a leather jacket with fringe.

"Where'd you get that?" Amy had asked.

"I bought it. Used."

"Where?"

"Like it's any business of yours."

And her daughter had stalked away, the fringe along the back swaying as she did so.

Jeanine from FNN never called her back. Amy wasn't sure she even expected her to.

"God loves weary people," Amy said as she looked down into the faces of the church women. "Whatever it is you're carrying, it's not too big for God. Let's pray."

After a few moments of prayer led by Amy, the president of the Ladies Missionary Circle, a woman named Beatrice, who wore a frowzy skirt and black rubber boots with buttons on the sides, clapped her hands together and said, "Thank you, Amy. We always enjoy hearing you. It was wonderful to hear what the Lord has laid on your heart." Then she turned to the women. "Ladies, wasn't that *good*?" They all smiled and clapped. "And we'll be praying for you, Amy. God has really put you in a mission field. I never thought of it that way before. Ladies, don't you agree?" And they all clapped their hands again. Amy said thank you and sat down. She could not stop her eye from twitching.

Coffee and food was next. Amy rose, got in line, smiled, and shook hands and hugged ladies, carefully avoiding making eye contact with Lenore Featherjohn, who stood directly behind her at one point. Despite Rube and the board, the rumors of Ben's demise and their impending move were still rampant. In front of Amy was Kate Nation, Rose Nation's niece, who was a first-year teacher in Amy's school.

Later, when Amy was standing by herself, Kate came up to her. "You need to take your own advice, Amy."

Amy steadied herself at the table. "What?"

"You're tired. I can tell. I see you every day in the staff room. I can see it in your eyes now."

Amy chuckled. "Tired, yes. I guess I will have to follow my own advice. Or get some new eye drops."

"But it seems as if something is bothering you, beyond just being tired." Kate said.

Why is she saying these things? "Oh, you know. A few challenges…," Amy said. "A teenager at home. She's fourteen going on twenty. I feel like putting her in a box and leaving her there until she's thirty." Amy chuckled again.

"When I was that age, I gave my mother grief, I tell you."

"She wants to find her birth mother." Amy covered her mouth with her hand then.

"Oh?" Kate looked at her. "Blaine's adopted?"

Amy nodded. "And now she has this big idea…" Amy rubbed her eyebrow, hoping to minimize the eye-twitching.

"Oh, that's just kids," Kate said. "Adopted or not, kids have to find themselves. They all go through this. Did you know my older brother's adopted? Colin? And the Browngreen twins? They're teenagers now. I remember when the Browngreens went to Romania to get them. And Pearl Sweet, she put her baby up for adoption. It takes a special person to take a child and raise her as her own. Amy, you're a very special person." Kate touched Amy's arm. It was all Amy could do to keep from bursting into tears.

52

S o that's all it was." May was crestfallen when Jake told her that Ben had written her name on a slip of paper and given it to Tolita Shenk.

"Apparently," Jake said.

"Well then. I guess that's that."

"May, you'll find the sniper," he said. "He's out there. Two things we learn in police work: there is always someone who knows, and secrets wear on people. Eventually someone will tell that secret."

May sighed. "So Tolita goes to Ben and tells him Blaine's mixed up with the wrong people, people who are stealing babies, and is in some kind of danger. That her whole family is in danger."

"That's about the gist of it. I don't know where the stealing babies thing comes in," Jake said.

The two of them were in the sanctuary of the Purple Church, a place they kept mostly closed up in the winter. Jake was atop a ladder that leaned against the wall near one of the stained-glass windows. They planned on selling it in order to pay for the cross-country skis. When they'd purchased this building, the sellers, who just happened to be the Featherjohn brothers, hadn't realized the value of the stained glass. May immediately did. Their window broker was driving up from Boston this afternoon to take a look.

"Watch yourself on that ladder, Jake. We don't need you crashing through our source of revenue."

"Not to mention what would happen to me."

"What does it look like up there?"

"The window looks good. No flaws that I can see. I think he's going to like it."

So far they'd sold a huge three-paneled stained-glass window that had been at the very front of the church behind the dais. With the price they got for it, they were able to completely renovate the building. Along the sides of the church were tall windows. On one side were the apostles, a window for each one, and on the other were various scenes and portraits depicting the life of Christ: the Nativity, the Crucifixion, the empty tomb, the Ascension. Their appraiser-broker had told them it would be better to sell the apostles as an entire set. He could get a high price for them, higher than what he got for the shepherd and the sheep in the front.

"That'll be our retirement fund," May told Jake.

They'd also sold two side windows, the funds of which had gone into refurbishing *The Purple Whale*, the former lobster boat they used for whale watching, and a dozen rental kayaks.

Jake frowned. "False alarm," he said. "I thought I spotted a crack. But no. It's fine." He looked down to where she was holding the ladder.

"My case notes are still missing, Jake, and I worry, at my age, when I lose things. Did you know my mother had Alzheimer's when she died? She was my age when the symptoms first began."

"May, you're fine. The notebook'll turn up. I wouldn't worry. If I can't read your shorthand, how will anyone else?"

She shrugged.

Jake had his favorites among the windows. He liked the Nativity scene. He didn't even mind the huge halos they all wore. The Crucifixion scene made him wince, but for some reason he didn't want to let that one go any more than he wanted to let the empty tomb scene with the angel go. And then there was the Ascension, although in Jake's estimation, that one had Jesus looking a bit too effeminate.

May? She didn't care about any of the pictures. To her they were nothing but revenue. She wanted to keep a few of the windows as a tourist draw. A whale-watching, sporting-goods store with stained-glass windows of biblical saints was a bit of an oddity, which they played up in their ads.

"I've looked everywhere," she said.

"You're the healthiest person I know," Jake said. "You'll be solving crimes after I'm long gone. Still going strong at ninety. A genuine Miss Marple you'll be. Don't give me any of your guff about your age. Hold the ladder steady. This window looks flawless."

"Maybe we'll be able to pay for the skis and that plumbing fiasco in the basement."

"First we have to sell this thing."

When they got to their office, still talking about stained glass and money and missing notebooks, Carrie had made fresh coffee and was spooning Coffee-mate into a mug.

"Hey," she said when they entered. She grinned at Jake, and he smiled back.

"What's up?" May asked

"I've got some information for you," she said. She opened up a packet of sugar and began to stir it in. "I called FNN—you're going to find this interesting—they have no one in their employ named Jeanine Bowman. Nor Ted Sorensen. They have dispatched no one to Fog Point to cover the story of the angel or the ice. Although now they might," she added.

"Really!" May said.

"So I called a few old friends in Detroit. No one's heard of Jeanine Bowman."

"So she's not from FNN," Jake muttered as he pondered the implications.

Carrie continued, "My old friend at the paper is running her name through the paper's archives. I'll let you know what I find out."

"So," May said, "she's hanging around here in Fog Point, asking a whole bunch of questions, and she's *not* working on a story? What's she up to?"

53

After Carrie left, May pressed the telephone message button. There were two. One was from Colin, asking Jake to come down to Pop's boatyard if he had a chance. It was important, he said. He had Kayla with him, so if Jake wanted to bring Jana, that would be okay. The second was from someone named Doreen Jesper from Barrhead, Alberta. On the way to Pop's with Jana in tow, he called Doreen on his new cell phone. She introduced herself as Tully's foster mother.

"Tully?"

Doreen quietly laughed. She had a gentle voice, soft and calming. "Tolita. That's her name. But everybody knew her as Tully. We were her foster parents for a number of years. I am so, so sorry to hear what happened."

"Are you surprised she was out here?"

"Very." She chuckled again. "I wouldn't have said she even knew where Fog Point was!"

"How long was she with you?"

"Maybe five years. Off and on. She blossomed here on the farm with us. She was a very, very smart girl. Her father died in a farming accident, but the rumors have always been that he took his own life. There was some business deal gone bad with the Shenk brothers. They are a big and powerful family here. Plus there were some allegations of a rape…"

"He raped someone?"

Jana looked over at him, her eyebrows raised.

Doreen continued, "There was a rape in the family, but I don't know who raped who. It's old, old news now, and I don't have the whole story. I don't know which one was blamed—I didn't grow up here, you see. There was a rape, and Henry supposedly pointed the finger at one of his brothers, and the brother retaliated, and Henry killed himself. But the whole story might not even be true. Tully's mother has been in and out of psychiatric wards for all of Tully's growing-up years. I'm afraid Tully Shenk's life has been marked by tragedy. Poor thing. We've had Coralee—that's the mother—out here at the farm a time or two recuperating as well. I always felt sorry for Coralee—she's such a sad, sad soul—and for Tully."

"Some of our information suggests she had a brother. Maybe a younger brother?"

"No. She was very much an only child."

"Why do you say 'very much'?"

"Because her parents could barely take care of one child, let alone two."

Jake thanked Doreen and closed his cell phone. A runaway child, a throwaway child.

He parked behind Pop's boatyard. While he was here, he may as well check on his own boat. Last spring, before launch, he'd repainted the whole thing, but he wanted to have a look at some trouble spots. What he didn't need was for it to sink like Carl and Earl Featherjohn's monstrosity of a schooner that had sunk right at the wharf, just the wooden masts jutting out of the water, while a group of eager whale watchers looked on to see Carl swear and curse about kids from Ridley Harbor who vandalized boats on a regular basis. But everyone knew the real reason it sank: the pumps had stopped running, and so the old wooden boat had simply filled with water.

Colin was at the far end of the boathouse, sanding a sleek kayak with six-hundred-grit sandpaper. He was a craftsman when it came to boats. One of his finest, one that Jake had displayed in the front of the Purple Church, had sold for an exorbitant amount of money.

Colin's daughter, Kayla, sat in a large playpen surrounded by brightly colored plastic toys. Jana immediately went to lift her out.

"Be careful with her," Jake said. "There's lots of sharp stuff around here that she could get hurt on."

The baby took a few steps with the help of Jana, who held the baby's hands in her own.

"I'll be careful, Dad. She likes me to do this with her. Don't you, Kayla? We walk together all the time in the nursery."

"Stay at this end of the building," he said.

Colin looked worried. And while Jana and Kayla walked around the room, Jake said quietly to Colin, "You needed to see me about something?"

"Jake." Colin put his sandpaper on a table and wiped his hands on his jeans, "I asked you to come because Marnie's really freaked. I mean really freaked about that newslady."

Was this the time to tell him she wasn't a newslady? "What's the problem?"

"This morning Marnie's out at the Shop 'n Save with Kayla in the shopping cart there. And Marnie turns around to get a can of peas. And she turns back, and that lady from the news is holding Kayla."

"What?" Jake blinked his eyes.

Colin unscrewed a thermos and poured some coffee into its lid. "You want some coffee? I'm thinking it's probably pretty innocent, but Marnie's totally freaked. She didn't even want to leave Kayla with the sitter when she went to work."

"What did the woman say?"

"Well, Marnie says she screams, and the newslady just laughs and says Kayla was so cute and she loves kids so much. She didn't mean any harm. And she was really sorry, she didn't mean to upset her. But Marnie's so upset, she's telling me we should call the police. But I don't think what she did is any crime. I mean, maybe where she's from, people do that. And she *is* with a news station. So I thought I'd maybe talk to her, so I call the B&B and find out the FNN people have checked out. Then I thought, I'd talk to you."

Jake frowned. Jeanine had checked out of Lenore's?

"I'm thinking of calling FNN, Jake, just to make a complaint. What do you think?"

"That won't do you any good," Jake said. "She's not with FNN and never has been. She's not who she says she is."

At this point Jana and Kayla giggled their way into the conversation. Jana had placed a plastic ring on top of Kayla's head. "Don't you think Kayla looks like an angel?" Jana asked.

As Jake looked at the baby, he was reminded, ever so slightly, of the baby picture Lenore had given them, the baby picture that had looked so familiar to him.

54

I wake from my afternoon nap. I don't know who this little tyke is who is standing at the foot of my bed asking something about e-mails. Is it Roger or Tim?

"Did you read all the Nancy Drew e-mails? Did you, Grandpapa? Did you?"

I look at him blankly. There's something I'm supposed to be remembering. Something important. The little tyke keeps shifting from foot to foot, impatiently. At the foot of my bed and all around me are papers. What are these? Had I slept here all day with all this paper? I sit up, confused, and they crinkle and crunch underneath me.

"Help me," I mutter. "Clean off all these papers. Get rid of this clutter. If Glad comes in now, she'll have my head on a platter. She hates clutter, that woman."

"Grandpapa?"

My head is hurting, and I close my eyes briefly. I can hear movement from somewhere outside this room. Are Reeny and the baby still here? Is the nurse with them? Has she buried the baby in the alders? Has she done that yet? I need to tell someone. She came to Glad with stories that the Shenk boy raped her. Not Henry, but the other one. The one who's mayor now. But it would do no good for it to get around that the mayor raped a poor retarded girl like Reeny. I need to tell Glad this, but there are these papers everywhere. She won't listen to me unless I get this place cleaned up.

And then suddenly a woman comes and puts an arm around the little tyke and leads him out of the room, and he is saying, "But all his e-mails!"

"There are no e-mails. Just scraps of paper. I'll clean them up later when Great-Grandpapa gets up."

"But, Grandma, they're from Nancy Drew…"

"He told you they came from Nancy Drew?" She is quiet for a moment, then she says, "You know, Jonah, how sometimes you get a sore throat or earache? Sometimes your body gets sick. Well, that's what's the matter with Grandpapa, except with Grandpapa, it's his mind that's sick. Sometimes he doesn't think so clearly." Their voices fade. Or maybe I am trying to make sense of them and can't anymore.

I gather up the papers and put them in a pile under my pillow before Glad comes in from planting her peas. I'll get up. Have some coffee with fresh cream. Then I need to get out to the barn. Lots of work to do today. Four new calves were born last night.

When the papers are safely stowed, I call out, "Reeny!" And then it is Reeny who stands there saying to me very firmly, "I'm not Reeny, Dad. Reeny's dead. I'm Bobbie."

"Where's Reeny?"

"She died, Dad. We've been through this. Reeny is dead."

But I can see her so clearly, the way she never looked at you straight in the eye when she talked, but always down.

I look outside the little window in my room to the gray cold, and it surprises me. It should be summer. Glad's out planting peas, isn't she? I remember the hot night when Reeny's baby died. They found Reeny and her baby in the milking barn, Reeny holding and crooning to that little bundle. And then Glad came and wrested the dead thing out of her arms. She didn't want to surrender it. She was wailing by now.

Crib death. That's what Glad said it was.

People said it was a mercy. The little one was a product of a rape. Products of rape never grow up to be much in this life. They're cursed right from the beginning. And Reeny's accusation that it was one of the Shenk boys who raped her was never proved, but Reeny kept insisting.

Even then, you didn't cross the Shenk boys.

No one talked about it after that. But I always wondered whether it was Reeny herself who did something to the baby that night.

That was the beginning of it, I thought. The beginning of the people in Barrhead ignoring the Henry Shenk side of the family.

A graveside service for the baby nobody wanted was performed by the Anglican priest on a day when the sun burned down and scorched all the fields.

Glad was there, too, when the other baby died, the baby Reeny took. But there was no service for that second one, just the nurse burying the poor little boy in the backyard under the alders. I thought it odd that Reeny took the baby from the very people who came to her defense in the rape. Way back then, it was Henry who stood up for Reeny, confronting his brother, wanting him to take responsibility right off the bat. Henry was good then, a good, strong farmer who thought right was right and wrong was wrong. That was before The Terrible Thing happened.

Surrounded by memories, I stand at the window and wait for Glad to come in from the peas.

55

I t was meant to be a date night, just the two of them, away from the kids for a while, away from Charlie and his video games, away from Blaine and all her problems, and even away from everything that had been happening in Fog Point of late. Amy looked across at her husband in one of Ridley Harbor's fanciest restaurants and wondered if she loved him anymore. If she had to name a time and a place when she came to this understanding, she wouldn't be able to. Maybe she was working too hard at school. Add to that the pressures of having to be home every evening by herself, night after night, helping the kids with their homework and putting them to bed while Ben headed to another church meeting. Possibly it was having to be the perfect minister's wife and feeling that she never ever measured up, no matter what she did. Perhaps it was having too many questions and not enough answers. Maybe it was the slow realization that whatever spark of Christian faith she possessed as a youngster was dangerously close to being extinguished. No, there was no specific time or date for what owned her now.

Across from her, Ben's head was bent into the menu, and he was frowning.

She wasn't particularly hungry, and nothing on the menu appealed to her. Crab-stuffed chicken breasts, filet mignon, mushroom caps, the finest of wines, mussels in white wine sauce, veal medallions, and all she kept thinking and worrying about was Blaine. When they left the house, Blaine had been in deep conversation on her cell phone. She was watching Charlie for the night.

That worried Amy. Could she trust Blaine not to run off and leave her little brother? Could she really trust her as a baby-sitter anymore?

Last night Blaine had been out until quarter to one with no explanation of where she had been. Amy and Ben had been frantic, especially Ben, who had yelled while he paced in front of her. Even Amy was surprised at the harshness of his outburst. And, of course, this resulted in a lot of slammed doors by Blaine. Later, when they were alone, Amy had said, "Don't you think you went a bit overboard with her?"

He was sitting on the edge of the bed, leaning forward, his face in his hands. "There are things—" His voice broke. "Things you don't know…"

"So, *tell* me, then!"

He looked at her helplessly. Then he got up, brushed his teeth, and climbed into bed beside her, without praying. She turned away from him.

And now they were on a nice little date night.

A candle on the table flickered, shadowing Ben's face. "Amy? Do you know what you want yet?"

She shook her head.

"I know you're concerned about Blaine—we both are."

She managed a smile and ended up ordering crab-stuffed chicken breasts.

"If it's any consolation," he said after their waiter left. "I think the rumors of our moving have pretty well died down."

"But these rumors start, Ben, they start in the first place when one or two or a dozen people aren't happy. If everyone loved us here, there would be no rumors."

Ben covered her hand with his. Soft music was playing, and their waiter came with a basket of bread and a bottle of wine. Amy said, "Maybe we *should* move." She looked away from him. "Get away from everything. Start over. Start completely over."

She pulled her hand away from his, chose a whole wheat roll from the basket, and spread butter all the way to the edges, making sure every milli-meter was covered.

He looked so sad, so little-boy-like as he looked at her. "Are you that unhappy here, Amy? Do you really think we should move?" He paused, then said quietly, more to himself than to her it seemed, "I could, you know. I could call the denomination office tomorrow. See what's out there."

She didn't respond. Did she really want to move, or was she just testing him? She had a good job here, a job she was good at, a job she liked. It wasn't so easy to move into a new place and get a teaching job as good as the one she had here.

"I don't know," she said. "Maybe not..."

They didn't say anything for a while. When their salads came, Ben said, "I brought you here because I need to tell you why I've been so crazy as far as Blaine is concerned. Maybe overly protective, or too much of a disciplinar-ian. I know you've been hurt, and I want to explain."

Amy met his eyes.

He placed his salad fork neatly beside his plate and wiped his hands on his napkin before he began. "I never told you this," he said. "And I'm sorry. But the girl who died, she came to see me at the church. I didn't know she'd talked to Blaine. I didn't know any of it then. I thought she was a crazy friend of Blaine's who was playing some sort of a practical joke." He stopped for a moment. His eyes looked ghostly in the candlelight. "She wanted to come back the next day and tell me something. She had something important to show me. She said it concerned Blaine. I forgot about it when she didn't show up. I figured it was all a joke. Then a couple of days later, I found out she was dead."

He told her everything he had told Jake and the police, leaving nothing out, and by the time he finished, Amy felt as if a rock had lodged in her stom-ach. She couldn't move. She couldn't look at him. She couldn't even breathe.

"But I don't…" he stopped, blinked, picked up his salad fork, placed it down again. There was the twinkle of laughter from another table. "I don't know what any of this has to do with Blaine. That's the part I don't understand. That's the part the police don't understand."

Amy looked at him and said quietly, evenly, "Maybe I know."

Their waiter came, saw they hadn't finished their salads, so smiled and left again.

"I believe," Amy began again, her voice barely a whisper, "that Jeanine, that woman from the TV, is Blaine's mother. I'm quite sure of it. That could be the key to this whole thing,"

"But that's not possible. I've seen her. She could be Blaine's grandmother."

"I've thought about this, Ben. People give up babies for adoption for all sorts of reasons. Maybe being too old to raise a child is as good a reason as being too young."

"But what does Tolita have to do with it? The girl who died?

"I don't know."

They finished their salads. When their main courses arrived, Ben said, "None of this makes any sense, you know."

"I know."

Over dessert, Ben put his hand on hers again. "Maybe getting all this out is just what we need. We can work together on this. We can pray together on this. Now that we know what we're dealing with."

"But," Amy paused. "There's something else…"

"What? It's okay, Amy. Is there something more about Blaine?"

"No. Ben, I don't know how to say this, but I will, I just will." She took a deep breath. "Ben…" What she meant to say was, *I don't believe in God anymore.* But what came out was, "Lately, I've been having a little trouble with my prayer life." Certainly that was true. Not the whole thing, but true enough. A starting point.

He took her hand again. "I think that happens to everyone, that feeling that your prayers aren't making it through the walls. Or that God isn't listening. I feel that way sometimes. Maybe this is something we could work on together. I admit I've been feeling out of my element with Blaine lately, but we both love God. That's the starting point."

But Amy wasn't looking at him. She dipped her spoon into the crème brûlée. Who does a minister's wife talk to when she doesn't believe in God anymore?

56

L enore was polishing her grandmother's silver when the police came yet again. She'd been thinking about the minister's wife. She knew Amy didn't care for her, the way she never spoke to her in church. Lenore was at church just like everyone else, just to learn about God. What was wrong with everyone that they got upset at her when all she was doing was minding her own business? She sniffed and dumped more polish onto the decorative edges of the tray. The other night, at the Ladies Missionary Circle meeting, Amy had given a really good message, and Lenore had purposely gotten in line behind her. She'd wanted to say how much she enjoyed it. She also wanted to apologize about Sunday. Carl had told her Amy had stopped by to see her, but he said that Lenore couldn't be disturbed, as she was taking a long-distance call. But Lenore would have come out of her room and made tea if she'd known. Lenore was also sorry about the rumor. She knew now that Norman wouldn't come here. The whole thing had been a mistake. She had made a mistake. And this realization was a new emotion for her. Where had it come from? Lenore didn't know. So she got in line behind her in church, but Amy never even turned around. She must've seen her there, yet she hadn't acknowledged Lenore's presence at all. Lenore eventually moved to stand with some ladies who would talk with her, Eloise and Enid.

When the police knocked on the door again, she sighed, put down her rag, wiped her hands on her apron, and let them in.

It was Bill and a young man she hadn't met before. She just went to the counter and plugged in the kettle. One of these days they would quit coming around.

Bill cleared his throat. "You did a great job with the sketch artist."

"Thank you."

"Now we're interested in the two from FNN."

"They checked out a couple of days ago." She put her basket of herbal tea bags on the counter. "I'm making tea, and there's coffee in the pot."

Bill got up, pulled two mugs out of the cupboard, and poured two coffees. He'd been here so many times, he knew where everything was. He gave one to the other officer who introduced himself as Stu. They sat down again. Lenore remained standing.

She said, "But I have to tell you I was quite surprised when they checked out, particularly since they were paid up for two more days."

Stu wrote that in his notebook.

"It was nice that FNN chose this place," she said. I've never had celebrities stay here before. CNN came, but I don't think they stayed anywhere overnight. They just whipped in, took pictures of the snowbank, and whipped out again. The people from FNN just stayed and stayed."

Even as she said it, she was glad Jeanine and her snooping ways were gone from her house. Hopefully, whatever story she was working on would never be on the air. She'd had FNN on all day and hadn't heard any stories about Fog Point. Good! Maybe Lenore could escape going to prison after all.

They wanted to see the registration book and the guest book, so she got them from her front hall.

Then Bill asked her, "Was there anything strange about them? Did you have any trouble with them? Anything strike you as strange or odd behavior?"

Lenore thought about Jeanine's snooping through Earl's computer and also all the baby pictures she'd found, but said sweetly, "No, nothing. They were wonderful guests."

The police took the guest card Jeanine and Ted had filled out when they'd checked in. They were also interested in the Visa number they used.

"Why are you interested in the people from FNN?"

"Because they're not from FNN," Bill said.

She blinked at them. "What? Who are they then?"

"That's what we're trying to determine."

"Oh dear, oh my." She put a hand to her chest. What was Jeanine doing on Earl's computer if it wasn't a story about the girl?

57

I think I have figured out where your picture was taken and maybe when."
The photo expert, someone named Emory Royale, was on the phone.

"Great," Jake said. "I'm taking notes."

"Ah, no. No no. I need to *show* you. And also give you a bit of a lesson on how dating is done. You can really do it on your own if you know how. You're a private investigator, right? I could give you some tips."

Twenty minutes later, Jake and Jana were in the car and driving through recently plowed roads out to the highway, then a right at the first exit, and eventually down a crooked road that led to Emory's place, "a lovely little spot in the woods," as he said. As they picked their way down the ice-encrusted, rutted, snow-covered dirt path that served as Emory's driveway, Jake was glad he had a truck. At times the road narrowed so much it looked as if they were being welcomed into a lair of snow-covered bones.

"Are we on the right road, Dad?" Jana asked when a branch whipped and scratched at their windshield.

"I think so."

She looked out the window. "I love being on an adventure with you. I used to love Nancy Drew, you know."

"There's a world of difference between Nancy Drew and real life."

"I know."

"And I would never take you on an adventure that was remotely dangerous…"

At that, the truck thunked over an icy root, and Jana said, "So much for not being dangerous."

But finally, just as Emory said, the road widened into a clearing, and in the middle of the clearing stood a tall, narrow three-story house that looked suspiciously like the Bates Motel.

Emory opened the door before they had a chance to knock. "Hello!" he said, clapping his hands. "Hello. Come in. Hello. Come in. Welcome to my warren."

He was small and chubby and wore a plaid shirt. A pair of glasses perched on the top of his head caused bunches of his hair to stand up crazily. Jana blinked and looked at her father, a bit of a smile in the corner of her mouth. Jake winked down at her. Father and daughter entered through his front hall and into an alternate reality.

The rambling house was piled high with the paraphernalia of his trade. Coffee tables, card tables, chairs, upended boxes were all heaped with cameras and camera equipment. Photographs covered every spare inch of wall space. The subject of the photos ranged from people to still lifes to storms and scenery.

One coffee table was piled with old, black, boxy cameras. Jake thought he recognized some from the seventies. Another table seemed to be devoted to thirty-five millimeter cameras and telephoto lenses. They looked scratched and old. A cluster of tripods leaned against the fireplace like pokers, and a box of what looked like undeveloped film sat in a shoe box just in front of the grate.

"Come, come, come," Emory moved quickly through the house on tiptoe, clapping every so often.

"Wow," Jana uttered. "You have lots of cameras."

"They're all for sale," he said. "I buy and sell cameras. On eBay."

"Do you take pictures with all these?" Jana asked.

"Oh, I have my favorites for that. But I don't take a lot of pictures, anyway."

"What about all the pictures on the walls?" Jana said, looking around her.

"Oh, those aren't mine. I buy photographs I like. I like the cameras, and I like to examine photographs. Vintage ones."

"What about the picture I gave you?" Jake asked.

"Your picture. Yes, your picture. More than twenty years old, I would say. At least twenty. I'm thinking between twenty-five and twenty-eight. I must tell you, I found your snapshot quite a challenge."

"It's old?" Jake stopped. "We were under the impression that this was a baby."

"Well, it is a baby. In the picture anyway. So, obviously it used to be a baby." And he chuckled. "But whoever he is, he's not a baby now. Come with me."

They followed him into the small room off the kitchen. Like the others, the walls were thumbtacked all around with photos. There were also several large sinks, leading Jake to think this had been a darkroom at one point. Emory led them to a draftsman's table. Above it, the baby picture was held to a corkboard by tiny straight pins.

"Okay, now, do you see the slight reddening of the image?" He handed Jake a magnifying glass. "Come closer. Have a look. Do you see it?"

Jake bent forward. "I noticed that. I thought that might be from being in a wallet too long."

"That might account for some of it. But sometimes photos take on a reddish tinge with age. And I'll bet my bottom dollar"—he tapped a finger on the corkboard—"this was taken with a thirty-five millimeter camera, which are a dime a dozen, and were back then, too."

"So why else do you think it's old?"

Emory put his hand up. "We can get a certain amount from the photo itself: the type of paper it was printed on, the size, whether it has a date printed along the side..." He winked at Jana. "That's always a great help. But more often we look to context, what else was in the picture at the time, that sort of thing. Do you see this metal bar in the corner?"

"I wondered about that."

"I've taken my magnifying glass to it, and I'm fairly certain it's the edge of a baby carrier and guess what! They're all plastic now and have been for quite a while. Here, take a look." He opened a laptop computer, and with a couple of clicks they were online and looking at baby carriers. "I'm guessing by this Web site that this baby carrier was manufactured around 1980, maybe a bit before. Plus the style of T-shirt sleeper."

"A baby T-shirt has a style?" Jake said.

"Oh yes. I don't know a lot about babies, but in looking up baby styles, I found that the split-neck style and that pattern print of circles haven't been made for many years."

"Did you find out when it was made?"

Emory shook his head. "I'm not that good. Often it's a process of elimination. Now, if the mother took some fabric from wherever and sewed her own baby clothes, then everything's out the window. But I would say that based on the reddish tinge, the size of photo, the style of baby clothes, and the fact that he's in a metal baby carrier, the baby you're looking for is more than twenty-five years old."

"So this baby we're looking at is a twenty-five-year-old man."

"Right!" Emory said grinning and clapping his hands once. "Or maybe even older."

58

To RoryB22—

I'm at an Internet café. Bus ride is long. I'll write more later.
NancyDrew2

To RoryB22—

If it wasn't for the book and stuff you gave me, I'd be
nowhere! Thanks so much. It's a long trip across the country. But I've made it! Bus was boring. I have the books and
the pictures and am keeping them hidden.
NancyDrew2

To RoryB22—

I'm here! I'm in Fog Point! Whew, what a trip. I haven't
met the woman from the Web site yet, but your book is
safe. I made sure of that!
NancyDrew2

To RoryB22—

She's still not here. Well, I'm here earlier than I said
I would be. I'm getting a bit nervous. Thanks for all the

money you gave me for this trip. I'm being careful with
it. And as soon as I find Seth, I'm planning on going
back to Vancouver and getting a job. I promise I'll pay you
back.

NancyDrew2

Dear RoryB22—

I'm getting nervous. That woman hasn't come yet. I've
still got the book. She said no police, so I haven't called
them.

NancyDrew2

Dear RoryB22—

They're letting me use the computer at the Dew Drop
Inn. Please write. I'm getting sort of scared. I met with B.
Also, the ring, although I don't know why that's so impor-
tant. Please write!

NancyDrew2

Dear RoryB22—

People are following me. Please write.

NancyDrew2

Dear RoryB22—

I spoke to B's father. Still haven't gone to the police,
and I've told everyone not to, but will you do me a favor? If I
don't e-mail you in two days, will you call the police? I don't
know who to trust.

NancyDrew2

The woman whose name I remembered this morning as Bobbie is standing in my bedroom holding a fistful of paper. "What have you got yourself mixed up in, Dad? What *is* all this?" She waves the papers under my nose and says, "Dad, what is this? Who *are* these people?"

It's the girl. It's Tully. I am remembering now. Tully who I thought was gone. "Tully," I say. "It's Tully."

"Tully!" Bobbie says. "What do you mean, it's Tully? You mean Tully Shenk? Tolita Shenk from town?"

I nod. "She was here last summer. I told you."

"What do you mean she was here last summer?"

Little tyke is standing behind his grandmother now, looking around at me.

"I told her about Reeny."

"What does Reeny have to do with anything, Dad?"

"Reeny took the baby."

"What baby? What are you talking about?"

"Tully is looking for the baby. And she's found him, but it's dangerous. We have to find Tully. Call the police. She wants us to call the police now. There are people who want to kill her."

59

The three of them—Jake, May, and Jana—were in the kitchen of the Purple Church, drinking hot chocolate and eating microwave popcorn, while outside the wind blew against the building. With the heat cranked up, the high windows along the wall were steamy. Jana had hooked her iPod into small speakers, and they were listening to ZOEgirl. On the table was Jake's model boat, spread out on a sheet of newspaper. Jana was painting a miniature sailor with a paint brush so tiny it only had three or four bristles.

Jake had gotten out his tugboat to try to clear his mind. He now had more questions that demanded answers. The baby they had assumed was Tully's was in his mid- to late-twenties. The police were looking for Mal Barcklay, whose picture was being plastered all over the news. Jeanine and Ted, who weren't Jeanine and Ted, had checked out of Lenore's B&B and effectively disappeared from the planet. And the fact that Tully had been looking for her brother also had the police looking for a mysterious older brother, even though Tully was an only child.

The police sketch of Mal Barclay was on the table in front of May, and she drummed her fingers along the sides of it.

She looked up at them, "You want to hear the latest?" May said, picking up her hot-chocolate mug. "No one in the Shenk family has come forward to claim the body. They all know it's her, but no one wants to take responsibility for her. Or pay for anything."

"What about her mother?" Jake asked, looking up from his boat.

"Coralee's her name, and apparently she doesn't have two dimes to rub together. She's appealing to her so-called family to help. Which includes the mayor. There was some sort of falling-out a long time ago between her dead husband and his brothers. Talk about your Hatfields and McCoys."

She rubbed her knee. Even through her jeans, it looked swollen. Jake worried about his friend. When she was involved in a case, everything else, including taking care of her health, took a backseat.

"So, what will happen to her?" Jana asked.

May shrugged. "The information I got from the police is that Doreen Jesper and her husband will be paying for the body transport and the burial costs. What is it with these Shenk people anyway? I'd like to go out there and throttle the lot of them. Don't these people realize family is everything? Family is not to be taken lightly." She took off her glasses and rubbed her eyes.

This outburst was interesting, coming from May, who had no family and spent Christmas with him and Jana. In their four-year partnership, he hadn't met one relative of May's. Yet he understood. Jana and Alex were the reason he came home from the Caribbean. After Connie left him, Jake quit the police force, walked away from God, climbed aboard his sailboat *Constant,* and took off down the coast. A year later he was in the Caribbean living on rum punches and living the life depicted in Jimmy Buffet's "Margaritaville." One morning he woke up and couldn't remember what his daughters looked like. He went ashore and called his old house from a pay phone. After a pause, Connie said no, he could not speak to Jana and Alex. She would not allow that. Other words were spoken, like where had he been for Christmas and birthdays? No cards? No presents? No financial support? Who did he think he was to phone out of the blue and ask to speak to them now? There was no way on God's green earth that this deadbeat dad would ever be allowed near his daughters again, and furthermore, Keith had filed adoption papers. He had a pretty good chance, too, of adopting Jana and Alexandra, considering Jake's total noninvolvement and lack of support.

That afternoon Jake sat in the cockpit of his boat in the eye-splitting splendor of the Caribbean and cried into his fists for an hour. In two days his boat was ready and provisioned, and he started the trip up through the Caribbean into the Bahamas, across to Florida, and up the coast. He was ready to do whatever it took to get his daughters back. Yes, family was important.

"We could do that, couldn't we?" Jana said. "We could have a funeral for her? How much would it cost?" Jana held up a tiny figure to the light to dab a bit of blue onto his jacket. "I think Reverend McLaren should do the funeral and she should be buried here. I think we should be her family."

May said, "There's a lot more involved than just saying you'll do it. It's a lot like custody of a living person. You can't always get what you want. So she was a runaway. So she wasn't the top of the heap. So the family's nutso about some stupid thing, whatever it is, that happened years ago. Tully is still family."

Jana said, "What about her brother?" She got up and put another bag of popcorn in the microwave. "Tully told Blaine she was looking for her brother. Does her brother know who she is?"

"Her brother," May grunted. "Now that's a whole other jar of pickles. You want to hear my latest theory?" She put the photograph of the baby picture down next to the artist's sketch of Mal Barcklay. "Are these one and the same? Is Mal Barcklay our mysterious grown-up baby? Tolita Shenk's brother? Is he the one she came here looking for? And did she unfortunately find him?"

60

"You had a brother," I told Tully a week before she left. "Your parents named him Seth. He disappeared during a baby shower many years ago, a long time ago now."

It was warm and summer, and we were sitting on a log at the front of the barn. From where we sat, we could see the whole farm spread out—the patchwork fields, the barns and the outbuildings, the garden, the two dark blue silos. I remember her freckles and her face in the light of that sunny morning. I remember her hair that hung in a ponytail over one shoulder. She had a thick blue elastic band around her thumb, the kind they put around broccoli. She kept playing with it, snapping it. I was hot. Hot and dry. Like the weather.

"Your mother never told you about him?" I asked, although I knew the answer. It was something no one talked about. No Shenk, certainly.

Tully looked away from me. I could tell she wasn't sure she believed me, the way her eyes didn't meet mine, the way she snapped the elastic. Well, why should she? I'm an old man who's outlived my allotment of years on the planet. "You should believe me," I said to her. "Because I'm telling the truth."

"I know you're telling me the truth." She said it quietly. "It makes sense. It's the first thing that's made sense in my whole stupid life. I knew there was something. No one would tell me. Not my mother. No one." She turned to me. "His name was Seth?"

I nodded. "Seth."

"And he got lost at a baby shower?"

I nodded again.

She leaned forward and put her hand on my knee. It was unexpected, and her hand felt warm, like a heating pad. The sudden contact electrified me. My own grandchildren, they weren't like that. No one touched in this family. No hugs. Well, they got all that from Glad. Her legacy. I looked down at her small round hand, the skin so smooth.

"How could a baby get lost at a baby shower?" she asked.

"It was a community one," I told her. "They had them then in the old community hall, the one they use for bingo now. Everyone from this end of the lake got together for baby showers, and the baby was passed from lap to lap." I didn't tell her that this baby shower represented the coming together of two feuding factions of the Shenks. It was kind of like a starting-over place. That Reeny was actually there, at this baby shower, that she was actually allowed to attend, was something in itself. And this baby, Seth, represented all of that, a healing in the community.

Reeny's baby was dead. The accusations that had flown hot through the whole of the previous two years were dying. People wanted healing. They wanted to put it all behind them. The Shenk boy, the one who was accused, was newly married and was farming with his brothers. He didn't need that hanging over his head for the rest of his life. He's the mayor now. I didn't tell any of this to Tully. I would later, but not now, not while we sat on the log and the insects whined high and loud in the trees.

"You were there?" Tully asked.

I shook my head. "That was just a thing for the ladies then. How old are you, Tully?"

"I just turned eighteen."

I nodded. She was born eight years after her brother disappeared. Eight years of looking, eight years of hiring private investigators and following leads and tips until finally they gave up. Then Coralee and Henry decided to have another child. I remembered the day Glad told me. It was an afternoon on a day much like this, a summer day, a day when the insects droned in the fields and the tomatoes on the vine were warm to the touch. "Henry and Coralee are having another baby," she said.

I didn't say anything.

Glad was sitting out by the barn, shelling peas and throwing the pods into a bucket for the chickens. " 'Bout time those two got on with their lives. Another child will do them good. That Coralee, she just can't get over it, but Henry, he's getting a handle on his drinking now. This'll be good for them. Another child."

I still didn't say anything. I was remembering what happened and my part in it, how I'd helped Reeny and Glad, how by my silence I hadn't done what was right.

"Don't you just stand there not talking to me!" The peas snapped between sturdy, hard fingers. "Don't you stand there pretending to be all honorable and good. That baby died. There was nothing to be done about it. And you're just as much to blame as me."

I walked away from her.

A year later the cancer came for Glad. She never saw the baby, Tully. Not once.

I didn't tell any of this to Tully. I thought about it, with Tully sitting in the same place Glad was that day when she was shelling peas in her wide cotton apron.

"Both of them were heartbroken," I said. "They looked and looked. So did the police. Someone even hired a private investigator. I remember that. But it was like the baby just vanished. No one ever found your brother."

"My brother." She shook her head. "I had a brother. I thought maybe my mother had miscarriages before I was born. Not this. It all makes sense now." She snapped the elastic harder now. "Because you know what I was? I was the replacement child. But it didn't work out so well, because my father got thrown into his combine, and my mother had her many nervous breakdowns, and I ended up living with strangers my whole life."

"Your father didn't die that way." I needed to tell her more of the truth. "He killed himself, shot himself. He just couldn't cope with the loss of your brother."

She stood up suddenly. "But what about me? What about the loss of me! He lost me. They both did! I never understood why my mother could never love me."

After a few minutes, she said, "I've never even seen a picture of him. My brother. Seth."

"I have some things," I said. I told her to wait, and I got up and went into the coolness of the house. I went into my little room off the family room and dug in the back of my closet for the book and the pictures and the film and the ring I'd kept all these years. I gave her everything, and she sat and looked at the picture of her mother holding baby Seth.

The brother she'd been robbed of by me and Glad and Reeny.

There were times after Glad died when I would walk along the place under the alders. Did the nurse put the baby in a wooden box? Glad never told me, and I never asked. All I knew was that the baby had been buried under the alders at the back edge of the house. I would kneel there sometimes and pray for the poor baby's soul. Sometimes I think about that nurse. She worked at a Christian home for unwed mothers in Edmonton that our church supported. She was just out of nursing school. Once when she left her ring in the soap dish in the bathroom, I put it in my pocket.

It's winter today, and I can't seem to find the energy to get out of bed, so I lie here and think about long-ago things. These are the things that are clear to me, when everything else isn't. I can't remember the names of the people who come into my room and lift spoonfuls of tomato soup to my mouth, but I can remember things long past. After Glad died, Bobbie took over the house and decided to build a gazebo out there under the alders. I tried to tell them no. No! What if they found that poor baby's bones? What if he was really there? What would happen to the farm? And to us? *And to me?*

I kept trying to persuade them not to build there. Anyplace else. Not there. But once Bobbie gets an idea, nothing else will do.

They called the contractors, who dug a foundation. I sat on the porch in a rocking chair, playing with a piece of string and waiting. But they never found the body that day.

I guess that's when I really began to wonder if the baby had actually died. It was something I'd suspected, something I'd thought about, but did this prove it? I had never seen the dead baby. I had never seen anyone digging out there, had never seen any evidence of the earth being dug up, no tamped-down places under the trees. It was then I began writing down my account of what happened in a school notebook I bought down at the pharmacy. I had other things, too. Her ring. And of course the film I'd never developed.

Things are hazy in my mind this morning. A woman who is a stranger to me contrives to spoon soup into my mouth. I'm having trouble swallowing. I don't know when that simple action became difficult, all consuming, a mission, something to accomplish and feel proud about afterward. She clinks the spoon against the bowl in an impatient gesture.

"Come on, Dad, eat up. You can do it."

I look at her face, and it's the face of Reeny. I won't eat. Not if it's Reeny who's holding the spoon. And she drops the spoon, and the red tomato soup slops over the side.

It looks like blood.

61

Amy drove directly to Lenore's after school. She knew that if she got home and began supper and got started on all the evening things she did every day, she'd never get back to Lenore's. Ben would surely talk her out of it. Last evening, after their dinner, she'd turned on the late news and learned that Jeanine and Ted were wanted by the police for questioning. They were not with FNN, nor were their names Jeanine and Ted. Their Visa card, which they'd used in a number of business establishments in Fog Point, had been stolen. Surprise, surprise. Ben had persuaded her not to go to the police with her conviction that Jeanine was Blaine's biological mother. In light of this new development, he was sure that Jeanine was not Blaine's mother, but Amy still wondered about that. What did she want with their daughter?

Because of this perceived thread, she and Ben had decided they needed to watch Blaine. They weren't convinced that a police car driving by every so often constituted safety for their daughter or their family. Ben would drive her to school in Ridley, and they would take turns picking her up. Until the police found Jeanine or this other fellow they were looking for, they wouldn't let their daughter out of their sight. Of course, Blaine called the whole idea stupid, but Amy saw something in Blaine's eyes that looked like relief.

And now Amy needed to talk with Lenore. Maybe the woman knew something about Jeanine that she didn't even know she knew. Maybe, too, it was time to have a chat with the woman who'd caused her and Ben so much heartache with her rumors and her complaints about the church furniture and all the things Ben had ever tried to do in this church.

It was misty out, and the cold hung on the tree branches like a living, writhing thing. The frost fogged her windshield, and the engine of her car sounded far away. She thought about Blaine as she drove. And she thought about Ben. How she missed them both. She missed the way they used to be—Blaine, the pretty dark-haired little girl who sang the loudest in the Sunday school class in her patent-leather shoes. She also missed her husband. She missed the long-ago Ben who shared everything with her, the team they were back then. During their night out, he tried to open up. She could sense that. Yet he'd kept so many secrets from her. Had she become someone he couldn't trust with the truth? Someone he thought too weak to handle hard things? He seemed able to tell Jake things he couldn't tell her—what kind of a marriage was that, where others knew more than she did about her own husband?

Yet she kept her own secret. When was she going to trust Ben enough to tell him the most important secret of her life?

As she neared Lenore's B&B, she began to think about the woman. She knew a little of Lenore's history, how she'd married an alcoholic and was forever trying to live that down. Well, things could be worse for Amy, couldn't they? At least she had Ben. Maybe it was time to give everyone around her—Blaine, Ben, and now Lenore—a bit of the benefit of the doubt.

She turned into the B&B driveway and parked next to the woman's big Lincoln Town Car. Several bouquets of flowers, frozen in the snow, and a few teddy bears dotted the snowbank. She faced the door and knocked. No answer. She waited, lifted the huge brass knocker again. Still no answer.

Lenore's back porch ran the full length of her house. Amy walked to the end of it and tried to peer into the various windows. Nothing at the far window. But at the kitchen window she saw Lenore at the table, her head bowed in her hands. Praying? Amy watched her for several seconds, envious of anyone's ability to pray for answers. In front of her on the kitchen table was a small decorative box.

Lenore looked up, and Amy waved through the glass. Lenore seemed confused. Almost flustered. She put a lid on the box, got up, grabbed a Kleenex, and blew her nose before she finally answered the door.

"Yes?" Surprise glittered in the woman's eyes as she let her in. Frizzy red hair showed white roots all around. She kept blinking as if she were trying to rid her eyes of tears.

Amy took a deep breath. "Lenore...I—"

"Come in. I'll get some tea on."

"I'd like to talk to you about Jeanine."

"I'm afraid she's checked out, dear."

"I heard that on the news. I just need to know if you know anything about her, or if she ever talked about Blaine."

Lenore looked at her confused. "Blaine?"

"Yes, my daughter, Blaine."

"I know the name of your daughter, but why do you ask about her in connection with the woman from FNN? Correction, the woman who pretended she was with FNN."

"She spoke with her on several occasions. I just wondered if there was anything in her belongings about Blaine or if she ever mentioned Blaine."

Lenore seemed about to say something and then didn't. "I'm afraid not, dear. Well, there's the kettle. You'll have tea? Sure you will." Lenore fluttered her badly manicured nails toward the kettle. "Have a seat, dear. I'll get the tea things."

Amy sat down in front of the box she had seen from the window, a decorative keepsake box covered in gaudy tulips.

"I've got fresh-baked scones," Lenore singsonged. "Just made them today. I'll set some out, and you can help yourself. Clotted cream, too. It's a nice afternoon snack."

Next to the box on the table was a photo of a little girl, around four, maybe five, wearing a VeggieTales T-shirt. Her dark hair made Amy think of Blaine at that age. Blaine playing the piano at her piano recital. Blaine racing home to show her mother the stone she'd found. Blaine riding atop Ben's shoulders.

Amy picked up the photo. It made her sad suddenly, but she kept looking at it, thinking of Blaine, wondering if Blaine was in trouble.

"That's my granddaughter," Lenore said brightly. "Isn't she beautiful? Her name is Alyssa." She put a plate of buttered scones on the table.

Lenore poured boiling water into the teakettle. Then quietly she said, "You'd think a son would at least live close to his mother, wouldn't you? There should be an open-door policy when it comes to family, don't you think?"

She turned back to the counter after she said this. Amy put the picture down. She didn't know whether Lenore was addressing her or talking to herself, so she didn't say anything.

Lenore put the tea service in front of Amy with a thump of its silver tray. "I didn't mean to say that. My son Norman is a wonderful man of God who is serving the Lord. My daughter-in-law is quite thoughtful. She always remembers to send pictures of the children. I got that one just this morning. I just printed it off. It was waiting for me at my computer after I finished my morning chores." She took a hand and ran it through her no-style hair.

Amy put the picture down.

"Did you know that Norman is a minister in a megachurch? Imagine if everyone in the entire town of Fog Point went to the same church. That's how big his church is. He's very successful." She looked up. "Do you know the head minister of his church? Maybe your husband does. He's very famous and writes books." She looked down at the picture of the little girl when she said this. "I know he relies on Norman a great deal. They have twenty ministers there. MarieAnn—that's Norman's wife—she manages the Christian bookstore that's part of their church. She always sends me a copy of his books when they come out." She turned and looked toward the snow. "They're so busy out there. Busy, busy, busy," she said, her voice lilting up at the end.

Amy said, "Lenore, I need to be upfront about something with you. We really need to talk—"

"Oh, where's my head? We need the peach jam. You can't have scones without peach jam, can you?"

"You must enjoy your grandchildren very much," Amy said.

Lenore brightened. "I do. I *do*. I get pictures every Christmas. And that VeggieTales shirt? I bought her that. I got it over at the Christian bookstore in Ridley. And MarieAnn took a picture of her in it to send me. That's how thoughtful my daughter-in-law is. Plus, their school pictures. I get those every year too. For Christmas. I can always count on their school pictures for Christmas. And just a little while ago, not more than half an hour before you knocked on the door, I got video camera pictures of them. Right on the computer. Little Alyssa dancing. You should see her! I have three grandchildren. Jonathan, he's how old now? Oh my, he must be nine by now." Lenore counted on her fingers. "How time flies! The last time I saw him, he was three. Jonathan's on the swimming team. And then there's Bradley. He's seven. He was just a baby when I saw him last. Oh my, he was barely walking. But he's a little water rat too. He plays Little League. They have a children's team at the church. They're so involved in the church. Busy little bees, they are."

Amy put down the picture. "You've never seen this little girl in person, have you?"

"I get lots of pictures. My daughter-in-law is so thoughtful that way. I got a whole new batch just the other day, and I get Earl to print them all off for me. And they send me Christmas presents, usually handmade by the children. And always something for my birthday and Mother's Day."

Amy stared at this woman, not comprehending. Certainly she had the money to fly. "Don't you go and visit?" Was she afraid of flying? Even when they didn't especially feel like it, even when it wasn't particularly convenient, each year she and Ben and the kids drove a thousand miles one way to Ben's parents and then a thousand miles in the opposite direction to visit hers. It's what you did. It's what families did.

"I used to." She picked up a scone and broke it in two and spread a knife full of peach jam on it. "They have him working so hard in that megachurch. They really don't have time now. And me, I'm an old woman who'd just get in the way."

"And they don't come here?"

"Well, how would they ever find the time! The church is such a growing concern out there. I got a magazine. MarieAnn sent me a copy. It's a Christian magazine, quite a famous one, and the whole thing is about their church." She rose. "Here, let me show you."

"I don't think so. I don't want to see the magazine," Amy said.

Lenore's eyes filled with tears. She got up quickly, upsetting her chair so that it fell backward with a loud crash to the floor. "I'm sorry," Amy said. "I didn't mean to hurt your feelings… I'd be happy to look at the magazine."

"It's not your fault. Look at clumsy me. I'm no good for anything. No wonder they don't want me to visit, clumsy old woman that I am. Oh, and would you look at my eyes watering. I have such allergies in the winter. Just park me in front of the Kleenex box this time of year. That's what I always say."

Amy stood up and righted Lenore's chair for her. Then she touched her shoulder and felt the soft wool of Lenore's sweater. She found herself saying, "It's okay, Lenore."

Lenore settled back down into her chair. For several moments neither said anything. Then Lenore said, "I was supposed to marry a minister. Did you know that? I was engaged to one. Instead, I run off with Harlan, the town drunk. That's why Norman doesn't come home. Sometimes there's just too much to live down. Oh, my dear, I'm babbling. I'm such a sick old babbler. Can't get these allergies to stop. Can you hand me my handkerchief, dear?"

"Lenore, I'm so sorry."

"Oh my. What you must think. You are so fortunate dear, for marrying a minister—" She stopped suddenly, didn't continue.

Amy found herself crying too then, wiping her eyes as she sat next to Lenore. "It's not all...it's not all it's cracked up to be."

A few minutes later Amy said, "Would it be all right if I came to visit you every so often?"

"I would love that, dear. And bring your children, would you?"

62

I t's cold in my room this morning. A woman is humming in the kitchen. I smell coffee. And something greasy, like bacon. It's making my stomach turn. Lately more and more things are making my stomach turn. She hums and washes dishes, and I sit here. I look at their anxious faces in the kitchen. Little Tyke. That name comes to my mind. I don't know why.

"It's getting worse," I hear one of the women say to the other woman. "He's getting delusional. Talking about the police coming and murders and people after us."

"You may have to begin thinking about a nursing home for him. The one in town is quite nice."

"That will be hard on him. This farm is his life."

"He wouldn't be far, though."

"He'd be in town. He's never lived in town."

I sit on the chair next to my television and look out at the gazebo under the alders and wonder and wonder.

"All he does is sit there day after day," I hear the woman say. "Is his mind empty? How can he do that?"

"Let him be. He's lived a good, long life. I'll read to him later. Have you gone to the police about the e-mails?"

"Not yet. I'm not sure what they mean. Or who they're from. I find it hard to believe that these e-mails have anything to do with Tolita Shenk. I'm afraid the police will laugh off the whole thing, thinking she was up here last summer. Here's what I think…" I hear clatter and water running. They're washing dishes, cleaning up. I don't turn to look at them. Some days it's too much effort to move my head. So I don't even try.

"I think he came across an article in the paper about Tully being murdered and somehow it triggered something in his mind and his poor addled mind made up the rest."

"Still, you should probably get them to the police."

I'm trying to make sense of what they are saying, but I have this fuzzy old brain that has carried too many thoughts in an entire lifetime and is now shutting down. An old engine can only work so long before it quits.

During that whole Terrible Time so long ago, I came up with all sorts of plans. I would go into the hired man's house when Reeny was sleeping and steal baby Seth and drop him off at the hospital anonymously. No one would ever have to know. Glad's honor and standing in the community would therefore be preserved. I stayed up at night and thought up plans. In the end, I did nothing. Glad said she would return the baby as soon as he was well. I should never have believed that.

The story was that Reeny had taken Seth outside for a walk during the baby shower. It was too hot in the community hall. I heard her tell Glad all of this in the kitchen of the hired man's house. She had picked up the baby and the baby carrier and taken him outside and sat with him under a tree. Poor, troubled Reeny had no idea that in the hall a drama was unfolding, and when the baby's mother and Glad had come outside along with the other ladies, Reeny hid him. She wasn't ready to give the baby back yet. Seth was sleeping, she didn't want to disturb him, so she put the baby carrier in some high grass and joined the ladies down in the hall.

When the police came, she was afraid they would hurt the baby, so she took him into a grain silo. She heard their heavy boots just inches from where she crouched in the loose grain. He was waking up, hungry, and she held him tightly to her. He silenced, long enough for the police to leave.

Then she hitchhiked back to the farm where she was staying in the hired man's house. If a local had picked her up with the baby in the carrier she held on her lap, if someone from Barrhead or in any of the communities north of Barrhead had picked her up, the story would have turned out completely different. But a stranger in a pickup truck, an American on his way up north to Slave Lake on a hunting trip, had picked her up. He had a long way to go. And he drove Reeny and the now crying and hungry baby to our farm. She found an old baby bottle in the main house and took it over to the hired man's house where she heated milk on her stove to feed little Seth. There was lots of milk. There's always lots of fresh milk on a dairy farm.

"I was looking all over for you, Reeny! I came home because I was looking for you!" Glad yelled at her when she finally got home.

"I had to take care of my baby. I had to take her home. I hitchhiked."

"What? What?" Glad said. I came out of the house then, too.

"I found my baby. Look. It's Marissa! I found her!" And Reeny held out the bundle for the two of us to see.

"What have you done, Reeny? Oh, what have you *done?*"

"But, it's Marissa." And she cradled it all the more in her arms and wouldn't give it to Glad when Glad tried to wrest it out of her arms. Reeny screamed and cried and wailed. I looked on uncomprehending. Until Glad explained. Baby Seth had gone missing at the shower, and the police had been called. That was why she was so late getting home.

"I'll go call the Shenks," I said. I picked up the phone to make the call, but the Hemphills from the next farm over were on it. It was a party line in those days. I could have butted in, said it was an emergency, but Glad grabbed the phone from me. "Let me take care of this. Let me talk to Reeny. After Reeny and I have a good talk, we'll call the Shenks."

But the next morning baby Seth was still with Reeny, and the next after that and after that.

"What is the baby still doing here?" I asked Glad one morning.

"There's something wrong with it," Glad said. "It's sick now and needs to be cared for."

It made no sense to me and still doesn't. Yet Glad had her reasons for protecting Reeny. Reeny wouldn't let go of that baby. Reeny said she would kill herself if Marissa was taken away from her a second time. Glad always had her reasons. And then Glad brought that nurse in because the baby was sick, the one who stayed with us when she and her husband spoke at our church.

"It's the cow's milk," the nurse said. "This baby needs formula, not cow's milk."

By then, by the time baby Seth got better, it was just too late to return him. People would have asked questions, called the police. We would have gone to jail as kidnappers.

The woman takes my cold coffee cup, and I turn to her and say, "It's because it was cow's milk." I say it three times, but the woman just smiles and pats my shoulder. "It's all in the book I wrote," I say. "It's all there."

63

Sometime during the time Amy and Lenore were inside, a sharp-fisted, sleety rain had started. The stuffed bear in the snowbank had blown backward and lay belly up in the wind, its soggy ribbon partially submerged in the wet snow, the edges of it frozen down. If it weren't sleeting so hard, Amy would have gone over to right it. She pulled the neck of her coat tightly up around her chin and stepped carefully, gingerly, through the slick ice toward her car. She'd have to scrape the windows.

She'd come back here. She told Lenore she would, and she meant it. Because when she thought about it, they really weren't all that different from each other. Both lonely, a bit friendless, maybe, both desperately trying to make the world believe everything was okay with them and that they were okay with everything and everyone.

As Amy carefully drove out of Lenore's ice-encrusted driveway, she thought about their conversation. Lenore had told her she was supposed to be a minister's wife. She'd had a lifetime of regret because she was supposed to be a minister's wife.

Lenore explained, "You are so fortunate. I should think it would be the highest calling for a woman, to be the helpmeet of a man of God."

Amy blinked at her and said, "It's not what you think."

Lenore sniffed and dabbed at her eyes. "I would have been the perfect minister's wife. I love to cook and entertain and have people over. I love my guests. Did you happen to see that Grape Vine article in the Ridley paper about my place here?"

"You already are a good hostess," Amy said. "Here. At your bed-and-breakfast. And everyone loves your"—she waved her hand around—"those cinnamon thingys."

"Cinnamon swirls." Lenore grinned. "They're my own invention."

"Well, they're wonderful. Everyone says so."

"Oh," Lenore said. And then two red patches appeared on her cheeks. "Oh, dear. They're nothing special. I've won ribbons for them, though."

In that glimpse of Lenore—her color high, the smile—Amy had seen the young Lenore, the teenage Lenore—pretty, with her freckles and strawberry hair, the small nose and bright eyes. The teenage Lenore who would give up everything to run off and elope with Harlan Featherjohn while she'd been engaged to a seminary student. Amy had heard the stories. Lenore, an only child, had been an embarrassment to the family—her minister father and her mother, her minister grandfather, her minister great-grandfather. Yet still she did it. As Amy eased into a stop at a red light, she thought that Lenore had probably shown more spunk, more independence in that decision, than any decision she'd ever made since.

She glanced at the digital clock on her car radio. She'd have to hurry. Ben would be bringing Blaine home soon. Charlie would be home soon too. He had floor hockey until five. She had to hurry. They needed supper on soon, because Ben had a board meeting at seven. There was always something, always some reason to rush.

Some of the widows in the church said that the dreariest part of their lives was going home to an empty house. But there were times Amy longed for this. To go home and have no one there demanding any attention. She'd kick off her shoes, pour herself a glass of white wine, and sit in front of the news. She'd have popcorn and crackers and cheese for supper. And later she'd pick up a romance novel and lie in a bubble bath until the water got cold.

Closer to her home she saw the misted edges of flashing red lights. Two police cars were parked in her driveway. And every single light in her house was on. Her first thought was of Blaine. She drove in quickly and parked next to the police car. Ben's car was there too. She glanced at her cell phone. Five missed calls. She'd left it in her car when she went in to talk with Lenore.

She raced to the porch, nearly slipping on the ice. She should have gotten here sooner. She should have come here right after school, like a good wife and mother. Blaine! What had happened to her?

A police officer stood on the front porch, someone she didn't know.

"Ma'am?" he said.

"This is my house. What's going on?"

"It's a crime scene, ma'am—"

She burst past him and flung the door wide open.

She was not prepared for what she saw. The entire inside of her living room looked as if it had been turned upside down, shaken, and then set right again. Books had been pulled off the shelves and lay in haphazard piles. The sofa was on its side, stuffing torn out, the cushions slashed. Glass figurines and candles and knickknacks were strewn about, and a framed photograph lay broken on the floor. She picked it up. It was a family picture, the four of them, taken two years ago at Christmas. She and Ben and a much younger and happy and smiling Blaine and, of course, Charlie. The glass was broken. A piece fell out. She tried to put it back in place, but cut her finger.

"Ben!" she called. "Ben!"

From the kitchen he emerged. "Amy! We've been calling you. I called the school. Where were you? Blaine's in the kitchen. So are the police. I picked Blaine up, and when we got home, we found it like this."

"What happened?"

"A break-in."

"I can see that!"

"They took the DVD player and some jewelry. Blaine's room got the worst of it. We're not supposed to be here," he told her. "They're taking fingerprints."

In the hallway beside the staircase, a man in a white suit was kneeling and dusting with a brush. A fine dusting of powder settled everywhere, as if her living room were a cake being sprinkled with powdered sugar.

"Where's Blaine? Is she okay?"

"We're fine. She's fine. She's in the kitchen with the police."

Amy raced to the kitchen where the devastation continued. Just about every plate, bowl, cup, and saucer had been smashed on the floor. The flour, sugar, coffee, and tea canisters had been upended and their contents dumped on the counter. At the table were two police officers. She recognized one as Bill. Angela, the big-boned policewoman with curly hair, was leaning forward and writing in a notebook. Blaine sat in stiff silence across the table.

"Blaine!" Amy rushed to her.

Blaine looked up. Her black-rimmed eyes were smeared and red. "Oh, Mom!"

Amy sat down next to her and put her arm around her shaken daughter, but Blaine turned her face away and looked down at her lap, long bunches of dark hair covering her face.

Amy turned to Bill and said, "Who did this?" She kept a hand on Blaine's shoulder, even though it felt uncomfortable there, even though it didn't feel welcome there.

"We don't know," Bill said. His glasses were up on his forehead. "We're working on that."

Blaine bent her head lower into her lap. Amy sighed. She removed her hand from Blaine's shoulder and felt the girl relax. Amy's eyes welled with tears; that her daughter felt so repulsed by her touch that she should visibly relax when Amy moved her hand away hurt deeply. There was a smear of blood on Blaine's shirt, and Amy was horrified that someone had hurt Blaine, until she realized the blood came from her own hand. She was still carrying the broken photo of her family. She got up and went into the small bathroom off the kitchen. She put the picture down, reached for a towel, dabbed at her throbbing hand, ran it under water, wept, tried to remove the glass but couldn't. She was shaking too badly.

"Here," Ben said. "Let me help." And he took her hand gently between his own and rinsed it off and removed the little shards of glass. He picked up the picture and took out the rest of the glass from the frame. The picture was scratched in several places. Ben's forehead was scratched, but the biggest gash was across Blaine's Christmas smile.

"I don't understand," she kept saying. "I don't understand." She was trembling. "I don't, Ben, I don't."

She came into his arms then, and he held her gently, tightly. He smelled of winter and of cold and the faint smell that was him.

"It's okay," he said. "It's going to be okay, baby."

64

On the day Carrie arrived with a file folder, Jake and May were in the office of the Purple Church. He was tapping a pencil on his desk and thinking. May was working on her paper-bag flow chart. She had added another line, "The Trashing of McLarens' Home?" The question mark was there because the police were of the opinion that the trashing may have been a high-school prank. But May wasn't so sure. Neither was Jake.

A blast of cold from the opened door, and there stood Carrie in her red wool coat and fuzzy hat. She was pressing a file folder to her chest.

"Hey," she said.

"Hi," he said and smiled. The sight of her always made him smile. She walked in and plunked the folder down on the *In Remembrance of Me* table. Jake closed his notebook. He hadn't been writing anyway.

"I found out some stuff for you guys." She pulled off her hat and fluffed out her hair. "I worked hard for all of this. Especially since I'm not a hotshot reporter anymore. And since none of them at the paper owed me favors, I had to beg and plead," she said, taking off her coat. "When you said the names Jeanine Bowman and Ted Sorensen, something twigged. All this was faxed to me this morning. Then I did some of my own Web surfing. It's all there."

May sat down across from Jake and opened the file. Several photocopied news articles and what looked like printouts from Web sites filled the file. Jake picked up the first one. It was from the *Edmonton Journal* and was dated more than twenty years ago. The headline read, "Adoption Home Shut Down."

Jake scanned the article. A place called the Mothers' and Children's Christian Home in Edmonton, Alberta, which provided adoption and counseling services for unwed mothers, was being shut down for nonpayment of back taxes. Twenty unwed mothers were left on the street with nowhere to go when the home was closed by the government. The place had been in receivership for some time. A lot of money had been raised for the home by area churches down through the years, but it wasn't enough. Part of the problem was they had never met the full requirements as a religious institution for charitable statutes and so owed tens of thousands in back taxes. The proprietors, Ken and Hazel Sugar, were unavailable for comment.

A follow-up article some days later stated that the police were investigating the unexpected disappearance of Ken and Hazel Sugar. The day the home was closed, a witness reported seeing them putting luggage in the trunk of their car, a blue Chevy, and driving away. Their whereabouts were unknown. Neighbors and area churches who supported the home were in shock.

A neighbor was quoted as saying, "They provided a home for those girls. Food, medical bills, they paid it all. They were selfless in that."

May said, "What do these people have to do with the price of tea in China?"

Carrie grinned. "Read on, my friends. You haven't come to the best part."

He laid the third article on the table; it was dated five years later, but written by the same *Edmonton Journal* reporter: "Sugars Linked to Adoption Ring. Sources close to the *Journal* have confirmed that the Sugars, who disappeared five years ago from the Mothers' and Children's Christian Home, may be linked to another adoption-home fiasco. The Boise Baby Home in Boise, Idaho, was recently shut down after five years when its owners, Kevin and Shirley Stewart, disappeared one day, leaving ten unwed mothers with no place to go. No explanation was given."

May glanced up at Carrie and raised her eyebrows. "And?"

Carrie drew out a Web site printout from the folder and laid it out where they could read it. It was a warning notice on a Web site called Victims of Adoption Fraud. There was a red flag at the top of the page: "The Tender Moments Adoption Agency in Fredericton, New Brunswick, Canada, and their proprietors, Jeanine and Ted Sorensen, have been red-flagged by VAF as an illegitimate agency. Keep checking back with this Web site for more information."

"What is this?" asked May. "This 'Victims of Adoption Fraud'?"

"As far as I can tell, it's a sort of watchdog Web site on illegal adoptions. It's pretty good," Carrie continued. "There's a whole section on foreign adoptions, information on baby stealing, and information for prospective parents and pregnant women."

But Jake was looking at the names. "Are these the people who were here? The FNN people?"

Carrie said, "I think so."

Jake frowned. "Why would they use the name Sorenson when they registered here? Why not another alias?"

"My guess is that they didn't realize they'd been flagged by VAF. When they found out, they packed up and hightailed it out of here. I called the reporter from Edmonton. He's been on the trail of the Sugars for a long time. He was very excited about this new development and plans to follow up. He thanked me for phoning. That adoption agency in Fredericton is up and running. This VAF Web site has a link to legitimate private adoption homes and agencies. I mean it's a massive undertaking when you think of it, to be constantly checking up on these places."

"Who operates this organization, VAF?"

"Someone named Diane White. There's a link to her story on the Web site. It's quite fascinating. I printed it off for you.

"When she was eighteen years old and pregnant, her parents kicked her out. She found the name of this home in Edmonton in the back of a maga-zine. She called it, told them about her situation and that she didn't know if she could keep the baby. They invited her up, took care of getting her across the Canadian border, and provided her with free room and board until it was time to deliver. They pressured her a lot, but she decided to keep her baby. Deep down she'd always wanted to keep the baby. Long story short, in the delivery room—which she said looked more like a back-alley office—they told her there were complications. She was anesthetized, and when she woke up, they told her that it was very sad but there had been something wrong with the baby and he died. The day after the baby was born, she was basically thrown out of the home. They needed the bed, they told her.

"She went back later to find something from her old room and ran into a couple of other young women. Their babies had also died. She did more research and was stunned to find that many women had the same story. If you wanted to keep your baby, there was always some emergency surrounding the birth, you were anesthetized, and when you woke up, the baby was gone."

Jake stared at the printout. Tolita Shenk had mentioned baby stealing to Blaine. It was as though a snowfall of puzzle pieces were settling around them. Even May wouldn't have enough colors in her Magic Marker box for all the radiating lines.

"I printed off their brochure from their Web site in case you're interested." She laid the pink-and-blue printout on top of the articles.

Tender Moments Adoption Home
Connecting Christian Parents with Children to Love

Thank you for taking the time to visit the Tender Moments Adoption Agency Web site. We are a legitimate private adoption agency with the gospel of Christ at the heart of our work. It's our hope and joy to unite babies with Christian parents. Whether you are a birth parent considering making an adoption plan or a prospective adoptive parent, this site will give you information to help you make an informed choice.

We also have a fully staffed Tender Moments Home for birth mothers, where girls who need a place to stay during their pregnancies receive the best medical care for their unborn babies, as well as counseling. You can rest assured that your baby will be placed in a wonderful, caring, Christian family.

There was a verse from the Bible at the bottom.

"Doesn't this sound nice?" Carrie said. "Just gives you the cozy willies, doesn't it?"

Jake continued reading:

Tender Moments wants to unite you with a child. We know how much you've been wanting a child. Birth parents routinely choose prospective adoptive parents from our group of approved families. We help you prepare a good profile for birth parents to review. Even if you have been turned down before, come to us. We can help.

The cost for a professional adoption varies according to what the birth parents are able to pay and any special circumstances. What we do ask is for a donation to the Tender Moments Home. For complete details and a confidential appointment, please e-mail: info@tendermoments.com.

May frowned at this. "Not even a name," she said. "Just this generic e-mail."

Carrie said, "I looked at some of the other adoption Web sites, and all of them have names and addresses and phone numbers. No wonder this has been red-flagged."

"And this Jeanine and Ted Sorensen are the managers there?"

She nodded. "That was easy to check out with a quick call to the Fredericton city hall. They're listed there as a legitimate business. And yes, its proprietors are Jeanine and Ted Sorensen."

May continued to read aloud:

How do I choose adoption for my baby?
Adoption is a loving choice for you and your baby. We at Tender Moments also know it is one filled with emotion. You may have mixed feelings, even now. That's understandable. Our experienced counselors will help guide you through this most difficult of choices. This is your choice. If you choose to keep your baby and raise your child on your own, Tender Moments will do all we can to help you with those most challenging first months. We have in place many programs for new mothers.
How do I pay for this?
You don't. This is the responsibility of your adoptive parents. If you choose to stay at Tender Moments, your expenses are fully covered by the adopting parents and Tender Moments.

May stopped reading at this point. "Carrie, is this normal? That the agency and the adoptive parents pay for everything?"

"Me, who has no children and suddenly I'm the adoption expert?" She grinned. "But this has been fun. Okay, my research seems to vary. What I did find, though, is that there are very few homes like this—homes for unwed mothers. Part of that could be because of the ease now of abortion. Unwanted pregnancies just aren't as difficult to deal with. But I think maybe a bigger reason is that society is more tolerant now. Very few parents are going to throw their pregnant daughters out into the street. But even the legitimate homes that are out there are different from this one. This is a full-service home where pregnant girls live and get all their medical care and basically everything for free. But the real difference comes after the babies are adopted. Other homes offer counseling afterward, because that's when a girl really needs it. They'll help with education and job skills. At Tender Moments, when the babies are adopted out, the girls are thrown on the street. They get nothing."

"What does this have to do with Tully and why she came here and why she died?" May asked.

"Maybe," Jake said, "these people had a secret and were willing to kill to keep it."

65

When Lenore heard about the trashing of Ben and Amy's home, she realized she had to do something, so she invited the McLaren family to stay with her in the bed-and-breakfast. Having the minister and his wife living under her roof made Lenore realize she should finally do the right thing. When she got right down to it, all of this bad luck, all of it had started, not when she married Harlan, as she liked to think, but when she moved that poor girl's body away from her sons' door. And maybe, just maybe, she needed to take some of the blame.

Starting to do the right thing also meant that Lenore needed to call May and tell her everything. From the beginning. Even if it meant she would end up in prison. And she probably would.

And while she waited for May to arrive, she fluttered around her kitchen, cleaning things, getting ready for supper, because now she had a houseful, didn't she? Earlier she'd even made whoopie pies for the young McLaren boy. He'd be the same age now as Bradley. Boys that age loved whoopie pies, didn't they?

May arrived a few minutes later, without Jake, which Lenore had been hoping for. When May sat down, Lenore hung a dishtowel on the stove and wrung her hands. "Oh, poor Norman," she said.

"Norman?" May looked at her.

"It won't do his reputation in church any good having a mother like me. Once this gets out. Once you hear what I have to tell you…"

May stood up and glared at her. "For once, Lenore, for once in your whole life, why don't you do something that's right and honest and good instead of what will benefit your sons? Stop making excuses for them, and let them live their own lives. All of them. And that includes Norman!"

Lenore sat down and said in a tiny voice. "I'm trying. That's what I'm trying."

"Trying, *trying*—there's no such thing as trying. You're either going to do it or you're not," May said.

"I called you, didn't I? I *am* doing the right thing. I'm trying." She dabbed at her eyes some more. The edges of her fingernails were rough and chipped. She needed a good manicure, but what with all the stress lately, no wonder her fingernails were breaking.

"Well, good then." May sat down. "It's settled. Now what is it you wanted to talk to me about?"

Lenore went to her breadbox and reached for the picture of Tolita Shenk she had put there so long ago. She set it down in front of May. Between sips of tea she told her story, right from the beginning, when she found Tolita's frozen corpse in the doorway to her sons' room. She didn't leave anything out.

May took off her Squirrels cap. "You moved the body?"

Lenore nodded.

"Well, I'm impressed. That's no mean feat."

"Well, it was kind of heavy, but I'm pretty strong. I've always taken my exercise."

But when she told May about the baby pictures in Jeanine's suitcase and the same ones in Earl's desk, May stared at her.

"We need to talk to Earl," May said.

"No," Lenore said.

"Oh yes." May grabbed her walking stick and started toward the basement door. "Is Earl home? *Earl!*" she hollered down the stairs.

"He's in Ridley," Lenore said.

"Fine then," May said. "Shall we go downstairs and have a look?"

Lenore had no choice but to follow. She was embarrassed by the smell of the place, but if May noticed, she was kind enough not to say anything. May hobbled over to Earl's computer and tables. "Show me what you found," she said.

But Lenore was nervous and opened the wrong drawer, the one with all the passports. She shut it quickly. "Wrong one."

"What were those?"

"Earl takes passport photos, so he gets to keep people's old passports."

"That's not how it works," May said. She opened the drawer again and pulled a few out. "These are terrible."

"What?"

"These are phonier than three-dollar bills. Look at the paper." May held up a few. "This is cheap photocopy paper on the inside, and you can get the paper for these covers at any Staples. What's he doing with these?"

Lenore shrugged. She really didn't know. She knew so little about what her sons did. Maybe she should take more of an interest.

"If he's a counterfeiter, he's really not a very good one," May added.

Lenore played with her rings while May put down the passports and rifled through the bottom drawer, the one with all the baby pictures. She pulled out a handful and laid them out on the desk.

"All these babies," May said. "What is Earl doing with these?"

"Does it have something to do with the passports?" Lenore ventured.

"Well, we'll know as soon as we talk to Earl, won't we?"

Lenore nodded and swallowed. What would her son say to these women going through his things? She didn't want to be here to find out. It was one thing to admit her own failings to May; it was quite another to implicate her sons.

Upstairs, the door slammed. Lenore jumped. "Oh no, it's Earl! It's got to be Earl. Let me run upstairs, give him tea, detain him. He can't know we've been here. We can put everything away, and you can go out the back door there." She pointed at the door on the opposite side of the room next to the big-screen TV.

"We're not going anywhere, Lenore. We're staying put. That son of yours has a lot to answer for."

In a few moments Earl thumped down the stairs carrying a large McDonald's bag. Lenore smelled greasy fries and burgers.

"Hey!" He stopped when he saw them.

"Hello, Earl." May made no effort to move.

"What're you guys doing here?" His eyes darted to the pile of fake passports on the desk.

"Earl," Lenore said. "What are you doing with all these people's passports?"

"Carl's kids made them."

Lenore stared at him.

"From the Boys and Girls Club. They were doing a project on other countries or other lands or some such. So they were making phony passports and money, too. Is that the big deal? You came down here because you thought I'd stolen a bunch of people's passports?"

"No," May said. "We're not here about the passports; it's about these baby pictures. All of these." And she pointed to them.

"They're for a Web site."

"What kind of a Web site?" May asked.

"I got a big contract a while ago. For an adoption agency Web site." He sat down in his chair and called up the Web site on his computer. Lenore was getting flustered. "But where did you get the pictures?" She was thinking about the baby picture that was in the same envelope as the one of Tolita Shenk.

May asked, "What adoption agency? Do you have a contact?"

"Sure. Tender Moments." He grunted as he sat down at the computer and called it up. "There was something kind of funny, though. They didn't want my name or Fog Point to appear anywhere on the site. Usually on the sites I manage, I've got 'Web site managed by Fog Point Designs' and my name and e-mail at the bottom, you know, so I can drum up more business. But they were quite adamant that it not appear. Well, actually, it did appear for a couple of weeks, before they told me to take it down. I've never met them, don't even know their names. I don't meet half the people I work for. They sent a bunch of photos as e-mail attachments for me to use for the Web site. They wanted a collage." He opened up his fast-food bag, unwrapped one of the three burgers he'd brought, and took a rather large bite. Lenore had to admit she was embarrassed. She'd taught her sons better manners than to wolf down their food.

"Surprise," May said. "You did meet them."

He looked up at her, uncomprehending.

"We believe," May said, "that Jeanine Bowman and Ted Sorensen were here pretending to be with FNN."

"Are you serious? Why didn't they say something to me when they were here, like their names, for example? I spent an evening with him. He wanted to see Web sites I'd done, so I invited him down here."

"Not down here," Lenore said. "Tell me you didn't take him down here."

He ignored her. "What you're telling me is that they run an adoption agency?"

"Not quite. And they're not with FNN. That was a ruse," May said.

Earl blinked at them.

"Ted Sorenson and Jeanine Bowman are really Ken and Hazel Sugar, who are wanted in two countries for human trafficking and tax evasion, among other things," May said. "Plus, we think they may have something to do with Tolita Shenk's death, or at least have information about it."

Earl scratched his head. "That's the girl who died in our backyard, right? The one the police keep hassling me about?"

"Right, Earl. And you had her picture," May said.

"I had her picture? What are you talking about?"

May put it down in front of him along with the baby picture that had been clipped to it. His eyes widened when he looked at it. "Where did this come from? I was looking for this. After the police left the last time, I got to thinking about these pictures. I was going to call them about it."

May sat down and took a fry from his supersize container. "Tell us," she said.

"That kid left it. He was here a few weeks ago. Weird kid. Never looked you square on when he talked to you. I come upstairs one morning, and he'd left these pictures on the counter underneath the newspaper he'd been reading. I called after him when I saw him leave, but I guess he didn't hear me. So I stuck them in an envelope and put them in my desk and forgot about them. Next thing I know, the artist's drawing of this guy is all over the TV and anyone with any information is supposed to contact the police. So I come downstairs, thinking I'll get the pictures and take them to the police, but I couldn't find them. Then I sort of forgot about the whole thing."

"And it didn't dawn on you that the picture he left was of the girl who died in your backyard?" May asked.

"I never made the connection. I guess I didn't look at it that long. And you're saying these pictures are a part of this whole murder thing?"

"That's exactly what we're saying," May said.

66

The police are here and reading my e-mails. They want to know about the girl who stayed here last summer, but my mind has gone fuzzy all around the edges. And a woman's voice is high and screechy at the end. It hurts my ears, and I put my hands over them. And then she goes and makes me a cup of coffee with lots of fresh cream. I like it with lots of cream. There's nothing like real cream in your coffee.

The police are out in the barn, and they come in breathing heavy from the cold, like cows do. I watch their breaths on them when they come through the door, and I say, you better take off those heavy boots of yours or Glad is going to have your head on a platter and then some. Glad is very particular about her floors. I mean to warn them about her.

One of the policemen comes over and sits down beside me on the couch. But it's not a man, it's a lady policeman. I think it's nice, them letting ladies be policemen these days. So I look at her and say to her, I think that's awfully nice. It's really quite nice. She looks at me with gentle eyes and asks me about Tully. And I try to remember.

She killed him. The nurse buried him. I finally get the words out. Underneath the alders in the back, beside the gazebo. But maybe not. I've never been quite sure about that. I wrote it all down and took her ring.

He's delusional, the other woman says. This is what he does. He makes things up.

Maybe, but maybe not. The police officer is smiling up at her. Let him talk, she says. Let him just talk. Her voice is so soft now it reminds me of cream. Ice cream. Homemade ice cream. We used to make homemade ice cream here. We had one of those ice-cream makers that you add the salt and ice to and then crank it. It seemed you had to crank it for hours to get any! But I remember it now. I remember that Tim would crank and crank, and then Ashe would demand a turn. I wonder where that ice-cream machine ended up. I haven't seen it in years. Where's the machine? I ask. You have to tell me where the machine is!

What machine? the woman asks me.

Have some coffee, Dad.

Did they throw the machine out? They shouldn't have, and I get agitated now, and I want to lash out at them for throwing away the machine.

He gets this way, the woman says. And there's nothing we can do. I don't think he's going to tell you anything.

The woman in the police uniform is still sitting beside me. She pats my hand. Maybe she's here about the machine. Maybe she's here because someone stole the machine.

I take a big gulp of my coffee. I have always liked coffee. It's been one of my favorite things. Glad used to say coffee kept her up at night. Well, I could drink it and drink it and then sleep nine hours easy.

I'm tired, I say.

And the woman says, you should come back in the morning. Sometimes he's brighter in the morning. You may get more out of him then.

Do you think there is anything to the story about the alders, one of the men asks. He's wearing a uniform. Three men dressed the same. And one of them a lady.

We'd be remiss not to try, not to see what's out there. He's obviously remembering something.

But that means digging, the woman says.

Yes, it does, they answer.

But I am remembering Reeny. I just can't form the words out loud. I can't say them. Maybe tomorrow. Maybe after some coffee.

Glad said to me, I want you to forget this ever happened. I just don't want you saying anything in town. We'll pretend this thing never happened. It was a tragic shame, but we need to put it behind us once and for all.

Then the other woman, the one who calls me Dad, she asks if they want sugar and cream in their coffee.

The police officer is still sitting here, and her hand is on my arm. This nurse who buried her baby. Do you remember her name?

Sugar! I look up and say the word loudly.

Dad, you don't take sugar. You've never taken sugar in your life.

It was her name! It was Sugar. I paractically shout the name, *Hazel Sugar,* and then more quietly, Hazel Sugar.

She was from the Christian home for babies, I tell them. Glad knew her from church. Hazel Sugar. I wrote it all down, every bit of it. I gave it all to Tully. It's in a book. With Hazel's ring. The one with her name on it. And the film. I made sure I had the film.

67

It was odd to Amy that she could actually feel content living in Lenore's B&B, but that's what she was. Content. Not happy, certainly, not with all that had gone on at her house, nor with Blaine, who still shrugged away from her. No, that didn't make her happy, but things were beginning to be different between her and Ben, and that was the only good thing in a sea full of bad things. For now, being content was a start.

It was early evening, and Amy was sitting on a Victorian loveseat in Lenore's grandest room, gazing out at the ocean. It wasn't all the way dark, and that cheered Amy. The seasons were changing. Soon it would be light longer, and this awful winter would be over. Charlie was downstairs watching videos with Lenore, who'd made a batch of cinnamon swirls with chocolate, especially for him. Blaine was at Jana's, and Jake and May were there too. It was a place Amy and Ben trusted, but otherwise they still demanded that Blaine be with them at all times. Blaine seemed oddly, almost happily, resigned to this fact.

Yesterday, Amy had heard Blaine on the phone telling one of her friends she couldn't come to a party. "With all that's happened at the house and everything, my parents are so worried about me. They're like totally not letting me go anywhere."

The odd thing was, Blaine had never approached her parents with any request to go to a party.

Also, Amy had decided to be truthful with Ben, and last night she finally told him she no longer believed in God. Late last night they had sat in the very loveseat she now sat in and held on to each other and talked and talked. Ben told her he had several drafts of a resignation letter on his computer, and in fact, had one in an envelope in his pocket at all times. She hadn't known that things weren't always perfect with him. She thought nothing ever bothered him.

"But you're so strong," she said. "You've always been so strong."

He'd looked past her, out the window, and said, "I'm not so strong." He paused and said, "Sometimes I envy you."

"Me?"

"You have a job in a seminormal place, away from the church and its problems. You don't have two hundred bosses, each telling you he or she wants a different form of worship. Or Bible study. Or Sunday-morning sermon. Or translation of the Bible. And then hearing the criticism that if I can't control my daughter then I shouldn't stay in the ministry..."

"People have actually said that?" Amy asked.

"I've heard comments. Even been quoted a verse in the Bible about it."

"Oh, Ben."

It was right after this that she told him she didn't believe in God anymore. She hadn't meant to. Clearly he had enough to deal with. Surely, if a wayward daughter would have him and others questioning his role in ministry, then how much more an unbelieving wife? But she had to. If they were ever to get their marriage back on track, she needed to be honest.

"Ben," she said, "you are being honest with me. I need to be honest with you. Totally honest."

He held her away from him slightly and waited.

"I don't...it's just...I'm not sure... You remember that pastor's wife? The one we met? The one who didn't..." She paused, groping for words. She tried to move away from him, but he brought her close.

"Amy, whatever it is, we can deal with it."

"Ben, I don't think I believe in God anymore."

For an instant he looked at her, but he didn't say anything. He didn't get up and walk away from her or suggest they pray. What he did was move closer to her and take her more tightly in his arms.

Finally she spoke. "I wish I believed in God, Ben. I wish I had that sure faith that everybody talks about. My father," she continued, "my minister father told me there had never been a time in his entire life when he doubted. Never one moment. Not even an instant." Amy was crying now, and Ben held her closer. She felt the nubby wool of his sweater against her cheek. "Every time I'm in church, I cry, because it's all so beautiful, and I so desperately want it. I want to have what all these people around me have. To actually believe."

Her words flowed more freely now. It was as if a dam had broken and she could finally speak, finally give words to all the stray and lost thoughts that had taken residence in her mind.

"Last Sunday we were singing." And she began to sing softly, "How deep the Father's love for us, how vast beyond all measure. That he should give his only Son to make a wretch his treasure..." Her voice faded to a whisper. "And Ben, I couldn't sing, because I was crying so hard, and I was crying because I thought, wouldn't it be wonderful if this were really true! To actually have the faith to believe it all. But I don't, Ben. I just don't. And...and... Ben, you deserve a wife who believes in God."

His hand was in her hair now, and he was stroking it. "I love you, babe, just the way you are. I wouldn't want you any other way. We're all we've got. We can't lose what we have."

"I don't want to either."

She thought about this as she sat in the window seat of Lenore's elegantly appointed master bedroom, looking out to sea in the far distance on this almost night.

Her cell phone rang, taking her out of her thoughts. It was Ben, and she needed to get over to the Purple Church right away.

"What's this about?"

"You just come, Amy. As soon as you can get here."

Something in his voice frightened her badly.

68

When Amy got to the Purple Church, there was already a collection of frowning people downstairs in Jana's bedroom. Jana and Blaine were sitting on either side of Jana's bed. Blaine's eyes were red, while Jana just looked surprised. Ben sat beside Blaine on the bed, his arm around her. Police officers Bill and Angela sat on folding chairs, which looked like they'd been lugged in here from the kitchen for this occasion. May was on an overstuffed chair, her cane leaning against the arm. Jake stood by the window, and Carrie stood next to him.

"What's going on?" Amy asked.

Ben pointed at the bed, at an old hardback school composition book with a black mottled design on the front. On top of it was a Kodak envelope full of photos, a school ring, and a black plastic film container with a gray lid.

Bill looked up. He had his glasses on his forehead again. "We believe this is what the thieves were looking for at your house."

Then Blaine said to Amy, "I didn't mean it, Mom! I didn't know!"

"I still don't know what this is all about," Amy said.

"The reason we were broken into," Ben said now, "was because Blaine had this stuff, this book. And someone wanted it."

"The Sugars, namely," Carrie said.

"I didn't *know*, Mom!"

"Sugars?" Amy said.

And then all of them, at once it seemed, were telling her an amazing story about a baby who was stolen at a baby shower some twenty-six years ago and later sold, or presumably sold. Or adopted, maybe, by people who didn't know he was stolen. There could be all sorts of circumstances. It could be, even, that he was dead, but excavations around the property in Alberta revealed nothing. And it was his sister who found something that brought her to Fog Point to look for a grown-up brother.

Amy put her hand to her forehead. A buried baby? A stolen baby? A grown-up baby living here in Fog Point?

Carrie told Amy that one of the people Tully met here in Fog Point was Blaine. It hadn't been a one-time contact. They had e-mailed for months after meeting in the chat room of a Web site called Victims of Adoption Fraud. Blaine kept her head down through the explanation. Amy's eyes were wide. *Victims of Adoption Fraud?* But she and Ben had adopted Blaine through a legitimate public adoption agency.

"When Tully came to Fog Point," Bill explained, "she brought these things with her. She gave them to Blaine—"

"Why?" Amy said. Her voice was louder than she intended it to be, a bit like a screech. "Why would that girl put my daughter in danger like that?"

"Mom!" Blaine looked up. "It's not her fault! I offered. She went to see Dad even..." Amy looked at her husband's hollow eyes. Blaine continued, "She knew my dad was a minister, and she thought maybe they'd be safe in a church. But in the morning, before school, she gave all the stuff to me. I told her she shouldn't leave them with my dad because he wouldn't know how important all of this stuff is." She looked at her father. "Sorry, Dad."

Ben spoke now. "And later that day she was killed."

Amy moved closer to her daughter. "Oh, Blaine," and she put her arms around her. This time her daughter didn't shrug away.

"I got scared then," Blaine said. "People were following me. Like that lady, Jeanine, from the news. I figured it would be safe here because Jana's dad is a detective. That's practically like the police. Remember when I snuck over here on that Sunday morning? That's when I brought the stuff. I put it all under Jana's bed."

Amy picked up the envelope. No one stopped her. She took out the photos and flipped through them. Women and girls sat on folding chairs in groups. Some of the girls wore loose-fitting T-shirts and leg warmers, and quite a few of the women wore those shoulder pads so chic during the eighties. A couple of shots featured a table filled with gifts: baby layette sets, toys, hand-knit sweaters. A couple of pictures showed a baby being held by various women. In one, a young girl held him carefully on her lap. But there was one photo Amy looked at longer than the others. In it a thin woman with long hair held the baby on her lap. She wasn't looking at the camera but down at the baby. One hand held the baby while the other touched the baby's forehead. The tender gesture entranced Amy, and she could not take her eyes away. "This is the baby's mother," she said.

"We think so," Angela said. "We think that's Coralee Shenk, Tully's mother. There are still a whole lot of missing pieces. We think this baby would be Tully's brother, and that's why she had these pictures."

Amy looked back at the picture. She thought about the first time she held Blaine. How would she have felt if Blaine had been taken from her? But then how would she feel if she knew the baby she had so lovingly and so innocently adopted had been stolen? The thought sent a chill up her spine. She put the photos back in the envelope. The ring was a class ring from a nursing school in Edmonton dated 1980 and inscribed with the name *Hazel Sugar*.

She picked up the book. It was old, the pages soft and gray with age. Amy opened it and slowly read the scrawly handwriting aloud.

The Story of What Really Happened to Seth Shenk
from My Point of View
by Rory Black

I met Hazel and Ken Sugar when they came to our church in 1979 and spoke about their home for unwed mothers. They seemed like a very nice young Christian couple. Ken Sugar was a new doctor and Hazel was studying to be a nurse. They felt their life calling was to help young women who were in trouble without the benefit of marriage. They were collecting donations to begin their home, and they were in our church to speak and get support for their ministry. They stayed with us on the farm for a night with their baby son. We had a lot of people in—visiting missionaries and the like. Glad liked that. I always think Glad thought she might get a better place in heaven if we entertained missionaries and visitors. Hazel and Glad seemed to hit it off. Maybe Glad felt some sort of motherly attraction to Hazel, I don't know.

So, a year later when we found Glad's niece, Irene Johnson—Reeny—in the hired man's house with Seth Shenk, Glad called Hazel in Edmonton and apprised her of the situation. I was upset and angry that she didn't phone the Shenks right away. Poor Coralee and Henry! They were beside themselves with worry. But Seth was sick. He was vomiting, and Glad didn't want to return him until he was well. Glad and I had a huge disagreement. But Glad wondered how it would look. Here we'd had the baby all along. Glad was a good church woman and well respected in the community.

"Let's get the baby well. Then we'll give it back," she said.

The thing I noticed right away was that Glad always called the baby "it." I know Reeny stole the baby from the shower to begin with because her first baby had died. I think part of Glad's reasoning came from the fact that she didn't want anyone to think that what happened to Reeny's real baby was her own fault.

You see, Reeny had never been quite right in the head since her baby had died of crib death two years before. Glad felt a responsibility toward her. Glad's sister, Reeny's mother, had died of cancer, and Reeny really had no one else. And Reeny, well, she wouldn't let baby Seth out of her sight. She kept calling him Marissa and said she would kill herself if anything happened to Marissa again. And she meant it.

So, when baby Seth began vomiting, Glad didn't call a nurse from Barrhead, because if she did, they would be reported right away, and they'd had Seth a week by now. I remember coming in from the field one afternoon and seeing a strange car in the drive. Glad wasn't at the house. I called for her there. I went over to the hired man's house, and there was Reeny and Glad and Hazel Sugar. Hazel was sitting on a rocker feeding baby Seth a bottle and talking and rocking the baby like he was hers. I stood there for a long time not saying anything. My rage was such that I couldn't. The baby should have been returned a long time ago! We had talked about this! Reeny wouldn't be implicated. We'd just drop the baby off at the hospital anonymously. No one needed to be the wiser.

So when I saw the three of them there, I stormed into the room and said, "What's going on? Why is that baby still here?"

"He's sick," Hazel responded promptly. "Reeny fed him cow's milk. Babies need formula. This baby is probably allergic to cow's milk."

And then Glad said to me, "I called Hazel. She's a nurse and my friend."

"You need to give the baby back. I'm going to call the police. I'm going to do it now," I said.

When I said that, Reeny began rocking back and forth in her chair, keening like a caught wolf cub, her fists pressed against her mouth.

"You will do no such thing," Glad said under her breath. "This isn't the perfect situation, but we've got to make the best of it. Yes, we should've returned this baby the moment Reeny brought it here. But we didn't, and now the baby's sick. We're going to get this baby well and then return it. Think of it, Rory, if this baby dies—and Hazel says he's not far from it—we will be arrested for murder."

The whole time Glad was lecturing me, Reeny sat on the couch, thumping her fists into her mouth and wailing, "Marissa, Marissa," and Hazel Sugar was rocking the baby, feeding him a bottle and singing to him. But something about her singing grated, something about it felt wrong. I couldn't put my finger on it at the time. Hazel looked up, pointed at me, and said, "Rory, I was never here. You remember that. Whether this baby lives or dies, I was never here."

I went back to the main house, still fuming, still enraged, because of course, I would do what Glad wanted. I always did what Glad wanted. I made a pot of coffee. I drink the stuff like water. While I was spooning in a dollop of cream, I noticed Glad's camera on the counter on top of an envelope of photos from the drug store. I opened the envelope and flipped through them. They were pictures of the baby shower. I don't know how Glad got to keep these pictures when everybody else's had to go to the police, but that's Glad for you. The whole thing gave me an idea. I took the camera out to the hired man's house and shot pictures of Hazel Sugar right through the window holding that baby with the shirt with the little circles on it. Next time I was in town, I'd take that film in and get it developed. I finished off the whole roll. I also kept the pictures Glad took of the baby shower. And Hazel's ring. She left it by the sink in the bathroom of the main house. I slipped it into my pocket. I don't know why I kept it, but I did.

I have to explain that at this time of the year I was very busy, too busy with the farm to pay much attention to anything else. We hadn't had a hired man for a year, and I was so short-handed that a lot of things escaped my attention then. I'm not trying to make excuses. There's no excuse for what I did.

Two days later, when Glad came to me and told me that the baby had not recovered, I said, "We have to tell them now."

"He died, Rory. He died. Don't you realize what this means? We will be arrested for murder. Both of us. Think about it. Think what this will do to our children."

"What did you do with him?" I asked. "His body?" My voice was strangely flat. I was having trouble breathing.

"Hazel buried it out under the alders. She gave it her own Christian service."

The whole thing made me sick. And I could remember Hazel saying to me, *"I was never here. You remember that."* But I had the film. I'd get it developed; then everyone would know. But then the thought came to me that if I took it down to the drugstore in Barrhead to get it developed, they would see what the pictures were. And it would all come back to destroy us. So I became like Glad then and kept all this in myself.

I am writing this in April 1990, almost nine years after all of this happened. Glad died yesterday from the cancer, and tomorrow is her funeral. But I have to get this all down because it has been eating at me for all these years about how we never talked about it. Never. Not once.

A few years after it happened, I decided to call the Sugars in Edmonton to find out what really happened to Seth. You see, I'd started having my doubts right away about his death. I'd been out to the alders and had done some digging. I couldn't find anything. But when I phoned, their secretary told me they were on vacation.

"Where?" I asked.

"Boise, Idaho."

"What are they doing down there?"

"Vacation," I was told.

It wasn't long after this that the whole place was shut down, and it was in all the papers and on television.

The Shenks have another child now, a little girl named Tolita, but things have never been quite right between them since losing baby Seth.

This is my honest and true account. I swear on the Bible and in front of my God.

　　　Rory Black

Amy closed the book and looked at the assembled group in Jana's bedroom. She felt tears welling in her eyes and said quietly, "What a tragic story." She inhaled deeply and glanced over at her daughter. Tears rimmed Blaine's eyes as well. "So," Amy began, "how did Tully get this book?"

"Tully stayed with him." Blaine offered. "With Rory Black, when she first ran away. She was there when I met her on the Internet. He gave it to her and she gave it to me. She didn't even know she had a brother. Her mother never told her. No one did."

"If this is true, then it's so sad." Amy wiped the tears away from her eyes with the corner of her sleeve.

Carrie handed her a Kleenex and said, "I've done a bit of research into this in the past few days. From what I understand, Tolita Shenk read this story and determined to find her brother, who would be twenty-six by now. She contacted quite a few adoption agencies on the Web."

"The police out in Alberta have Rory Black's computer now," Angela interjected. "And they're going through all of Tully's e-mails."

"One of the agencies," Carrie continued, "is VAF or Victims of Adoption Fraud. When Tully looked through all the red-flagged private adoption agencies, she discovered the Mothers' and Children's Christian Home in Edmonton and contacted the head of that organization, a Diane White, who is an amazing lady with contacts all over the place. Tully learned through Diane, and through tracking down various records, that one of the babies ended up out east about the time Seth went missing. "

Jana leaned forward, her head in her arms, and began to cry. Jake went to her. "It's my fault," Jana said. "All of it's my fault."

"Jana, no," Jake said.

"It was me who got Blaine asking about her real mother, after we watched that *Oprah* program."

"It's nobody's fault," Carrie said.

"What I want to know," Ben said, "is why she was asking about the Featherjohns? She specifically asked how to get to Featherjohn's."

Carrie answered, "Jeanine and Ted made one rather foolish mistake. They hired Earl from Fog Point to do their Web site. We think that Tully probably saw his logo on the site before he had to take it off. The Sugars gave Earl lots of baby pictures to use as part of a collage of pictures for the Web site. The baby picture of Seth was among them. Whether this was a mistake or not, we don't know. Anyway, she may have seen this picture and figured it was as good a starting point as any. Plus, Diane indicated that Seth may have been adopted by someone out east. Tully's mistake was blabbing all of this in the very public chat rooms of VAF. When Blaine found someone asking questions about Fog Point, she immediately answered, and they had many public conversations about Fog Point. It would be nothing for Hazel Sugar to hack in to those chats."

Amy put her hand up. "Wait. Jeanine and Ted, the ones from FNN?"

"They weren't from FNN."

"But I saw her talking to you," she said to Blaine.

"She was warning me. At first I thought she really was with the news and wanted me for a story, but then she told me that if I knew anything about where Tully's things were, I should get them to her right away. I was so freaked. That's when I decided to bring them here."

"Oh, Blaine," Amy said.

"We're pretty sure the Sugars were responsible for the break-in at your place," Bill said. "We think Mal Barcklay is connected somehow. Find him and we may find some answers."

"But where is Seth Shenk?" Amy asked.

"That we don't know," Jake said. "At least not yet. But I have a feeling that by the time this story breaks, we will. Someone in Fog Point adopted a baby from that home in Edmonton twenty-six years ago."

"What do we do now?" Amy asked

Carrie linked her arm in Jake's. "Jake and I are desperate to adopt a baby. We're Mr. and Mrs. Jack Corcoran from Muskogee, Oklahoma, and we heard about the Tender Moments Adoption Agency. We already have an appointment in Fredericton in two days to meet the Sorensens."

69

Mid-February is not the height of the tourist season in Fredericton. Jake wondered about the wisdom of coming up here when blizzards threatened, as he and Carrie and May drove the Trans-Canada Highway toward the city. He wondered if they should have thought this trip through a bit more. Yet there would be no telling Carrie that. She was on the trail of a story. He'd never seen her quite this up before, happy, as she carried around her notebook. If this could draw her back to her chosen profession, it was worth it. As they crossed the Canadian border at Houlton, Maine, and headed down the four-lane but very desolate highway toward Fredericton, every so often they glimpsed the wide, frozen St. John River far down to their left. Signs and high moose fences along the highway bespoke the province's wildlife. Jake kept a vigilant watch as they drove.

Tomorrow they had an appointment at Tender Moments in downtown Fredericton, and they wanted to have a look, if they could, at the home where the girls lived. The two were not at the same location. The Tender Moments Adoption Agency had an office in the same building that housed the Pregnancy Crisis Centre.

"I wonder if they know," Carrie mused as Jake accelerated to pass a huge truck with Day & Ross along the side. "I wonder if the Pregnancy Crisis Centre knows that it's sharing its office space with human traffickers and baby thieves?"

"They may not know now, but hopefully, after we're done, they'll find out," May said from the backseat.

Although the police hadn't officially sanctioned this meeting, when Bill realized that Carrie was coming regardless, he shrugged and said he'd see what he could set up. The Fredericton police had listened to the fantastic story about their good corporate citizens and read the news stories Carrie had found. They didn't quite believe it but promised to be there on the spot if needed.

With the help of their MapQuest printout, they easily found their way off the Trans-Canada, down Regent Street, and to the Beaverbrook Crowne Plaza Hotel, where they had booked two rooms, side by side. The hotel was across the street from the large, stone government building.

All the city seemed covered with a sheen of winter. Snow was piled along the roadways and onto places that Jake was sure would abound with gardens in the summer.

They checked into their hotel and ordered room-service suppers. "It would serve no purpose," May said, "for the three of us to be seen together. I'm pretty sure that that Jeanine person has seen me. You guys go for a walk. Enjoy the nightlife, such as it is. I'm staying here."

She also wanted to take advantage of the city of Fredericton's free wireless service to do more Web searching. Like the police and everyone else, she was looking for that elusive Mal Barcklay. She still held to the idea that he was Tolita's brother.

"But why would her brother kill her?" Jake had asked.

"I don't know motive. It's just a theory, Jake. Just an idea."

Jake wondered if her leg was giving her problems and that was why she was begging off their evening out. She needed to stop several times on the car trip up to walk off the pain. No wonder she was sometimes crabby.

When Jake asked the girl at the front desk where the safe and unsafe places to walk were, the girl said. "Take normal precautions, but it's a pretty safe city all over. Especially in winter. You can walk anywhere—as long as you don't freeze. That would be the problem more than crime." She gave Jake and Carrie a map.

The two joined a small group of walkers on this Thursday night, all bundled against the cold. Thankfully, there was no wind, which made it not unpleasant. It was just as cold as Fog Point, but the air seemed more open, somehow less closed in and dense, leading Jake to further wonder about May's pronouncement that Fog Point had been transported into an alternate Chronicles of Narnia reality where the snow would never end and spring would never come.

The iced-up St. John River was to their right as their boots crunched on the sidewalk snow. Downtown, tiny blue lights—thousands of them strung high on leafless elms—cast shadows on ice skaters who circled the smooth square pond beneath the lights.

Carrie took Jake's arm. "Oh, Jake, we should've brought skates."

"Maybe there's a place we can rent them."

But after numerous queries, Jake discovered that everyone who wanted to skate brought their own skates from home. So Carrie and Jake held hands and walked around the pond. A mother and father and two girls skated by. Children chased and called to one another on the ice. Couples skated arm in arm, as if dancing, and a woman in a long red scarf skated close past where they stood watching. They could feel the breeze of her passing and hear the blades scratch along the surface.

"Isn't this nice?" Carrie said to him. He pulled her arm through his, held her hand in both of his, and rubbed her fingers through her mittens to warm them. Sometimes he found himself comparing her to his ex-wife. He hated himself for doing that, but how does a person not do that? Connie was small and wiry. A little Peter Pan pixie, he used to call her, always moving, always having things to do and places to be. She would never just stand like this. Carrie was bigger, sturdier, more solid in body and soul. And he was finding that he liked that. As they stood watching the skaters, he realized he liked that a lot.

"Look, Jake." Carrie pointed. In the very center of the ice, a young woman in a large, white wool sweater twirled. Then both feet were square on the ice again, and she glided backward. She raised one leg behind her at a perfect right angle before changing positions again, leaping, spinning once in the air, and landing with grace. The two white wool ball tassels attached to the top of her knit hat danced around her face as if with their own free will.

Carrie shivered beside Jake, but he could tell she was smiling. He pulled her close to him. Above them, the blue lines of lights twinkled like some alien language written across the sky.

Through her mittens Jake fingered the wedding ring Carrie wore while they watched the dancer. He wore one too. They had put them on before they left the hotel. It had been a long time since he'd worn a wedding ring, and it felt strange on his hand. But May thought that to play the part, they needed rings. So to the dollar store in Ridley they went.

He was about to tell her how perfect the night was, how happy he was, how right this all felt to him, how beautiful she was. He was about to tell her he loved her when she leaned up and whispered, "I'm starving. Let's get cheesecake." Letting go of his hand and laughing, she ran toward the lights of a nearby coffee shop. "They have cheesecake," she said to Jake. "I saw a sign."

By the time they were sitting, drinking coffees and sharing a piece of chocolate cheesecake, he'd lost the moment.

After they finished their coffee and cake, they decided to walk back to their hotel by way of the Tender Moments Home. Jake checked the address and the map. To get there, they would only be going out of their way by a few blocks. They easily found the house, a huge, old white home that looked very much like Lenore's Victorian B&B. Its wooden front porch looked more suited to rocking chairs and long summer nights than as receptacles for snow shovels and snowshoes. The house was on a street of other historic clapboard homes, most of which had been well maintained. There was no signage out front of this one, but he double-checked the address. This was the place.

"Are you going to knock on the door?" Carrie asked.

"I don't know."

"It looks so—how shall I put it?—normal," Carrie said. "Hard to believe that babies are bought and sold from this nice-looking house in this city that's so safe you can walk any place at night."

"Maybe this is the perfect place," he said. "A place no one would suspect. Plus, have you noticed the number of churches in this city? I bet they contribute to this ministry with great gusto."

They were about to walk on past when Carrie said, "Wait!"

"What?" Jake said.

She whispered, "Someone's sitting on the porch."

"Outdoors? In this weather?"

"Well, look."

Carrie was right. A small someone, bundled in an overcoat, was sitting on the porch steps. They approached tentatively. They'd seen several street people in the downtown core. Maybe this was someone looking for a place to rest for the night. It was a girl who sat there, shivering, hugging her knees, rocking back and forth. Her wool coat was twice her size and looked like it had come from a thrift store by its wear. She was also very pregnant.

"Hello?" Carrie said.

The girl continued to rock, didn't look up. She hummed something tuneless.

"Are you okay?" Carrie asked. "Are you locked out? Can we do something for you?"

"I have a cell phone," Jake offered.

The girl sniffed a few times and wiped her nose on the sleeve of the coat. "Just waiting for someone," she said.

"Should you be outside? It's really cold."

"I'm okay."

"Do you live here?" Carrie asked.

"If you want to call it that," she mumbled.

"Do they treat you well?"

She shrugged. "Better'n home I guess. My mom kicked me out. So I came here."

"She kicked you out because you were pregnant?"

The girl shook her head. Her hair was long and in strings. "No. Way before that."

"When is your baby due?"

"Three weeks." She reached down to scratch a knee. Her legs were bare underneath the coat and skinny.

"My name is Karen," Carrie said, sitting down beside her. "And this is my husband, Jack. We have an appointment tomorrow with the Sorensens."

"You want a baby?"

Carrie smiled and looked at Jake. "We want a baby very much; that's why we're here. We're hoping to adopt a little baby."

The girl pulled the coat more tightly around her. "Well, you're not getting mine."

"Well, of course we don't want a baby that a mother wants to keep."

She looked into the far distance and didn't say anything for a while. "I'm waiting for my boyfriend. He's a bartender at Sweet Waters."

"What's your name?" Carrie asked gently.

"Lucie. Spelled with an *ie,* not a *y.*"

"Can we come in, Lucie," Carrie asked, "and see where you live?"

"You're not allowed."

"Really? You're not allowed to have people in your home?"

"Not with weirdo Al around." Her face was pale, almost translucent by the street light, as if they could see the bones beneath.

"Al?"

"The guard. Security guy. He'd freak if he knew I was out here waiting for my boyfriend. The jailer, we all call him."

"You all. How many of you live here?" Carrie asked. Jake was surprised at all her questions. He'd never seen the reporter side of Carrie before. The girl seemed to be warming to her.

She shrugged. "Five of us now. I'm the one most far along. The rest are just new. There's this one girl who's Chinese? She cries all the time. I don't think she speaks English."

"And you're planning on keeping your baby?"

She bent her head into her knees and didn't say anything for a while. Jake was getting cold. He shuffled his feet. Finally, she said, "I have to talk to my boyfriend. They said there might be something wrong with my baby. They're going to do more tests tomorrow."

"I'm so sorry to hear that," Carrie said.

"That's why I was waiting for my boyfriend. I have to see him. To tell him. As soon as the baby comes, we were gonna move into his place." She bit her lip and blinked rapidly. "I can't live with him now 'cause he shares an apartment with a bunch of other guys. But we're going to get our own place soon."

A light came on inside. "You better go," she said. "Al will be here any minute. If he checks my room and I'm not in it..." She made a cutting motion with her hand across her neck.

"We'll be praying for you," Carrie called.

"If you think it'll do any good, be my guest."

70

The following afternoon at twenty after four, Carrie and Jake sat on comfy overstuffed chairs in the Pregnancy Crisis Centre, which shared the building with Tender Moments Adoption Agency. Theirs was the last appointment of the day. One couch and several chairs made this room feel less like a waiting room and more like someone's living room. Carpet covered the floor, and paintings of flowers and children decorated the walls. Pamphlets and magazines on parenting and pregnancy were scattered on a wooden coffee table in the middle of the floor. Carrie picked up a *Christian Parent* magazine and began leafing through it while they waited for Jeanine Sorenson. Even though the door had been opened, no one seemed to be around.

Jake fervently hoped that Jeanine hadn't seen them around Fog Point. But to be on the safe side, Jake wore an old pair of glasses with thick black plastic frames that Carrie said made him look like a college professor. And Carrie didn't wear her red coat and hat, so recognizable in Fog Point.

When they'd gotten back to the hotel last night, May was tapping furiously on her computer keyboard.

"Any luck?" Jake had asked.

"Not so far. But I'm finding a lot of usable information on the Sugars. I found pictures." She clicked on her screen. "I don't have my printer with me or I'd print them off for you. Here, do these two look like the FNN people or what?"

Jake looked at the picture of the couple who, the site said, managed the Boise Baby Home. The woman had dark short hair and the man, clean-shaven, wore a cowboy hat.

"Since I never met the famous people from FNN, I've no way of knowing."

"I've already e-mailed these to Bill."

"Where'd you get them?" Carrie said. "I thought the Sugars were camera shy."

"It was on a victims' blog Web site. I'm learning a lot, and I hope to learn a whole lot more," she'd said.

Two other people waited with Jake and Carrie this afternoon. A young woman sat very still, her hands on her lap as she looked straight ahead. Her hair was black and spiky, and her glasses' frames were patterned with something that looked like tweed. Jake kept looking at her glasses wondering where one purchased such eyewear. Next to her was an older woman, her head bent into a *Reader's Digest*. No conversation passed between them, yet by their proximity, Jake guessed they were mother and daughter. Pregnant, counter-culture daughter and unhappy mother. He wanted to laugh because they seemed so stereotypical, but he couldn't laugh at the sadness surrounding them.

Tender Moments brochures and parenting magazines were liberally spread out on the tables. A Mr. Coffee on a far table looked as though it was set up for clients. Jake looked at Carrie, she nodded, so he got up and poured two Styrofoam cups, added powdered cream to both, and brought them back.

A tall woman with tiny reading glasses perched on the end of her nose and a swinging full skirt came into the room and introduced herself to Jake and Carrie as Nancy Webb, coordinator of the Pregnancy Crisis Centre.

"Oh, I'm glad you found the coffee. It's not too bad, but if you want something better, there's a Tim Hortons down the street." She laughed. "I've been told I'm not the best coffee maker. You're here for Jeanine, right? She's on a conference call in her office but should be available soon."

They nodded.

"We all *so* love Jeanine around here. She and Ted do such good work. Taking in poor girls with no place else to go." Nancy shook her head and smiled.

"Are you connected with them?" Carrie asked. "Are they a part of Pregnancy Crisis Centre?"

Nancy shook her head. "Not at all. Two different boards, two different everythings. We just happen to have offices in the same place."

Carrie said, "They seem like remarkable people. I know my husband and I are impressed." Carrie squeezed Jake's hand. "But I wonder how they're funded? I mean, it must cost a lot to run a home like that."

"The Sorensens are such selfless people." She took off her glasses. "They'd made a lot of money in oil out west, and they wanted to give back. They have quite a lot of donors," she added. "But most of the money is what they themselves give selflessly to the work."

Jake looked at her and tried hard to keep the cynicism out of his voice. "That's nice," he said.

"Do you know much about the home?" Carrie asked. "How is it that they have an office with you here?"

"When you get right down to it, the work we do is connected to their work. When these poor, young women come here, they're so lost. We offer counseling, and some choose to give their babies up for adoption and some choose to keep them. We offer help in either case. Well, when the Sorensens came here, they had a wonderful vision for a home for runaway or homeless mothers. They presented it to our board of directors. We prayed about it and decided to let them use a room here as an office, free of charge, of course."

"Of course," Jake said.

"Do they live around here?" Carrie asked. "The Sorensens, I mean."

"They have a beautiful home across the river, next to the new golf course."

"Nice," Jake said.

"But I only know this because one of the board members lives near them. The Sorensens like to keep a low profile."

"I bet they do," Jake muttered.

"What about the young women who may decide to keep their babies?" Carrie asked. "Does your organization help them? I mean like with baby clothes and equipment, that sort of thing?"

"Oh, that's one of the main things we do," Nancy said. "That's what we're all about."

"But I mean, have you helped any of the women from the home?"

She thought about it, twirling those little reading glasses in her fingers. "Not really, but that's because most of the babies from the home are adopted out."

"*All* of the babies are adopted out?"

"I don't know about that," Nancy said. "But that's the wonderful part of it, that the Sorensens are able to find so many prospective Christian parents."

Jake hoped no one could see his eyes rolling. Obviously Carrie noticed, because she gave him a quick tap on the hand.

"Have you ever visited the home?"

Nancy nodded vigorously. "Oh yes. Of course. When the Sorensens first arrived with their son, they took all of our volunteers on a tour of the place. They've done some wonderful things with the rooms. They want to make the girls feel at home."

"What about the doctors?"

"They use doctors from the hospital here in Fredericton, but sometimes they fly in their own doctor, for special cases."

"What kind of special cases?" Carrie asked.

But Jake had stopped on the word "son," and said, "Their son is here too?" He remembered from Rory Black's account that the Sorensons had a son.

"That would be Al. He works with them. He's—"

"He works at the home?" Jake interrupted.

"He's kind of a handyman extraordinaire. He has a few challenges, some learning difficulties, but he's blossomed here, and we all love him. He really keeps that place in tiptop shape. He does odd jobs for us, too—"

"He's the security guard there," Carrie said, reminding Jake of the girl's words from the night before about the man. What had she called him? The jailer?

Nancy laughed. "Well, one hardly needs a security guard here in Fredericton, so I wouldn't call him that. But, yes, he does look after the home."

"Do they have other children?" Jake asked.

Nancy shook her head. "It's sad. Jeanine, who loves children so much, only had one."

Just then the door to Jeanine's office opened, and a woman stood looking at Jake and Carrie. She had salon-styled blond hair and wore an expensive suit. For one horrible moment Jake thought she recognized them, the way she stood there staring at them, but then she said, "Mr. and Mrs. Corcoran? Come in, please."

They entered and sat in two chairs across from her desk. In the harsh morning light, Jeanine's face seemed drawn and hard. Jake thought about her learning-challenged son. Was that why she embarked on this life? Jake had been a police officer for long enough to realize that sometimes people do what they do out of sheer desperation. Who knows what was in her mind when she took Seth so long ago. Maybe, because she had one son who was a disappointment, she meant to keep Seth for herself? And then, realizing she could easily be caught and imprisoned, she sold him and pretended he had died. Was that the reason?

Jeanine pursed her lips and took out a pad of paper and the adoption application forms they had previously filled out and e-mailed from a dummy e-mail account.

"Now." She adjusted her glasses. "You are Jack and Karen Corcoran from Muskogee, Oklahoma. It says here you're in construction, Mr. Corcoran?"

He nodded. "Own my own company." He hoped his poor attempts at a midwestern accent weren't detectable.

"So tell us," Carrie grabbed Jake's arm. "We've been to so many agencies and have been waiting *such* a long, long time. We are so hoping, that's why we…well, me…why I was so determined just to pick up everything and fly out here."

Jeanine eyed them, brushed a piece of blond hair from her forehead. She picked up their form. "I have a Caucasian baby who might just be available in three weeks." She picked up another file from the desk and opened it.

"Really!" Jake thought Carrie said it just a little too loudly. He squeezed her hand.

Jeanine sighed. "Oh, wait. Oh, dear. The file is flagged."

"Is there a problem?" Carrie asked.

"Well," she laid the file on the table and ran manicured fingers over the edges of it. "We don't call them problems. We call them challenges. And we have a major one."

Carrie leaned forward. "Yes?"

Jeanine pursed her lips, sighed, and then said, "Usually we ask the prospective parents to pick up the cost of hospitalization and doctor fees. Plus, we ask for a small donation to the home. But," she looked back at the sheet. "This baby that will be born in three weeks is very healthy now, but, oh dear." She stopped, read through the sheet. "This one had a few problems in the beginning, requiring extra tests and sonograms. That cost has been quite hefty, I'm afraid."

"What's wrong with the baby?" Carrie asked.

"Nothing is wrong now. In the beginning, the mother had some cramping, and the doctor thought she might lose the baby. We had to run some extra tests to ensure the safety of the mother. The pregnancy has since progressed normally. The tests, though, can be quite expensive."

"We're willing to pay it," Jake said. "No matter what it is."

"We've been waiting so long, you see," Carrie said.

"Well, okay then." She peered at the file and scratched some figures on a notepad, then totaled them. "The tests come to one hundred thousand dollars."

"Hoo-ee," Jake said, shaking his head. "One hundred thousand dollars," he said loudly. "This is what babies *cost* these days?"

Jeanine said, "This one, I'm afraid so." She eyed them curiously in a way that made Jake nervous. He pushed his black plastic glasses up on his nose. "And we don't use the word *cost* when referring to a baby. What you're paying are the medical charges."

"So it's okay, Jack? We can have this baby?" Carrie said it so convincingly that Jake glanced at her.

"Sure, honey, if it's what you want." He turned to Jeanine. "Do you want the money now?"

"The usual practice is half now and the other half when the baby is delivered into your waiting hands."

"Our waiting hands," Carrie said.

He reached in his pocket and took out a phony checkbook, wrote a check for fifty thousand dollars, and handed it to her.

"When do we get to meet the mother?" Carrie said, clapping her hands.

"That's another prob—challenge," she said, putting up a finger. "The mother, sweet little thing, wants a completely closed adoption. She has asked not to meet the parents nor does she want any further contact. She only asks that her baby be placed in a Christian home."

"Well, we certainly fit that bill," Jake said.

On the way back to the hotel, Carrie said, "One problem, Jake, one serious problem. This is Canada, right? All of those expensive sonograms would be paid for by the government."

"Yeah, but we're just rich, stupid Americans. How are we supposed to know that?"

May was pacing in the hotel room when the two returned.

"I got something. Here, sit," she said, as she cleared papers off the bed.

Carrie sat on one of the beds, and Jake sat on a chair. May took a deep breath. "I found this on a blog. Blogs are such wonderful places for research. I'm convinced now that this is how Sol does it. You wouldn't believe the kinds of stuff people put out there on blogs. Names, places, pictures even. Well, I was linking through a bunch of adoption victims' blogs and—"

Jake put up his hand. "Whoa, they have adoption victims' blogs?"

May nodded. "There are blogs for everything, Jake. Anyway, I want to show you this." She clicked through her computer and showed them the screen:

The worst part about being at the Boise Baby Home was Mal Al. We all called him that. Mal is Spanish for bad. He's the Stewarts' son. We couldn't go out; that big lunk of a guy wouldn't let us... He was a weirdo with his two different-colored eyes...

"Do you see this? Al. Their son is named Al. They called him Mal Al. Bill told us he had two different-colored eyes. So I did some more searching and found that their son is Allen Barcklay Sugar."

"Where's the Barcklay come in?"

"That's his legitimate middle name. Spelled that weird way with the *c* and the *k* like that."

"He's here," Carrie said. "He works as a delivery boy for the adoption agency. The woman at the Pregnancy Crisis Centre talked about him."

Jake picked up the phone to make three calls, one to Bill, one to the local police, and one to the Canadian RCMP.

71

Allen "Mal" Barcklay Sugar was picking at threads on a brown afghan and watching an old taped episode of *Lost* when he heard a thunderous knocking on his door. Michael had just shot those two women in the hatch, and Allen wondered whether the thundering had something to do with Michael. Maybe Jack or Locke were on their way down. Allen didn't move, but sat rapt, not noticing the heap of brown yarn that lay unraveled at his feet.

The girl died! How could this happen? He wanted to yell at her to get up. He wanted to go right in there and kill Michael for doing what he did, because the thundering would not stop and that had to be the reason.

"Open up! Police!" He thought, at first, that this came from his television, but this was the wrong program. They didn't say that on *Lost*. Only on shows like *Law & Order* and *CSI*. And then, surprisingly, he heard his name being called. "Allen Sugar, open up! This is the police!"

He shoved the brown yarn and the rest of his afghan underneath the couch but didn't get up. *Lost* wasn't over yet, and he didn't want to miss the end. Not of *this* episode!

The police banged through his door, and all of them rushed over to him. A big one grabbed him and put his arms behind his back and put handcuffs on his wrists. Just like on television. He wanted to ask if he could go to the bathroom first but didn't. He'd never seen anyone do that on *Law & Order*, and he was fairly sure it wouldn't be allowed. Besides, he had to remain quiet.

Those were always Mother's strictest orders. "When they take you away, never say anything. If you say something—anything—I will not be able to help you."

He wanted to yell out, "Don't be loud! The girls need to be quiet!" But since he couldn't speak, he tried to make faces to let them know what he meant. They ignored him. He also wanted to ask what would happen to the girls, but when he tried to move his wrists to point to the rooms, they must've thought he was trying to get loose, so they held his shoulders all the tighter and told him he was being arrested for the murder of Tolita Shenk.

His apartment was in the back by the kitchen, and therefore, they marched him right through the house, right in front of the girls. And he didn't want that! He didn't need the girls knowing he wouldn't be there to protect them. They would be afraid at night without their protector.

A cluster of girls stood in the living room and watched as he was marched by. He wanted to offer some words of reassurance, that he'd be back to take care of them. But he remembered Mother's stern warnings and said nothing.

This had happened to him before. Lots of times. Once for breaking into a doctor's office. They thought he was stealing drugs. He wasn't. He was finding file folders for Mother. She needed him to destroy some adoption records. So he did, right in the office's own shredder. He was able to do this before the police came.

He didn't say anything then. And within two days, Mother was there and paying for him to come out.

"He's troubled, officers. He has a long history of mental illness; I have a doctor's letter. You can release him into my care," she'd said.

Later, in the car, she gave him a hug and told him what a good boy he was for being so quiet and obedient. And then later, just to make sure it stuck in his brain, she came into his room and screamed again, "If you speak! If you say anything! If anything comes out of your mouth, we won't be able to help you. You'll be on your own. Finally, in the big world, on your own. And how will that suit you?"

He would be quiet this time, too. He would push all the sounds of the room and the talking of the girls and the hard talking of the police out of his mind and just wait for Mother. If he thought hard enough, he could go to a place in his mind where he barely heard the things around him, and even time moved more slowly. As they led him out into the night, he began going to that place. He hardly felt the cold, didn't need a jacket, and didn't even have to go to the bathroom anymore.

He remembered Tolita Shenk. Mother had firmly scolded him for killing her. All he was supposed to do was get the book and the ring and the pictures and the film, and instead he'd killed her. But the girl wouldn't give them to him. What else was he supposed to do? So he'd put his hands around her neck, and still she wouldn't tell him where they were. Mother needed those things! Hadn't she understood when he told her that?

After he phoned Mother and told her what he'd done, she scolded him harshly and told him that now he needed to go to the girl's motel room and get rid of all the girl's identification. Damage control, she called it. So he did that. Mother had taught him carefully through the years how to do the things she needed him to do.

Still, when he arrived home, she looked at him, took his face in her hands, and screamed at him. Somewhere he'd lost his contact lens and now everyone could see that his eyes were two different colors. Where did you lose this? How did this happen? And she screamed at him, *"Freak! Freak!"*

He hated that word; it made him remember all the times the boys in his class would call him that, because of his eyes and because he couldn't talk right.

"M-maybe it c-c-came out," he stammered. "When we were in the…in the…in the…in the snow."

"How could you be so stupid? Freak! Freak!"

He wanted to run from Mother, but there was no running from Mother. Even Father couldn't run very far from Mother.

"*Now we have to go there,*" she'd yelled at him. "*Now your father and I have to go there and find it and fix up your mistake.*"

Even though Tully was dead, Mother still needed her things. He had to find the book. And Mother wasn't pleased about this either. She commanded him to go through that pastor's house there until he found it. "I don't care what you do—trash the place—but find that book!"

"We've got the PI's case notes, isn't that enough?" his father said. "I got those when we were there."

"Yeah, and I can't read them, can you?"

Allen listened to them argue and knew his mistake was the cause of it all. For punishment he had spent three days in the basement of their house across the river with no food and only one bottle of water a day. He was not to kill people. Not unless authorized by Mother. But while he was being punished, it wasn't himself he thought about but the girls. How would they survive without someone to look after them? He thought of nothing else for the three days he spent in the basement.

And when Mother came down to let him out, his first thought was the girls and their safety. Even before he got something to eat, he drove his truck across the river to the house to check on his girls. Only when he was satisfied that they were safe and healthy could he go down to Tim Hortons and get some chili and a bagel and a coffee. Only then.

The streets were filled with flashing police cars when they held his shoulders and led him outside. One of the cops, a big one who smelled like garlic, put his hand on Allen's head and made him sit in the backseat of a car. He wondered why there were so many cars. Were more people getting arrested?

But he wouldn't ask. He couldn't. He would remain quiet.

"*Say not a word, Allen. Not a word. Mother will come. If you leave the talking to Mother, Mother will come and help you. Just wait.*"

72

This shirtless little man with the head bowed low and the bald spot was not at all what Jake expected Allen Sugar to look like. Being a cop for so long, and now a PI, Jake had some knowledge of criminal types, and this unassuming young man did not fit that bill. But, then again, murderers came in every shape and size.

As soon as he'd made the call to Bill back in Fog Point and Bill contacted the Fredericton police force as well as the RCMP, Jake, May, and Carrie grabbed their jackets. No way were any of them going to miss this. They'd parked their car a block away from the Tender Moments Home, so as not to impede police traffic, and clomped through the snowy sidewalk to where the action was likely to take place. Already three police cars were parked in front of the home, their lights flashing. Jake knew that the same number, or more, were being dispatched to the Sorenson's luxury home on the north side of the city.

By the time they got to the home, Allen Sugar was being led out. Jake, Carrie, and May stood as if at a parade and watched. Jake knew that the three of them would be called upon to offer testimony. He anticipated a long night at the police station, where they would go over their testimony in minute detail.

They were not the only rubberneckers. Porch lights were coming on up and down Charlotte Street. A man in a bulky jacket came out and stood beside Jake. "I bet it's drugs," he said. "That man's the bane of his parents' existence, I would say."

Another neighbor, who wore a ski jacket over his bathrobe, agreed. "I always figured that place was a front for drug dealers. Never felt it was that home for girls like they said it was. All along I had my doubts." His black hair stuck out at odd angles, and he kept shaking his head.

A woman from one house over joined in the conversation. "You try to raise kids right and look what happens to them. His parents? Pillars. And look at him. Guy can't even talk right…"

"You're wrong," a young woman said. "His parents are such big shots in town. They're oh so generous with their money and want to do *everything* to help poor young pregnant girls, but this son of theirs? Is he ever in the pictures in the paper with them? Nope. Is he ever mentioned? Nope. He's an embarrassment to them. So no wonder he turned out the way he did."

May turned to her. "It sounds like you know him."

She put her hands to her ears to warm them, and shifted from foot to foot. "A little. We've talked. Or rather I've talked. He has a bit of a speech impediment. But when you do get him to talk, it's *Mother* this and *Mother* that. Guy can't even take a whiz without getting his mama's permission…"

This got Jake thinking about children who were a disappointment. According to Nancy at the Pregnancy Crisis Centre, the Sugars had wanted more children but couldn't have any. How much of who Allen was came from feeling as if he was a disappointment? Given one chance, and he blew it. Then he thought of Tully, never able to be fully loved, because no matter how much she tried, she could not replace her brother. He thought about Lenore and her three sons, the two youngest never quite measuring up to the one with the big church and all the children. He thought about children everywhere forced to bear the burden of their parents' aspirations and expectations.

And then a thought struck Jake. If Allen was a product of his parents, what if they used him, right from the beginning, to do their killing for them?

He was the perfect scapegoat when you thought about it: a bit simple, with a speech impediment. What if they saw in him a way to carry out their own plans? No, surely no parent would do that, would they?

The patrol car drove away, the street quieted down, and the people went back inside to their warm bedrooms.

Carrie reached for his hand as the last police car drove away. "It's over," she said.

"Not quite," Jake said. "They still have to arrest the Sugars."

73

L enore used her trowel to dig up the teddy bears, candles, ribbons, crosses, and flowers—fake and real—from her snowbank. It took two green garbage bags to cart away the junk. At one point she briefly thought about washing up one of the particularly nice and new teddy bears—drying it, fluffing it out, putting on a new ribbon, and setting it on one of the beds in her guest rooms—but then, just as quickly, she changed her mind. She didn't need to be reminded of any of this.

Her guests were gone now. The last of the photographers and newspeople had left, and the McLarens were back in their own house. She always felt this sense of letdown when her last guest left. The only way she knew to get out of it was to plan and work hard for the next season, trying new recipes, quilting new pillows, scouting around for more antiques and curios for the guest rooms.

She put the trowel away and got out her rake from the shed to smooth the snow flat. No more impressions of angels. No more people bowing in her snowbank. It wasn't working anyway. Rose Nation's arthritis was back worse than ever. If anyone else came, if any more busloads of church people came, she'd tell them it was closed. The police had told her she had every right to do that. There was one funny thing though. Nootie told her that little Amber's allergies were doing a whole lot better since she'd come with her mother to the snowbank.

"But how could she," Lenore asked, "since I made the whole thing up?"

Nootie's only comment was, "Who knows the ways of God?"

The young woman Violet finally checked out and went home. Lenore had discovered that Violet's need for a cane was part of suffering from multiple sclerosis. Before Violet left, Lenore packed up a full box of cinnamon swirls for her to take with her on the train. She encouraged her to find a church in her town, too.

"But I don't have faith," Violet said, her pretty eyes wide. "If I had faith, I would have been healed!"

"Shush, shush, dear. None of us have much faith on our own. If we all had to have faith before God took a look at us, there would be no faith anywhere and no hope."

"So how do we get faith?"

"I don't know, dear. Not entirely. But I'm looking too."

They were going to keep in touch by e-mail. That would be nice, Lenore thought. After she raked the snow clear, she kicked it around a bit with the toe of her boot. She'd had a long talk with the police, after which she was certain she was going to be carted off in handcuffs to prison. They'd told her about a charge called "interfering with a dead body," but so far no one had come for her. She wondered if she could be like Martha Stewart in prison and teach her fellow inmates how to make cinnamon swirls.

The police had actually thanked her for being so accurate in the composite drawing. A lot of people couldn't remember details like she did, they told her. Especially the part about the two different-colored eyes. Because of her drawing, they'd managed to arrest the fellow who'd murdered Tolita Shenk. They'd found a contact lens on the body with enough DNA to positively prove that Allen Sugar had killed Tolita Shenk.

She dragged the trash bags out to the curb, waved to Enid, who was sweeping her walkway, then went back inside. Did her work ever end? No. Her sons were in the kitchen, eating peach pie at the table. Perfect. She needed to tell these boys of hers a few things.

"Carl. Earl." She pulled off her boots and took off her coat. "I see you've found the pies."

"Peach, my favorite," Earl said.

"But where's the ice cream?" Carl asked.

She sat down across from them. "I need to speak to you both."

"Can't now," Carl said, taking a drink of his coffee. "Got to get to my Boys and Girls Club."

She pointed at him. "Stay!"

He stayed. Earl continued eating his pie, his left arm around his plate on the table as if protecting it.

Lenore quieted her voice. "This won't take long. What I want to say is this." She took a deep breath. "How proud I am of you two…"

Earl's fork stopped halfway to his mouth. He turned his head her way. Carl, both hands on his coffee cup, just stared at her.

"Carl, you've come a long way, and I'm proud of all you do with the Boys and Girls Clubs. They speak so highly of you down there."

"Mother?"

She turned to Earl. "And, Earl, I never realized what all you do down there, you doing up people's Web sites the way you do. You do such a nice job."

Earl still hadn't placed the fork in his mouth.

"Also," she dabbed the corners of her eyes. "I've also never thanked you both for staying here in Fog Point with me. A mother likes her children close. A mother likes to know her children will stay beside her when she gets old."

"Well," Carl said.

"Um," Earl said.

"One more thing. I'm going to give you boys one month, and then I'll be charging rent for the use of the basement."

Earl put the forkful of pie back on his plate, and Carl set his coffee cup down.

"And if you eat my food, it's more. You have one month's grace. Oh, and another thing. I had a contractor look at the basement. He's found dangerous levels of mold and other stuff down there. He's even thinking a rat or two may have died in the walls, which would account for the smell. You're going to have to find a new place for the months of March and April. I'm getting it completely torn apart and redone. I've already hired him. The whole foundation of this great old house is in peril. And I need to have it ready for the summer season. You can rent one of my attic rooms if you choose. But, Earl, I'd suggest you rent one of the downtown storefronts for your business. You don't necessarily have to go on the boardwalk, which is expensive, but there are plenty of other places available."

The two looked at each other. Then Lenore rose. "One month's grace." Then she turned the TV on to a cooking show and made a pot of tea for herself.

I have something for you." Ben stood in the doorway of Amy's classroom and held out a small, square parcel wrapped in brown paper. She'd been grading math papers and had lost track of time. Most of the other teachers had gone home by now. The monthly calendar had flipped another full page, and the sun had come to melt the ice in the harbor, the way it always eventually did. Outside her classroom windows the world dripped. It was still light, and the late-afternoon sun slanted in and warmed her desk. But that was what always happened. Spring always followed winter. Summer always followed spring.

The funeral for Tolita Shenk had been more than a month ago, and Ben had officiated. Coralee, her mother, had asked for that, and Tolita's foster mother agreed. Everyone from Fog Point attended, it seemed. Stone Church couldn't hold all the people, so Earl Featherjohn had rigged up speakers and a video monitor in the gym of the school. And even so, several of the larger classrooms also had to be employed. The girl who'd come here looking for her brother had made an impression on everyone.

All the regulars from Stone attended, as did May and Norah and many people who didn't ordinarily go to any church. The police attended in full dress, as well.

Amy had sat in her customary place, four rows from the front and on the right, glad she'd taken Ben's advice and gotten there early. Blaine, Charlie,

Jana, Jake, and Carrie sat next to her. Lenore was directly behind her, next to Enid and the Noonans. Both of Lenore's sons were busy with the technical aspects of the services, so they couldn't sit with her, a fact she freely told everyone in attendance.

Ben gave a stirring message titled "The Parable of Tully," about how this girl that no one knew captured all of their hearts. Amy was proud of her husband and told him so after the service.

Two people flew out from Barrhead for the service: Coralee Shenk was a thin shadow of a woman who hung closely to the arm of a woman who was introduced to Amy as Doreen Jesper, friend of the family and Tully's foster mother. Amy remembered the photo she'd seen of Coralee, the way she held her baby, her left hand touching the side of his face, the way she'd looked down into the face of the son who would be taken from her only moments after the picture was taken. Amy had heard more of the story than what she read in Rory Black's notebook, bits and pieces that filled in the gaps. How the baby's abductor was the niece of this man who was now suffering from Alzheimer's in a nursing home in Barrhead. Amy had read many times the long account that Carrie Maynard had written up. The story had been published as a "special" to the *Boston Globe,* and she'd shared the byline with a reporter out in Edmonton, Alberta, where the whole thing started. Somehow the baby had ended up in an orphanage in Edmonton and then was adopted by Shirley and Gus Nation from Fog Point, who had no idea that their newly adopted son, Colin, was part of the Sugars' baby mill.

At the reception after the service, Amy leaned against the wall under the basketball hoop, a cup of coffee in her hand, and thought about these things as she watched people. A man named Allen Sugar had been arrested for Tully's murder. His parents, who had run at least three illegal baby mills in the past thirty years, had fled and were nowhere to be found. When police arrived at their home the night their son was arrested, the house was vacant. Jake had said that in a year or so they'd probably surface in some unsuspecting town, opening a home for unwed mothers. But this time the police would be waiting for them.

Allen, their son, apparently hadn't said a word since being arrested more than two months ago, not to anyone. No one knew quite how to proceed with a case when the accused would not speak. He'd been through three public defenders already, all of whom had given up on him.

Amy wondered about this as she put her empty coffee cup down on a nearby table. She watched Colin Nation approach Coralee and Doreen. Doreen talked to him for a few minutes, and he nodded. Coralee managed a smile—her Seth, the son she had lost all those years ago at a baby shower—and finally they hugged each other. Coralee's thin shoulders heaved, and Colin wiped his eyes. They hugged again, even more tightly.

Finally, Colin's wife, Marnie, approached with baby Kayla in her arms. More words that Amy couldn't hear, but there was no disguising their body language. Doreen spoke now, and Marnie handed Kayla to Coralee. A wide smile broke out on Coralee's face, the first Amy had seen. The baby girl grabbed for Coralee's glasses, the ends of her hair, her necklace.

In a few moments, Colin's parents and his sister Kate came over, and they all shook hands. Shirley Nation and Coralee hugged each other briefly. Amy wondered how that would feel. Maybe there would be a day when she'd find out. Amy turned away then and went back to the refreshment table. She heard Lenore telling Eloise and Beryl that her two sons were responsible for the whole setup here, the whole thing. Amy smiled.

Amy smiled more these days. She loved her daughter beyond all loving yet knew her hold on Blaine was tenuous, as was the hold on any child, adopted or natural. It was sort of like God's hold on her. Sometimes he let her go to find her own way, to trip and fall, to look for a so-called *real* God. And just as she would be waiting for Blaine, God was waiting for her. She knew that. She also knew that God would be patient.

She looked up from her school papers at Ben, who walked toward her and held out a package. "Open it," he said. He pulled up a child-size chair and sat beside her. He looked funny, this long, lean husband wrapped around a student's chair. A crazy grin stretched across his face.

She undid the wrappings. The picture of her family, the one taken two years ago at Christmas, the one that had been scraped and broken during the breaking and entering, had been perfectly restored.

"Our family," Amy said running her finger across the glass. "Thank you."

ABOUT THE AUTHOR

Award-winning author Linda Hall has written twelve novels, including two Christy-nominated novels, *Steal Away* and *Sadie's Song*. She and her husband, Rik, live in New Brunswick, Canada. When she's not writing, they enjoy spending time aboard their sailboat, *Gypsy Rover II.*

For more about Linda, her boat, her blog, and the official recipe for cinnamon swirls, she would be delighted for you to visit her at www.writer hall.com.

Book one
in the
Fog Point series

"Dark Water *is a triumph*" —JANE KIRKPATRICK, bestselling author

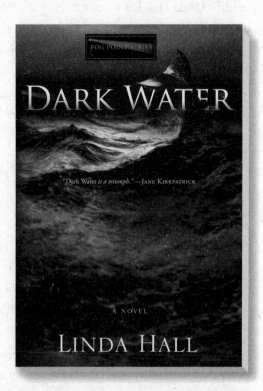

When jewelry designer Elise St. Dennis hires PI Jake Rikker to find an ex-con who is stalking her, he becomes entangled in a mystery that could destroy them both.

Available in bookstores and from online retailers.